CRUSADE

THE CHRONICLES OF THE BLACK LION, BOOK TWO

RICHARD CULLEN

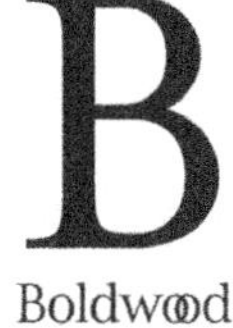

Boldwood

First published in Great Britain in 2025 by Boldwood Books Ltd.

Cover Design by Colin Thomas

Cover Images: Colin Thomas

A CIP catalogue record for this book is available from the British Library.

Paperback ISBN 978-1-83603-366-0

Large Print ISBN 9978-1-83603-365-3

Hardback ISBN 978-1-83603-364-6

Ebook ISBN 978-1-83603-367-7

Kindle ISBN 978-1-83603-368-4

Audio CD ISBN 978-1-83603-359-2

MP3 CD ISBN 978-1-83603-360-8

Digital audio download ISBN 978-1-83603-362-2

This book is printed on certified sustainable paper. Boldwood Books is dedicated to putting sustainability at the heart of our business. For more information please visit https://www.boldwoodbooks.com/about-us/sustainability/

Boldwood Books Ltd, 23 Bowerdean Street, London, SW6 3TN

www.boldwoodbooks.com

PREFACE

In 1213, Pope Innocent III issued a papal bull, a written decree known as *Quia maior*, in response to the continued Moslem presence in the Holy Land, and its challenge to Christian interests in the region. Pope Innocent, who had already organised the Fourth Crusade, which infamously resulted in the razing of Constantinople in 1204, saw it as his duty to continue the crusading tradition and unite Christendom against what he viewed as the Islamic threat.

The Fourth Crusade had weakened the Byzantine Empire, creating a power vacuum in the region. Additionally, the Ayyubid dynasty established by the legendary Saladin, which controlled Egypt and much of the Levant, began experiencing internal strife, as his sons and brothers fought over who should succeed him. Pope Innocent's successor, Honorius III, and other Christian leaders saw this as an opportune moment to launch a new campaign.

The Fifth Crusade began in 1217, with armies departing from various parts of Europe, and the strategic decision was made to target Egypt, rather than directly attacking Jerusalem. This plan was based on the belief that controlling Egypt would provide a stronger base for eventually recapturing and holding the rest of the Holy Land.

The crusaders besieged the Egyptian port city of Damietta in 1218 and were met with determined resistance from the sultan, al-Adil, brother of Saladin. Unfortunately, in his seventies, the ageing al-Adil was in no condition to face such a determined invasion and died during the siege. Without its figurehead, the surrender of the city seemed inevitable.

But al-Adil's son, al-Kamil, had other ideas...

PROLOGUE

EGYPT – 1219AD

The sun glared down with a wrathful eye as the two warriors rode west. To their right, the waters of the Bahrat al-Manzilah glinted like a sheet of silver, but Kashta took no joy in the sight. His thoughts were troubled, his eyes fixed on the road that stretched before them, winding into the barren hills.

Many miles behind lay Damascus, with its gardens and minarets, the souk with its bright silks and spices, the very heart of the Ayyubid Sultanate. A heart that beat slower now, since just days before they had laid their sultan to rest. Al-Adil. The man they had called Sayf ad-Din – the Sword of Faith. The ruler who had held the Frankish besiegers at bay for so long, was no more.

Now Kashta and Wasim rode back into that firepit, to join al-Adil's son al-Kamil at his camp to the south of Damietta. To pledge their swords anew, and stand against the invaders who still laid siege to that proud bastion on the Nile. The great tower of Burj al-Silsilah – the chain tower that had held the invading fleet at bay – had already fallen to the Franks, and with it the sultanate's hold on the city grew more tenuous by the day. They could only keep faith that their new sultan might yet turn the tide. But then, looking at his riding companion, Kashta knew that faith was something he did not put much store by.

'Here.' Wasim nudged his horse closer to Kashta's, offering his waterskin. 'Wet your throat, my friend.'

Kashta eyed the proffered skin, knowing full well what it contained. Buzah – a potent beer brewed by the Turks. A foul concoction, but what could one expect from such dogs?

'Keep it,' he replied. 'I like my wits about me.'

'And I like a little joy in my life,' Wasim countered. 'Who knows when we'll next have cause for it?'

He upended the skin, throat working as he swallowed. Wasim ibn Shakil was a man who seized his pleasures where he found them, whether they were considered haram or not. He was striking to look at, his name meaning handsome one, son of the handsome one. Certainly he was blessed in that regard, but it was only one blessing among many. Wasim's skill with the sayf was unparalleled, and along with his steely nerve it had seen him raised into the ranks of al-Adil's jandariyah, the elite guard of the sultan himself. But skill with a blade had not seen the Sword of Faith spared from the ravages of age, nor the savagery of the Franks. Their sultan had died despite their efforts to secure him a victory, and now they looked to his son for redemption.

Wasim eventually lowered the skin with a satisfied sigh. 'You're thinking again, Kashta. I can smell the smoke from here.'

'One of us has to.'

Wasim tilted his head, sweeping a hand through sweat-dark locks. 'Cheer up, my friend. Our journey's almost at an end. We are about to pledge ourselves to a new master, and who knows what riches he might bestow upon such revered and storied men as us.'

Kashta knew the truth of it. Storied they may be, but revered? Not so much. The dark of Kashta's flesh was something that would always set him apart. His grandfather had been one of the few al-Sudan to remain loyal to the great Salah ad-Din during the Battle of Slaves, fifty years earlier. His father had likewise grown up as a loyal servant to the Ayyubids, though never treated as an equal. In his turn, Kashta had carried on that loyal tradition, despite the hardship it promised.

A lesser child might have broken beneath the yoke of such service. Instead, Kashta had bent, supple as the steel of his blade. He had risen by degrees, from the dung-spattered yards of the hujra to the ranks of the jandariya, loyal unto death. Drilled and honed to a killing edge, his life was bound to the will of his sultan. Soon he was accounted one of the finest warriors in the jund, second only to Wasim himself.

'Storied and revered we may be,' Kashta said. 'But invincible we are not. And here we are riding back into the teeth of our enemy. I see little to smile about, no matter the riches that await us. The crusading Franks will stop at nothing until Damietta is theirs. And if it falls? Then what?'

Wasim waved a hand dismissively. 'Do not pretend you are afraid, my friend. I do not believe it. And in turn, I am not afraid. For why would I be, with the great Kashta ibn Assad to watch my back? Besides—' he patted the leather bag at his horse's saddle '—I always come prepared for the worst.'

Kashta knew exactly what Wasim meant by that. In his bag was but one item – a white strip of linen to wrap his corpse in should he fall. It was common practice among the Saracens of the Ayyubid to carry such a shroud, but one that Kashta had failed to adopt. He saw preparing for one's death in such a way too much a temptation of fate. Although some might have considered riding directly toward a horde of besieging Franks something of a greater temptation.

As if summoned by that thought, Fariksur came suddenly into view before them. One moment, endless emptiness had stretched to the four horizons, the next, the plain ahead was teeming with men and beasts – the comings and goings of a town set on a war footing.

Both men quickened the pace of their steeds, eager to reach their goal. The gates were guarded, but their entry was not impeded, and in short order they were trotting through the packed streets, assailed by the sights and sounds. The deeper they rode into the town, the more they saw that chaos reigned; a maelstrom of jostling bodies and barked orders. Everywhere Kashta looked, he saw men girding for war: hammers clanging against anvils as armourers laboured to repair dented helms and notched blades, fletchers bent to their task as they churned out arrow after arrow to let fly at the Frankish horde.

To the west, the vast encampment was protected by the torrent of the Nile. To the north, a great trench had been dug and fortified against attack. For now, though, they were safe while the crusading westerners battered at the walls of Damietta, five miles further along the river. For now. Once the city was taken, and a foothold established, the armies of Christendom would eventually turn their eyes south. And so they had to be stopped, no matter the cost.

'Look,' Wasim said, gesturing through the press toward a distant parade of pavilions. 'Our journey's end.'

Kashta spotted a yellow flag flying above the press, a red eagle emblazoned upon it. The symbol of the Ayyubid sultans. Wasting no time, they steered their horses toward it, seeing the way was guarded by men in armour bearing their long rumh lances, with sayfs at their side. At their approach, one of the guards stepped forward, polished jawshan winking in the sunlight. Beneath his armour was a distinctive coat of blue and gold, his steel baydah bearing a horsehair plume, marking him as a mamluk of al-Kamil's askar.

'Your business?' The slave warrior's voice was harsh as a desert storm.

'I am Wasim ibn Shakil and this is Kashta ibn Assad.' All mirth had now vanished from Wasim's voice as he spoke. 'Sworn swords of the Sayf ad-Din. We have come to pledge our steel to the sultan, Malik al-Kamil, in his hour of need, and to stand with him against the infidel tide.'

The guard regarded them, dark eyes flickering over their travel-stained clothes and the glinting hilts of their blades. For a long moment he seemed poised to refuse them, to turn them away like beggars come to scratch at the door of their betters. But then he grunted and stepped aside, jerking his head towards the pavilion.

'Your sultan awaits,' he said curtly.

Wasim dismounted, Kashta doing the same. Together they approached the largest tent, the presence of mamluks growing thicker with every step. Plush carpets had been laid upon the dusty earth, the perfumed smoke of censers permeating the air and hiding the sweat-stink of men preparing for war.

At the edge of the tent, they knelt together, a perfectly synchronised gesture of submission, before finally Kashta allowed himself to look up. He had only ever glimpsed al-Kamil from afar, and then in happier times. His sultan's son had been little more than a stripling youth the last time Kashta laid eyes on him. In the intervening years, al-Kamil had transformed into something truly formidable.

He sat cross-legged on a low divan, swathed in robes of peacock blue and cloth-of-gold that could not quite disguise the hardness of him. Like his father, his face seemed carved from weathered stone, eyes remote and unknowable as the stars, as he regarded them from the interior of the pavilion.

'So.' Al-Kamil's voice was soft as a snake's hiss. 'Two mighty warriors come to prostrate themselves. I must be blessed indeed, to warrant such an honour.'

'Great Sultan, Malik al-Kamil Naser ad-Din Abu al-Ma'ali Muhammad.' Wasim raised himself up but remained on his knees. 'We come to serve, as we served your most exalted father before you.'

'Is that so?'

'Yes, Great Sultan.' Wasim continued. 'We are your servants, as we were your father's. Point us at your enemy and we shall run them through, crush them into the dust, fling them back into the sea from whence they came.'

'Bold words.' Al-Kamil leaned back on his cushions, a mirthless smile curling his lips. 'And who are these men, who would rid me of the Frankish curse that afflicts my lands?'

'Wasim ibn Shakil, and Kashta ibn Assad, the Lion of the Sudan.'

'Lion of the Sudan?' Al-Kamil looked Kashta up and down, as though assessing him at market. 'He certainly looks the part. Tell me, Wasim ibn Shakil, is your slave as fierce as he looks?'

They spoke as though Kashta could not understand their words, as though he was simply chattel, but it was not the first time he had faced such insult. And when those words were spoken by the sultan, it was best to swallow them down, rather than take issue.

'Great Sultan,' Wasim said, his voice ringing clear across the hushed confines of the pavilion. 'Kashta is no mere mamluk. He is a free man, who comes before you of his own will, to offer his blade in service to the sultanate. We have both stood upon the walls of Damietta. Both bled to defend them. We know this enemy, as we know the beating of our own hearts, and we are ready to face them once again.'

Al-Kamil steepled his fingers, the rings upon them glinting in the muted light. 'And such loyalty... it comes with a price, I assume?'

Wasim's grin widened. 'Everything has a price. From the lowliest beggar to the mightiest sultan, all must pay for what they desire.'

'And what is your price?' al-Kamil asked, his voice low and dangerous. 'Gold from my coffers? The company of women, soft and willing in the night?'

Kashta felt a surge of anger at the sultan's words, at the implication that their loyalty could be bought so cheaply. He rose to his feet, his chin raised, his jaw tight. At his sudden movement, every warrior about the pavilion suddenly tensed. All but al-Kamil.

'Land,' Kashta said, the word carrying its own finality. 'I would ask for a place to plant my feet, to till the soil and watch the crops grow tall beneath the sun.'

Al-Kamil regarded him for a long, tense moment. Then, slowly, he nodded, a smile curving his lips that did not touch the coldness of his gaze.

'Land you shall have, Kashta ibn Assad. A fitting reward for a lion's service, and for the blood you will spill.' He leaned forward, his robes whispering softly with the movement. 'I look forward to seeing how fiercely you roar, when you tear out the throats of the infidel.'

With a languid wave of his hand, he dismissed them. Kashta and Wasim bowed low, then turned to stride from the pavilion, the rich carpets muffling their footsteps as every eye watched them go.

As they emerged from the guarded compound, ready to retrieve their horses, Wasim clapped Kashta upon the shoulder, his grin wide and triumphant. 'See, my friend? I told you the sultan would welcome our aid, that he would see the value in the swords we laid at his feet. I would have preferred coffers of gold to land, but still...'

Kashta said nothing, his gaze fixed north, toward where Damietta lay beyond the bright horizon. The sultan had agreed to their price readily enough, had promised them the reward they sought, but as he stared, Kashta couldn't help but wonder...

...what would they be called upon to pay in return?

PART ONE: THE SHORES OF OUTREMER

CYPRUS – 1219 AD

1

A salt breeze gusted off the wine-dark waters, as Estienne gazed over the battlements of Gastria. The Templar stronghold stood like a raised fist upon the rocky coast of Cyprus, as defiant as the Order that had built it.

The sun beat down, but after his long journey south across the sea, and days acclimatising to the hot conditions, he scarcely felt it any more. His skin had darkened to a burnished bronze, his dark hair kissed blond in places by the relentless sun. In this place, so far from home, Estienne felt like he had been born anew, much different to the sallow, half-starved boy who'd stumbled into William Marshal's service a lifetime ago.

Just shy of his twentieth year, he now stood taller than most men, shoulders broad, hands callused from daily weapon work. Gastria was a temple filled with pious warriors dedicated to God and their holy purpose, and Estienne had fitted in here like a fist in a mailed glove. Since his arrival, he had seen it as his duty to hone his body and mind, so that he might become an instrument of war. But he knew it would soon be time to leave. Time to put himself to the test.

In the distance, the island's green hills rolled away, dotted with olive groves and sun-baked vineyards. A far cry from the rain-lashed moors of home. Estienne drank in the sight, committing every detail to memory. Who knew when he might see such serenity again, once he had left these shores.

The harbour below swarmed with activity, as ships jostled at anchor. Sailors flooded the decks, surrounded by knights and men-at-arms, destriers and pack mules. The entirety of Christendom looked to be gathered, bound for Outremer, ready to wrest the Holy Land from the grip of the Saracens. And Estienne would be among them.

That realisation sent a tingle down his spine, anticipation and unease twining in his gut. After so many years striving in William Marshal's shadow, fighting for the soul of England, he would finally take up the crusader's cross in truth. Fulfil the highest calling of his knightly oaths and prove himself worthy of the spurs he had been granted.

Estienne touched the scar that split his cheek, tracing its ridge with a callused thumb. A parting gift from Ilbert FitzDane, the man who had tormented him for so long. The man whose skull he had staved in on the deck of a ship, before consigning his corpse to the depths. It was a reminder of who he had been. And who he was no more. He was done chasing old ghosts, scratching at the wounds of his youth. In Egypt he would forge a new path. Carve out a legacy worthy of the man who had raised him. Let the Saracens tremble at his coming, for by God, he would put the fear of the Almighty in their heathen hearts...

'Taking in the view, my friend?'

The voice made him start, and he turned to see a familiar figure climbing the steps to the rampart – Brother Hoston, adorned in the black cappa that marked him as sergeant of the Order, blood-red cross vivid against the dark fabric.

'Aye, while I can,' Estienne replied. 'It is a view I would remember.'

The grizzled Templar joined him at the merlon, eyes scanning the teeming harbour. 'Well, enjoy it while you can. Our supplies are almost loaded, and my brothers champ at the bit. We make sail with the next tide.'

Estienne nodded, glancing back over his shoulder at the green hills and groves. 'And I share their impatience, but I'll miss this place. It has a... serenity to it.'

'Aye, that it does.' Hoston's thick fingers drummed against the sun-baked stone. 'But our task is not one of peaceful reflection. Best we leave that to the monks and scholars. Ours is a different calling.'

'To bring the light of God back to Outremer,' Estienne murmured. 'By the sword, if need be.'

'Just so.' Hoston clapped a hand to Estienne's shoulder. 'Come, we've preparations yet to make before we depart.'

He led the way down from the battlements, and Estienne followed. As they wound their way through the fort, he couldn't help but feel a twinge of trepidation. This fortress had been a refuge, if only for a little while. A chance to catch his breath before plunging headlong into the maelstrom of war once again. Now, with each step, he knew he was drawing closer to that peril.

Ahead, the chapel door stood open, the soothing lilt of plainsong drifting out into the sun-drenched yard. Estienne caught a glimpse of white-robed warrior monks, heads bowed in prayer, and felt a sudden urge to join them.

'Should we?' he asked as they passed, jerking his chin towards the kneeling figures. 'Surely a few moments in prayer couldn't go amiss.'

Hoston shook his head curtly. 'There'll be time enough for

prayer afore we leave. First, I would show you a different sort of sanctum.'

Estienne was about to ask what that meant, when Hoston turned and continued through the stone passageway of the fort. With a last glance at the chapel, Estienne followed, still none the wiser. Hoston led him deeper, down from the courtyard into a torchlit corridor beneath the bowels of Gastria. He took one of those torches and led Estienne to where stood a huge oak door, which Hoston opened with an iron key. A creak of hinges, and Estienne realised what the Templar had meant.

The armoury within was a cavernous space, the air heavy with the stink of oil, leather and steel. Racked along the walls, piled in corners, heaped in sprawling profusion, was an arsenal to beggar belief. Estienne had seen the Marshal's collection of arms, had spent long hours as a squire oiling hauberks and sharpening swords in the armoury of Pembroke, but it was a mere store cupboard compared to this. Everywhere he looked, steel winked in the guttering torchlight. Ranks of spears clustered on racks, blades honed to wicked points. Crossbows hung from hooks, wooden shelves groaned beneath the weight of helms, as maces, picks and horseman's axes jostled for space.

And the swords... by God, the swords. Dozens upon dozens of them, from humble arming blades to massive two-handers. They gleamed like bright flame in the light of the torch, racks of them marching away into the shadowed recesses.

'I've never seen such wealth of arms,' Estienne breathed, turning a slow circle. 'Not even in the Marshal's service.'

Hoston placed the torch in a sconce on the wall, before spreading his thick arms. 'The Temple is not meagre in its riches, lad. What sort of holy warriors would we be, if we lacked for weapons?'

Estienne regarded a hauberk on its stand, marvelling at the

fineness of the links, the leather trim. 'I suppose I shouldn't be surprised. The Order's coffers are said to be bottomless.'

'Perhaps not quite bottomless, but they're deep enough.' Hoston regarded that fine coat of mail. 'Aye, looks about your size. You shall have it.'

'My... my thanks, Hoston,' Estienne replied, not quite sure how to accept such generosity. 'But surely one of your brother knights has more need?'

Hoston shook his head. 'You were squired to the great William Marshal. Besieged at Dover, fought at Lincoln and saw the French defeated off Sandwich. You are a knight more than worthy of the name.' He thrust a great helm into Estienne's hands. 'What kind of man would I be if I saw you off to battle in nothing but sackcloth?'

Estienne swallowed as he gazed at his gift. The mail shimmered, each ring perfectly worked. The helm was plain black, with an elegance to its simplicity. Armour fit for any lord, and yet freely given.

'This is... I am honoured, Brother Hoston. Truly.'

The Templar offered a rare grin. 'Save your thanks, Ser Estienne. You'll earn that armour in the weeks to come. Of that, I'm sure. But that's not all.'

With that, he turned and stalked deeper into the dark of the armoury. Estienne followed as Hoston drew up before a battered rack. Upon it, sheathed in boiled leather, hung the biggest damned sword Estienne had ever seen. Fully four feet in the blade, with a grip designed for both hands, it looked more fit for a giant than a man.

'This,' Hoston said, taking up the weapon with a grin that held no mirth, 'is what you'll be wanting when you face those godless Saracens.'

He placed the sword into Estienne's hands, and he wrapped

both fists around the leather-bound grip. To his surprise it was lighter than it looked, and he could tell without drawing the steel the fineness of its balance.

'I have never fought with such a formidable weapon.'

'The great sword of war. It may take some getting used to, so I suggest you learn quick.'

Estienne gazed down at the weapon, imagining driving it through mail and bone, and his stomach roiled. The hammer Goffrey had gifted him was a brutish tool, but this... this was an instrument of purest butchery, forged for no other purpose than to cleave men in half. It would take time to grow accustomed to its brutal heft, but once he did...

'It's a mighty gift. I pray I prove worthy of it.'

'You will,' Hoston said with iron certainty. 'Your arm will be strong because your cause is righteous. With this blade, you'll smite the enemies of God. It is what you were made for.'

His words hung heavy. In that moment, staring into the pitiless sheen of his new sword, Estienne couldn't escape the feeling that a mantle of terrible purpose had settled upon his shoulders.

'I will... seek to prove you right.'

'Seek and ye shall find, young Wace,' Hoston replied, eyes glinting with zeal in the light of that single torch. 'Now come. Let's see how things proceed at the dock.'

Estienne laid his new weapon down beside the hauberk upon its rack, and followed Hoston from the armoury. When they reached the dock it seethed with activity, as sailors swarmed over the decks and rigging of the great dromonds and galleys, tightening lines, trimming sails, stowing barrels and bales that would feed the crusading army when they arrived at the mouth of the Nile. Grooms and horse-boys wrestled with destriers and sumpters, fighting to load the recalcitrant beasts up the gangplanks and into the dark holds that would be their home until they reached land once more.

Estienne drew up at the edge of the jetty, watching the orderly pandemonium unfold. 'So many willing knights. And not just of your Order.'

'Aye,' Hoston replied. 'Half of Christendom, it seems, all bound for the same bloody shore. And more besides already besiege Damietta's walls, the grand master of the Templar Order among them. Question is, are you ready for it, lad?'

Estienne gazed south across the wind-whipped sea. At what waited beyond that horizon.

Was he ready? In truth, he didn't know. In his years of service to the Marshal, he'd waded through blood and shit. He'd felt the crunch of bone beneath his hammer, watched the light leave men's eyes. He was no stranger to battle, but this... this felt different. Before he had done his duty to king and country; now he was to fight for the Holy Cross. For God. And no matter how much Estienne told himself this cause was righteous, he couldn't quell the worm of unease burrowing beneath his ribs.

'It will be unlike anything I've faced before,' he said at last, the words feeling like an admission of weakness that shamed him.

'Aye, that it will. The Saracen fights like no Christian knight. They are swift horsemen, keen archers and their blades cut like razors. All the tourneys in the world couldn't prepare a man for their like.'

It sounded like a challenge. One Estienne was not about to balk at. 'I will not falter. When the time comes, I will fight as God demands, no matter the foe.'

A slow smile curved Hoston's lips. 'That you will, Ser Estienne. That you will. I've no doubt you've got the Marshal's own steel in you, and I'd wager you'll put the fear of the Almighty in the hearts of any Saracen you face.'

With that, he turned and strode back toward the fort, leaving Estienne amid the bustle of the dock. Overhead, gulls wheeled and keened, looking and sounding much like the birds that had circled Pembroke, a lifetime ago.

The sudden memory of Eva, of her dark hair and quicksilver smile, flashed before he could quell it. Immediately, he pushed it from his mind, a door slamming shut. There could be no room for sentiment where he was bound. No softness in the face of what was to come. He was a weapon in the hands of God now, and he would not rest until Outremer was free.

The past was gone.

All that remained was Holy War.

2

Estienne stood at the prow of the dromond, wind whipping his hair into a flurry. They had sailed no more than a mile inland, the banks of the river almost too distant to see, but now as he squinted against the glare off the water, one hand lifted to shield his gaze, he drank in the sight of the city they had come to conquer.

Rising beside the glittering expanse of the Nile, stood Damietta. The port city's high stone walls were starkly pale against the darkness of the river, its towers and battlements jutting like a jaw of broken teeth. Even from this distance, Estienne could see the tiny black specks of figures moving along the ramparts – Saracen warriors battling against the onslaught that threatened to consume them.

'Quite the sight, isn't it?' Hoston's gruff voice at his shoulder.

'Aye,' Estienne replied. 'Though not a welcoming one.'

'No, I don't suppose it is.' The grey-bearded Templar narrowed his eyes at the oncoming shoreline. 'The Saracens have held fast thus far, despite our best efforts.'

Another Templar, a hawk-faced man named Andre, sidled

up to join them at the rail. He jerked his chin towards the centre of the river, where a great blackened tower rose from the swirling waters like a charred stump.

'See that keep? Bastards used it to string a great chain across the mouth of the Nile, blocking our ships. We had to destroy it just to get this far.'

Estienne frowned, eyeing the ruins. 'But still Damietta stands?'

'For now. We have surrounded the city, but those walls are thick, and the Saracens fight like demons. But we'll have them yet, mark my words.'

The ships pressed on, the rhythmic slap of the oars and the creak of timber a counterpoint to the cries of the gulls wheeling overhead. As they drew closer to the shore just north of the city, Estienne could make out the sprawl of the crusader camp along the bank. A sea of tents and pavilions, flags snapping in the breeze, the tiny figures of men and horses swarming the dockside. And in the distance, the dull boom of siege engines hurling their payloads against Damietta's unyielding defences. Estienne watched a boulder arc through the air to shatter against the battlements in a spray of shards. If the barrage had any effect, he couldn't see it, the walls as unyielding as the relentless sun.

The ships cruised into the makeshift bay, activity on deck becoming frenetic as orders were shouted, oars raised and mooring ropes thrown ashore. Estienne stepped across the gangplank as the work to unload the ship began, the crunch of dirt beneath his feet a welcome sound, despite the foreboding sight of Damietta in the distance.

He watched as squires and serving-brothers led snorting, stamping warhorses down the gangplanks, the beasts' hooves churning the sand. Wagons were piled high with barrels and sacks, supplies to feed the relentless war machine of Christendom.

As he cast his eye over the shore, a curious sight caught his attention. A group of shipwrights laboured over an immense, ungainly looking vessel. Beams and planks lay scattered beside two cogs lashed together with thick rope.

Estienne nudged Andre, tipping his head towards the river's edge. 'What's that they're building?'

Andre squinted against the glare. 'Ah, that. Some fool notion of siege craft the Frisian shipwrights have concocted. They plan to sail it against the city walls like a siege tower. Damned thing doesn't look fit to float, let alone assail a wall.'

Estienne regarded the strange sight for a long moment, a sense of unease trickling coldly down his spine. The mission seemed clear – take Damietta in the name of the Almighty and put the fear of God into the hearts of the heathens. But standing here, the scale of it, the thousands of lives all turned to the same task, and the thousands more standing opposed to it... it suddenly felt like a goal beyond the reach of even these doughty soldiers of God.

No time to think on it further, as another order was shouted, and their train of supply wagons began to move from the dock-side. Estienne mounted a waiting horse and followed Hoston and the others into the teeming throng of the camp, as the wagons rolled.

The place was a roiling hive, a sea of tents flapping in the breeze, air thick with the stench of horseflesh, sweat and rot. Flies buzzed in clouds and gathered upon every surface, Estienne more than once having to swat them from his view. They picked their way through the mud and filth between the tents, trying not to inhale too deeply. All around him, men jostled and cursed, voices raised in a clamour of different tongues – Italian, French, German, a smattering of English.

Estienne had imagined the servants of God would be a disciplined lot, filled with pious zeal, but the reality was far different. Everywhere he looked he saw signs of degradation. Drunk men slumped in the open, their piss drying in the sand. A group of soldiers diced and squabbled, coin changing hands in quick succession. Wild-eyed preachers ranted from atop barrels, their words lost amid the clamour.

'Has it always been like this?' he murmured to Hoston, as they rode around a pile of reeking horse shit. 'Since the beginning?'

The older knight grimaced. 'Aye, more or less, though it looks worse than when I was last here. Men grow restless with inaction, and this siege has dragged on longer than most. Idle hands turn to vice all too easily.'

Andre spat into the muck. 'And disease hasn't helped. The bloody flux has swept through the camp like a scythe. We've lost hundreds to it.'

'The Almighty tests our resolve,' Hoston replied. 'But those with true faith will endure.'

Estienne wasn't so sure. Faith felt a paltry shield against the reek of desperation that hung over this place like a pall. Nevertheless, they continued through the degradation, every step bringing yet more questions to the fore. Eventually he saw a group of tents that stood a little apart from the rest, their banners bearing the crossed keys of the Holy See.

'Who holds command here?'

'The papal legate, Pelagius Galvani,' Andre replied. 'The leader of this whole affair, despatched by Pope Honorius himself to be the guardian of our faith. Though I use that term loosely.

Man's more concerned with his own comfort than the state of his followers.'

Hoston shot him a chiding look. 'Have a care how you speak. The legate commands in the Holy Father's name.'

Andre grumbled something under his breath, but Estienne got the gist of his attitude toward their divine leader.

'So this is only a portion of our forces?' Estienne asked as they wended their way through the seething sprawl.

'Indeed,' Hoston replied. 'The Italians hold this northern camp, under Pelagius. To the south of the city, the French and their Pisan allies camp under the command of John of Brienne, the King of Jerusalem. And to the west, across the Nile, the German Order of Saint Mary are led by Grand Master Hermann of Salza.'

'So many factions,' Estienne murmured. 'And they are all of a single purpose in this?'

Andre grinned, raising an eyebrow that suggested they were not. 'As often as not. But Pelagius and John of Brienne rarely see eye to eye. The legate is as uncompromising as the hand of God itself. He sees this crusade as his way of bringing the undisputed authority of the papacy to the Holy Land. John simply wants to reclaim what is his by right – his throne in Jerusalem. But fear not, you won't need to get mired in such fractious nonsense. You're with us.'

'So where are we headed?'

Hoston jerked his chin east along a road that wended its way southeast. 'The Templar and Hospitaller camp. We'll have a proper welcome there. The grand masters keep their knights in better order than does Pelagius.'

Estienne couldn't help but feel relieved. Surely among Hoston's knightly brethren, the highest virtues of the crusade would hold sway. He could only hope it was a far cry from the deprivation that had so far welcomed him.

Soon they left the northern camp behind, following a short trail towards wooden fortifications in the shadow of the city's eastern wall. All the while, Damietta loomed, and Estienne wondered how long it would be before he added his number to those assailing it. The prospect made his insides roil. The chance to prove his worth in the eyes of God and man, warring with the inevitable dangers of throwing himself against an unknown enemy. He bristled at the very thought, impatience warring with good sense.

When they finally reached the Templar enclave its difference to the northern camp was stark as night from day. Passing through the stout wooden palisades that encircled the orderly rows of tents, Estienne felt his tension ease fractionally. Here there was no drunken carousing, no piles of waste rotting in the sun. Men went about their business with purpose, hauberks and helms polished to a hard sheen, weapons close at hand. Estienne saw knights conferring over maps, squires and pages loading ammunition for the mangonels and trebuchets that squatted at the perimeter like brooding beasts.

Hoston surveyed the bustling scene with a grunt of approval. 'See, I told you. The grand masters run a tight ship.'

Estienne could only nod, drinking in the sight. This was what he'd imagined when he'd left the familiar shores of England, bound for the glory of God's own war. Here were men united by holy purpose, prepared to lay down their lives for the faith. It filled him with a sense of determination unlike any he'd known before.

Voices called out in greeting as they approached the heart of the encampment. All about, the banners of the Templars and Hospitallers flew above a cluster of sturdy pavilions, the red cross on white, and white cross on black, flapping gently in the breeze. Grim faces eyed them as men raised their hands in welcome. Hoston, Andre and the others acknowledged those greetings in kind, and Estienne suddenly felt a stranger among these brothers, keenly aware that he would have to prove himself worthy to be in their company.

The wagons came to an abrupt halt, and the Templars began to unload in disciplined order. Hoston clapped Estienne on the shoulder as he dismounted.

'Come,' Hoston said, leading him away from the train of wagons. 'There is someone you should meet.'

Estienne followed, and as they entered the central enclosure of the camp, he saw a group of knights clustered around a large table strewn with maps. At one side stood a thickly bearded man in a white cappa, the crimson cross bold upon his chest. He glanced up at their approach, piercing brown eyes narrowed against the glare.

'Brother Hoston,' he called out in greeting. 'It is good to see you again. And with a new companion.'

'Yes, Grand Master,' Hoston replied, with a curt bow. 'Pierre of Montaigu, may I present Ser Estienne Wace, formerly squire to William Marshal himself.'

Pierre's gaze sharpened, fixing on Estienne like a hawk sighting prey. 'The Marshal, eh? A great man. And bonded to us in brotherhood near his end. It must have been a great honour serving as his squire.'

'It was, my lord,' Estienne replied. 'And his loss is felt keenly by all of England, but I know he rests with God now.'

'As will we all, in time.' Pierre gestured to the man standing at his right hand, a looming figure with a nose that looked to have been broken more than once. 'My brother, Garin of Montaigu, Grand Master of the Knights Hospitaller.'

Garin offered a nod, his eyes keen within a sun-weathered face. Estienne struggled to stand tall as the two grand masters regarded him. Here were men who had seen more battles than he'd seen summers, warriors of God tempered in the crucible of the Holy Land, and Estienne suddenly felt out of place. What could a fledgling knight offer them but another sword arm, another body to throw into the breach? Would he even make a difference?

His doubt spurred him to speak. 'It is my honour to serve beside you, Grand Masters. I only hope I may prove myself worthy of God's grace, just as the Marshal did. I'll fight with every ounce of strength the Almighty has granted me.'

Pierre studied him for a long moment. 'Bold words, young Wace. Let us hope your blade is as keen as your tongue. Damietta's walls still stand, despite our best efforts. The Saracens are dug in like ticks and show no sign of yielding. So there'll be no shortage of opportunities for you to prove your words.'

As if to punctuate his claim, the deep thud of a mangonel sounded from the perimeter, followed by the now-familiar whistle of a payload arcing through the air. As Estienne heard the dull thud of impact, Hoston clapped a hand to his shoulder.

'Best we go find you somewhere to bed down, lad.'

Pierre and Garin had already turned their attention back to the table once more. Estienne followed Hoston, leaving the grand masters to their strategies. All the while he wondered how he might possibly prove himself to such men, so uncompromising in their faith.

Quickly he quelled that flicker of doubt, locking it away. He was a soldier of God now, a holy warrior pledged to the highest of callings. He could not falter, not when he was to soon embark on his greatest test.

3

Days had bled into one another since their arrival, each as stifling and uneventful as the last. The city stood defiant, its battlements unbreached, despite the constant barrage from the siege engines. The Templar camp bustled with its usual activity as the day waned, men going about their duties with grim determination, and as night fell Estienne found himself sitting between Hoston and Andre at one of the many campfires. As they settled around the flames, a young squire brought them bowls of a thick, tasteless stew. Estienne took his portion with a nod of thanks.

When night fell over the crusader camp, an unexpected sound drifted on the evening breeze. From the south, where John of Brienne's forces were encamped, a song rose into the darkening sky. The melody was unfamiliar, but the words, though indistinct at this distance, spoke of home and hearth, of green fields and forests so far removed from this harsh, sun-baked land.

The song swelled as more voices joined in to the south, a chorus of homesickness given voice. It tugged at something deep within Estienne's chest, stirring memories of home, and for a moment, he was transported back to Pembroke, to the life he'd left behind. A life he could never regain.

As that noise still drifted on the desert breeze, a new song suddenly erupted from the north. This one emanated from Pelagius' camp – a hymnal, solemn and reverent. The two songs clashed in the night air, each fighting for dominance. One seemed to speak to the heart, to the longing for home and the simple pleasures left behind. The other called to the soul.

Estienne sat frozen, caught between these competing melodies, and as he listened, he felt the vast distance between himself and everything he'd once known. These songs, so familiar yet so out of place. The desert night, the looming walls of Damietta, the holy assembly of men from all corners of Christendom – all of it felt suddenly so foreign. And yet… despite their varied origins, they were all here for a common purpose. The songs, even in their contrast, somehow underscored this shared mission.

When he looked to his left, he saw Andre was watching him, a wry smile on his lips. 'That happens from time to time. Stirring, isn't it?'

Estienne opened his mouth to reply, when a flash lit up the night sky. In the next moment, fire licked at the air, the western barricade bursting into bright flame. He leapt up, hand instinctively reaching for a weapon that wasn't there.

Hoston was already moving, his voice rising above the sudden clamour of shouts. 'We're under attack. To arms, brothers. To arms.'

The camp erupted into chaos. Men scrambled for weapons, their shouts of alarm mixing with a sudden howling from beyond the perimeter of the camp. Estienne's heart hammered in his chest as he tried to make sense of the mayhem surrounding him.

Another flash illuminated the night, followed by a whoosh of fire. Estienne watched in horror as a tent burst into flames, the canvas consumed in seconds.

'What devilry is this?' Estienne gasped, the acrid stench turning his stomach.

'Naptha,' Hoston barked in reply, glaring into those flames. 'The Saracens hurl it from their walls to repel us, but now they use it to attack our camp. Move, lad. We need to defend the wall.'

They sprinted through the chaos, dodging panicked men and flaming debris. The air filled with smoke, choking and disorienting. Somewhere in the distance, Estienne heard the thunder of hooves.

'They've breached the defences,' someone cried.

'More men to the western wall!' screamed another.

Andre appeared at Estienne's side, his sword already drawn. 'We need to stem the tide before they overrun us completely.'

Estienne nodded, suddenly aware of his own vulnerability. 'My weapons... they're in my tent.'

'Go!' Hoston barked. 'And be quick about it, boy. Andre, watch his back.'

As Hoston rushed towards the sounds of battle, Estienne and Andre sprinted in the opposite direction. Estienne heard the whistle of an arrow a split second before it thudded into the ground at his feet, but he carried on regardless. They both dashed through the rows of tents, before skidding to a halt at his own shelter.

'Be quick, lad,' Andre growled, as his eyes scanned the dark. 'We're needed at the defences.'

Estienne burst through the flap of his tent, fumbling in the darkness for a weapon before his hand closed around the hilt of his great war sword. When he rushed out into the night once more, he could see the western perimeter was in flames.

'Move it.' Andre's voice cut through the din. 'Every man needs to—'

An arrow buried itself in Andre's throat with a sickening thud. The knight's eyes widened in shock, his sword falling from his grip. He reached for the shaft protruding from his neck, blood bubbling from his lips as he tried to speak.

'No.' Estienne lunged forward, catching Andre as he collapsed.

He lowered the dying man to the ground, unable to do anything but watch as the life drained from his eyes. Andre's body went limp, his final breath bubbling from his throat, and Estienne stared down at him, rage rising.

'Templars.' Pierre of Montaigu's voice cut through the cacophony of battle. 'To me. Rally to me.'

Estienne stood, grip tightening on his sword as he turned toward the grand master's voice. Then he was running, muscles straining as he sprinted through the camp, dodging raining arrows and leaping over fallen bodies. He could see little of the enemy through the black, but the weight of the war sword felt reassuring, and he could barely quell his eagerness to make it sing. Andre's lifeless eyes haunted him more with each step, fuelling a rage that threatened to overwhelm him.

A horse burst from the dark, its rider a silhouette against the flames in the distance. The Saracen warrior raised a curved blade high, war cry on his lips as he bore down on Estienne.

Time seemed to slow. Estienne planted his feet, his years at the sword taking over as he gauged the distance, waiting until the last possible moment, then pivoted, swinging his massive blade in a wide arc.

The sword bit through mail and flesh, the Saracen tipping backward from his saddle to hit the ground with a thud. Estienne dashed forward two steps before he skewered the man where he lay. There was a grunt, then a sigh as Estienne withdrew the blade, then silence.

He looked down at the corpse, its eyes staring at the dark heavens, all that was visible of the face behind the aventail. Estienne had killed before, but never like this, never so easily. The war sword's power was terrifying, unlike anything he'd wielded before, and he suddenly yearned to wield it again...

A scream from nearby snapped him out of his daze. Estienne turned to see a Templar knight struggling against three Saracen warriors as they battered relentlessly against his shield. Without hesitation, Estienne charged into the fray, his first blow catching one of them in the back, the massive blade cleaving through mail, and spine with it. The man fell without a sound, dead before he hit the ground. The other two turned to face this new threat, their eyes widening at the sight of Estienne's blood-drenched form.

What followed was a blur of steel, too fast for Estienne to even parse. Each swing a death sentence, before two more corpses lay in the dust. No time to gloat, no time to even think on what he had done, as the Templar turned, wide-eyed, and gestured for him to follow.

When they reached the perimeter, the scene was one of utter chaos. Templars fought desperately against a wave of Saracen attackers, the air thick with arrows, the twang of bowstrings a constant harmony with the clash of steel and screams of the dying.

Estienne threw himself into the melee, his war sword rising and falling in a deadly rhythm. A face leered at him from the dark, curved sabre raised, and he cut it down without thought, blade cleaving with relish. Another came lurching out of the night, and his huge sword swept left to right, doing God's own work, his arm fuelled with divine purpose.

He fought alongside men whose names he didn't know, united in their desperate struggle for survival as blood soaked the ground, the earth muddy with it. The night was tinged with a red hue as he fought, that blade singing in his grip as he lashed out at screaming faces beneath their domed helms. Their attackers looked desperate, frenzied as they flung themselves at the Templar lines, but Estienne felt no sorrow for their plight. No compassion. All he saw were enemies of God standing in his way, and his only purpose was to cut them down in the name of Christendom like so much wheat.

A Saracen's blade suddenly slipped past Estienne's guard, opening a gash along his ribs. He barely felt the pain, lost in the frenzy of combat, and his return stroke took the man's head clean off his shoulders.

'Stand fast.' Pierre's voice cut across the defensive line. '*Deus vult*.'

The shout was returned by a hundred Templars and Hospitallers alike, spurring them to greater effort against the Saracen onslaught. Estienne found himself caught up in it, spurred on by the red surge of righteous fury, thinking only of God's glory as he swung that huge blade again and again.

As dawn's first light began to creep over the horizon, Estienne found himself fighting back-to-back with Hoston. The older knight's sword was notched and blood-stained, his black surcoat now a gory mess.

'There's too many of them,' he shouted over the din. 'We can't hold much longer.'

Estienne risked a glance beyond the perimeter. His heart sank at the sight of even more Saracen warriors pouring towards their position. It seemed for every enemy they cut down, two more took his place.

'Aye. We're going to be overrun,' Estienne growled, cold reality sending chills down his back.

Hoston nodded grimly. 'But we'll make the bastards pay for every Christian soul they take.'

As the sun crested the horizon, casting its light over the blood-soaked battlefield, Estienne allowed himself a moment of grim acceptance. If this was to be his end, at least he would meet it with a sword in his hand. Perhaps not the glorious death he had envisioned, but it would have to be enough.

The blast of a horn cut through the din, its clear note a stark contrast to the relentless clash of steel. Estienne turned to the south, squinting through the meagre dawn light for the source of the sound. Then he heard it – the thunder of hooves, growing louder with each passing heartbeat. The Saracens heard it too, their attack faltering as they turned to face this new threat.

Mounted knights galloped from the gloom, charging across the sand, their armour gleaming in the dawn light. At their head flew a banner Estienne recognised – a black cross on a white field... The Order of Saint Mary had come to their aid.

Lances slammed into the Saracen flank, that seething mass of horseflesh and armoured might crashing down like an avalanche. They shattered on impact, sending Saracen archers flying from their saddles, and those who survived the initial charge found themselves trampled beneath iron-shod hooves or cut down by the knights' swords. Estienne watched in awe as the knights carved through the Saracen ranks, their discipline impeccable, each man moving in concert with his brothers.

Around him, a cheer went up from the Templar lines, hoarse voices finding new strength in the face of salvation.

'For God and the Holy Land!' Pierre bellowed, raising his

sword high and striding across the fallen defences. 'Drive the bastards back.'

The Templars surged after him, catching the disorganised Saracens between hammer and anvil. Estienne threw himself into the fray with renewed vigour, his war sword rising and falling in great sweeping arcs. Quickly, the Saracens' will to fight crumbled in the face of the onslaught, and what had begun as an orderly retreat quickly devolved into a rout. They fled in all directions, abandoning weapons and wounded comrades alike in their desperation to escape.

But Estienne's blood was up and singing for vengeance. Gripping the sword tighter, lest it slip from his grip, he gave chase, feet pounding across the plain. So focused was he on the hunt that he failed to heed any shouts of warning, or see there were no others at his side.

His lips curled back from his teeth in a rictus snarl as he ran. Those heathen bastards were just ahead of him, and he would have his due. He would slay them all for the glory of God. For the death of Andre. For—

Suddenly his path was blocked, by a rearing horse, a knight of Saint Mary sitting proudly astride. The horseman reined in sharply as Estienne stumbled back.

'Easy there, brother,' the knight called out. 'The day is won. And if you run much further you'll be sitting on the lap of the enemy.'

Estienne blinked, suddenly aware of how far he'd strayed from the Templar lines. He lowered his sword, chest heaving as the red tide of battle began to ebb.

'My thanks,' he managed between ragged breaths. 'I was...'

Foolish, was the word he was looking for. Too consumed by his own ardour for blood to control his urges, but he said nothing more. In response, the knight grinned knowingly from within his open-faced helm. He was young and handsome, with a squarer jaw than Estienne had ever seen.

'Best you get back to the safety of camp, my friend,' he replied. 'Before the Saracens decide to take one more Christian for their tally.'

With that he reined his horse around and headed back toward his fellows.

Estienne followed, and by the time he reached the perimeter of the camp once more, he saw Grand Master Pierre deep in conversation with a tall, broad-shouldered man with a long moustache, whose white surcoat bore the black cross of Saint Mary.

'...lucky we were visiting John's camp to the south when we heard the commotion,' the knight was saying, German accent thick. 'We rode as soon as we realised you were under attack.'

Pierre clasped the man's arm, his relief evident even through his exhaustion. 'Your arrival was truly God-sent, Marshal Hermann. We owe you a great debt.'

'We are all servants of Christ here,' Hermann replied. 'Today it was our swords that turned the tide. Tomorrow it may be yours that save us all.'

The knights began to mount up, and Estienne watched exhausted, as they rode away, their white surcoats soon lost to the haze of dust and smoke that still hung over the battlefield.

Once they had disappeared into the distance, the rush of blood that had sustained Estienne through the long night finally began to ebb. His limbs were heavy, the great war sword, which had felt so light and deadly in the heat of battle, now dragged at his arm like an anchor.

'Wace.'

Estienne turned to see Hoston approaching, his face grim.

Blood had dried in his beard, and a nasty gash across his forehead spoke of a close call during the fighting.

'Hoston. Glad to see you alive.'

Hoston's eyes swept over the carnage surrounding them. 'Aye. We lost many brothers this night. Good men, all of them.'

'Andre,' Estienne replied. 'I saw him fall. There was nothing I could do.'

Hoston laid a hand on Estienne's shoulder. 'He died as a warrior of God, defending his brothers. We can ask for no better end.'

The sun had fully risen now, its harsh light revealing the true extent of the devastation. Bodies littered the ground as far as the eye could see, Christian and Saracen alike rendered equal in death. Before he had come here, Estienne had relished the prospect of his first battle. Of a chance to prove his devotion to God and to do his part in returning the Holy Land to Christendom. Now the grim reality of that task was writ large before him, and he knew it was but the first step on his journey.

'What now?' Estienne asked.

'Now we bury our dead. And pray that their sacrifice was not in vain.'

As if suddenly spurred by Hoston's words, men began to move through the camp, gathering the bodies of fallen Templars. Estienne joined them, lifting broken corpses and laying them out in neat rows. With each fallen brother Estienne helped carry, he felt a piece of himself harden.

So many dead, and still they had not breached the walls of Damietta. And in the distance, those walls loomed on. A perpetual reminder of the task that lay ahead.

4

Both Templars and Hospitallers had been summoned north on a morning marred by cloud, and Estienne joined the contingent on the road to Pelagius' camp. As he entered the northern base, riding alongside Hoston, the place seemed even worse than when they'd had first arrived. A miasma of unwashed bodies, rotting food and human waste assaulted his nostrils, and he fought to keep his face impassive, not wanting to appear weak in front of the veteran knights he rode with.

All around them, the camp seethed with activity. Men-at-arms lounged in the shade of makeshift shelters, gambling and drinking despite the early hour. Camp followers darted between tents, carrying baskets of bread and jugs of wine. The air rang with discordant voices shouting in half-a-dozen different tongues, and the sound of someone frantically coupling resounded from a nearby tent. A far cry from the orderly rows and quiet discipline of the Templar encampment.

'Not what you expected from God's holy warriors?' Hoston's eyes crinkled with amusement as he noted the look of disgust on

Estienne's face. 'More like Babylon itself, than the encampment of a righteous army.'

Estienne shook his head. 'I already knew there were... excesses. But this... seems to have got worse.'

'Aye, it's a sorry sight,' Hoston agreed. 'But men grow restless in siege. And Pelagius has a looser hand on the reins than our grand masters. He surrounds himself with just as many sell-swords as pious men. And this is what happens.'

They rode on, picking their way through the press of bodies and makeshift structures. As they neared the centre of the camp, Estienne caught sight of a large pavilion flying the papal banner. A group of richly dressed men were gathered outside, their faces grim as they conferred in low voices. Estienne watched as the grand masters, Pierre and Garin, dismounted and made their way toward the others.

'The war council gathers.' Hoston nodded to a tall, bald man with a heavy beard. 'John of Brienne is already there. Along with Hermann of Salza and the other leaders.'

Estienne leaned forward in his saddle, straining to catch a glimpse of the legendary King of Jerusalem. Beside him he recognised Hermann of Salza, the tall knight with his drooping moustache who had ridden to their aid not five nights before.

'They may be some time,' Hoston said, dismounting with a grunt. 'Perhaps you'd like to have a look around while we wait? Get the lay of the land?'

Estienne hesitated. Part of him yearned to stay and witness the deliberations of these great men. But he knew his place. He was here to serve, not to meddle in affairs beyond his station.

'Yes, that might not be a bad idea,' he said at last. 'I'll leave my horse with you, if that's all right?'

Hoston nodded, taking the reins. 'Mind yourself. This camp's not as friendly as ours.'

With a final glance at the command tent, where the great and good of the crusade were now gathered in conference, Estienne set off into the bustle of the camp. The further he ventured, the more his initial impressions were confirmed. The air was thick with the reek of unwashed bodies, the constant keening of gulls punctuated by bursts of raucous laughter and angry shouts. Men sprawled in the shade, faces flushed red from drink despite the early hour. In one corner, a pair of knights grappled in the dust, urged on by a ring of jeering onlookers.

Was this truly God's army? These men seemed more interested in vice than virtue, more concerned with earthly pleasures than heavenly rewards.

A flash of crimson caught his eye, and he turned to see a banner snapping in the hot breeze – a golden lion rampant on a field of red. Estienne's heart quickened... he knew that device.

Sure enough, beneath the banner sat Savari of Mauléon, surrounded by a group of richly dressed knights. He was sprawled in a chair, a goblet of wine in one hand, his saturnine features creased in laughter at some jest. It was a far cry from when Estienne had seen him last at the monastery of Saint Albans, when King John had set him to curb rebellion in the south of England. They had not spoken a word back then – Estienne had only been a squire and not in a position to add his voice to proceedings – but perhaps there might at least be some accord here. They had both fought on the same side during that troubled time, and now they were equals under God. Surely even a man of status like Savari would welcome a fellow servant of King John.

Estienne hesitated, torn between caution and a need to make a connection, to find his place among these seasoned warriors. Drawing a deep breath, he approached the group.

'My lord Savari,' he said, offering a small bow. 'I don't know if you remember me, but I was a servant of William Marshal during the rebellion in England. You and I were at the muster in Saint Albans, though I was not yet knighted. It's an honour to see you here.'

Savari's eyes flicked towards him, narrowing slightly. 'Is it, now? Your face rings no bells. I'm afraid I don't recall every squire who fetched a cup for me.'

A ripple of laughter ran through the gathered knights and Estienne felt heat rising that he was quick to quell.

'I... I have earned my spurs, my lord.' Estienne kept his tone as even as he could manage. 'I fought at Lincoln, at Sandwich—'

'Of course you did, boy.' Savari cut him off with a wave of his hand. 'I'm sure you were very brave. Now run along and let the men talk.'

More laughter, crueller this time. Estienne's hands clenched into fists, and he wanted nothing more than to lash out, to slap the grin from Savari's face and prove the truth of his words, but he knew that way lay ruin. He was a knight now, not some hot-headed squire to be goaded into a brawl.

With a stiff bow, he turned and walked away, the mocking laughter of Savari's men ringing in his ears. Each step was an effort of will, but he kept walking, jaw clenched so tight it ached. He would prove his worth on the battlefield, not in some drunken scuffle. Let them laugh. When the time came to face the Saracens once again, he would show them what he could do.

As he walked, trying to master himself, a new sound reached his ears – a voice raised in fervent prayer. Intrigued, despite his sudden dark mood, he followed the sound to its source.

A crowd had gathered, where a tonsured monk stood preaching. His voice rang out clear and strong, filled with passionate conviction as he exhorted his listeners to cast aside worldly concerns and embrace God's love.

'Brothers and sisters,' the monk cried, arms upraised, 'you stand on the threshold of paradise. Cast off these shackles of sin, embrace poverty and humility, and you shall know the true glory of our Lord.'

Estienne edged closer, drawn by the monk's words. All around him, knights and men-at-arms had gathered beside spellbound camp followers and other penitents, all listening with rapt attention, many kneeling in the dust. It was a stark contrast to the debauchery he had witnessed earlier. As he watched, men and women in simple robes moved among the crowd, offering blessings and prayers. Their belts were carefully knotted in three places, and they moved with an air of quiet reverence.

'Quite a sight, isn't it? How he holds them in the palm of his hand with naught but a word.'

Estienne started at the voice spoken in a thick German accent, though the Latin was impeccable. Turning he saw a familiar figure at his shoulder – the handsome face of the knight of Saint Mary who had stopped him racing into certain danger during the recent battle. Up close, Estienne could see he was young, perhaps no older than himself, with clear blue eyes and a shock of black hair.

'It is,' Estienne agreed. 'And I should thank you. For what you did during the fight at the Templar camp. You likely saved my life.'

The knight shrugged, a small smile playing at his lips. 'All part of my duty, brother.'

Estienne nodded, feeling a sudden spark of kinship with this fellow warrior.

'I'm Estienne Wace,' he said, offering his hand. 'Formerly of William Marshal's household.'

'Amalric von Regensburg,' the other knight replied, grabbing

Estienne's outstretched hand before offering a crisp bow. 'Of the Teutonic Order of Saint Mary.'

Estienne jerked his chin towards the preaching monk. 'Who is he? I've never seen one man command such attention.'

'That's Francesco,' Amalric explained. 'A rich man's son turned hermit, now something of a prophet. He draws quite a crowd wherever he goes.'

Estienne's brow furrowed as he watched the robed figures moving through the throng. 'And those others? I've never seen monks and nuns mingling so freely.'

'Not monks and nuns, my friend. Those are the Brothers and Sisters of Penance. See how their belts are tied? Three knots – for poverty, chastity and obedience.'

Estienne shook his head in wonder. 'I would not have expected to find such piety here. When last I passed through, this camp was a den of vice.'

'The crusade attracts all sorts,' Amalric said with a shrug. 'Saints and sinners alike. But Francesco... he has a way of reaching even the most wayward of sinners.'

As if to prove his point, a burly knight near the front of the crowd fell to his knees, great sobs wracking his body as Francesco laid a comforting hand on his head. All around, men wept openly, caught up in the fervour of the moment.

Estienne felt a sudden longing for such certainty, such faith. He had come to this land to serve God, to prove himself worthy of His grace, and had thought himself on the righteous path. But in the face of such devotion, his own convictions seemed paltry and weak.

'Wace.'

The sharp call cut through the reverent atmosphere. Estienne turned to see Hoston approaching, his craggy face set in its usual stern lines.

'We're about to leave,' the older knight said, jerking his head back towards the command tent. 'Best say your goodbyes.'

Estienne nodded, turning back to Amalric and clasped the young knight's arm. 'It was good to meet you. Perhaps we'll have a chance to speak again soon.'

Amalric bowed again. 'God willing. May He watch over you, brother.'

'And you, my friend.'

As Estienne fell into step beside Hoston, he cast one last glance over his shoulder. Francesco was still preaching, his voice rising and falling in a lilting cadence. For a moment, Estienne wished he could stay, to lose himself in that fervour, that passion, and forget the weight of expectation he had placed upon himself.

Instead, they made their way back through the camp, and as they neared its edge, Hoston broke the silence. 'The council is concluded. We attack on the morrow.'

Estienne's pulse quickened. 'How?'

Hoston jerked his chin towards the harbour, where a cluster of ships sat at anchor. Estienne recognised them as the same vessels he had seen when they first landed – but now there were four great cogs lashed together, with a raised wooden scaffold erected across their decks. Upon that scaffold, scores of men might stand shoulder to shoulder, fully armed and armoured, at a height with the high walls of Damietta.

'Those ships. That's our way to breach the city. We'll assault the walls from the river. All we need now are men with enough faith to stand atop those platforms and weather the Saracen fire.'

Estienne's heart leapt. Here, at last, was his chance to prove himself. To show anyone who doubted him that he was a knight worthy of renown. Worthy of God's grace.

'I'll do it,' he said, the words tumbling out before he could consider their weight.

Hoston raised an eyebrow, studying Estienne with those piercing eyes. 'It's no small thing you're volunteering for, lad. Any man who stands up there will need the Almighty's own protection. And God's own luck to survive.'

'Then I'll find out if I'm such a man,' he replied, willing his voice not to waver.

For a long moment, Hoston said nothing. Then, slowly, he nodded. 'Very well. I'll speak to the grand master. But know this – once you're up there, there's no turning back. You fight, or you die. Simple as that.'

'I understand,' Estienne replied.

And he did. This was what he had come for, what he had trained for all these long years. A chance to prove his worth, to carve his name into the annals of history. But beneath the exhilaration, a small voice whispered doubts. Was he truly ready for this? Could he live up to the legacy of the great William Marshal? Or would he fall, forgotten and unmourned, on some foreign shore?

Estienne pushed the thoughts aside. There was no room for doubt now. He had made his choice. All that remained was to see it through… and do his best to survive.

5

The Nile's murky waters churned beneath the lashed galleys, waves lapping against hulls as a hundred oarsmen rowed towards Damietta's looming walls. Estienne stood rigid among the press of bodies atop the makeshift platform, his arming sword gripped tight in his right hand, shield hefted high in his left bearing the red crusader cross. The familiar weight of Goffrey's hammer hung at his hip – a reassuring talisman in the face of the nightmare to come. He'd left the great war sword behind, much as it pained him. In the crush of men and the chaos of battle to come, it would be unwieldy and more hindrance than help.

The stench of fear permeated the air. All around him, men muttered prayers or exchanged grim looks. Some retched over the side, whether from nerves or the lurching sway of the ships, Estienne couldn't say.

A whistle split the air, followed by a dull boom as the crusader artillery on the western shore launched its salvo. Stone and flame arced through the sky to smash against the battlements in front of them. Clouds of dust billowed up, subduing the defenders for precious moments, allowing them to approach unmolested, but it would not be long enough. No sooner had the dust begun to settle, than Estienne heard the Saracens barking at one another, their archers moving into position.

'Shields up!'

The cry rang out, and Estienne raised his shield just as the first volley of arrows hissed from across the water. Shafts thudded into wood and mail alike. A man to Estienne's left screamed, an arrow protruding from the slit in his helm. He toppled backwards, nearly taking Estienne with him as he fell.

Gritting his teeth, Estienne planted his feet wider as the ships rocked. The walls loomed closer with each passing heartbeat, and he could make out individual figures now – armoured men scurrying along the battlements, readying for the assault to come.

Another volley of stones smashed into the walls. A section of crenellation crumbled, sending defenders tumbling to their doom, their screams high-pitched as they fell to the hungry waters of the Nile.

'*Deus vult*!' someone bellowed.

The cry was taken up by a hundred throats, swelling to a deafening roar. Estienne remained silent, conserving his breath. His eyes never left the approaching walls, searching for any sign of weakness, any gap in the defences he might take advantage of. Then came a shout from below for the oarsmen to cease their relentless pull. The galleys slowed until their prows struck against the wall below with a teeth-rattling impact, and Estienne almost lost his footing. Grappling hooks sailed out from the front of the platform, biting into the battlements.

This was it. The moment of truth.

'Attack!'

The command came like a smack of freezing water, spurring the crusaders into motion. Estienne surged forward with the tide of men, his feet thundering across the wooden platform. As he reached the wall, a gout of flame erupted from his left, liquid fire splashing across shields and armour. Men screamed as the unstoppable heat consumed them, writhing in agony as their flesh burned.

Estienne's shield bloomed into flame, the acrid stench of burning wood filling his nostrils. He hurled it aside without a second thought, not stopping in his advance as he vaulted the parapet and crunched down onto the walkway beyond.

An arrow whipped past his head. Another clattered off the battlement beside him, just as a Saracen warrior charged, sabre raised high. Estienne met the blow with his arming sword, and lashed out with a vicious kick, catching the man in the knee. As the Saracen stumbled, Estienne's blade found his neck.

Hot blood sprayed across his black surcoat as Estienne wrenched his sword free. He had struck the first blow for his Christian brothers, but there was no time to think. No time to breathe. Only kill or be killed.

He spun, barely deflecting a spear thrust aimed at his gut. Closing the distance, he rammed his shoulder into the spearman's chest and the man fell back. Questing fingers found the hammer at his hip, and he pulled it loose from his belt before bringing it down with all his strength. It struck the Saracen's skull, bone giving way beneath the blow. Once. Twice. Three times, until the man's face was a ruin of pulped flesh.

Estienne staggered back a pace, trying to get a sense of the battle. All around him, crusaders and Saracens fought and died. The air rang with the clash of steel, punctuated by screams of agony and mangled war cries. There was no sense to this. Only chaos. Only the need to fight.

There, he saw an archer taking aim from along the walkway, and charged forward, the arrow zipping past him. The distance closed in a heartbeat and Estienne's sword hacked in, cutting the bow in two before slicing clean through the man's arm. It should have shook him, horrified him, but as the man fell screaming, Estienne was gripped with a sudden fervour.

'For Christ!' he roared, his voice barely recognisable to his own ears. '*Deus vult.*'

He whirled, searching for his next target, and through the haze of smoke a flash of movement caught his eye – two figures back-to-back, locked in desperate combat amid the chaos.

One was a giant of a man, his ebony skin glistening with sweat and gore as he battered aside crusader after crusader with sweeping blows of his massive sword. Beside him fought a smaller warrior, his movements liquid grace as he wove through the melee. His lamellar armour glinted in the sun, intricate patterns etched into the metal plates. His straight blade danced, opening mail and battering at shields with a perfect combination of brutality and precision.

At the sight, Estienne's heart beat all the faster. Here were foes worthy of his steel.

He charged toward the giant Moor, bellowing a wordless battle cry. The huge warrior turned, eyes widening in surprise as Estienne swung at him, only just managing to raise his oval shield in time to catch the blow, steel ringing from steel.

The Moor wasted no time, swinging back with his massive, curved blade, forcing Estienne to duck, hearing the sweep as it cut the air an inch above his helm. Then he struck again, this time with the hammer, denting the Moor's shield and forcing him on the back foot.

Both men paused, eyeing one another warily, circling, looking for an opening, any sign of weakness to exploit. But there was no weakness here.

'Come on then, you heathen bastard,' Estienne snarled. 'Let's dance, you and I.'

Whether he understood the insult or not, the Moor's eyes blazed with fury. He lunged forward, his great sword cleaving the air. Estienne darted aside, the blade missing him by a hair's breadth. He countered with a quick swing of the hammer that clanged against the shield, forcing the bigger man back a step.

They traded blows, neither able to land a decisive strike. Estienne's arms burned with exertion, sweat stinging his eyes. In contrast, the Moor seemed tireless, his attacks coming with unrelenting force, as all around them violence reigned.

Movement to his left. Estienne barely had time to register the swift Saracen's approach before the man's blade slashed at him, ringing off the mail of his shoulder. His armour turned the worst of it, but pain still blazed white-hot along his arm.

Estienne stumbled back, nearly falling, and the Moor pressed his advantage, his sword arcing down in a killing blow... to be met by Estienne's upraised blade. The weapons locked together, ringing a dulcet tune as each man strained against the other. Estienne barely had a chance to see the huge Moor bearing down on him...

A pair of spears drove in, two knights of the Hospital charging forward to drive the Moor back. As he retreated under the sudden onslaught he bellowed at his Saracen friend, urging him on, and the smaller warrior darted in, his blade a silver blur. Estienne twisted desperately, almost knocked off his feet as the sword slashed wildly at him. His own blade moved with economy, managing to parry as best he could, but this warrior was simply too fast, too skilled.

With a flourish, the blade cut in again, but Estienne managed to strike true, swords ringing as their cross-guards locked. Then he lashed out blindly with his hammer, feeling the satisfaction of it finding a solid target, the spiked head driving through the domed helm and into skull beneath.

The Saracen's sword fell from nerveless fingers and he dropped to his knees, face twisted in shock and pain. Their eyes met for the briefest moment, and Estienne saw fear there. Desperation. A silent plea for mercy.

He granted none.

His sword punched through the Saracen's armoured chest, lamellar plates splitting asunder. When he wrenched it free the warrior collapsed in silence.

A howl of anguish tore through the din of battle. Estienne's head snapped up to see the Moor charging towards him, eyes blazing with murderous rage. He barely managed to bring his sword up in time to deflect the first blow. The force of it numbed his arm and he staggered back, the Moor's fury lending him impossible strength. Each strike threatened to shatter Estienne's guard as his enemy roared and spat.

Estienne's back hit the parapet. There was nowhere left to retreat and he steeled himself for the killing blow—

A flash of white. The ring of steel.

The Moor was suddenly assaulted from all sides as a group of Templars rallied to Estienne's defence. He could only watch as the huge warrior lashed out at the valiant knights attacking him, driven from the parapet. Their swords battered at the huge oval shield, and despite his fury the Moor was forced back.

Estienne heaved in air, the helmet now stifling in the heat and smoke. He could see the Saracens rallying. More and more were coming to defend their city, and it became obvious in moments the wall would be lost. There were simply too many, too savage in their defence. But he would not be denied. He was an instrument of God and he would fight till his last breath to prove it...

'Fall back.' The cry rang out from somewhere behind him, as he made to advance. 'To the ships. Fall back.'

Strong hands seized Estienne's shoulders, yanking him backwards. He stumbled, nearly falling as he was dragged away from the melee.

'No,' he snarled, struggling against the grip. 'Let me finish this. In God's name, I have to—'

But the knights around him paid no heed, dragging him towards the edge of the battlements. All around them, the crusaders were in full retreat. Men scrambled over the wall, heedless of the drop to the deck below. Arrows hissed through the air, felling stragglers as the Saracens pressed their advantage.

Estienne caught a final glimpse of the Moor, still bellowing challenges as his fellow warriors held him back. Then Estienne was over the edge of the wall, hitting the raised platform with a dull thud that clattered his teeth. The ship began pulling away, oars churning the muddy waters of the Nile as they retreated.

As Estienne staggered to his feet, he dragged the great helm from his head, desperate to catch his breath. The battle fury began to ebb, leaving him weak-kneed and trembling, and he became aware of a burning pain in his shoulder where the Saracen's blade had struck.

As the battle ardour faded, he saw the platform that had carried so many brave knights into battle was now a charnel house. Corpses lay strewn about, many still smouldering from the Greek fire. The air was thick with the stench of burned flesh and the crackle of flames. Of the hundreds who had set out to storm Damietta's walls, barely a quarter remained.

They had failed. All the bloodshed, all the lives lost, and Damietta's walls still stood defiant. But as the city receded into the distance, Estienne knew there would be another chance. And next time he would not be denied so easily.

6

The stench of death hung thick in the air, cloying and sickeningly sweet. Kashta stood motionless, surrounded by a sea of open graves that pockmarked what had been the lush gardens of Damietta's grand mosque. It was once a reverent setting, this place named the Amr ibn al-As, after one of the Prophet's closest companions. Now it was nothing more than a necropolis, a testament to the brutality of the Frankish assault.

Women wailed, their cries piercing, as they mourned over the shrouded bodies of their husbands, brothers and sons. The sound grated on Kashta's nerves, and he clenched his jaw, willing himself to remain stoic in the face of such overwhelming grief. No easy task, as he fixed his eyes on that single, open grave. Within it lay the body of Wasim, wrapped in the white shroud he had carried with him since they'd left Damascus. Kashta's throat tightened at the sight, memories of his friend's laughter and bravado coming in brief flashes.

They had prepared Wasim's body as tradition demanded, washing away the blood and grime of battle, binding his ankles, and placing his hands upon his chest. Now he lay on his right side, face turned toward Mecca.

Kashta's fingers clenched, longing to reach out and touch his friend one last time, to shake him awake from this nightmare. But he knew it was futile. Wasim was gone, cut down by Frankish steel on the very walls they had sworn to defend. As the imam's voice droned on, reciting prayers for the dead, Kashta barely heard him. His focus was fixed on the shrouded form before him, the friend who had been more than a brother. Wasim, who had stood by him through countless battles, who had shared his dreams of a life beyond war.

Now those dreams lay shattered, buried alongside Wasim in this blood-soaked earth.

A hand touched Kashta's shoulder, startling him. He turned to see an old man, his beard streaked with grey, holding out a shovel.

'It is time, brother,' the man said softly. 'Let us lay him to rest.'

Kashta nodded, unable to trust his voice lest it betray his sorrow. He took the shovel but for a moment stood frozen, unable to begin. Unable to say that final goodbye. Then, with a deep breath, he plunged the blade into the mound of earth beside the grave. The scrape of metal against soil was jarringly loud in the relative quiet, drowning out even the weeping for a heartbeat. When he hefted the first shovelful of dirt, he felt something inside him crack. His fortitude beginning to crumble. His vision blurred, and he blinked rapidly, refusing to let the tears fall.

The Quran spoke of patience in the face of loss, of the virtue in restraining one's desire for vengeance. But as Kashta watched the earth fall upon his friend's shrouded form, he knew that patience was a luxury he would never allow himself. The rhythmic thud of earth hitting cloth filled Kashta's ears, each impact driving home the reality of what he must do.

As he worked, his mind drifted back to the chaos of the battle. The air had been thick with the screams of the dying and the acrid stench of naphtha, as he and Wasim stood shoulder to shoulder, locked in glorious combat. And then, through the smoke and confusion, he had seen him. That knight in black, his garb emblazoned with a lion. The warrior had moved with brutal efficiency, cutting down defender after defender, hammer and blade swinging with the strength of ten. It was only right that the city's most renowned defenders should face him. And face him they had... to Wasim's ultimate loss. Cut down without mercy.

The memory of that cruel end burned white-hot in Kashta's mind, fuelling a rage that threatened to consume him. He drove the shovel into the earth with renewed vigour, each thrust as unpitying as the one that had ended his friend's life.

'I will find you,' Kashta growled through gritted teeth. 'I swear by the Prophet, I will hunt you to the ends of the earth and beyond, if I have to.'

And with those words he knew that the sultan's cause no longer held any meaning for him. His loyalty had died with Wasim, replaced with but a single goal. He would find the black knight, the lion of the Franks, and he would make him pay for what he had done.

As the last of the earth settled over Wasim's grave, Kashta stood back and stared at the mound of freshly turned soil, all that remained of his closest friend.

'Rest easy, brother,' he murmured. 'I will not let your death go unanswered.'

With a final, lingering look at that grave, Kashta turned away. He strode from the makeshift graveyard, his hand absently drifting to the hilt of his sword. Soon, it would once again taste Frankish flesh. For Kashta ibn Assad would roar once more. And this time, he would not stop until he found the black knight and slaked his vengeance in blood.

7

The familiar stench hit Estienne before he and the Templars even reached the edge of the northern encampment. Sweat, piss and something fouler – a reek of discontent and desperation. He wrinkled his nose, exchanging a knowing glance with Hoston as they rode within its defences. Tents sprawled haphazardly, their guy ropes tangled like spider's webs as men lounged in whatever shade they could find, dice rattling in grimy hands. The air rang with bellowed curses in a dozen different tongues. A bitter edge to the irregular laughter.

'God's teeth,' Hoston muttered. 'Has Pelagius lost control entirely?'

Estienne said nothing as his gut churned with a familiar unease. He'd seen this before, in the days of King John's reign – the slow rot that set in when men lost faith in their leaders. It never ended well.

They picked their way through the squalor, horses snorting nervously at the press of unwashed bodies. A fight erupted to their left, two men grappling in the dirt over some petty slight. No one moved to break it up.

'Come on, lad,' Hoston urged.

Estienne tore his gaze away from the brawl and nudged his horse back into the column of Templar knights. Everywhere he looked, he saw signs of a crusade unravelling. Women of ill virtue plied their trade openly, coin changing hands without a pretence of shame. The reek of cheap wine cut through the stink. Rumours of unrest had been enough to urge the Templar grand master to come north with all haste, but Estienne doubted he had expected things to be this bad. Whatever his thoughts, it appeared they had arrived just in time.

Pierre ordered his men to dismount, and serving-brothers were quick to take their horses as the Templars made their way further into the encampment. Soon they reached what passed for the camp's centre, where a crowd had gathered. At its heart stood Pelagius, resplendent in his cardinal's robes. The contrast between his finery and the rabble surrounding him was almost comical. Almost.

The mob barracked Pelagius mercilessly, their words a tangle of demands and accusations.

'Where's our pay, you fat bastard?'

'The Saracens bleed us dry while you feast.'

'Give us battle or give us leave to go home.'

Pelagius raised his hands, trying to placate the angry horde. His words were lost in the din, but his face was a mask of barely contained panic; this was a man used to commanding respect through the weight of his office alone. That spell was breaking before Estienne's eyes.

A stone arced through the air, missing the legate's head by inches. The crowd roared, whether in approval or dismay, Estienne couldn't tell. His hand instinctively went to his sword hilt, but Hoston's iron grip on his arm stopped him short.

'Not our fight,' the Templar warned. 'We don't want to be seen to draw steel on our fellow crusaders if this goes bad.'

Estienne nodded, forcing himself to relax, but the air crackled with the promise of violence barely held in check. Pelagius' guards closed ranks around him, hands on weapons, and for a heartbeat, it seemed the crowd might surge forward, consequences be damned.

'Quite the circus, isn't it?'

The raised voice at Estienne's shoulder nearly made him jump out of his skin, and he turned to find Amalric grinning at him.

'That's one way to put it,' Estienne replied. 'Though more like a bear baiting, if you ask me.'

'It's been like this for days,' Amalric replied, brow furrowing in concern. 'The common folk formed their own council, if you can believe it. They're demanding action. They have grown sick of throwing themselves at the walls of a fortress, and now they want to strike out into Saracen territory instead.'

'And Pelagius allows them to voice such dissent?'

'Allows? He has no other choice. Half the army would desert if he tried to silence them.'

'Enough!' A new voice cut through the chaos, deep and commanding.

The mob parted, revealing a tall figure striding purposefully towards Pelagius. Even at a distance, Estienne recognised the heavy beard and regal bearing of John of Brienne, titular King of Jerusalem.

The crowd's mood shifted palpably. Where Pelagius inspired only contempt, John commanded genuine respect, and the crowd fell silent, hungry for whatever words the king might offer. John of Brienne reached Pelagius, and the two men conferred in low, urgent tones. After what felt like an eternity, Pelagius raised his hands once more. This time, the mob heeded his signal, hungry for whatever pronouncement might fall from his lips.

'My brothers,' the legate began, his voice carrying across the throng. 'I hear your concerns. I feel your frustration. But take heart. For God has shown us the path to victory. Even now, al-Kamil cowers in his camp at Fariksur. He thinks us weak, divided. But we shall show him the terrible might of a united Christendom. Tomorrow, we march. We shall smash al-Kamil's forces and open the road to Cairo itself.'

The crowd erupted in a deafening roar. Men brandished weapons, caught up in the intoxicating promise of imminent glory. Even John of Brienne, usually so stoic, allowed himself a fierce grin.

Estienne found himself swept up in the moment, his pulse quickening at the thought of battle. This was what they'd come for, wasn't it? A chance to strike a decisive blow against the Saracen? But even as his blood sang with anticipation, a small voice in the back of his mind urged caution. As much as he hungered for another chance to prove himself, he remembered the screams upon the walls of Damietta. The slaughter, the sacrifice. This was not something to rush into blindly at the behest of an unruly mob.

Turning to Amalric, he saw the knight's eyes shone with an eager light. 'Finally, a chance to prove our mettle, eh?'

Estienne forced a smile, pushing down his misgivings. 'Aye. God willing, we'll send al-Kamil running with his tail between his legs and—'

'Stop!'

The crowd's noise was cut short by the single, piercing voice. Estienne searched for the source of the interruption, and as the mob parted, it revealed a lone figure striding purposefully towards Pelagius and John of Brienne. Even at a distance, there was no mistaking the man in his simple brown robe, the tonsured head, the burning intensity in his eyes – Francesco, the monk Estienne had seen preaching days before.

'What in God's name is he doing?' Amalric muttered.

Estienne said nothing, gripped by the monk's audacity. Francesco pushed through the ranks of onlookers, planting himself squarely before the legate and the King of Jerusalem.

'My lords,' Francesco's voice rang out, clear and unwavering. 'I beg you, reconsider this folly.'

A ripple of angry muttering passed through the crowd. Estienne tensed, acutely aware of how quickly the mob's mood could turn, but Francesco seemed oblivious to the danger, his focus entirely on the men before him.

'This attack is doomed to fail,' the monk continued, his words laced with conviction. 'How many more must die before we see the error of our ways? I have prayed to the Lord, and He has shown me a better path. Let me go to al-Kamil myself. I will open his eyes to the truth of Christ's word, and end this bloodshed without another drop spilled. I will baptise him in the name of the Lord. He will become as a brother to us, not our enemy.'

The crowd's muttering grew louder, taking on an ugly edge, but Francesco seemed to draw strength from the hostility surrounding him. He turned to face the mob, arms spread wide in supplication. 'Brothers. Sisters. Is this truly what we came here for? To visit death and misery upon our fellow man?'

A storm of jeers answered him, and a transformation came over the crowd. Where moments before they had been united in bloodlust against the Saracen, now they found a new target for their rage.

'Coward!'

'Heretic!'

'String him up!'

The shouts grew more vicious, and Estienne felt his chest tighten, torn between admiration for Francesco's courage and fear for the man's life.

'Peace, brothers,' Francesco cried, his voice straining to be heard above the din. 'We are called to be fishers of men, not butchers. Let me show you a better way.'

But his words were lost in the rising tide of anger. Men surged forward, some faces twisted with hate while others laughed at this prattling monk. The mob closed in, and Francesco was swallowed up by the press of bodies.

This was none of his concern. Estienne should have let the mob have its due, but that was not how he had been raised. William Marshal had taught him a code, instilled the tenets of it into every fibre, and Estienne could not merely stand by and watch as a man of God was beaten, perhaps to death, by a baying crowd.

He stepped forward to help, but before he could push his way through the mass of bodies he felt a firm hand grip his arm.

'There is nothing you can do, my friend,' Amalric said. 'There are too many.'

'Like hell there are.' Estienne snatched his arm free and bulled his way into the crowd.

Angry jeers surrounded him, men jostling to vent their anger on the beleaguered monk. Estienne grabbed one of them by the scruff and dragged him aside, planting his open hand into another's face and pushing him out of the way. Though Estienne had not yet seen his twentieth summer, he was still taller and stronger than any of this mob, and he managed to reach Francesco before they could do him permanent harm.

'What the fuck are you doing?' someone snarled, as Estienne dragged the monk to his feet.

Francesco pawed at Estienne's gambeson, his mouth and nose bleeding, his eye already swelling shut. Without a word, Estienne glared about in wordless challenge, one hand gripping Francesco, the other his sheathed sword, as though offering a silent promise of violence should any challenge him. It quelled the ire of the mob, and he was able to guide Francesco back to the safety of where Amalric stood, followed by the wrathful glares of the crowd.

'My thanks,' Francesco said, managing to stand of his own accord. 'May God bless you.'

'Just make yourself scarce,' Estienne replied. 'Save the blessings for another time. I think you've said enough.'

Francesco nodded his understanding. 'I will. But I owe you a great debt, my friend. I will pray to our Lord God that one day I may be allowed to pay it.'

With another bow, he made his way from the gathered throng. Estienne just caught sight of that tonsured head disappear, before Pelagius raised his arms, demanding calm.

The legate's face was a mask of cold satisfaction, all trace of his earlier discomfort gone. The baying of the mob faded to a dull murmur. Where before he had seemed uncertain, even fearful, now the legate radiated an almost palpable authority.

'My brothers, our path is clear. That mad priest would have us cower in the face of the Saracen, but we are the soldiers of Christ. And we know no fear.' A ragged cheer went up from the assembled throng. 'Tomorrow, we march on Fariksur. Al-Kamil's defeat will secure the Holy Land once more. And then, Cairo will tremble at our approach, and throw open her gates to welcome her true king.'

The legate's words whipped the crowd into a frenzy. Estienne felt the pull of it, the intoxicating promise of glory, but Francesco's words still echoed in his mind, a discordant note in this symphony of bloodlust.

As the crowd began to disperse, buzzing with anticipation of the coming battle, Amalric clapped a hand on Estienne's shoulder. 'Well, my friend? Ready to retake Outremer for God and the Holy Roman Emperor?'

Estienne forced a smile, hoping it didn't look as hollow as it felt. 'Aye.'

Amalric frowned, clearly sensing Estienne's doubts. 'You seem troubled.'

'Aren't you? I cannot help but think that after what we have seen here, perhaps our fellow crusaders are not such a righteous bunch. Their motives might not be altogether... pious.'

'Of course. I'm not blind to the excesses we've witnessed. But what choice do we have? We've come too far to turn back now.'

'I know. It's just... did you hear what that monk said? About converting al-Kamil peacefully?'

'Madness,' Amalric scoffed. 'The ravings of a fanatic.'

'Perhaps. But what if he's right? What if there's another path?'

They stood in silence for a moment, the sounds of the camp washing over them. Finally, Amalric spoke, his voice suddenly sombre. 'Even if there is, it's not for us to walk it. As the legate said – we're soldiers of God, and our path is set.'

Estienne nodded, not trusting himself to speak. He knew Amalric was right, at least in part. They had sworn oaths to raise their swords in the name of God, pledged their lives to this cause. But still he couldn't shake the feeling that they were hurtling towards disaster, and perhaps the monk Francesco was right after all.

8

The road south to Fariksur wound through deep ravines and across narrow canals. Always the Nile flowed to their west, the glimmering waters taunting them and their parched throats. Estienne rode close to the front among the Templar vanguard, not far behind Henri of Bohun, the appointed leader of this expedition, his azure banner flying with six lions rampant. As Earl of Hereford, Henri was a senior knight among the crusader host, and had been chosen by the legate himself to ride at the head of their army. Most likely he had taken the Cross as a form of penance, after siding with Prince Louis in the recent uprising against King John. Estienne thought him a poor choice to lead them, but who was he to question the orders of the legate.

Beside him, sitting proudly astride their destriers, were the grand masters of the knightly orders – the brothers Montaigu and Hermann of Salza. Estienne should have felt safe amid such stalwart knights, and with the reassuring bulk of Hoston at his side, but there was an unnerving feeling to all this. They were but a mile south of their temporary crusader camp and already he felt so exposed it may as well have been a thousand. The thirst clawed at him, his gambeson and hauberk baking him so much he was already sodden beneath it. Even the righteousness of their cause could not assuage the misery that hung over him.

Ten thousand of them had set off on this journey, or so someone had guessed. Ten thousand warriors ready to face down al-Kamil and reclaim the Holy Land for Christendom. Ten thousand. And still Estienne could not shake the feeling it would not be enough.

He turned to the north, craning his neck to take in the winding road and the sea of banners that filled it. Among that crowd the golden cross of the Kingdom of Jerusalem flew most prominently, John of Brienne just visible atop his steed. Beyond it were other banners, including that of Pelagius himself, along with the patriarch Ralph of Jerusalem and James of Vitry. Interspersed among them were the heraldic devices of a score of noble houses from across Christendom, all united in this holy cause.

And bringing up the rear, just hidden from view, were wagons and pack animals, along with the women – laundresses, cooks, and those of more questionable virtue. A city on the move, ten thousand strong.

The relentless sound of hooves took on a hollow timbre as they crossed another narrow canal, the crusader army swinging inland, away from the Nile. Estienne squinted against the glare, the landscape ahead shimmering in the heat. Then suddenly his heart quickened as he saw, rising from the barren plain half a mile hence, a cluster of tents.

'Hoston,' Estienne said over the jingle of harness and creak of leather.

'Aye, I see it,' the Templar replied.

And he was not the only one. A ripple of unease passed through the vanguard, as Henri of Bohun raised his arm for the column to halt. As they watched, figures began to emerge from the tents – men scrambling to gather belongings, horses being led out and mounted with haste. It was clear the enemy had spotted the advancing crusaders and were choosing flight over fight.

Despite the speed of their retreat, unease prickled along Estienne's spine. This felt too convenient, too much like a trap waiting to be sprung. It was obvious he was not the only one who thought so, as murmurings spread through the ranks, word of the enemy's flight passing back along the column.

The orderly march faltered, men craning their necks to catch a glimpse of the abandoned camp, while at the head of the column, the grand masters and Henri huddled in urgent conference.

'Will we attack?' Estienne asked.

Hoston shook his head. 'Not if we've any sense. We'd be exposed on that plain, and we're nowhere near al-Kamil's main force yet.'

A sudden cry from among the crusader ranks. Estienne didn't recognise the language but the intention was clear – an encampment was being abandoned and there was loot for the taking.

They moved from the main column in small groups at first, before scores of crusaders broke, running full tilt toward the enemy tents. Shouts of warning went up, urging them back in line, but it was too late. Some waved weapons, eager for plunder, while others stumbled, hands outstretched, moaning of thirst and the promise of water.

'God blind them,' Hoston snarled. 'Have they no discipline?'

But his words were lost in the rising din. More and more men streamed away in a ragged flood, all thoughts of cohesion and order forgotten as they crossed the plain. They swarmed the camp like ants on a carcass, and in moments the first fights were breaking out over the spoils.

Estienne looked to Hoston, seeing his own fears mirrored in the older knight's eyes. This was madness, a disaster waiting to happen. How could they hope to face the enemy when they turned on each other at the first temptation?

'We should stop them,' Estienne said.

Hoston opened his mouth to reply, then froze, head whipping around at a sudden clamour from the rear of the column. Shouts of alarm, underscored by a rising crescendo of screams in the distance.

'Merciful Christ,' the Templar breathed. 'We're under attack.'

Estienne rose in his stirrups, straining to see through the billowing dust. There, where the women and baggage train rode, a swarm of enemy horsemen had struck like wolves. The women's screams carried across the plain, shrill with terror, piercing Estienne to his core. He watched helplessly as the distant cavalry cut through their meagre defences, trampling the fallen, their wicked-curved blades flashing in the sun.

All along the column, the fragile threads of discipline unravelled. Men milled in confusion, shouting to one another, some trying to turn back to aid the rear, others still intent on reaching the abandoned camp ahead. Orders flew, contradictory and panicked. The army was coming apart at the seams.

'We must help them,' Estienne shouted to Hoston over the growing tumult.

But before the Templar could answer there came a barked order for attention. Riding back along the column came Pierre of Montaigu, the grand master standing tall in his saddle.

'We hold,' he yelled, his voice cutting through the confusion. 'We are the vanguard. Our purpose is to defend this column from the front, and if we break, all is lost. We will guard the way.

Allow the rest of the army to retreat. Hold here, men of Christendom. For God and Outremer.'

Estienne bit back a curse, every instinct screaming at him to wheel about and charge to the aid of those defenceless souls behind, but he had to trust in the grand master's will. Trust that the other orders would hold firm in the face of this onslaught.

A flurry of movement behind – John of Brienne breaking from the column at the head of his knights, sword brandished high. The King of Jerusalem was rallying men to him as he rode, his voice booming over the fray.

'To the rear! Drive them back! For God and the Holy Land!'

Cheers answered him as more crusaders fell in behind, streaming back the way they had come. But even as Estienne watched, pockets of panic bloomed among the foot soldiers and commoners. The column began to crumble, men stumbling against each other in their haste to flee the spectre of further danger and reach the far-off promise of shelter.

'This is madness,' Estienne snarled, frustration boiling up in his breast. 'We're split in two, our flank exposed. Can't they see this is exactly what the enemy wants?'

'Hold your nerve,' Hoston spat, eyes scanning the ridge to their west.

Estienne forced himself to calm, gripping the sword in his hand, trying desperately to control his breathing. Beside him, the Templars and Hospitallers sat grim and resolute, a bulwark of steel and faith against the disintegrating strength of their army.

Behind, the sounds of the onslaught grew – the screams, the clash of steel, the pounding thunder of horses. Then from beyond the next rise, a new sound of hooves approaching fast. Estienne saw the first of the enemy horsemen crest the desert hill. The sun flashed off their spear tips and the cruel edges of their swords. He felt his stomach lurch as he realised how exposed the crusaders' flank was in that moment. There was no time to redress the lines against this threat...

'*Deus vult!*'

The grand master's cry tore at the sky, echoed by hundreds of knights as the enemy struck like a storm unleashed. From the east, a hail of arrows fell upon the crusaders' exposed flank. Men cried out, tumbling from saddles, hands clutching at the shafts blooming from eye, throat and chest. Horses screamed, staggering as the missiles found flesh, crashing into their fellows in a tangle of limbs.

The Saracens attacked in small groups, whooping as they struck lightning-fast. Then they were gone, riding away as swiftly as they had come, loosing arrows in their wake. Fire suddenly bloomed along the column, and Estienne struggled to control his mount. Balls of acrid smoke erupted from the line of men as screams peeled out. Greek fire...

'Hold ranks,' came the cry, but the centre of their line was already wavering, resolve crumbling in the face of this hellish onslaught. Some cast away weapons and fled. Others milled in maddened confusion, heedless of their superiors' bellowed commands.

'Attack,' came another cry, taken up by another voice, and another.

Horses tore from the main defensive line, a galloping charge at the darting Saracen lines. It was folly, the archers too quick atop their swift steeds, and the attack faltered. A hundred men on horseback, charging at nothing but a rain of arrows.

Estienne heard sudden cries in Italian, and the infantry bringing up the rear of the vanguard began to peel off in ones and twos at first. Then full flight, as the hissing arrows of the Saracens brought down a storm upon them. Panic spread like an infection; Estienne saw even the stalwart Hospitallers consumed by it, some reining their horses north and setting off at a gallop.

He clung to his reins, fighting to steady his mount as it shied and fought the bit. His instincts screamed at him to attack, to charge the oncoming enemy and meet their steel with his own, but he knew it would be suicide. Cut off from support, without the strength of his brothers beside him, he would be torn to bloody ribbons, and so he held his ground, though every sinew and bone howled at the wrongness of it.

'Damn it,' the grand master snarled, wheeling his horse about amid the confusion. 'Withdraw. We withdraw.'

Even as the knights began to gradually pull back, the Saracens took their advantage, raining more arrows. Estienne still struggled with his mount, an arrow hissing into his shield as he wheeled about.

At first their retreat was orderly, but Estienne could sense that even the grim veterans of the Templars were wavering on the edge of panic. Their steady withdrawal began turning as their ordered trot turned to frantic canter. Slowly, disciplined order was replaced by turmoil. Even Hoston, riding close to Estienne's side, put heels to flanks, urging his destrier away faster from the wicked arrows that harried their every step.

There, up ahead. Like an oasis of steel amid the swirling insanity, Estienne spotted a formation of men holding against the tide. Black and white surcoats. Pisans and Germans standing shoulder to shoulder, even some of the Hospitallers who had managed to master themselves and halt their panicked rout. The bulk of Templars surrounded them, and Estienne reined in alongside.

'We hold here,' came the sharp bellow of Pierre of Montaigu.

'Stand your ground,' followed the guttural snarl of Hermann of Salza.

Estienne cast his eye over the defensive line, seeing scores of knights of the Order of Saint Mary. Amalric sat astride his huge horse, his brothers alongside. No time for acknowledgment. Only time to heave in breath as he glared at the dust cloud they had left in their wake, listening to the thunderous noise that followed them. The Saracens were coming, relentless in their pursuit. But surely the crusaders would stand. This gathering of Christian might would drive them back. It had to.

No more time to think as the Saracen cavalry burst from the choking cloud. A roar went up – crusader and Saracen alike – as battle was joined. Estienne sunk his heels, planting himself astride the saddle as he felt the first impact of a spear against his shield. His sword lashed out on instinct, ringing off metal, whether helm or shield or blade he had no idea amid the confusion. No chance to think, just fight. Killing and hacking and striking again. The song of steel against steel rang in Estienne's ears, clamour unending. Roars, screams, the brutal meaty sounds of blades puncturing mail into flesh. The wicker and scream of horses as they fell. A reign of violence and confusion, but despite their brave stand, they gave ground by inches.

And still they came.

And still the crusaders gave ground, reluctant step after reluctant step.

Another spear lanced at him from the confusion, and Estienne rocked back in the saddle, its tip scraping against his helm. For a moment he thought he might topple from his horse, before a strong arm grasped his surcoat, holding him aloft.

His vision cleared enough to catch a glimpse of a white surcoat and black cross. Amalric, face visible from within his open-faced helm, teeth gnashing.

'Come, Wace,' the German snarled. 'We must go.'

Already Estienne could see the Templars were withdrawing. Rank upon rank of horsemen peeling away from the fight.

He put spurs to flanks, riding alongside Amalric, galloping the long road they had travelled, back toward their fortified camp. No longer any order. No more barked commands. Now they rode for their lives, every man thinking only of himself as he raced for the safety of those distant fortifications.

At last, the camp was in sight, its ditch and makeshift rampart promising a desperate sanctuary. What had been a fighting retreat was now fractured into a rout, and men hurled aside sword and shield, fleeing like rabbits before hounds. They trampled one another to cross the narrow bridges that spanned the vast defensive trench, such was their desperation, but still there were so many more to go.

Estienne pulled hard on his rein, and Amalric did likewise. Squinting, he saw the grand masters, Pierre, Hermann and Garin, had reached the ramparts before them, and even now they sat as a bulwark, defending the way. Estienne nudged his horse closer, turning to face the coming onslaught. Templars, Hospitallers, the Knights of Saint Mary, all ready to face their attackers to the end.

'We stand,' Hermann of Salza cried.

If he was going to say any more it was drowned amid the thunder of hooves. The Saracens fell upon their line, heralded by a torrent of arrows, and Estienne barely had time to bring his shield to bear. Horses screeched, many of them falling to the ground, before the sound to charge rang out. Estienne's destrier bolted forward, and he squinted from within his helm looking for the first of the enemy to engage. It was then he noticed Amalric was no longer by his side.

He tugged back on the rein, looking about. Men fled around him, still desperate to escape Saracen fury, but amid the panic he saw Amalric rising to his feet, his huge horse lying riddled with shafts.

Estienne spurred forward, holding out a hand to his friend. 'Come on.'

Before Amalric could reach out, agony exploded in Estienne's side, as though a fire had been ignited in his hip. He looked down, uncomprehending, to see an arrow shaft in his side, crimson blooming against the black of his surcoat.

The world turned to a blur as he slid sideways. Then he hit the earth hard, barely comprehending his horse bolting, the men fleeing all about.

Hands seized him below the arms, hauling him upright. Amalric's voice roared in his ear, though he couldn't make out the words. The world swam, edges greying, as he was dragged across the trampled earth and over the slick wood of the drawbridge.

Both men collapsed on the other side as figures raced past, smudges of movement, as the last stragglers stumbled to safety. Across the fortification, Estienne glimpsed the Templars, grim and determined as they held the foe at bay.

Then his sight blurred, bleeding away at the edges like ink in rain. He was suddenly cold, and so very tired. Amalric shook him, saying something, but Estienne could hear no words, as though he were listening from below the surface of a quiet pool.

His last thoughts as he slipped away were of Francesco's dire warning that this had all been doomed. And damn him, he was right...

9

Pain. The first sensation that greeted him as consciousness slowly seeped back into his battered body. A throbbing ache radiating from his side, pulsing in time with his heartbeat. He groaned softly, eyes opening to see the world was a blur of shadow and flickering light. Distant voices murmured, echoing strangely as if from the bottom of a deep well.

As the world slowly resolved itself, Estienne realised he was lying on a rough pallet, staring up at the stained roof of a tent, the air thick with the stench of herbs. Turning his head, he saw a face that swam into focus – gaunt, bearded and distantly familiar.

'Francesco?' he asked, throat parched as the desert sands.

The monk smiled. 'Welcome back, my friend. You had us worried for a time.'

Estienne's last thought had been of this very man. Strange that he was the first thing Estienne saw upon waking.

He tried to sit up and immediately regretted it as agony lanced through his side. He fell back with a hiss, hand going to the source of the pain. His fingers brushed against the coarse weave of bandages.

'Steady now,' Francesco cautioned, placing a gentle but firm hand on his chest. 'Your wound was deep. You're lucky the arrow didn't pierce anything vital, but you lost a great deal of blood when we cut it out of you.'

Memories rushed back in a dizzying tide. The disastrous march on Fariksur. The Saracen ambush. Amalric's determined face as he hauled Estienne across the narrow bridge to safety. Then nothing but a haze of pain and confusion.

'Where am I?'

'You are at the camp of John of Brienne, south of Damietta. You and some of the other casualties were brought by wagon along the road north. I was asked to help tend the wounded. A task which I and my brothers and sisters were only too glad to help with. When I found that you were among them, the man who liberated me from an angry mob and saved my life, I realised God had given me the chance to repay my debt to you.'

'As happy as I am he afforded you such an opportunity, it would be nice if he'd made it slightly less painful.' Estienne adjusted himself, sitting up a little. 'How long have I been here?'

'Four days since the army retreated. If one could even call it that any more.'

'What do you mean?'

Francesco sighed, running a hand over his weary face. 'The army... what's left of it... is in a sorry state. Men are deserting by the score, slipping away in the night. Morale has never been lower.'

Estienne closed his eyes, but it could not shield him from the disappointment. Their crusade was in shambles, their grand purpose reduced to ashes. God's holy work left to crumble into ruin and disgrace.

'But do not despair, my friend,' Francesco said. 'At least your wound is healing well. A small miracle amidst all this misery.'

The monk gently peeled back the bandage from Estienne's side. The wound beneath was an ugly, puckered thing, the flesh a mottled purple and angry red, but the stitches were neat and even, and there was no telltale stench of putrefaction.

'Sounds like we'll need more than small miracles to salvage this endeavour,' Estienne hissed through gritted teeth.

'Perhaps.' Francesco sat back on his haunches, gaze distant. 'Or perhaps we've been going about it all wrong from the start.'

Estienne frowned. 'What do you mean?'

The monk leaned forward. 'This violence, this ceaseless bloodshed... what has it brought us? Nothing but death and ruin. As you witnessed, I tried to persuade Pelagius days ago that there is another way. A path to peace.'

'And I understand the sentiment, but peace with the Saracens is impossible. They'd sooner put us all to the sword.'

Francesco shook his head. 'Not all of them. And I think not al-Kamil. I intend to meet with him, to negotiate an end to this madness. More than that, I will show him the glory of Christ's love. I will open his eyes to the true faith, so that we may live together as brothers. This, I truly believe, is our only hope.'

Estienne remembered how this monk had tried to turn them all back from the path of folly that had brought him here. And still, after all they had suffered at the hands of the Saracens, Francesco thought he could achieve peace. Such conviction seemed insane, but at the same time it might merely be divinely inspired purpose.

Sunlight slanted into the tent as the flap covering the entrance was moved aside, dust motes swirling in its warm glow. Someone entered, their shadow looming, before Estienne recognised a tall, handsome figure clad in a familiar white surcoat.

'Amalric,' Estienne said. 'You are a sight for sore eyes.'

'As are you, my friend. For days now we thought that Saracen arrow might take you from us.'

'It will take more than that,' Estienne replied, although from the pain in his side he wasn't so sure.

He struggled to sit up, and Francesco helped him settle more comfortably. A drink of water soothed his parched throat, before he looked to Amalric once more.

'I hear things are not going well among the leaders of our crusade. What word from the grand masters?'

'Still determined to regain the Holy Land. But after the defeat on the road to Fariksur, their enthusiasm is not shared. I never thought it would come to this. All those grand speeches, all that talk of glory and God's will...'

Estienne could feel the bitter taste of defeat in Amalric's tone. 'Then what will they do?'

Amalric shook his head. 'I wish I knew. John of Brienne and the other lords meet daily to discuss our next move, but there is little agreement. Some want to launch another attack on Fariksur. Others counsel withdrawal. Each day more men slip away on ships back to their homelands. Discipline is in tatters.'

Estienne glanced toward Francesco, who tinkered with herbs at a small table. 'There may be another path. Francesco has spoken of meeting with al-Kamil to discuss terms for peace.'

Amalric's face twisted in confusion. 'Has the sun addled his wits? Meet with the infidel sultan? He will be slaughtered.'

'He believes it may be our only choice.'

'Then he's mad,' Amalric said, seemingly unconcerned that the monk could hear every word. 'There can be no parley with the heathens. No peace while they occupy sacred land. Outremer must be returned to Christendom. Our oaths demand no less.'

'And where have our oaths gotten us so far?' Estienne snapped. 'How many more good men must we see butchered before—'

His words cut off, as a distant commotion erupted outside the tent – the rising sound of angry voices, the clatter of arms and shouts of alarm. Amalric was on his feet and Estienne gritted his teeth and struggled to swing his legs over the edge of the pallet, ignoring the tug of his stitches.

'Help me up,' he demanded. 'I need to see.'

Amalric looked like he might argue, but with a muttered curse, he gripped Estienne's arm and hauled him upright. The world swam dizzyingly, and for a moment Estienne thought he might fall, but Amalric's strong arm kept him steady. Together, in lurching lockstep, they made their way to the opening of the tent while Francesco looked on with concern.

Peering out, Estienne saw the encampment he had been resting in for the past days. All about chaos reigned, as a milling mass of confusion and brewing violence snaked its way between every fluttering tent. Men shouted, shoved and jostled, tension palpable, as a steady tide of them marched west, towards the distant ships docked upon the shore of the Nile. All propriety abandoned as they made for the promise of home.

'It's all coming apart,' Estienne breathed.

Amalric said nothing, but in his silence was a bleak certainty – if ever they needed a miracle, surely it was now.

The heavy tread of footfalls distracted Estienne from the sight. Approaching the tent, he saw Hoston, his black cappa stained, weathered face set in a grim expression until he set eyes on Estienne.

A smile of relief crossed his face. 'You're alive, lad. And on your feet. God be praised.'

'And I have the monk Francesco to thank for it.'

'Aye,' said Hoston. 'He took it upon himself to see you cared for personally. But now back to your bed or his work will have been for nothing.'

Estienne didn't argue, allowing Amalric to help him back to the pallet. He winced as he lay down again, but the pain seemed more bearable with every passing moment. Francesco made him drink more water, and he felt almost invigorated by it.

'It seems our endeavour falters,' Estienne said to Hoston. 'But I take it you remain stalwart.'

'It's a bad business,' Hoston replied. 'But the grand masters will remain. Our campaign is far from over.'

Estienne struggled to sit straighter, fighting a wince. After all he had seen, all he had suffered, his mind was now made up. There was only one path forward.

'Francesco means to treat with al-Kamil. He believes there may yet be a path to peace. A way to salvage something of worth from all this. After all he has done for me, the least I can do in return is go with him. See him safe as best I am able.'

'You cannot be serious.' Amalric snapped. 'Estienne, you can barely stand. And the very idea... it's madness.'

Estienne shook his head. 'No. Madness is what is happening around us – abandoning all that we have fought for. All that we swore to accomplish in God's name.'

Francesco had turned now to regard him, a look of surprise and gratitude on his face. 'My friend, there is no need for you to—'

'There is every need,' Estienne replied. 'I would be dead without your help. This is the least I can do.'

'God's name?' Hoston growled. 'You think the Almighty will smile on such folly? Treating with the heretic? It's suicide.'

'I think...' Estienne forced down the pain. 'I think Francesco has the right of it. The path we have trodden thus far has brought us only to ruin. Perhaps it's time we sought another way.'

Hoston's face was unreadable, until something flickered in those stern eyes. Something like a grudging understanding. 'On your head be it then. I cannot stop you.'

'Madness,' Amalric grumbled. 'You're in no condition for this fool's errand. The stitches will tear, the wound will reopen...'

'Then you'd best pray Francesco knows his needlework.' Estienne smiled, despite his discomfort. 'We'll need horses for the journey south.'

Hoston nodded. 'You'll have them. Though it galls me to see you undertake this doomed journey.'

Estienne inclined his head in a gesture of gratitude, before struggling up once more. As he stood, bracing himself against Amalric's steadying arm, he felt his conviction embolden. Everything he had strived for and suffered since leaving home had brought him here. This chance at deliverance, not only for himself but for all Christendom. Perhaps this, at last, was the true purpose to which he'd been called. The sacred charge placed upon him by God.

He turned to Francesco, seeing his own conviction mirrored in those dark, fathomless eyes. 'I'm ready.'

The monk smiled, but there was a look of uncharacteristic steel to his eyes. 'Then let us go forth, and place our trust in the Almighty.'

10

The road stretched out before them, looking almost endless beneath the unforgiving sun. Estienne squinted against the glare, the black of his surcoat drinking in the heat until it felt like he was being roasted alive. Sweat ran in rivulets down his back, plastering the fabric of his gambeson to his skin. Each plodding step of his horse sent a jolt of pain lancing through his side, the wound from the Saracen arrow still throbbing. But he would endure. He had to endure.

Beside him, Francesco seemed untroubled by the blistering conditions, his rough-spun robes billowing in the hot breeze. The monk's gaze was fixed ahead, towards the shimmering horizon where al-Kamil's camp lay waiting within the bounds of a fortified town.

'Feels like we are being watched,' Estienne said, though he had spotted no sign of scouts on the path south. 'The last time I took this road it was right into an ambush.'

Francesco glanced at him, a wry smile touching his lips. 'Having second thoughts, my friend?'

'Let's just say I preferred facing the Saracens with an army at my back.'

'And how did that work out for you?'

'Point taken,' Estienne conceded. 'Still, it is easier to face them sword in hand.'

'Ah, but you do have your sword.' Francesco nodded to the blade hanging at Estienne's hip. 'And that surcoat, the fierce black lion. A symbol of your courage, is it not?'

Estienne's hand drifted to the heraldry that adorned his chest. 'Aye. A reminder of the vows I swore. The oaths I bound myself to.'

'And yet you ride with me to parley, not to fight.'

'I've seen enough fighting,' he replied. 'Enough blood spilled on these sands. If there's a chance for peace, however slim... I owe it to myself to try.'

'You're a man of honour, Estienne. Of conviction. Those are rare qualities in times such as these.'

'Honour,' Estienne muttered. 'Conviction. Kind words, but what good are they when the cause I champion falls to ruin?'

'The greatest good, my friend, for they are true. You fought for what you believed was right. And now you ride with me as my guardian, even when the Almighty himself watches over me.'

Estienne said nothing, turning the words over in his mind. His crusade, his grand quest in God's name... it had all seemed so clear when he'd left England's shores. So righteous. But with each passing day in this blighted land, those certainties had crumbled. The sins of the flesh, rampant in the crusaders' camp. The savagery and hypocrisy of the battlefield. And now this – riding to treat with the sultan himself, with death a real prospect.

He looked down at the black lion rampant on his chest, the emblem of William Marshal's legacy. The symbol of all he had hoped to become, all he had dreamed of since he was a lowly squire. What would the Marshal think of him now, riding into the enemy's arms with no mail or helm, and a vow to keep his sword sheathed? Would he see a man of principle? Or a fool? In truth, Estienne was no longer certain himself any more, but as the fortifications of al-Kamil's camp drew ever closer, he knew there was no turning back. Not now.

His heart hammered as they approached the main gate of the town, the hooves of their mounts raising puffs of chalky dust from the hard-packed earth. Every instinct screamed at him to wheel about, to put distance between himself and this enemy bastion, but he mastered the urge. He had made his choice. There was no undoing it now.

A shout rang out from the ramparts, sharp and guttural. Estienne's grip tightened on the reins as a group of Saracen warriors emerged, their curved blades drawn and flashing in the sun. They surrounded the two riders in a ring of steel, dark eyes glaring with suspicion from beneath turbaned helms.

Francesco seemed unperturbed, calling out to the guards in fluent Arabic, his words flowing rapid and melodic. The Saracen commander barked a response, but instead of ordering them cut down, he turned and waved sharply at someone behind the crudely built wall. With a groan of straining timber, the makeshift gates swung inward. Estienne released a breath he hadn't realised he was holding, as the warrior motioned for them to enter. He shot a glance at Francesco, but the monk's face held only serene calm as they rode right into the lion's den.

Within the walls lay an ordered sprawl of tents. The air was scented with cardamom and cinnamon, disguising the musky smell of men and horses. The quiet discipline of the place stood in stark contrast to the squalor and dissolution Estienne had left behind in the crusader ranks.

Movement at the periphery of his vision drew his focus, his jaw tightening as a trio of richly garbed figures approached, the warriors parting before them like waves from a ship's prow. At their head strode a man who could only be al-Kamil himself, sultan of the Ayyubid dynasty.

He was tall and regal, his beard close-cropped, features aquiline, but it was his eyes that struck Estienne most – dark and depthless, glinting with intelligence in a seemingly ageless face. He opened his arms as he drew nearer to them, smiling, speaking words of welcome that Francesco returned warmly before dismounting. Estienne struggled down from his own saddle, watching, fascinated, as the monk bowed low. When Estienne tried to mimic the show of respect he struggled not to groan as his stitches pulled and the wound in his side protested.

When al-Kamil's gaze fell upon him, it was an all-seeing stare, one that sent a shiver down Estienne's spine. He was in the presence of true power, and couldn't shake the feeling that the next few hours might shape the course of the entire crusade, if not Estienne's life.

'He wishes us to follow,' Francesco said suddenly. 'As his honoured guests.'

Estienne dragged his eyes away from the sultan. 'Did he know we were coming?'

'Why, of course. Your suspicions were correct. His men have watched our journey south for many miles.'

Estienne thought about the danger they had been in, and perhaps still were. But then... maybe not. As the sultan led them deeper into the fortified camp he realised if these Saracens had wanted them dead it would have happened on the road already. Either the sultan's hospitality, or his curiosity, was the reason they still lived. Hopefully he would not grow short on either.

The interior of al-Kamil's pavilion was a more opulent place than Estienne had ever seen. Rich carpets patterned in intricate designs covered the floor, their weave so plush he could feel their softness even through the soles of his boots. Tapestries on the walls, alive with scenes of the hunt and palace life, the greens and golds and crimsons near glowing in the muted light. The air was perfumed with drifts of incense, at once alien and intoxicating. At the centre of it all, a pile of cushions that looked so inviting Estienne could have laid his head down and slept for a month.

Francesco and al-Kamil sat cross-legged on the embroidered finery, and Estienne struggled to join them. They were surrounded by armed men, but not one had demanded to take the blade from Estienne's side. Clearly, al-Kamil felt comfortable in his own domain. Comfortable enough to allow an armed enemy to enter and treat with him.

Conversation between the men began, and Estienne understood not a word that passed between them. Nevertheless, he found himself transfixed by the back and forth of their expressions and gestures.

Francesco leaned forward, his hands sketching shapes in the air as he spoke, face alight with passionate intensity. Al-Kamil listened with a tilt of his head, stroking his beard, eyes glinting with what might have been amusement or challenge or both. At times he nodded as if in agreement, others he shook his head firmly and countered with a river of his own words.

As the time stretched, Estienne could only marvel as it seemed some manner of understanding began to bloom between these two men from such vastly disparate worlds. Where he had expected only rancour and mistrust, he perceived instead a burgeoning respect taking root, the mutual recognition of keen minds. It defied everything Estienne had been led to believe about the Saracen enemy – a heathen foe, barbarous and perhaps beyond reason or care. But as he watched the sultan pour tea for the monk with his own hands, as he witnessed the thoughtful crease of al-Kamil's brow and his gentle words, he began to see not a savage, but a man. Even a king, more noble than any he had ever met.

Eventually, Estienne began to shift on his cushion, trying to find an angle of repose that did not send spikes of agony through the wound in his side. The dull, persistent throb had escalated now to a hot coal lodged just beneath his ribs. He pressed a hand to the bandaged wound, feeling the heat of inflamed flesh even through the linen, and a sharp twinge tore through him forcing a hiss through clenched teeth. Al-Kamil's hawk-like gaze fixed upon him, a furrow of concern creasing the sultan's brow. He uttered a quick burst of Arabic to Francesco, who shot Estienne a look of sudden dismay before replying in low tones. Al-Kamil's frown deepened as he listened.

When Francesco had finished, he turned to Estienne, face still rapt with concern. 'The sultan asks what ails you.'

'And you told him? I am his enemy, Francesco. He most likely thinks me deserving of it.'

The monk raised an eyebrow knowingly. 'Quite the contrary.'

With a snap of his fingers, the sultan barked an order to one of the attendants hovering near the entrance of the tent. The man bowed low and hastened off, returning moments later with another figure in tow – a grey-bearded man in flowing robes, a leather satchel clutched in his weathered hands. Estienne tensed as the man approached, but Francesco leaned in closer.

'He is the sultan's own physician, my friend. You can trust him.'

The old man beckoned for Estienne to follow, and gingerly he rose, moving to the edge of the pavilion. As Francesco and al-

Kamil continued their conversation, the physician set his satchel down on a table and rolled up the sleeves of his robe. He looked to Estienne, dark eyes glinting with intelligence and something that might have been compassion, before gesturing to the black surcoat.

Estienne hesitated, every fibre of his being rebelling at the thought of baring his weakness to these people. But the pain in his side was almost unbearable and, begrudgingly, he shrugged out of surcoat and gambeson, gritting his teeth as the movement pulled at his stitches.

The healer's hands were cool and well-practised as he undid the linen wrap, gentle in their probing of the reddened, puckered flesh beneath. Estienne braced for the jolt of agony, for some sign of roughness from this man who should by all rights wish him only suffering, but it never came. The physician's touch remained delicate as he examined the wound, before reaching into his satchel, pulling out a small pot of salve and a fresh wrap. The strong, bitter scent of herbs filled the air as he smeared the ointment on Estienne's skin with deft fingers. Finally, he wound a length of clean linen around Estienne's torso, his ministrations as careful as if he were tending his own kin.

As he tied off the ends and stood back, Estienne flexed tentatively, steeling himself for the expected stab of discomfort. While a dull ache remained, the searing agony that had dogged him all day was gone, muted by whatever unguent the old man had applied.

'Thank you,' was all he could think to say.

There was a trace of a smile on the old man's face before he retreated, with a final bow to al-Kamil. Estienne merely stood for a moment, unable to reconcile this act of pointed kindness with all he had been taught to expect from the enemy. The world he had known, the truths he had clung to, seemed to waver. If he could be so wrong about this, about the capacity for mercy and wisdom in those he had been told to despise, then what other certainties had been built on foundations of sand?

As Francesco and al-Kamil resumed their conversation, their voices rising and falling in the incense-scented gloom, Estienne stood and watched. He had ridden into this camp ready to protect Francesco with his life. Now it appeared he was the one being offered protection. The last thing he had expected.

It seemed that there was much more to this crusade, and his own path on it, than he could ever have dreamed.

11

Estienne reclined against the plush cushions, feeling an unfamiliar sense of ease settle over him like a warm cloak. The wound in his side, once a searing agony, had faded to a dull ache under the ministrations of al-Kamil's physician. The bitter unguents and fresh linen wrappings worked wonders, leaving Estienne marvelling at the skill of these Egyptian healers.

Around him, the sultan's pavilion was a study in opulence. A low table nearby groaned under the weight of fruits, meats, and delicacies the likes of which Estienne had never seen. He reached for a dried plumb, popping the sweet morsel into his mouth and savouring the flavour. To think, mere days ago he had been subsisting on hard tack and salted pork, the crusaders' fare as meagre as their spirits. Now he dined like a king in the enemy's own camp.

Francesco sat across from him, deep in conversation with several of al-Kamil's advisors, the monk's face alight with passion as he spoke. Though Estienne could not understand the rapid flow of Arabic, he could sense the weight of the words exchanged. The potential for understanding, for a bridge across the chasm of faith and culture that divided them. And yet, despite the length of their first meeting, the sultan himself remained elusive. Al-Kamil had welcomed them with unexpected grace, offering his own physician to tend to Estienne's wounds, but he had yet to engage with Francesco's offer of conversion, the true purpose of their journey into the heart of the enemy's domain. Estienne could only hope that the monk's silver tongue would eventually sway the man. That a fragile peace could take root and grow.

The men suddenly laughed, Francesco clapping his hands in appreciation of something. Seeing Estienne's sudden confusion, Francesco leaned in with a grin.

'These men just shared with me a saying of the Prophet Muhammad: "Wisdom is the lost property of the believer. Wherever he finds it, he has a right to it."'

Estienne frowned, puzzling over the words. 'What does it mean?'

Francesco's smile widened. 'It means that wisdom, true wisdom, belongs to all of us. Regardless of faith or creed. We must be open to finding it wherever it may lie, even in unexpected places.' He gestured to the advisors, who had returned to their own quiet conversation. 'These men, they possess a deep understanding of the world. Of the human heart. Speaking with them, hearing their perspectives… it has opened my eyes in ways I never anticipated.'

A sudden commotion from outside the tent put Estienne suddenly on edge. Shouts in Arabic, the sound of a scuffle, and he sat up straighter, hand instinctively going to the hilt of his sword. Across from him, Francesco's brow furrowed in concern.

The tent flap was flung aside, and a figure burst in – a towering Moor, his skin black as night, eyes blazing with barely contained fury. He was a giant of a man, muscles rippling, a wicked sabre hanging from his hip. Estienne surged to his feet, ignoring the twinge in his side, as he realised their tenuous peace was about to be shattered.

The Moor's gaze fixed on him, eyes widening as they fell upon the black lion emblazoned on Estienne's surcoat. With a roar of rage, he jabbed a finger, words spilling from his lips in a furious torrent of Arabic. Estienne's hand dropped to the hilt of his sword, the leather wrap beneath his palm a reassuring sensation in the face of this stranger's rage. He held himself ready, not knowing what fresh madness was about to be unleashed...

Then he recognised that snarling face. Remembered when he had last seen it... upon the walls of Damietta. Among the smoke and blood and screams, this was the giant he had fought. This was the peerless warrior who had raged so furiously as Estienne had cut down the Saracen with his flashing sword.

Francesco placed himself between them. The monk's hands were raised in a placating gesture as he spoke rapidly in Arabic, his tone soothing even as tension grew like a gathering storm. Around them, the pavilion had erupted into chaos, guards rushing in from all sides, swords and spears glinting in the muted light. They formed a wall around Estienne, poised to strike at the slightest provocation, and the advisors scattered like startled birds, retreating to the edges of the tent.

Estienne held himself in check, even as the Moor continued to rage and spit. He willed his fingers to uncurl from his sword hilt, forced himself to stand steady under the weight of that murderous glare. He could only pray that Francesco would weave his words well enough to quell this imposing warrior.

Francesco turned to Estienne, his face grave. 'The Moor's name is Kashta. He says you killed his brother during the assault on Damietta's walls.'

Brother. Though it was obvious this Moor and the Saracen

he had slain were no kin by blood, Estienne knew of the bonds that a man could form in the crucible of war. It provoked a pang of regret that knifed through him, sharp and sudden. He met Kashta's accusing glare, seeing the raw pain etched into every line of the man's face.

'I...' Estienne swallowed hard. 'It was battle. My life or his. I never wanted...'

Even as he struggled with the words, he could see the futility of them. He had taken the life of this man's brother in arms. No appeal to the madness of war could salve that wound.

Francesco continued to speak, his voice low and urgent. Kashta snarled a response, every syllable dripping with venom and hate until finally, Francesco turned back to Estienne, his eyes bleak.

'He demands your life,' the monk said softly. 'As payment for his brother's death. He will have blood for blood. There is nothing I can say to dissuade him. All that stays his hand now are the vows of hospitality under which we reside. He fears his sultan's wrath, but how long that will stop him, I do not know.'

Estienne could still feel the throttling tension, the violence held at bay only barely. He had accompanied Francesco here to protect him, but quickly learned it had been a needless gesture. Now it was Estienne who jeopardised this uneasy peace.

'Then I must leave,' he said. 'Now, before blood is spilled. My presence here endangers us both.'

Francesco clasped his shoulder. 'As much as I wish you could remain by my side, that is for the best. Go swiftly, my friend. I will do what I can to calm the waters here, but you must away, before this tide of anger swells beyond our control.'

Estienne gripped the monk's arm in return. 'I pray your mission will yet bear fruit, Francesco. May the Lord watch over you.'

'May he watch over us both.'

With a final nod, Estienne allowed himself to be escorted from the pavilion. He felt the weight of Kashta's glare, hot as a brand, but he did not look back. He did not want to provoke the man any more than he had already done that day upon Damietta's walls.

As he emerged into the harsh sunlight, there was already a horse waiting, held by a grim-faced Saracen. Estienne swung himself into the saddle, ignoring the twinge of pain in his side.

He glanced back one last time, taking in the scene he was leaving behind. Francesco, still locked in intense conversation with Kashta and the advisors. The monk's face was drawn and weary, but his eyes still burned with that unquenchable fire. That belief in the power of words over swords.

Oh, to have such faith.

Turning his horse to the north, Estienne began to ride back toward Damietta. He had tried the route of peace, and it had got him nowhere. It now seemed he was bound to war, whether he wanted it or not.

12

Rain lashed against Estienne's face as he stood at the edge of the Templar encampment. The sky above Damietta roiled with angry clouds, flashes of lightning illuminating the distant horizon. Thunder rumbled in the distance, a low growl that seemed to echo the unease that lingered over the crusader camp. Since his return, there had been no movement within the city, nor any further attempt to assault it. Now they were mired in a stalemate, while the heavens raged on.

Beside him, Hoston's eyes were narrowed against the downpour.

'Still no word from Francesco?' he asked above the storm's fury.

Estienne shook his head, water running in rivulets from his sodden hair. 'Nothing. Not since I left al-Kamil's camp. I am starting to fear the worst.'

'But you say they treated you with... kindness?' The scepticism in Hoston's tone was palpable.

'Aye. Al-Kamil's own physician tended my wound. They fed us from the sultan's table. It was... unexpected.'

Hoston grunted. 'Unexpected indeed. These are strange times, Wace. I felt sure you would be staked out for the carrion birds. Instead, they see to your care better than we can. Such strange days these are.'

Estienne's hand drifted to his side, where the Saracen arrow had struck. The pain had faded to almost nothing, thanks to the skilled hands of al-Kamil's healer. The kindness of that act still bewildered him, at odds with everything he'd been taught to expect from their sworn enemy.

'I can't help but wonder if we've been wrong about them. About all of this.'

'I know you've seen things that trouble you, Estienne. But we must hold fast to our purpose. We are God's warriors, here to reclaim the Holy Land for Christendom.'

Estienne wanted to argue, to give voice to the doubts that had taken root, but before he could, a new sound cut through the storm. A bell, high and urgent, rang out from within Damietta's walls. Both men turned toward the city as alarm spread through the Templar camp, shouts of surprise and confusion rising above the rain's steady drumming.

'What in God's name...?' Hoston murmured through gritted teeth.

A rider, white gambeson sodden and filthy, emerged from the gloom to the west, his horse's hooves throwing up great gouts of mud. The man reined in hard before them, chest heaving, rain streaming down his face.

'The city,' he gasped. 'Damietta's defences... they've been breached.'

'What did you say?' one of the Templars barked back at him.

'The way lies open,' the messenger replied, pointing back toward the vast city. 'We can ride right through the gates.'

A shout went up, calling them to arms, and the Templar

encampment erupted into frenzied activity. Knights scrambled for their horses, their shouts barely audible above the storm's fury. Estienne felt his blood course through him, his body responding to the call to arms even as his mind reeled.

Grand Master Pierre's voice cut through the chaos. 'To me, brothers. The time is upon us. We ride for Damietta.'

Estienne exchanged a quick glance with Hoston before both men sprinted towards their tents. Inside, Estienne's hands moved with practised efficiency, buckling on his hauberk despite the protestation of his healing wound. Outside once more, the rain had intensified, turning the ground into a quagmire. Estienne splashed through the mud before swinging himself into the saddle of a waiting destrier, grimacing as the movement pulled at his side. Around him, the Templars formed up, a sea of white cappas and red crosses, each man a bastion of faith and steel.

Hoston appeared at his side, rain streaming down his weathered face. 'Stay close, lad. We don't know what awaits us in there.'

Estienne nodded, gripping his reins tighter. The memory of his last assault on Damietta's walls flashed through his mind – the chaos, the blood, the warriors he'd cut down without a second thought. Acts that had earned him Kashta the Moor's undying hatred. He swallowed hard, pushing the guilt aside. There would be time for regrets later. Now, there was only the prospect of an end to all this killing.

At Pierre's signal, the Templar force surged forward. They thundered across the rain-soaked ground, hooves churning mud, lightning casting their silhouettes in stark relief against the stormy sky. As they neared the city walls, Estienne expected a hail of arrows, a storm of Greek fire raining down from the battlements, but nothing came. The walls loomed before them, dark and silent, offering no resistance to their advance. Then, through sheets of rain, Estienne saw it. The great gates of Damietta stood open, yawning wide like the maw of some great serpent.

'Hold.' Pierre's command brought the column to a halt, mud spraying from beneath iron-shod hooves.

A murmur of disbelief rippled through the ranks. Estienne shared a bewildered look with Hoston. After months of siege, after so much blood spilled on both sides, could it truly be this easy?

'It has to be a trap,' someone muttered nearby, giving voice to the fear that haunted them all.

'We've come too far to falter now, brothers,' Pierre's voice rang out, steady and resolute. 'Whatever awaits us beyond those gates, we face it together. For God and the Holy Land.'

Murmurs of assent rippled through the gathered knights, their fervour overcoming their apprehension. Estienne felt no such certainty as they formed up to enter the city, his grip tightening on his sword hilt, but with a prayer on his lips, he urged his mount forward. The Templars advanced as one, passing beyond Damietta's walls and into the unknown, the rain-slick ground echoing with the sound of their advance. A grim percussion to herald their long-awaited victory. Or perhaps, Estienne thought with a chill that had nothing to do with the rain, to announce their damnation.

But only silence greeted them as they entered Damietta, more unnerving than any battle cry. Estienne's eyes darted from shadow to shadow, every sense straining for some sign of an ambush, but there was only the steady drumming of rain and the snort of uneasy horses.

As they pressed deeper into the city, the true nature of this victory revealed itself by ever more horrifying degrees. Bodies lined the streets, hundreds of them, their emaciated forms a testament to the siege's cruel efficiency. The rain washed rivers of filth through the gutters, carrying with it the nauseating stench of decay. Estienne's gorge rose, and he swallowed hard against it. This was not the glorious conquest he had imagined when he'd set out on this crusade. This was not God's work. This was suffering, raw and undeniable.

'Sweet Jesu,' Hoston breathed beside him, his usual stoicism penetrated by the horror that surrounded them. 'No wonder they fled this place.'

Movement caught Estienne's eye – a flutter of rags, a trembling hand reaching out from a doorway. It seemed that despite Hoston's words, not all had fled after all.

The survivors emerged slowly, like wraiths materialising from the gloom. Their eyes were sunken, faces gaunt with hunger, and Estienne felt his heart sink at the fear etched into every trembling line of their bodies. They murmured quiet pleas, sinking to their knees, weeping in terror as the Templars rode by. These people, these ordinary folk, clearly expected to be slaughtered where they stood.

A woman stumbled forward, clutching a bundle to her chest. For one terrible moment, Estienne thought it was the corpse of a child, but as she drew nearer, he saw it was nothing more than a collection of rags. Perhaps all that remained of a child she had lost during the siege. Her eyes, haunting in her hollowed face, fixed on him with a desperate intensity.

'Mercy,' she croaked in heavily accented Latin. 'Please, mercy.'

Estienne was almost overwhelmed by the weight of her plea. He had come here to fight the Saracen, to strike a blow for Christendom, but this... this broken soul before him was no enemy to be vanquished. She was simply a victim of their war.

Before he could respond, Pierre's voice rang out. 'Hold, brothers. These people are not to be harmed. They are under our protection now.'

Estienne felt a surge of relief, grateful that at least this small mercy would be granted. As the knights began to disperse, securing the city and tending to the survivors, Estienne dismounted. His boots squelched in the muck as he led his horse on through the abandoned city. More crusaders had come now, entering from the north and south. Men rode their destriers, banners raised proudly, but there was nothing noble to this. In larger numbers were men who ran rampant through the rain, entering houses to loot whatever they could, only to emerge moments later empty handed. If there had been anything of value within the walls of Damietta it was gone now. All that had been left behind was misery.

The rain had begun to slacken, but its patter still echoed through the empty streets like a mournful dirge. Estienne stood amidst the desolation, his surcoat sodden, as heavy as his heart felt. All around him, crusaders moved with purpose, securing buildings, gathering the weak and wounded.

He turned to see Hoston nearby, still atop his horse, eyes scanning the scene wearily.

'What does this mean?' Estienne asked.

The old knight's uncertainty was evident from the way his eyes darted from one scene of sorrow to the next. 'It means we've won, lad.'

'Have we?' Estienne couldn't keep the bitterness from his voice. 'Look around you, Hoston. Is this what victory is supposed to look like?'

Hoston's brow furrowed. 'It's not for us to question God's plan. We've struck a blow against the heathen this day, reclaimed a piece of the Holy Land for Christendom.'

'And what of them?' Estienne gestured to a group of survivors huddled in an alleyway, their eyes wide with fear and hunger. 'Are they the heathens we've come to vanquish? Women, children, the old and weak?'

'War is never clean, boy. You know that as well as I do.' Hoston's tone was gentle, almost paternal, but it did nothing to soothe the turmoil in Estienne's heart.

'This isn't war,' Estienne spat. 'This is slaughter. We've laid siege to a city full of innocent people, starved them into submission, and for what? So we can plant our flag on a pile of corpses and call it righteousness?'

'Mind your words, Wace.' Hoston's tone had turned serious. 'Such talk borders on heresy.'

'Heresy?' Estienne barked. 'And who decides what is heresy? Who decides who the enemy is? We painted these people as wicked, but I have seen the truth of it. They are just like us, in every way. Capable of both kindness and cruelty in equal measure. So I ask again, who decides which side has the right of it? God? The Pope? You?'

For a long moment, Hoston said nothing. When he spoke again, his voice was low, tinged with a sadness Estienne had never heard from him before. 'I don't have the answers you seek, Estienne. None of us do. We can only trust in our faith, in the righteousness of our cause.'

'And if that faith is misplaced?' Estienne asked, more to himself than to Hoston. 'If our cause is not as righteous as we believed?'

The older knight had no response to that. He simply tugged on his rein, his warhorse plodding away, leaving Estienne alone to watch as the rain washed the filth from the street.

13

The stench of rot and human waste assaulted Estienne's nostrils as he picked his way through the streets. The corpses that choked the city were now gone, but everywhere he looked, evidence of the siege's brutal toll still assaulted him. The constant hum of flies played its dirge, the fat black insects flocking in clouds. Skeletal dogs fought over scraps in filth-clogged gutters, their ribs stark beneath mangy hides. The residents who remained – those too weak or too stubborn to flee – huddled in doorways, hollow-eyed and trembling.

A group of holy men in stained habits shuffled past, distributing meagre alms to the starving. One, a wizened old friar with a face like crumpled parchment, pressed a crust of bread into the hands of a weeping Saracen woman. She clutched it to her breast as though it were the most precious thing in the world, her gratitude a low keening that set Estienne's teeth on edge.

The friar murmured a prayer, tracing the sign of the cross in the air before moving on to the next outstretched hand. Estienne watched him go, feeling a little hope despite the degradation. Perhaps not all was lost. Perhaps there was still room for compassion amid the rubble of their grand crusade.

That optimism shattered as he rounded the next corner. A group of men, their surcoats stained and tattered, were brawling outside a half-collapsed building. The cause of their dispute lay scattered around them: bolts of once-fine cloth, now trampled in the mud, and a handful of tarnished silver coins.

'Thieving bastard!' one man bellowed, driving his fist into another's face with a sickening crunch. 'It's fucking mine!'

Estienne's hand went to the hilt of his sword, every instinct screaming at him to intervene. But what good would it do? There was no justice to be found here, no righteousness in this petty squabble over the spoils of war, if they could be called that. And so he walked away, leaving them to their quarrel.

This was what they had fought for? This was the glorious victory they had been promised? Damietta lay conquered, yes, but at what cost? The place was in ruins. The streets that might have once bustled with life now ran with filth and blood. And for what? So that men who called themselves warriors of God could squabble over scraps like animals?

He tried to dismiss such thoughts as he neared the centre of the city. The streets grew busier as he reached a market square, the noise louder as voices mixed in a host of dialects. It heartened Estienne to see that charity was the order of the day here, more priests and knights of the holy orders were present, handing out bread to the very people they had spent so long trying to conquer.

A flash of white caught his eye – a surcoat, miraculously unstained amid the general squalor. Estienne could not suppress a smile as he recognised Amalric kneeling beside a young boy, no more than six or seven years old, offering him a hunk of bread and a cup of water. The child snatched at the offerings with trembling hands, gulping down the water so fast he choked.

'Easy there, little one,' Amalric murmured, his voice gentle. 'Not so fast. There's plenty more where that came from.'

Estienne approached, that smile still tugging at his lips. 'Your actions do you credit, my friend. It's good to see some kindness amid all this bedlam.'

Amalric stood, his own smile tinged with sadness. 'And yet it is not enough.'

The boy scampered away, clutching his meagre feast, and Estienne clasped his friend's shoulder. 'It's more than most are doing. I've seen precious little charity since we entered these walls. Mostly just looting and fighting over scraps.'

'We were supposed to be better than this,' Amalric replied. 'We came here to liberate, not to pillage. To bring the light of Christ, not to...' He gestured helplessly at the devastation around them.

'I know,' Estienne replied. 'I was taught that a true knight should show both martial prowess and compassion. But since we arrived on these shores, I've seen hardly any of the latter.'

Amalric nodded, his eyes distant. 'Perhaps that's why we're here. To remind our brothers of what it truly means to be a warrior of God.'

They stood in silence for a moment, watching as the boy shared his bounty with a group of other children huddled in a nearby doorway. It was a small act of generosity, but it struck Estienne deep. Here, amid the ruins of their grand crusade, a starving child showed more humanity than many so-called holy warriors.

'Come,' Estienne said, suddenly feeling the need to be liberated from the bustle of the square. 'Let's walk, you and I.'

Amalric nodded, following as Estienne led them away along

the western throughfare, toward the river. As they picked their way through the debris-strewn streets, Estienne's mind churned with questions. The fall of Damietta had been meant to be a turning point, a great victory for Christendom. Instead, it felt more like the beginning of the end.

'What do you think is next for us?' he asked eventually. 'Have you heard any rumours about where we will go from here?'

'I'm afraid not,' Amalric replied. 'The crusade has... stalled. There's no other word for it.'

'Stalled? But how can that be? We've taken Damietta. Surely this is but the first obstacle to overcome before we strike out and retake the rest of the Holy Land?'

Amalric shook his head. 'It's not that simple. Al-Kamil has indeed offered terms. Generous ones, by all accounts. He's even willing to restore much of the Kingdom of Jerusalem to Christian rule.'

'But that's... that's everything we wanted. Isn't it?'

'It would certainly make for a good start. But Pelagius won't hear of it. He's refused to even consider the sultan's offer.'

'What? Why in God's name would he do that?'

Amalric shrugged. 'Most likely he believes we can take all of Egypt, given enough time and resources.'

'And what does John of Brienne think of this?'

'He's furious, as you might expect. From what I've heard, he and Pelagius have been at each other's throats over it. But in the end, Pelagius holds the Pope's authority. His word is final.'

Estienne felt a knot of frustration tighten in his gut. They had been offered peace – a chance to achieve their goals without further bloodshed – and Pelagius had spat on it. For what? The promise of greater glory?

'Perhaps Francesco was right after all. He said this crusade was doomed. That we were destined to fail if we continued down this path of violence and conquest. Everyone thought him a madman at the time, but now…'

'Have you had word of him since your return from al-Kamil's encampment?' Amalric asked.

Estienne shook his head. 'I have not. But since al-Kamil still stands against us, I can only assume Francesco failed to convert him to our faith.'

'Then I hope God is watching over him,' Amalric said, his voice grim. 'The Saracens aren't known for their mercy towards those who preach the word of Christ.'

'I wouldn't worry overmuch for his safety,' he said, trying to convince himself as much as Amalric. 'Francesco struck me as the type to bring people to his side, despite what you witnessed when he tried to turn us from our march on Fariksur. And al-Kamil… well, from what little I saw of him, I do not think he would harm an unarmed preacher of God's word.'

'Let's hope you're right,' Amalric said. 'But if Pelagius continues to refuse the sultan's terms, I fear Francesco's fate will be the least of our worries. The Saracens won't sit idle forever. Sooner or later, they'll strike back.'

They had almost reached the city walls. Ahead, the ramparts still stood strong, as they had done throughout the siege. Beyond them, the waters of the Nile flowed north to the sea. Both men took the stairs up to the walkway, looking down on the river. Estienne was reminded of the day he had fought upon these battlements. Had killed upon them. He could only wonder if all that slaughter had been worth it after all.

'Surely we can't just wait here,' he said eventually, breaking the heavy silence that had fallen between them. 'Something must be done, one way or another.'

'Oh, plenty is being done, my friend. The leaders of our glorious crusade talk and talk and talk. They sit in their fine tents, drinking wine and arguing in circles while the rest of us wait in this Godforsaken place with nothing to do but pray and grow old. And all the while, the Holy Roman Emperor? The Pope? The very men who sent us on this folly sit safe in their palaces, far from the stench of death and the cries of the starving. They make grand proclamations and issue holy edicts, but when it comes to doing something...' He trailed off, shaking his head in disgust.

'You sound as though you are losing your faith in this endeavour, my friend.'

Amalric shook his head. 'Ach, my faith is still strong, Estienne. I am just frustrated. We sit here in this foreign land, far from home, while nothing gets done.'

The word 'home' suddenly stirred memories Estienne had tried so hard to bury. Images of green fields and grey skies, a stark contrast to the sun-baked desolation that surrounded them. And with those images came a face – perfect in every aspect, framed by dark hair that seemed to drink in the light.

Eva.

Her name echoed in his mind, prompting a bittersweet ache in his chest. How long had it been since he'd allowed himself to think of her? Since he'd let himself remember the touch of her, the light in her eyes when she smiled? What was she doing now, he wondered? Had she married her Marcher lord, as had been arranged? Was she happy, or did she too lie awake at night, haunted by memories of what might have been?

'Wace?' Amalric's voice cut through his thoughts. 'Are you well? You look distant.'

Estienne blinked, forcing himself back to the here and now. 'I'm fine. Just... thinking.'

'About what comes next?'

Estienne nodded, not trusting himself to speak. Let Amalric

think he was pondering the future of their crusade. It was easier than admitting the truth – that he was lost in thoughts of a past he could never reclaim, a future he had sacrificed for this... whatever this was.

He looked out over the Nile, its waters glinting in the fading light. How different it was from the river that flowed past Pembroke Castle. And yet, for a moment, he could almost imagine himself back there, standing on the battlements with Eva at his side, their whole world stretching out before them.

The illusion shattered as a gull's harsh cry echoed across the water. Estienne closed his eyes, willing the memories away. Whatever dreams he had harboured of Eva were just that – dreams. And dreams, he had learned, were a luxury he could ill afford in this unforgiving land.

'Do you ever think about what might have been?' Estienne asked, still staring out at this alien land. 'If you had walked a different road, I mean?'

Amalric shrugged. 'Not really. There were not that many different roads open to me. I am the fourth son of a wealthy burgher, but I was never going to follow in the footsteps of a merchant. And so I learned to fight. To ride. But never abandoned God's path. Eventually I pledged myself to the Order of Saint Mary, and here I am.'

'I'm sure there's more to that story,' Estienne replied.

Amalric offered a knowing grin. 'And maybe one day I will tell it.'

Estienne stifled a laugh. He was tempted to unburden himself. To tell Amalric all about his own past. The family he had found among the Marshals. How he had lost them for reasons he had been cursed never to learn. Instead, he satisfied himself with silence, but for the sound of the river flowing by.

'Perhaps we should pray?' Amalric said finally. 'It might help to clear our minds, to remind us of our purpose here.'

Estienne hesitated. What good had prayer done them so far? But when he saw the earnest look in Amalric's eyes, the fact his faith remained unshaken by the horrors that surrounded them, he knew he could not refuse. In that moment, Estienne envied Amalric that certainty more than he could express.

'Very well,' he said at last. 'Though I fear God may have turned a deaf ear to our pleas by now.'

'He hears us always, my friend,' Amalric replied, voice filled with certainty. 'Even when we doubt. Perhaps especially then.'

They knelt together at the edge of the city, overlooking the vast river. Amalric bowed his head, his lips moving in silent invocation. After a moment's hesitation, Estienne followed suit, closing his eyes against the fading light.

How many times had he knelt like this in the chapel at Pembroke, his heart full of certainty and purpose? It seemed a lifetime ago now. Still, his lips moved silently, forming prayers even as doubt gnawed at his heart. Prayers for the souls of those lost in this senseless conflict. For the restoration of the Holy Land, though he was no longer certain what that truly meant. And, unbidden, a prayer for Eva – that she might find happiness, even if it could never be with him.

'Amen,' Amalric finished, crossing himself.

'Amen,' Estienne echoed.

They rose slowly, Estienne feeling somehow lighter. As if the familiar ritual had lifted some small portion of the weight that pressed down upon him.

Amalric smiled, clapping a hand on Estienne's shoulder. 'There. Do you not feel more at ease now, my friend?'

'Perhaps,' he admitted. 'Though I fear it will take more than prayer to see us through the trials ahead.'

'Faith, Estienne,' Amalric said, his voice firm. 'Faith will see us through, as it always has. So shall we do this again tomorrow? It might help to make it a daily practice, especially in these trying times.'

'Yes.' Estienne nodded, surprising himself with his eagerness. 'Yes, I think I'd like that.'

As they turned to make their way back through the darkening streets, Estienne found himself envying Amalric's certainty once more. His own faith felt as fragile as spun glass, ready to shatter at the slightest touch. And yet... there was comfort in the ritual of prayer, in the shared moment of reflection.

As they parted ways for the night, his mind still echoed with the words he had spoken, his thoughts turning back to Eva. He wondered if she too was praying, somewhere across the sea. And if so, what... or who... she might be praying for.

14

A month since they had taken Damietta, and slowly, ever so slowly, it seemed the city was returning to life. Estienne took a deep breath as he made his way through the streets for his nightly meeting with Amalric, the evening air heavy with the mingled scents of unwashed bodies, horse dung, and the distant waft of spiced meat on the air. Somewhere nearby, a dog barked, the sound sharp in the gathering twilight.

Estienne passed what must have once been a thriving marketplace, now nothing more than a stretch of abandoned stalls and wind-blown debris. A tattered awning flapped forlornly in the breeze, and he caught sight of a child's toy – a crude wooden horse – lying forgotten in the dust. A reminder of the lives upended by their holy war.

As he rounded a corner, the sound of raucous laughter drifted from a nearby alley. A group of men huddled around a small fire, passing a wineskin between them. Their faces were flushed, eyes bright with a desperate sort of mirth.

The further he wandered from the city's centre, the more oppressive the silence became. Here, the evidence of a city defeated lay everywhere. Doors left ajar, personal belongings scattered in the street – it was as if Damietta's inhabitants had simply evaporated, leaving behind the ghostly remnants of their lives.

Estienne paused before one such home, its windows dark and empty. For a moment, he allowed himself to imagine the family that might have lived there. Had they fled in terror at the approach of the crusader army? Or had they simply melted away into the desert, taking with them whatever meagre possessions they could carry? He could only hope that in the coming days that house would be occupied once more and filled with the joy of kinship.

A woman's cry split the air, high and desperate.

Estienne's hand gripped his sword, his body tensing as he tried to pinpoint the source of the sound. For a heartbeat, nothing but silence. Then the cry came again, muffled this time, but unmistakable in its distress.

Estienne broke into a run, his footsteps echoing off the mud-brick walls as he raced towards the sound. The door of an abandoned house hung askew on its hinges, the noise of muffled whimpering coming from within.

Taking a breath, he stepped inside, greeted by a jumble of shadows and half-light, the last rays of the setting sun slanting through gaps in the shuttered windows. As his eyes adjusted to the gloom, he saw three men looming over a huddled figure in the corner. The woman's habit marked her as one of the Sisters of Penance he had seen in the company of Francesco the monk, her face a mask of terror as she pressed herself against the wall.

One of the mercenaries had his hand fisted in the woman's hair, his face flushed with drink and cruel intent. The other two stood back, leering, hands already fumbling with the laces of their breeches.

The sight sent a surge of white-hot rage through Estienne's veins. They were here to exact a holy purpose, and yet these men had stooped to the vilest of sins. The hypocrisy of it burned in his throat like bile.

'Step away from her, bastards,' Estienne growled, his voice satisfyingly low and dangerous in the stillness of the room.

The mercenaries turned as one, surprise quickly giving way to contempt as they took in the lone knight before them.

'Piss off, boy,' the largest of the three spat, his accent sounding Genoese in origin. 'This doesn't concern you.'

Estienne took a step forward, his hand gripping tight to his sword. 'I won't ask again. Let her go and leave this place. Now.'

The mercenary holding the woman in his grip laughed. 'Or what? You'll report us to the legate? Go on then, run along and tattle. We'll be done here soon enough.'

'I am no teller of tales,' Estienne said, his voice steady despite the fury building in his chest. 'But I was squired to William Marshal, the greatest knight in all Christendom. And if you don't let that woman go, I will kill you all.'

For a moment, uncertainty flickered across the mercenaries' faces. Then one scarred brute with a patchy beard stepped forward, drawing a wicked-looking dagger from his belt.

'Big words from a pretty boy. Let's see if you can back them up.'

As they began to advance, memories of his training under the Marshal flooded back. That familiar voice seemed to whisper in his ear, *When faced with more than one foe, control the space. Make them come to you.*

Estienne took a deliberate step back, drawing the mercenaries away from the cowering woman. His eyes scanned the room, taking in potential dangers and anything that he might use to his advantage – an overturned table to his left, a pile of broken shelving to his right.

'Last chance,' Estienne said, his voice cold as the steel still scabbarded at his side. 'Walk away now, and we'll speak no more of this.'

The scarred mercenary's face twisted into an ugly grin. 'Fuck your chances, boy. We're gonna gut you like a pig and leave you for the rats.'

As the man lunged forward, dagger flashing in the dim light, Estienne felt a familiar calm settle over him. He'd tried reason. He'd offered mercy. Only violence remained.

Steel sang as Estienne's blade cleared its scabbard. The scarred mercenary's dagger thrust forward, seeking flesh. Estienne's sword lashed out, taking that hand off at the wrist. The mercenary's scream was cut short as the backswing took him in the throat, and blood painted the wall in a glistening arc. The man fell, gurgling, clawing at his ruined neck.

No time to think. The second mercenary charged, face contorted in rage and fear. Estienne sidestepped, using the man's momentum against him. His knee came up, catching the mercenary in the stomach. As he doubled over, Estienne brought his sword pommel down hard on the back of his skull. Bone crunched, and the man dropped like a stone.

The third mercenary, eyes wide with surprise, scrambled for the door. Estienne's sword flashed out, catching him in the back of the leg and he went down screaming. As he crawled desperately for the open door, Estienne strode after, each step measured and inevitable as death itself.

'Please,' the mercenary sobbed, rolling onto his back. 'Mercy.'

Estienne looked down at the broken man, sword spattered red. For a moment, he saw not a mercenary, but a boy – young and afraid, pissing himself in terror. Then he glanced across the room, to where that woman of God still cowered. These men had offered her no mercy. There might well be none to be found in his whole Godforsaken land.

His sword fell.

The room went silent.

Estienne stood amid the carnage, chest heaving, ears ringing in the sudden quiet. He'd killed before, more times than he could count, but never like this. Never with such brutal efficiency. Never with such a lack of emotion.

A soft whimper from the corner brought him back to reality. The Sister of Penance huddled there, her habit splattered with blood, eyes wide and unblinking as she stared at the bodies strewn across the floor.

'Are you hurt?' Estienne asked, his voice sounding strange and distant to his own ears.

The woman shook her head mutely, then burst into tears. Great, heaving sobs wracked her body as she curled in on herself, face buried in her hands.

Estienne took a step towards her, then stopped. What comfort could he offer, standing there with a bloody sword and three corpses at his feet? He was no saviour, no holy warrior. Just a man with blood on his hands and a gnawing emptiness in his gut.

'I… I'm sorry,' he whispered.

The woman looked up at him, her face streaked with tears. 'Bless you. God bless you.'

God? Was he even here any more? Despite days of praying on the wall of Damietta, he wasn't sure God had heard even a single word.

'Go,' Estienne said, gesturing towards the door. 'Find the others of your Order, but speak of this to no one.'

The woman nodded, stumbling to her feet. She paused at the door, looking back at Estienne with a mix of gratitude and something else – fear, perhaps. Then she was gone, into the gathering darkness.

Estienne turned back to the corpses. The stark evidence of what he had done. There would be a reckoning for his actions if he was found out, and he could only pray that the price would not be too steep.

'Christ's bones. What in God's name happened here?'

Estienne started at the words, raising his sword as he turned back toward the doorway. Amalric's ample frame filled it, his face a mask of shock as he took in the carnage.

Estienne felt a wave of relief wash over him, followed immediately by a surge of shame. Of all the people to find him like this, it had to be Amalric – his friend, his brother in arms, the one person whose good opinion he valued above all others.

'They were... they were attacking a woman. One of the Sisters of Penance. I had no choice.'

Amalric's eyes narrowed as he stepped into the room, carefully avoiding the expanding pools of blood. 'No choice? Estienne, there are three dead men here.'

'Mercenaries,' Estienne spat. 'Genoese dogs who thought they could prey on the weak.'

He watched as Amalric crouched beside one of the bodies, examining the fatal wounds. When he looked up, his expression was grim.

'They won't be preying on much now,' Amalric said. 'This was a slaughter.'

'Would you rather I had left them to their sport? Let them defile a woman of God?'

'Of course not,' Amalric replied, rising to his feet. 'But this... this complicates things. The Genoese will demand blood when they learn of it. And there is only so much sway the grand master can leverage...'

The implications hung heavy in the air between them. Estienne had killed fellow crusaders – men who, despite their sins, were still considered soldiers of Christ. The punishment for such an act could be severe, perhaps even mortal.

'What do you suggest?' Estienne asked.

Amalric was silent for a long moment, his eyes roaming the blood-splattered room. Then, with a heavy sigh, he removed his surcoat and knelt beside the corpse nearest the door.

'Are you going to help me, or not?' he asked. 'This one looks heavy, and the river is at least fifty yards away.'

Estienne blinked, scarcely able to believe what he was hearing. 'You... you're going to help me cover this up?'

Amalric grinned. 'You're my brother. I won't see you hanged for defending an innocent.'

Estienne mirrored Amalric's grin, and together, they set about the grim task of covering up what had happened. As they hauled the first body out into the darkened street, Estienne felt a surge of gratitude towards his friend. But with it came a gnawing sense of guilt. He was dragging Amalric into his mess, forcing him to compromise his own honour.

'You don't have to do this,' Estienne said as they made their way towards the Nile. 'If we're caught...'

'If we're caught, we'll come up with something,' Amalric grunted, adjusting his grip on the body. 'Now save your breath. We've a long night ahead of us.'

The streets of Damietta were mercifully quiet as they made their grim journey to the city's walled perimeter. With a grunt of effort, they heaved the first body over the edge and into the river. It hit the water with a muffled splash, the current carrying it quickly northward.

Three times they made the journey, each one leaving them more exhausted than the last. By the time they dragged the final corpse to the water's edge, both men were out of breath. Once the Nile swept away the last evidence of their grim work, both men stood silent, watching the quiet waters. Then Amalric turned to Estienne, his face grave in the starlight.

'As though it never happened,' he said.

'As though it never happened,' Estienne repeated.

But it *had* happened. The memory of it still lingered. The blood still stained his tunic. He had killed those men without a thought. As though they had deserved it, and he was their executioner ordained by God himself.

And deep down, he knew he was not done yet.

PART TWO: THE SANDS OF AL-NAFŪD

EGYPT – 1220 AD

15

The midday sun beat down as Estienne walked the streets, the heat heavy and oppressive even in the shade of the date palms that lined the thoroughfare. Around him, the city was slowly coming back to life, like a slumbering old man, rousing from a long and terrible dream. The filth and debris of the siege had been cleared away by work parties of foot soldiers and penitent citizenry. In their place, hesitant signs of normalcy were emerging – the clatter of a blacksmith's hammer ringing out from a nearby forge, the cry of a hawker touting his wares, the laughter of children chasing each other through the winding alleys. Both Egyptian and westerner went about their business in peace, as though the months and years of strife between them had never happened.

Yet, beneath this veneer, Estienne could sense an undercurrent of disquiet that clung to the place. It was there in the way the market stalls stood half-empty, their owners casting wary glances at the wandering knights and mercenaries. In the way the laughter of the children held a brittle, fractured edge, as if they had forgotten how to be young. In the hollow eyes of the beggars who clustered in doorways, hands outstretched in wordless need.

As he walked on, the great mosque rose up before him, its dome and minarets soaring into the cloudless sky. But no longer did the muezzin's call to prayer echo from its heights. Instead, the clang of church bells rang out, announcing the transformation of this once-proud centre of Moslem faith into a cathedral for the victorious crusaders.

Estienne paused in the shadow of the towering edifice, his gaze travelling up the intricately carved walls, the graceful Arabic script now obscured by the banner of the cross. There was no denying the raw power of the symbol, the weight of the victory it proclaimed. And yet, as he stared up at that stark white standard, he couldn't suppress the flicker of doubt that stirred in his heart.

In the weeks since Damietta's fall, he had watched the city change, watched as many of the jubilant conquerors departed, their places taken by fresh-faced recruits thirsting for glory. These newcomers moved through the streets with the swagger of victors, eyes alight with righteous zeal, but Estienne wondered if they truly understood. If they had seen what he had seen, the drawn faces of the starving, the piles of the dead, the shattered remnants of lives upended, would their faith be quite so unwavering?

Shaking off the dark turn of his thoughts, Estienne pressed on. Overhead, a pair of swifts darted and swooped, their chittering cries bright in the heavy air. He envied them their freedom. What he would give to soar above the doubts that plagued him, to see the clear path ahead.

Those doubts faded as he reached his destination – the temple to which the grand master, Pierre of Montaigu, had summoned his Templars and all those who followed them. The makeshift church was already crowded when Estienne mounted its stairs, the assembled knights standing shoulder to shoulder beneath the arched ceiling. Shafts of sunlight slanted through the high windows, catching motes of dust in their golden beams and casting the white cappas of the Templars in a soft glow.

As he moved through the press of bodies, Estienne caught snatches of murmured conversation – speculation on the reason for their summons, rumours of discontent among the ranks, whispers of coming glory. He could feel the tension in the air, a palpable current of anticipation that raised the hairs on the back of his neck.

'Do you know what this is about?' he asked Hoston as he came to stand beside him.

Hoston shook his head. 'No more than you, lad. But I'd wager we're about to find out.'

The low din of voices fell to a hush as the grand master strode to the front of the temple. He mounted the steps of the altar and turned to face the assembled knights, hands spread wide in a gesture of greeting.

'Brothers,' he began, his voice filling the hall. 'I have called you here today because the time has come for us to act. For too long, we have languished within these walls, resting on the laurels of our victory, while the enemies of Christ continue to pollute the Holy Land with their presence.'

A ripple of assent ran through the gathered knights like a rustle of wind through leaves.

'God has granted us this city, this foothold in the land of Our Saviour, but now it is our sacred duty to carry the banner of the cross further toward the Holy Land and reclaim what is rightfully ours.'

As he listened, Estienne felt something akin to hunger, a yearning for purpose that had lain dormant since the fall of

Damietta. For all his doubts, all his questions about the righteousness of their cause, there was a part of him that still craved the chance to prove himself, to carve his name into the annals with deeds of valour. Yet even as that old desire kindled, he couldn't shake the memory of Francesco's words, the monk's conviction that there was another path, a way to bring light to the darkness without bloodshed.

'And so, my brothers, I come to you with glad tidings,' the grand master continued, his voice ringing with conviction. 'Our next conquest has been decided. While the rest of Christendom's armies languish idle within the walls of this city, our holy Order will strike out and claim what is ours by right of God. We set our sights on the port of Tinnis, nestled eastward on the shores of Lake Manzalah.'

A great roar of approval surged from the assembled knights. Swords were drawn and thrust aloft, the rasp of steel on leather echoing from the stone walls. But even as the tide of fervour swelled around him, Estienne felt a cold weight settle in the pit of his stomach. Tinnis. Another city, another stronghold of the enemy to be breached and broken. More blood to spill, more lives to shatter in the name of their righteous cause.

He thought of Damietta in the aftermath of the siege, the hollow faces of the survivors huddled in the ruins of their homes. The terrible silence that had fallen over the streets, broken only by the keening of the bereaved and the hungry cries of children. Was this truly the work of God, to visit such devastation upon the innocent?

Yet for all his doubts, Estienne could not deny the thrill that sang in his blood at the prospect of battle. The sense of purpose that came with fighting for a cause greater than himself. There was a purity to it, a clarity that he craved, even as he questioned the very foundations of their holy war.

Around him, the cheers of the Templars reached a crescendo. As the grand master stepped down from the dais, the knights began to disperse, the buzz of excited chatter filling the air. Estienne stood motionless amid the swirl of white cappas, his thoughts churning. Beside him, Hoston turned, fixing him with a searching gaze.

'What say you, lad? Will you sail with the Templars to Tinnis, or stay here to hold Damietta with the rest?'

Estienne felt the weight of the question settle on his shoulders. To stay here, in this city that felt more like a mausoleum than a bastion of their faith? To walk streets haunted by the ghosts of the slain while the spectre of his own doubts dogged his every step? Or to push onward, to seek some measure of meaning in the crucible of battle, even as he questioned the very nature of their crusade?

He thought of Francesco again, the man's unwavering belief in the power of compassion, the possibility of a different path. If he stayed, perhaps he could carry on that legacy in some small way, be a voice of mercy in a world gone mad with zealotry. And yet, even as the thought took shape, he knew it for a hollow hope. He was a warrior, not a priest. His hands were made for the sword, not the cross.

Estienne met Hoston's gaze. 'I'll join you.'

Hoston nodded his approval. 'Aye, I thought as much. The Black Lion still wants to roar.'

Together, they turned and strode from the church. In the sudden sunlight, Estienne could only think himself a fraud. Hoston had called him the Black Lion, but he could not know the doubt that went along with the fury.

'There is an appointment I must keep, Hoston. Please excuse me.'

Hoston nodded his understanding, as Estienne left the

grounds of the Templar church and made his way west through the city. The last rays of the setting sun painted the sky gold by the time he reached the walled extent of Damietta. Upon it, Amalric was already there, kneeling at the parapet that looked down upon the river. The young knight's head was bowed, lips moving in silent prayer. For a moment, Estienne hesitated, struck by the serenity of the scene. It seemed almost a shame to disturb such peaceful devotion.

'I was beginning to wonder if you'd forgotten our appointment,' Amalric said, sensing he was being watched.

Estienne managed a wry grin. 'Not forgotten, just... delayed. The grand master of the Temple summoned us to a meeting.'

Amalric's brow furrowed. 'What news? Has something happened?'

'The Templars have decided to strike out from Damietta. They mean to take Tinnis for Christendom. And I've decided to join them.'

'When do you leave?' he asked quietly.

'Soon. Within days, most likely.'

Amalric rose to his feet, taking hold of Estienne's shoulder. 'Then I wish you well, my friend. Truly. I hope you find what you're looking for on this journey.'

'My thanks. And who knows? Perhaps our paths will cross again before long.'

'I've no doubt they will,' Amalric replied.

They stood in companionable silence for a moment, then Amalric straightened, his face taking on a more solemn cast. 'We should pray one last time together, before you embark on this new journey.'

Estienne nodded, grateful for the familiar ritual. They knelt side by side and Amalric's voice, when he spoke, was low and fervent.

'Heavenly Father, we come before you with hearts filled with gratitude. We thank you for the brotherhood we have found in this far-off land, for the strength you have given us to face each new challenge. And now, Lord, we ask for your blessing on our brother Estienne as he prepares to set forth on a new path. Watch over him, we pray. Guide his steps and his sword. Grant him wisdom in times of doubt, courage in the face of danger, and compassion when his battles are done. And if it be your will, Lord, direct him to more peaceful shores when his task is over.'

'Amen,' Estienne murmured, the word barely more than a whisper.

As they rose, Estienne felt a sudden urge to say more, to somehow convey the depth of his appreciation for Amalric's friendship. But before he could find the words, Amalric pulled him into a fierce embrace.

'Until we meet again, brother,' Amalric said.

Estienne returned the embrace. 'Until we meet again.'

And then it was over. Amalric stepped back, as Estienne nodded once, then turned to leave. As he walked away, Estienne tried not to think on the friendship he had lost, but what he might gain in the days to come. That sense of purpose. Of faith.

On the walls of Damietta and the road to Fariksur he had fought without mercy. In the aftermath of it he had been filled only with doubt. Was he a soldier of God, or merely pretending? He could only hope the answer might be found in Tinnis, for good or for ill.

16

The deck heaved beneath Estienne's feet, rolling like an angry beast desperate to shake him loose. He clung white-knuckled to the rail, salt spray and rain lashing his face. All around the tempest howled, an unholy din of creaking timbers, thrashing waves and barked commands ripped away by the gale.

They never should have sailed with the impending storm's jaws poised to snap shut, but the grand master's command had been absolute – muster the fleet on the northern coast, then onward east to seize Tinnis in the name of the Holy Cross.

Estienne's gut lurched, and not just from the ceaseless pitching of the ship. Their holy purpose seemed a distant thing now, drowned out by the shrieking storm that had blown them miles off course. Somewhere out there, across the heaving expanse of the wind-whipped Mediterranean, Hoston and the other ships of their vanguard fought to stay afloat. He could only hope their galleys fared better than this one.

'For the love of Christ, secure that line!'

The shout snapped Estienne from his musing. Sailors scrambled across the deck, struggling to hold fast the rigging as the gale clawed at the straining sailcloth. Estienne's stomach attempted a rebellion of its own, nausea swelling with each sickening roil, but he blinked rain from his eyes and fixed his gaze on the ever-darkening horizon.

The clouds hung heavy and purple-black, the sea and sky bleeding together until he couldn't tell where one ended and the other began. No land in sight, no stars to steer by. Only the hammer of the waves and the high keen of the wind. And beneath it all, threading through the marrow of his bones, a growing sense of dread. An icy certainty that this was no ordinary storm. That some vast, uncaring force had marked them and meant to drag them down to the bottomless deep. Estienne's fingers tightened on the rail, slick and chilled to the bone. At that moment, with the sea writhing like a nest of serpents, the salvation promised by this war in the Holy Land had never seemed more distant and unreachable as God's own grace.

A blinding flash of light heralded a boom like the world splitting in two. Estienne staggered, nearly pitched headlong by the thunder that cracked above the ship. No sooner had its violent echo faded than the bow shook as the ship's hull struck some obstacle hidden beneath the churning waves.

'We're taking on water,' came the immediate cry.

'All hands to the hold! Bail, you bastards.'

Screams erupted from below. Estienne lunged for the hatch, feet skidding on rain-slick boards as he half-climbed, half-fell down the narrow ladder to be met by a scene of chaos. Men thrashed and floundered, fighting the gushing torrent that poured in through a jagged gash in the hull. Barrels and crates bobbed in the rising water, and the horses – God Almighty, the horses. They screamed like damned souls trapped in their pens, eyes rolling white, hooves flailing as they strained against their ties. Estienne splashed through the knee-deep water, snarling curses as he fought to keep his feet. The sharp reek of fear filled his nose, ripe and rotten. If he didn't free the beasts, they'd surely drown.

'Help me, damn you,' he roared at a sailor struggling past, but the man didn't even turn, scrabbling for the ladder with a pitiful wail.

Estienne drove a shoulder into the nearest stall door, wood crunching beneath the impact. The horse within reared, screaming, and he ducked beneath its hooves.

'Easy, easy now...'

But the animal knew only blind panic, and strained until its tethers suddenly snapped. Estienne could only lurch aside as it bolted like a demon loosed from hell. He grunted as he was thrown hard against the stall by another wild list of the ship, breath whooshing from his lungs. Water churned around his thighs now, icy and grasping. Above, feet pounded on the deck, and a new note entered the chorus of screams.

'Abandon ship. Every man for himself.'

The hull groaned like a dying beast, timbers creaking as it listed hard to larboard. Estienne swore, struggling to keep himself upright. The world tilted sickeningly, and he almost fell as he was thrown sideways.

Another keening shriek from one of the other stalls, but there was no time left to save those beasts. No bloody time. The sea frothed around his waist, clawing at his chest, so hungry. And it would not stop until it had swallowed him whole.

Abandoning the steeds to their fate, he fought his way toward the ladder. Other men clawed toward it, one grasping his shirt to haul him back, but Estienne was the stronger. He grasped the first rung, hauling himself up, almost slipping as he focused on the open hatch above.

Lightning sheeted across the sky as he emerged, painting the world stark silver. For a moment, Estienne viewed it all with searing clarity – the ship, fast submerging, waves grasping at her sides. The rigging snapped like old bones, masts swaying drunkenly. And the faces of men he'd sailed with for two days, their features contorted in terror as they flung themselves into the seething maelstrom.

Estienne crawled his way up the canting deck, muscles straining as he fought the tilt of the ship. The rail was near, and he could see the white churn of the waves beyond as he reached out to anchor himself to something, anything. His feet slipped and he crashed hard to hands and knees. The fall saved him, as a sliding crate hurtled past, missing his head by a handspan before splintering to kindling against the mast.

'Christ Jesus…' His curse was lost to the gale.

The ship was almost on its side as the sea reached up to claim her, and men leapt overboard without hesitation, taking their chances in that icy embrace. But Estienne couldn't find it in himself to follow. The cold truth of it seized him – for all his skill with blade and horse, he was no strong swimmer. In that roiling abyss, what hope would he have?

Yet what choice remained?

Stay and sink with the ship, or meet his end embraced by the deep? The deck lurched further, and the choice was made. He tumbled, frantically scrabbling for purchase on slickened wood, and for a moment, he was weightless as a sigh.

Then the sea slammed up to meet him, and the whole world went black and cold and roaring. The impact spun him sideways, ripping breath and sense asunder, and he was sinking, down and down into the frigid dark. The cold was like a razor, knifing in to bite deep into flesh. His chest heaved, desperate for air, and saltwater flooded his throat. He kicked wildly, flailing against the consuming dark but every movement was sluggish, laboured, as though the sea itself sought to pull him down into its inky-black belly.

Lungs aflame, spots crowding the edges of his vision, he clawed upward with the last of his failing strength. And just when that strength was near spent, when his limbs had turned to lead and his mind spiralled toward oblivion, he broke the surface. A gasping, spluttering eruption, and air, sweet mother of Christ, air in great whooping lungfuls.

He floundered, tossed like a cork on the waves, saltwater sloshing into his nose, soaking his tunic and making it impossibly heavy. The sea heaved around him, towering swells crashing and roaring, and for one gut-wrenching moment he was sure he would be dragged back under. But through the stinging film of brine in his eyes, through the whipping froth and foam, he saw it – a darker shape bobbing on the water, riding the surging tide.

Estienne kicked for it, every stroke a battle against the sea. His fingers probed the murk and closed on soaked, splintered wood – a scrap of decking, a shattered spar, he knew not which. All he knew was that it felt solid, and real, and he clung to it with a drowning man's desperation as the waves battered and rolled.

As he lay there, desperate among the raging tempest, the cold sank deeper, leeching the feeling from his limbs, turning his mind to a grey fog. He blinked against the pelting rain, peering into that impenetrable, heaving night for any sight of the other men, but there was nothing. Nothing but the hunger of the sea and the howling fury of the storm.

All he had left was to pray, through chattering teeth. Not for salvation, not for rescue from this hell of cold and wet, but for understanding. For some sign, some scrap of certainty that this was all part of God's plan for him. That the path he'd walked, from England to Outremer, from squire to knight to battered castaway, had meaning. He prayed until the storm relented, until the sea calmed. Until he was left alone in the cold and the dark, gripping onto a meagre sliver of driftwood.

When the mercy of exhausted sleep began to overwhelm him, he could only succumb to it, and hope that he would eventually wake and not be committed to the bottom of the sea.

17

Consciousness returned at a slow, shuddering crawl. His first sensation was the taste of sand, gritty and foul on his tongue. Then came the dull throb of pain, radiating through every inch of his battered body. He groaned, the sound little more than a croak.

Sunlight seared his vision as he cracked open salt-crusted eyes. A rapid blink and tears streamed down his cheeks, the world swimming into hazy focus. An azure sky, so bright it hurt to look upon, the susurrus of waves lapping at his legs.

Before he could appreciate his miraculous survival, his stomach lurched. Only enough time to raise himself on hands and knees before he vomited seawater through mouth and nose, the sting of it making him moan pitifully.

With a grunt, Estienne rolled onto his side, the beach finally coming into full clarity around him. Memory crashed over him like a wave, as violent and cold as the storm that had dragged him down into the abyss. The lightning-split sky, the ship's timbers cracking like bones, the frantic press of bodies as men leapt into the churning sea. His own desperate struggle, clinging to a bit of flotsam as the frigid water battered him senseless.

He shoved himself upright, hand splayed on the sand to steady himself while his head spun. As his vision cleared, he could see the full scope of the devastation wrought by the tempest's fury. The shore was a tableau of ruin, littered with the broken remnants of their ship. Splintered planks and shattered spars jutted from the sand like the bones of some long-dead leviathan. Tattered shreds of sailcloth fluttered forlornly in the salt breeze and everywhere, strewn across the beach as far as the eye could see, the bloated and battered corpses of men and horses, surrounded by flies humming in celebration of the feast.

Nausea rising, Estienne staggered to his feet. He recognised the faces of some of the dead. Men he'd sailed with, Templars he'd fought beside, shared meals and japes and tales of home. Brothers of the sword, sworn to the same holy cause, now lying cold and still, glassy eyes staring sightlessly at the pitiless sky.

Grief knotted in his chest, twining with a sickening sense of guilt. Why had he alone been spared, when so many good men had been claimed by the deep? What had preserved him to be washed up on this unknown shore? But in truth, he wasn't sure he wanted to hear what reasons. His guilt only deepened as he felt a selfish notion of relief that he alone had survived.

Quashing it down, he gazed about him, trying to quell the sense of nausea and better gauge his surroundings. One step, followed by another as unsteady as the first. His legs threatened to buckle beneath him as he staggered along the tideline. The sun beat down, merciless in its intensity, and sweat trickled down his back, his face, the salt of it stinging his eyes and mixing with the brine that soaked his tattered tunic.

Estienne squinted against the glare, trying to get his bearings. The coastline stretched on in either direction, an unbroken line of white sand bordered by scrubby dunes. No landmarks, no sign of settlement or civilisation. Just an endless, unfamiliar expanse that mocked him with its vastness.

Was this Egypt still? The Holy Land? Some nameless stretch of the Levantine shore? The storm had blown them wildly off course, and Estienne had no way of knowing how far it had carried him from their intended path. Wherever he was, he could not muse on it forever. If he did not find some sign of life soon, it would not matter where he was.

He scanned the beach, the dunes, the distant line where the sand met the scrub and rock of the interior. Searching for any sign that might mean salvation – the glint of a river, the smoke of a cookfire, the distant mast-top of a ship. Nothing, save the shimmer of heat-haze and the mournful cry of gulls wheeling overhead.

Estienne knelt for a moment, knees sinking as the sand yielded under his weight. Clasping his hands tight he closed his eyes.

'Dear Lord, I thank thee for my liberation from the depths of the ocean. Now I pray I might be offered further salvation. Grant me the strength to endure. A chance to carry on as your mortal sword and strike down thine enemies. Guide my way, o Lord, that I might continue my path as your faithful knight.'

Then he stood, no more time for prayers. Step by stumbling step, he pressed on, his mind roiling as bleakly as his gut. If he could just find some scrap of shade, some shelter from the sun's unrelenting glare... but there was no respite to be had on this barren stretch of sand. And with each passing moment, each aching stride, the temptation of giving up loomed larger. To simply lie down upon the beach, close his eyes against the hammer of the sun, and wait for the oblivion that surely beckoned.

A clench of fists and teeth, and Estienne pushed those dark thoughts aside. He was a knight, a holy warrior sworn to God's service. He had not survived the maelstrom's wrath only to expire here, alone and unmourned in some forsaken land. He would walk until his strength gave out. Crawl, if he must. He was not ready to face his maker yet.

On he walked, at first fearing to leave the beach. Surely if he continued along the coastline he would find some fishing village or even a port. But the farther he stumbled, the longer he went without seeing any sign of life, the more he was forced to fight his despair.

Veering inland, he left the sand behind to walk the scrubby ground, eyes squinting in the glare, scanning for any signs of salvation. For hours he wandered the desolate plain, never allowing himself to give up hope, until finally he saw something.

At first he thought it a mirage, a trick of the heat shimmering off the sand and his own fatigue. But as he stumbled on, daring to hope, the distant smudges resolved into the unmistakable shapes of human figures. He allowed himself a glimmer of hope. Surely God in his mercy had sent these people – fishermen perhaps, or even fellow crusaders washed up by the storm as he had been.

Estienne raised a hand, a painful cry tearing from his throat, little more than a dusty croak. He quickened his pace, stumbling in his haste, his rescue so close he could almost taste it, but as he drew closer, his stirring hope turned to a sinking dread. These men wore curved blades at their hips. He could hear them now, and there was an aggressive lilt to their voices, raised in a shout as they spotted his approach. These were neither fishermen nor crusaders, they were Saracen fighters, and despite the hospitality he had been shown by al-Kamil, Estienne knew he had to be cautious. His life would depend on it.

He stopped cold, heart drumming. Instinctively, his hand went to his hip, searching for the sword that had been his constant companion, but his fingers closed on empty air. He was defenceless.

The men drew close enough that Estienne could see the glint of pitiless eyes, the hard set of mouths in sun-weathered faces. They barked words at him in a harsh tongue that he could not comprehend.

'Wait,' he croaked. 'I am...'

What? What would he say? That he had come here to this place to claim Outremer for Christendom? That despite his intention to conquer they should still treat him with friendship, as their sultan al-Kamil had? Even if he could have spoken their language, he doubted they would listen. The best he could hope was to be ransomed back to his crusader brethren, but how would he explain that to these men?

They were within a few feet now. One of them was smiling a toothless grin, but there was nothing friendly about it. Two more closed in on either side, making no pretence, their eyes showing nothing but wicked intent. A fourth moved so near the stink of his breath was palpable, his face a blank mask, before he struck Estienne with the back of his hand.

It was not a hard blow, but in his weakened state, Estienne's legs buckled. He snarled as he fell to his knees, determined to stand, to fight back, but he could hardly raise his hands. Another slap, a kick, and one of them laughed. Estienne heard the telltale ring of a sword being drawn, and he realised this was it. He was to be slaughtered in the sand, so far from home, as his killers laughed at his demise.

But the final stroke never fell. As Estienne knelt in the sand, head bowed, bracing for the inevitable, rough hands seized him instead. They dragged him upright, iron fingers digging into his arms, wrenching them behind his back. He cried out as his shoulders screamed in protest, the sound cut off by a blow to the head that made stars explode across his vision. Reeling, he could only gasp as his wrists were bound tightly with coarse rope, the fibres biting deep.

The Saracens hauled him along, and he could only stumble after. They were shouting, harsh syllables flying back and forth above his bowed head, but he could make no sense of them. Their tone told him all he needed to know – he was a prisoner, his life entirely in their hands, to be ended or spared on their whim. But they had chosen to spare him, at least for now, though to what purpose, Estienne could scarcely imagine. Did they mean to toy with him, a mouse dangled in the paws of a cat before the killing bite? To parade him before their fellows, a trophy of their prowess and his disgrace? His answer came starkly, as he finally saw where he was being led.

Across the scrub, a road. And on that road stood yet more Saracens leading a cart drawn by two horses. Behind it, a pitiful trail of misery. More prisoners, their faces wan, clad in rags, all tied to one another. Men, women, children, each with their gaze drawn to the ground lest they catch the eye of their captors.

Estienne saw a cruel whip on the belt of one man standing in wait for his fellows to return. Those men barked more words at one another, more laughter, no doubt congratulating themselves for their good fortune in finding one more slave.

With a slap against the rump of a horse, the cart began to trundle on. Along with it, the human chattel bound to its rear.

And Estienne with them.

18

Estienne stumbled onward, feet dragging in the dust. Each step was agony, his muscles screaming in protest, the rope around his wrists rubbing his skin raw and bloody. How many days had it been since the Saracens had taken him? He'd lost count, the endless march south blurring into a haze of exhaustion and despair.

The cold nights offered no respite, huddled amongst the other captives for warmth, teeth chattering, stomach cramping with hunger. But the heat of day was like a smothering embrace that sapped the strength from his limbs and the moisture from every pore. He could feel it now, searing through the threadbare remnants of his shirt, baking him alive inside his own skin.

A sharp prod between his shoulder blades jolted him from his misery. One of the guards barked something, the words harsh and guttural. Estienne didn't need to understand to know it was a command to keep moving, and he gritted his teeth and obeyed, too weary to earn another beating. On they trundled, this stinking row of misery. On towards their fate.

Then, as he squinted against the glare as he had done countless times, he saw it rising from the shimmering heat-haze ahead. A city, sprawling and unfamiliar, its minarets thrusting into the cloudless sky. The sight filled him with a dull dread, each step bringing him closer to those high walls, to the final seal on his fate. As they neared it, their captors grew more vocal with excitement, but Estienne could sense the apprehension in his fellow prisoners, the heightened sense of fear.

The press of bodies as they entered the city gates was suffocating, the din of voices clamouring in unknown tongues. Estienne felt like he was drowning, the strangeness of it all crashing over him in waves – the pungent aroma of spices, the braying of camels, the flashes of colour from robes and veils and buildings. It was a world so alien from the green fields and grey skies of home that it might as well have been the surface of the moon.

They were led along those streets to a central market square. Here the city folk went about their business seemingly oblivious to the procession of sorrow being driven through its midst.

Estienne barely resisted being shoved into a holding pen, stumbling against the other captives, a jumble of faces both fearful and defiant. There were Nubians, their skin black as polished ebony, Saracens in tattered robes, even a smattering of pale-skinned Europeans, their shared misery a language all its own. Estienne locked eyes with one, a gaunt man with lank hair and a matted beard.

'God help us,' he croaked, his accent marking him as from the south of England.

Estienne opened his mouth to reply, to find some kinship in this man from his home, but before he could, a guard lashed out with the butt of his spear, catching him across the face. He reeled back, blood filling his mouth, the stark order for silence well received.

As he huddled there, breathing hard through the pain, the

terrible reality of his predicament crashed over him. He was no longer Estienne Wace, the Black Lion, knight crusader of Christ. He was chattel, a thing to be bought and sold, his fate bound to the whims of men he once would have called enemy.

Looking around at his fellow captives he saw faces that were a portrait of despair, eyes dull and without hope, shoulders slumped in weary resignation. Was that how he appeared now? A pitiful wretch? A hollow shell of the man he'd been? He almost couldn't bear to consider it, yet it was there – the knowledge that in this strange and merciless land, he was now truly, utterly lost.

When the sun had risen to its zenith, the cage was thrown open, and the slaves were goaded out at spearpoint. The market square seethed with activity now, a clamorous din of vendors and patrons, and among it all Estienne and his fellow captives were arranged in a line like so many head of cattle, ready for inspection by discerning buyers. He squinted against the harsh sunlight, his bonds chafing as he shifted from foot to foot. The indignity of it all was almost too much to bear – that he was reduced to an object to be poked and prodded, his worth determined by the strength of his back and the health of his teeth.

As if on cue, a group of men approached, their robes richly embroidered, their eyes hard and appraising. They moved down the line, examining each captive in turn, feeling the jut of ribs, the curve of spine, the swell of muscle. Estienne fought the urge to recoil as their hands pawed at him, fingers thrusting into his mouth to inspect his molars, running over him as a merchant might run hands over prized silk. His cheeks burned with humiliation, his pride screaming at the violation, yet he stood mute and still, knowing that any resistance would only earn him more pain.

Finally, the inspection was done and the buyers conferred among themselves, gesticulating and arguing, their voices rising and falling like the ebb and flow of a tide. And through it all, Estienne remained still, seething so intensely his nails bit crescents into his palms.

A sudden commotion caught his eye. A new group of men had entered the square, their bearing hard and purposeful, faces scarred and weathered. At their head strode a giant of a man, his bald pate gleaming in the sun, a wicked scar cleaving his face from brow to jaw. He radiated an aura of menace, of leashed violence barely held in check.

The brute's eyes raked over the line of captives, settling on Estienne with an intensity that made his skin crawl. He said something to his companions, voice harsh and grating, and they laughed, a sound devoid of mirth. Then began the haggling, the brute and Estienne's current owner facing off like two dogs fighting over a bone. Their voices rose, the words flying fast and hard, punctuated by sharp gestures and the occasional snarl. Estienne couldn't follow the rapid trading of words, but he understood the tenor of it all too well – his fate was being bartered away, his future traded like so much coin.

At last there came a final emphatic word from the scarred man, a grudging nod from Estienne's seller. Hands were clasped, palms slapped together to seal the deal, and it was done.

He felt something within him go cold and numb, frost spreading through his veins. This was it, no longer a captive but a slave, his life measured out in silver. As he was led away by the scarred brute and his men, he couldn't help but wonder if death at sea might not have been a mercy compared to what awaited him now.

They were almost to the edge of the square when more

commotion broke out behind them. Shouts rent the air as the crowd parted like water before the prow of a ship. Estienne craned his neck, trying to see past the broad backs of his captors. Something was happening, something that had the whole market abuzz.

And then he saw him – tall and imposing enough to make Estienne's blood run cold.

Kashta, the Moor who'd confronted him in al-Kamil's own tent, advanced with eyes that blazed with the promise of vengeance. He was here, pushing through the throng like a giant among mortals, his face a thunderhead of fury.

Estienne felt bile rising in his throat as his new master turned, brows furrowed in annoyance at the interruption. When Kashta reached them, words spilling from his lips in a furious torrent, the slaver's expression shifted to one of wary focus. The argument that erupted was a maelstrom of guttural Arabic, voices raised in anger, hands slicing the air in sharp, emphatic gestures. Estienne could only watch, heart pounding, unable to understand the words but grasping the tenor of it – Kashta wanted him, wanted the vengeance he'd been denied for the death of his brother in arms, and he meant to have it no matter the cost.

The two men were nose to nose now, spittle flying, fists clenched. The slaver's hand hovered near the hilt of his blade as Kashta's body tensed like a snake ready to strike. The air was alive with the promise of violence, the crowd drawing back, sensing a storm about to break.

But the moment never came.

Just as suddenly as it began, the confrontation ended. The slaver spat a final word, a clear dismissal of Kashta's claim. For an instant, Estienne thought the Moor would lunge, witnesses be damned. Draw his sword and strike his fateful blow. Instead, he stepped back, rage and frustration etched into every line of his face. Then his eyes found Estienne's, and the promise in them chilled him to the bone. This was not over. Not by a long measure.

Then Estienne was yanked around, the slaver pulling him roughly away. He stumbled, but he didn't resist. There was no point, not now.

As he was led toward the outskirts of the city, Estienne couldn't shake the image of Kashta's eyes boring into his, couldn't quell the icy certainty that this was only the beginning. Somewhere out there, the Moor was watching, waiting. A shadow at his heels, a spectre of promised retribution.

The noise of the marketplace receded behind them to nothing more than a distant hum. Estienne was led, along with the brutal slaver's other purchases, to a shaded area, where they were driven to their knees. As their captors set about securing their carts and goods for the road, Estienne took in the other slaves he was with. It was a rich mix of men, women and children. Some with skin darkened by the sun, others pale as though plucked from the north of the Mediterranean.

'Fortune seems to have abandoned you this day, friend.'

The words, spoken in fluent Latin, startled him from his thoughts. Estienne turned to find one of the other slaves regarding him with a wry, weathered smile. He was a small man, wiry and sun-browned, with a mane of curly hair and a face that looked to have been carved from old leather.

Estienne frowned. 'That much is obvious.'

'Is it?' The man chuckled. 'That al-Sudan back there, the one with murder in his eyes? He wanted your head. Wanted it so bad I thought he'd take it right there in the square. A shame for you he was persuaded otherwise.'

'I don't follow. How would that have been any better than this?' Estienne held up hands still bound tight.

'It would have been better that than what lies ahead. Take it from me.'

Estienne felt a prickle of unease. 'What lies ahead?'

The man nodded eastward. 'The Silk Road. A thousand miles of misery, and us driven every step by the whip. In the end, you'll wish that al-Sudan had opened your throat.'

The thought of such a journey almost unmanned him, but Estienne wrested his wits from the edge of despair. Still, he could not shake the notion he was being punished. And if this was to be his penance, his trial by fire, how was he to endure it? How was he to keep his faith, when every step along this Silk Road might carry him further from God's grace?

'Where are we now?' Estienne asked, keeping his voice deliberately low so as not to alert their new masters.

'Why, you are in the city of al-Mansurah. Where now resides the sultan, Malik al-Kamil.'

Not forty miles south along the Nile from Damietta. So close, but he may as well have been a thousand miles away. To add insult, it seemed that al-Kamil was also here, but the chances of him being able to benefit once again from the sultan's good grace looked slim.

Taking a cleansing breath, he turned back to the old man. 'My name is Estienne. Estienne Wace. And you?'

'Isaac,' the man replied after a moment. 'Isaac ben Berachiyah.'

'Well, Isaac ben Berachiyah,' Estienne said, forcing a note of conviction into his voice that he didn't fully feel. 'I swear to you, we will survive this. Whatever lies ahead, whatever we must face... we'll see it through. God will watch over us.'

Isaac looked at him, something like pity mingling with the

weariness in his eyes. 'God, you say? I fear he's long since abandoned us, friend. Best not to put your hope in him any longer.'

Before Estienne could answer, a guttural order was barked. The other slaves were quick to rise, Isaac along with them, and Estienne followed suit. With the crack of a whip, the lead cart trundled off along the road from the city.

Estienne followed, his only thought now of survival.

19

Kashta stood at the eastern boundary of al-Mansurah, eyes fixed on the road where the slave caravan had disappeared into the heat haze. The arid wind whipped about him, but he barely registered its touch. His thoughts were consumed by a single, searing notion – the reckoning that had been snatched from his grasp yet again.

The confrontation with the slavers replayed in his mind, taunting him. He had been so close, the Frankish knight who had slain Wasim almost within reach, but those slavers had closed ranks. His demands for them to hand the knight over had only been met with refusal. His offer of payment laughed at as paltry. His claim that he was favoured of the sultan ignored. When appeals to their better nature were rebuffed, he had resorted to intimidation, but those slavers were not to be cowed. To challenge their claim further would have meant his own death, cut down in the dust of the market square for all to see.

Frustration rose, bitter and impossible to quell. The knight, the Black Lion whose name he had learned was Estienne, had stood there bound and helpless. In that moment it had taken every ounce of Kashta's self-control not to lunge for his throat, but what good would it have done Wasim if he'd thrown his own life away in a moment of blind rage? His brother's shade would find no peace in such a reckless sacrifice. And so Kashta had stepped back, and watched as his chance for retribution was led away along the Silk Road.

Around him, the city's clamour brought him back to the present – the braying of animals, the traders peddling their wares, the ceaseless thrum of life going on, heedless of the tempest raging within him. With a snarl of disgust, Kashta turned his back on the road and made his way into the city. His heart was heavy with the weight of his failure, but there was still a flicker of determination. This was not the end. Somehow, he would find the Frankish knight again, and when he did...

The streets of al-Mansurah teemed as Kashta stalked through them, his stride purposeful yet directionless. Children darted between food stalls with shrill laughter, and the air was thick with the scents of spices and roasting meat. To Kashta, it all felt distant, as though he moved through a world separate from the vibrant tapestry around him. This city, the refuge al-Kamil had chosen after the fall of Damietta, was meant to be a haven, a place to regroup and rebuild. But for Kashta, it felt more like a gaol that held him prisoner. Everywhere he looked, he saw reminders of what had been lost – in the empty space beside him where Wasim should have stood, in the absence of his brother's ringing laughter and ready grin.

Unbidden, memories rose to the surface, vivid as fresh wounds. He and Wasim, standing shoulder to shoulder, swords flashing in the sun as they faced their enemies. The long nights spent huddled around campfires, trading jests and dreams of the lives they would build when their time as warriors was done.

Now those dreams were scattered on the winds. Wasim was

gone, cut down by Frankish steel, and Kashta was left alone. The thought was a spear through his heart, a pain that stole the breath from his lungs.

He paused in the shadow of a crumbling archway, his chest heaving as he fought to master himself. Around him, the city's life continued its relentless pulse, heedless of his grief. An unending din that grated on his raw nerves. What was his place in this new world now his was lost to him? Now their sultan had succumbed to defeat and given up the very city Wasim had wasted his life to defend?

It had been months now since they had slunk from the city of Damietta in the dead of night. Fleeing in the storm that hid their passing, so they might come here to al-Mansurah and wait for the Franks to continue their advance south. How long were they to reside in this place, waiting for their fate to be decided by foreign invaders? The question haunted him as Kashta turned his steps towards the hujra, his mind awhirl.

But even as despair threatened to engulf him, a small, stubborn flame began to flicker in his heart. Wasim was gone, but his brother's spirit cried out for justice, for the scales to be balanced in blood. And it fell to Kashta now to see that debt paid, no matter the cost.

As he neared the hujra, Kashta slowed his stride, his resolve hardening. He knew what he had to do, even if the enormity of it gave him pause. The knight, Estienne, could not be allowed to escape, to slip through his grasp like sand. Kashta would not rest until he had found him again, until he had looked into those pale eyes and seen the light of life fade. Only then would the scales be balanced. Only then would Wasim's spirit find peace.

The barracks lay still and quiet as Kashta entered. Around him, his fellow warriors milled, talking idly in their repose, but Kashta barely registered them, his focus turned inward to the journey that lay ahead. What tie did he truly have to this place anyway, save the memory of loss? His loyalty had been to his sultan, and to the warrior brother who had fought at his side. But al-Kamil was not the man al-Adil had been, and Wasim... Wasim was lost to him. There was nothing for him here now, no purpose or promise that could outweigh the debt he carried.

Entering his quarters, Kashta began to prepare for his journey. His own belongings were few, the spartan trappings of a life lived in service to the sultans of Egypt, but he would need little. For this journey, travelling light would be an imperative. He would take only what was needed. His sword, a horse, a supply of rations, a handful of coins, a waterskin.

He gathered them methodically, and as he did, he felt a sense of purpose settle over him, a grim determination that lent clarity to his thoughts. This was the path he was meant to walk, the only road left to him now.

Once he had prepared his horse and led it from the stable, Kashta paused as he breathed a silent prayer. He called on Allah to guide his steps, to lend strength to his arm and surety to his heart, for he knew the road would be long and fraught with dangers that would test him in ways he could not yet imagine. But he would endure, driven by the flame of his vengeance, the memory of his lost brother.

With that thought lodged like a shard of flint in his heart, Kashta turned his back on the hujra, and made his way back through the city. No one questioned him or thought to ask where he might be going. But then Kashta ibn Assad had always been a man apart from these Saracens. He had never been one of them, but his fierce reputation had ensured he was respected among their number.

A final glance around the barracks, then Kashta shouldered his meagre pack and led his horse out into the waiting day. The sun beat down, fierce and unrelenting, but he barely felt its heat. His blood was up now, his purpose a fire in his veins as he strode the streets toward the eastern road. When he reached it, Kashta paused, turning to take a final look over the city he had called home these past months. The minarets glinted in the sun, the domes of the mosques rising majestically above the jumble of flat roofs and narrow alleys. It was a sight that had once filled him with a sense of belonging. Now, it left him feeling hollow, and he turned back toward the Silk Road.

Somewhere out there the slave caravan wound its way along the Silk Road, and with it, the knight who had taken everything from him. Kashta would not rest until he had faced him in combat and righted the wrong done to him.

'I so swear it,' he whispered to the warm breeze.

With that vow, Kashta passed through the city gates, the walls of al-Mansurah falling away behind him. Ahead lay only the open road, and the promise of vengeance.

And he followed it gladly.

20

The sun was a merciless hammer that struck with every laboured step. Estienne trudged on, his feet dragging in the dust, even as his body cried out for rest. There was none to be had. The slave caravan forged ever onward, heedless of exhaustion or suffering, driven by the ruthless will of their captors.

He had counted eleven days since they had left al-Mansurah, a ceaseless cycle of scorching heat and freezing nights. His world had become the road ahead, the shuffling of feet, the crack of whips, and the dull throb of misery that pulsed through the ranks of prisoners.

Estienne had seen the toll this march was taking on his fellow captives. He had watched as men and women, at first strong, were reduced to shambling wrecks, their spirits broken by the unrelenting cruelty of their masters. He had seen them collapse in the dust, only to be lashed into motion by their snarling overseers, whips cutting bloody ribbons into sun-scorched skin.

Among the slavers, one stood out – the bald brute with the wicked scar cleaving his face from brow to chin. He seemed to take a particular pleasure in tormenting the prisoners, his whip always eager to bite. Estienne had felt its sting himself, when exhaustion made his steps falter. The pain was like molten metal poured over his flesh, but he gritted his teeth and endured, determined not to give the bastard the satisfaction of seeing him break.

As they crested yet another rise, the outline of a city shimmered into view. Estienne squinted against the glare, his heart leaping with a sudden, desperate hope. Surely this must be their destination, the end of this hellish journey. But even as the thought formed, he quashed it, not daring to let himself believe. Hope was a luxury he could ill afford now, a weakness that could crack the fragile shell of resolve that kept him putting one foot in front of the other.

Beside him, Isaac stumbled as he fought to keep his balance. Instinctively, Estienne reached out to steady him, his hand closing around a bony arm. Isaac looked up, nodding gratefully through his exhaustion.

'Careful there, friend,' Estienne murmured.

Isaac nodded. 'Thank you. Once again.'

It was not for the first time Estienne had kept the old man moving when it appeared he would falter. Not that he expected Isaac to be grateful. Seeing to this man's safety had diverted attention from Estienne's own struggle.

Their brief exchange was shattered by a vicious crack, the sound of leather snapping. Estienne flinched, turning to see the scarred slaver looming over them, his whip coiled in a white-knuckled fist.

He snarled something in Arabic, his eyes alight with malicious glee. Estienne understood well enough – stay silent, keep moving. Still, he bit back the retort that rose to his lips, knowing it would only earn him a lashing. Beside him, Isaac hunched his shoulders, his face tight with fear, and they fell back into the lurching rhythm of the march, the city ahead looming.

As they drew closer to the gates, Estienne's curiosity got the better of him, and he glanced sidelong at Isaac. 'This place, do you know it?'

Isaac nodded. 'Gaza. I used to trade here, in another life.'

Estienne felt a flicker of surprise. A trader? He wouldn't have guessed it, looking at the man now, with his ragged robes and sunken cheeks. But then, the march had stripped them all down to the bone, erasing the trappings of their former lives.

'The scarred one,' Estienne ventured, jerking his chin towards their tormentor. 'He seems to have it in for you.'

Isaac's mouth twisted into a bitter grimace. 'Alzeshi? Yes, that he does. We have a history, he and I. He was a rival of mine, back in my trading days. We competed along the same routes, for the same customers. But he was always one step ahead, always seemed to know just whose palms to grease.'

Estienne frowned, trying to reconcile this image of Isaac as a merchant with the broken man who shuffled beside him. Had he been a slaver too? Right now, it didn't seem to matter much.

'What happened? How did you find yourself here?'

Isaac shrugged. 'I made some bad deals. Got in over my head. And Alzeshi... he was there, watching, waiting. He's been biding his time for years, waiting for a chance to see me brought low. It's a bitter irony, isn't it? A man born of Judah, undone by poor accounting. You'd think we'd have a better head for such things.'

'You're Jewish?'

Isaac shot him a sidelong glance, a guarded wariness in his eyes. 'And proud of it. That a problem for you?'

Estienne shook his head. 'No judgement here. Just surprised, is all. I didn't know there were Jewish merchants plying their trade in these lands. They are persecuted enough in my own.'

'And we endure,' Isaac replied, a hint of pride creeping into his voice. 'We've been trading in Egypt and Syria since the time of the Roman emperors. Though fat lot of good it does me now. Moslem law forbids the enslavement of fellow believers. But us? We're fair game.'

Estienne fell silent, his mind whirling. He had never stopped to consider the tapestry of faiths and peoples that made up the Holy Land he had sworn to regain. To him, the Saracens had been a monolith, a faceless enemy to be defeated in the name of Christendom, but now, walking in bondage beside this man, he realised how blind he had been in his single-minded pursuit of a holy cause.

'I'm sorry,' Estienne offered, the words feeling inadequate, but what comfort could he offer?

Isaac merely shook his head. 'Don't be. We all have our burdens to bear. In this, at least, we're no different, you and I.'

'Aye. Seems we've both had our share of trials.'

Isaac huffed a sound that was almost a laugh. 'That we have. Though I can't say I ever saw this particular fate coming.'

The gates of Gaza yawned open before them, ready to swallow the wretched procession whole. Estienne felt a renewed sense of trepidation as they passed within, which only deepened as they were driven through the city streets, seeing the hungry faces watching their every step until eventually they entered the marketplace, where the auction block waited.

Alzeshi and his fellow slavers whipped them into order, separating some slaves from others, and choosing those to be sold. Estienne and Isaac were among a group corralled to the side, as the rest were presented to the crowd. One by one, they were dragged forward, prodded and poked, examined like livestock for signs of strength or infirmity.

Beside him, Isaac watched the proceedings with a grim set to his jaw, and Estienne leaned in close. 'Why aren't we for sale here? What makes us so special?'

Isaac's mouth twisted in a bitter smile. 'Special? No, I wouldn't call us that. Those he sells now are the weak, who will not make the rest of the journey. The ones who won't survive the long march ahead. Alzeshi is many things, but he's no fool. He'll save his prime stock for the markets of Damascus, another two hundred miles from here. That's where he'll get the best price.'

Estienne swallowed, the implications of those words sinking in his gut. The long march ahead... a death sentence for the frail and the sickly, a trial by ordeal for the rest of them. And at the end of it, what? A lifetime of servitude, of backbreaking labour and unending toil?

'No,' he said, more determined than intended, loud enough that some of his fellow slaves looked at him sidelong.

'No?' Isaac replied. 'You think you have some choice in this?'

'There is always a choice. No matter what you face, no matter the odds against you.'

'You speak as though you have faced worse.' Isaac raised a sceptical eyebrow.

Estienne turned, staring at the marketplace and its eager patrons. 'I have survived a siege. Broken one. Brought down an invading army, and survived a failed assault on the city of Damietta as the walls burned around me. I will not be sold at market. I will die first.'

The side of Isaac's mouth turned up. 'Then it has been good to know you, friend.'

Estienne ignored the quip. He could understand Isaac's

doubt. But he would prove the little man wrong. His chance would come. And when it did, Estienne would not hesitate.

21

The sun hung low, painting the sky in hues of amber, as Kashta stumbled through the gates of Gaza. His legs trembled with each step, muscles aching after days of relentless pursuit. The ten-day journey from al-Mansurah had taken its toll, leaving him gaunt, his once-proud bearing bent by exhaustion. His horse had perished on the road, serving to feed him rather than carry him, but now even those rations had dwindled to nothing.

As he entered the city proper, the bustle and clamour of Gaza's streets washed over him – merchants hawked their wares in a mix of languages, the air thick with the mingled scents of spices and roasting meat. Camels brayed, their bells tinkling as they swayed past, laden with goods bound for distant lands. In any other circumstance, Kashta might have marvelled at the sight of this fabled desert oasis, this jewel of the Silk Road, but now he barely noticed it. Instead, he listened intently for the guttural tones of the slavers he pursued as he wove through the press of bodies.

When finally he realised there was no sign of them, he paused at a fountain, cupping his hands to drink deeply of the cool water. As he straightened, wiping his mouth with the back of his hand, Kashta caught his reflection in the rippling surface. He hardly recognised the man who stared back at him. His face was gaunt, cheekbones standing out in sharp relief, eyes sunken and haunted. But this pursuit had changed him in more than body. It had hollowed him out until little remained but the burning need for vengeance.

Shaking off the thought, Kashta pressed on. The slave caravan couldn't be far now. He had pushed himself to the brink of collapse to keep pace with their swift journey along the Silk Road, and he wouldn't let them slip away. Not when he was so close.

As he rounded a corner near the city's eastern gate, he saw them – the slavers, preparing to depart Gaza and continue their journey. Kashta's breath caught in his throat as his eyes raked over the assembled group. The slavers moved with practised efficiency, checking bonds and readying their mounts, but it was their slaves that drew Kashta's attention, and what he saw made his brow furrow in dismay.

There were so few of them now. Where once there had been dozens of souls bound for the auction blocks of Damascus, now barely a score remained. Those left were haggard, their eyes dull with exhaustion and defeat, but their bodies still strong enough to fetch a high price.

And there, in the midst of the wretched group, stood the object of Kashta's relentless pursuit. The Frankish knight.

Even bound and in rags, there was no mistaking him. Kashta would have known that defiant bearing anywhere, would have recognised the set of those broad shoulders and the glint of those grey-blue eyes in his sleep. This was the man who had robbed Kashta of his brother in all but blood. Estienne. The one they called the Black Lion.

A shadow descended over Kashta's vision, and before he knew it, his hand had moved to the hilt of his sayf. It would be so easy. One swift charge, one clean stroke, and his vengeance would be complete. But even as his fingers closed around the weapon's familiar grip, Kashta held back. The rules of the siyar had been drilled into him since childhood, the code of honour that set him apart from common brigands and cutthroats. It whispered to him now, a quiet voice of reason beneath the roaring tide of his rage. He had not tracked this man across hundreds of miles, had not driven himself to the very brink of collapse, only to strike him down in bondage. No, when the reckoning came – and it would come – it would be blade against blade, warrior against warrior. Only then would the scales truly be balanced.

Kashta forced his hand away from his weapon. His body trembled with the effort of restraint, muscles coiled tight, and he tasted blood where he had bitten the inside of his cheek.

'Soon, Frankish dog.'

As if sensing Kashta's gaze, Estienne's head turned. For a moment, Kashta thought their eyes might meet across the crowded square, but before that could happen, one of the slavers barked an order, and Estienne's attention was diverted. Kashta took his chance to melt back into the crowd, and find a better vantage point from which to observe.

From the shadows of a nearby alleyway, he watched as the slavers made their preparations to depart the city. He had crossed vast stretches of unforgiving desert, pushed his body to its very limits, all in pursuit of this one man, but when would his opportunity for revenge present itself? He had not the coin to purchase Estienne from his enslavers. And were he sold at market, as was their intent, what then?

Kashta had to pray that an opportunity would present itself, and soon, lest he lose all hope, or even his life, in this deadly pursuit. One thing he knew – the hunt would continue. He would follow this caravan, shadow their steps until the moment was right. And when it came, and Estienne stood unbound and armed, then Kashta would have his reckoning.

With renewed determination, Kashta slipped away from his hiding place and made his way through Gaza's bustling streets. He had to prepare if he was to continue his pursuit into the unforgiving wasteland that lay ahead.

First, he sought out a well, quenching his thirst and refilling his waterskins. Then, to the marketplace, where he bartered what little coin he had left for dried meat, fruit, and dhourra – provisions that would sustain him on the long road to come.

With his preparations complete, Kashta made his way to the city's eastern gate. The slave caravan had already departed, but he could see the dust of their passage rising in the distance. He paused for a moment, taking a deep breath as he steeled himself for what was to come. Then, with a final adjustment of his pack and a hand on the hilt of his sayf, he set out once more into the unforgiving embrace of the desert.

For the rest of the day he kept his distance, always remaining just beyond the horizon, a shadow dogging their steps. The rhythm of his pursuit had become almost meditative – one foot in front of the other, eyes scanning the terrain for signs of danger, mind focused solely on the moment when he would finally confront Estienne. It was as he crested a low dune that he first noticed the change in the air.

A hot wind gusted across the sand, carrying with it an acrid taste – a change to the very atmosphere surrounding him. He paused, shielding his eyes as he gazed towards the horizon. There, in the distance, dark clouds were gathering, their edges tinged with an ominous yellow-green hue. A storm was brewing, and by its look, it would be a monster.

Kashta's heart quickened, a mix of anticipation and dread coursing through him. On one hand, the coming tempest could provide the chaos he needed to make his move. In the confusion of wind and sand, he might find the opportunity to separate Estienne from his captors, to finally face him as an equal. But the storm also presented new dangers, risks that could end his quest before it reached its conclusion.

As if sensing his trepidation, the wind picked up, whipping at Kashta's robes and sending the first stinging grains of sand against his skin. He pulled his hamtar tighter around his face, leaving only his eyes exposed so he could focus on the horizon, where he could just make out the distant silhouettes of the slave caravan, unaware of the fury about to be unleashed upon it.

'Come, then,' Kashta whispered. 'Let us see what Allah has in store for us both, Black Lion.'

With each step forward, the storm grew closer, the sky darkening to a sickly olive hue. That wind increased to a roar, drowning out all other sound. Ahead, the slave caravan had disappeared entirely, swallowed by the advancing wall of sand and dust.

Kashta plunged forward into the maelstrom, and as the storm engulfed him completely, his hand tightened on the hilt of his sword. Let the desert throw its worst at him. He would endure. He would persevere. And when the dust settled, his brother would finally be avenged.

22

The world had become a frenzy of howling wind and stinging sand. One moment, Estienne had been trudging along in the miserable procession of slaves, the next, a sandstorm hit with the force of a battering ram, engulfing the caravan in a suffocating cloud of grit and chaos.

His eyes watered as he squinted against the onslaught, struggling to make sense of the pandemonium erupting around him. Slavers shouted orders that were immediately swallowed by the roaring wind. Horses whinnied in panic, rearing and threatening to bolt. His fellow captives cried out in fear, their voices lost in the deafening howl of the storm.

Through the haze of swirling sand, Alzeshi's scarred face was a mask of rage and frustration as he fought to maintain control of his caravan. In that moment of distraction, Estienne's mind raced. This was it – the chance he'd been praying for. It might be his only opportunity to break free from this nightmare.

He turned to Isaac, the old trader hunched against the biting wind, looking frailer than ever. There was no time for words, no chance to explain. Estienne grabbed the man's arm and made his move.

'Come on,' he growled.

Their hands were still bound, but their legs were not, and in the confusion Estienne burst into action. He all but dragged Isaac from the road, unnoticed in the storm that raged all around them. In an instant, the world became a blur of stinging grit and disorienting noise. Estienne's lungs burned as he gasped for air, each breath bringing a mouthful of sand. He could feel Isaac stumbling beside him, the old man's slight frame buffeted by the relentless wind, but Estienne refused to let go. They would escape together or not at all.

His heart pounded a frantic rhythm in his chest. They were free – for the moment at least – but lost in a howling wasteland that could kill them as surely as any slaver's whip. Yet even that uncertain fate was preferable to the life of bondage that awaited them in Damascus.

'Keep moving,' Estienne yelled, not sure if Isaac could hear him. 'Don't stop, old man.'

On they stumbled, blind and choking, with only Estienne's iron grip keeping them together. Every step was a battle against the wind, every breath a struggle, but still, they pressed on, driven by the desperate need to put as much distance between themselves and the slavers as possible.

He had no idea how long they ran for, or in what direction. All sense of time and place was stripped away by the fury of the storm. For all he knew, they could have been going in circles, or heading straight back into the arms of their captors. Still, he didn't dare stop. Could not stop. To pause now, even for a moment, would mean defeat.

More than once, Isaac stumbled, nearly falling, and Estienne tightened his grip on the man's arm. He could feel Isaac's strength flagging, knew that they couldn't keep this pace up much longer.

'Hold on,' Estienne growled. 'We can't stop now.'

Just as Estienne felt his own reserves of strength beginning to ebb, his foot sensed a dip in the terrain, barely perceptible through the swirling sand. He stumbled, realising the ground was dropping away more sharply than he'd first thought. Together they slid down a steep incline, sand giving way to rock, until suddenly they found themselves in a dry riverbed carved into the desert floor by some ancient watercourse.

The relief was immediate. Though sand still swirled overhead, the high walls of the wadi provided a degree of shelter from the worst of it. The constant roar of wind was reduced to a muffled howl, and for the first time since their mad dash for freedom, Estienne could hear his own ragged breathing, and the wheezing gasps of Isaac beside him.

'Are you all right?' Estienne asked, turning to the old man.

Isaac nodded weakly, unable to speak as he fought to catch his breath. He looked even more frail now, covered in a fine layer of sand, his face etched with exhaustion, but there was a glimmer in his eyes – a spark of hope, perhaps?

Estienne helped Isaac to a seated position, propping him up against the rocky wall of the riverbed. Then he slumped down beside him, the thrill of escape beginning to ebb, leaving behind a bone-deep weariness. With what little strength he had left, he used his teeth to work at the bonds still chafing his wrists. It took some time, but after so many days the hemp was worn, and eventually he managed to free his hands. Sighing in relief, he then turned his attention to Isaac, who offered little resistance as Estienne managed to untie him too.

For a long moment, they simply sat there in silence, two unlikely companions united by their desperate bid for freedom. They had escaped, but they were also lost in the middle of a raging storm, with no food, no water, and no real plan. And yet, they had survived. They had found shelter. Perhaps luck – or God – was on their side after all.

'We made it,' Estienne said softly, almost to himself.

Isaac turned to him, a wry smile cracking his lips. 'For now, at least. Though I fear we may have simply traded one death for another.'

'We're not done for yet, old man.' Estienne surprised himself with the conviction in his voice. 'I for one don't intend to die out here in this Godforsaken desert.'

'Then I am truly lucky to have a companion with such confidence in his ability to cheat death.'

'We haven't cheated it yet. Rest while you can. We'll need to move quickly once the storm passes.'

As if in response to his words, a fresh gust of wind sent a cascade of sand showering down into their shelter. Instinctively, Estienne shifted, using his body to shield Isaac from the worst of it. The old man gave him a look of quiet gratitude as they huddled in their meagre shelter, surrounded by the muffled roar of the continuing storm.

As exhaustion began to overwhelm him, Estienne allowed himself a moment of cautious hope. They had survived this far. Perhaps, just perhaps, they might yet find their way to true freedom.

* * *

Estienne blinked awake, his eyes struggling to adjust to the sudden brightness of sunlight. They were surrounded by an eerie silence, as sometime in the night, the storm's fury had abated.

Cautiously, he rose to his feet, his muscles protesting after so long hunkering in the riverbed, and offered a hand to Isaac, helping the old man up with gentle care.

'Come on,' Estienne said, his voice rough as thirst clawed at his throat. 'Let's see if there's any sign of where we are.'

Together, they climbed out of the ravine that had sheltered them through the tempest. As they crested the edge, both men stopped short, momentarily stunned by the transformed landscape before them.

The storm had reshaped the desert entirely. Where before there had been a sea of undulating dunes, now great sweeping ridges of sand stretched as far as the eye could see. The terrain was unrecognisable, as if they had been transported to some distant land.

'We are truly lost,' Isaac breathed. 'How are we to reach safety now?'

'Fear not, my friend,' Estienne replied, trying his best to sound hopeful. 'We'll find our way out of this, I swear it.'

Isaac opened his mouth to reply, but whatever he was about to say died on his lips. His eyes widened, fixed on a point over Estienne's shoulder. A look of abject despair washed over the old man's weathered features.

Estienne turned, and there, emerging from behind a newly formed dune like spectres from his nightmare, were Alzeshi and his men. The scarred slaver's eyes lit up with malice as they fixed on his recaptured property. Behind him, his men spread out in a loose semicircle, effectively cutting off any chance of escape.

He knew what was coming now. Had seen how Alzeshi dealt with slaves who tried to flee. But as the slaver and his men advanced, something hardened within Estienne and he placed himself in front of Isaac, meeting Alzeshi's gaze unflinchingly. If they were to be punished, let the bastard focus his wrath on him.

'Let's get to it then,' Estienne said, his voice low and steady.

Though it was obvious he did not understand the words, Alzeshi's scarred lips twisted into a humourless smile. Estienne steeled himself for what was to come.

The first blow came without warning, one of Alzeshi's men hitting the side of Estienne's head with a bony fist. He tasted blood, his vision swimming as the rest of the men fell upon him like a pack of rabid dogs. Fists and feet rained down, each impact a shock of agony that threatened to drive him to his knees, but Estienne refused to fall. He locked his legs, gritted his teeth, but eventually he fell, the world spinning – a maelstrom just like the storm.

Through the haze of pain, Estienne was dimly aware of Isaac's voice, pleading for mercy in the Saracen tongue, and as suddenly as it had begun, the beating stopped. Alzeshi knelt beside him, grabbing a fistful of Estienne's hair and wrenching his head back.

'Dog,' he spat. One word Estienne could understand at least.

Through swelling eyes, he saw Isaac kneeling beside him, the old man's face a mask of anguish and guilt.

'I'm sorry,' he whispered. 'They would not listen—'

'No,' Estienne managed to croak. 'My choice. Not... your fault.'

Before Isaac could respond, grasping hands seized them both. Estienne bit back a grunt of pain as he was hauled to his feet and fresh bonds hastily tied around his raw wrists.

Alzeshi barked an order and they were shoved back toward the waiting cart and ordered into line with the other slaves. It was not until they had continued their journey for some time that Estienne's wits began to return, and he became aware of a growing sense of unease among the slavers. He caught snatches of worried conversation, saw the way Alzeshi's brow furrowed as he consulted with his men.

Slow realisation dawned, until Estienne finally understood the cause of their concern. The landscape around them was utterly unfamiliar. Gone was the well-worn path of the Silk Road. In its place was a vast, trackless waste that stretched endlessly in every direction.

They were lost.

Eventually, Alzeshi stopped the wagon, gesturing wildly as he argued in heated Arabic with one of his men. Even without understanding the words, Estienne could read the frustration and growing panic. These men, once so assured and in control, were now at the mercy of the unforgiving desert.

'This is bad,' Isaac murmured. 'Very bad.'

Estienne nodded, wincing as the movement sent a jolt of pain through his battered body. 'They have no idea where we are, do they?'

'No. And they have no idea how to get back on course.'

The column lurched into motion once more, but there was renewed tension in the air. The slavers' shouts were tinged with barely concealed fear, their whips cracking with increased frequency. As they trudged onward, the sun climbing higher in the merciless sky, Estienne found his thoughts turning to darker possibilities. What would happen if they couldn't find their way? Would Alzeshi and his men abandon them to die in the desert? Or would they all perish together?

'We have to be ready,' Estienne whispered.

The old man raised an eyebrow. 'Ready for what? Another escape?'

Estienne shook his head. 'I don't know. But we can't just keep wandering aimlessly. When the moment comes, we must be prepared to act.'

Isaac studied him for a long moment. 'Very well, my friend. But I doubt you'll survive another beating.'

'Let me worry about that.'

They fell silent then, saving their strength as the caravan pressed on.

23

The sun beat down upon the ragged line of slaves trudging through that endless sea of sand. Estienne's eyes swept over his fellow prisoners, only a dozen of them left, their gaunt faces etched with exhaustion and despair, and he tried not to think on those they'd left behind in the baking sun to die. Beside him, Isaac stumbled, his frail form swaying precariously. Estienne reached out instinctively, steadying the old man with a hand on his bony shoulder.

'Easy, my friend,' he murmured. 'Just a little further.'

Isaac's rheumy eyes met his. 'You... you say that every hour.'

It was true – he'd been making the same empty promise for longer than he could remember, even as their situation grew more desperate. He could see the toll their journey was taking on Isaac. The old man's skin hung loose on his frame, his steps growing more unsteady with each passing mile.

A crack split the air, followed by a pained yelp. Estienne turned to see Alzeshi, his scarred face twisted in a snarl, laying into one of the other slaves with his whip. The man, a Nubian with skin as dark as night, stumbled and fell to his knees, raising his bound hands in a futile attempt to ward off the blows.

Alzeshi roared, his words incomprehensible. Estienne felt his jaw clench, rage bubbling up inside him. He took a half-step forward, but Isaac's hand on his arm held him back.

'Don't,' the old man whispered. 'You'll only make it worse.'

Reluctantly, Estienne held back as the Nubian struggled to his feet, fresh welts visible on his dark skin. He hated this feeling of helplessness, of being unable to protect those around him. He was a knight, given a code to follow, but out here in this desert the only code that mattered was one of survival.

They trudged on, the sun climbing higher and baking the air until Estienne's lungs felt like they were on fire. His lips were cracked and bleeding, his tongue swollen in his mouth, and he could not remember the last time they'd been given water.

As they crested yet another dune, Estienne's heart sank. The landscape before them was identical to what lay behind – an endless expanse of sand stretching to the horizon, broken only by the occasional rocky outcropping. There was no sign of the well-worn path of the Silk Road, no hint of civilisation.

'We're going to die out here.' Isaac's voice was nearly lost in the whisper of wind over sand.

'If we do,' Estienne replied, 'we'll do it as free men, not slaves.'

'Free to die of thirst instead of beneath a slaver's whip,' Isaac chuckled. 'Some choice.'

Estienne was about to reply when Alzeshi's voice cut through the air, sharp and angry. As they resumed their endless march, he cast one last look at the horizon, searching for any sign of hope. There was only sand and sky, stretching on forever, indifferent to their suffering.

It wasn't until the sun had passed its zenith that Alzeshi

called a halt, his voice hoarse and strained. The slaves collapsed where they stood, too exhausted even to seek what scant shade the wagon might offer. Estienne eased Isaac to the ground, feeling how light the old man had become.

'Water,' Isaac croaked, his eyes rolling. 'Please... water...'

Estienne turned towards the slavers. Surely with their property on its last legs they would distribute what precious supply remained. But as he watched, he saw Alzeshi and his men huddle around the one remaining waterskin, passing it between them with greedy gulps. Not a drop was offered to the slaves and Estienne felt something snap inside him, a dam of rage finally giving way under the weight of his desperation.

'Water,' he shouted, his voice cracking. 'For God's sake, give us water.'

Alzeshi's eyes narrowed as they fixed on Estienne. Then the slaver strode towards them, the empty waterskin dangling from his hand like a taunt.

'Dog?' he sneered, the only word he knew Estienne would understand, before shaking the empty waterskin like a prize.

Estienne gestured to Isaac, prostrate on the sand. 'For him. He won't survive without it. Please...'

Alzeshi gazed down at Isaac, the man who had once been his rival. Then he shrugged, as though one more life didn't matter.

The casual brutality of it burned in Estienne. He had seen cruelty in his time, had witnessed the horrors of war and siege, but this utter disregard for human life seared him to his core.

'You can't...' he began, but Alzeshi cut him off with a backhand that sent him sprawling.

Estienne pushed himself up onto his knees, the taste of blood in his mouth. With a fluid motion, Alzeshi drew his sword and the curved blade caught the sunlight. He said something, goading, taunting Estienne as he knelt there on the ground, beaten and pathetic. But no. He was not beaten. Not until his last breath.

Legs trembling with the effort, Estienne forced himself to stand and meet Alzeshi's gaze. If this was to be his end, he would face it as a knight. As a free man.

'Well?' he said, gesturing for Alzeshi to strike. 'What are you waiting for?'

Alzeshi's eyes widened, clearly taken aback such a display of defiance. Then his face contorted with rage, and he lunged forward with a wordless roar.

Estienne braced himself for the killing blow, a strange calm settling over him.

It didn't come.

Instead, a noise split the air. The unmistakable sound of an arrow in flight, followed by a meaty thud. One of Alzeshi's men toppled backwards, landing in a puff of dust, shaft protruding from his chest.

For a heartbeat, the world froze: Alzeshi, arm still raised for the killing blow; Estienne, tensed for an impact that never came; the other slaves and slavers, faces masks of confusion and dawning fear.

The air erupted in a storm of arrows, each one finding its mark with deadly precision. Alzeshi's men fell in quick succession, their bodies thudding into the sand before they could even cry out. Estienne stood rooted to the spot, his mind struggling to process the sudden violence unfolding around him.

Alzeshi whirled, his blade flashing as he lashed out at nothing. His eyes were wild, darting in every direction as he sought the source of the attack. He bellowed an order, but his men were already dead, crimson blooming across the sand beneath their prone forms.

From the shimmering haze of the desert, a dozen horses

trotted into view. Estienne blinked, certain his sun-addled mind was playing tricks on him. The riders were no men he had ever seen before, no warriors he could put a name to. They were short and stocky, with high cheekbones, flat noses and narrow eyes. Their skin was the colour of burnished copper, weathered by sun and wind. Each rode a small, shaggy horse that seemed to float across the sand, barely leaving a hoofprint in its wake. But it was their bows that drew Estienne's eye. Gently curved like a lip, they seemed to be extensions of the riders themselves, a far cry from the long war bows used on the battlefields of England and France.

Seeing his men bested, Alzeshi let out a roar of defiance, and charged the nearest rider, sabre raised high. The horseman wheeled, avoiding the wild swing with effortless grace. In one fluid motion, he nocked an arrow and loosed it point-blank into Alzeshi's face. The slaver fell without a sound, his scarred visage pierced through by the force of the shot.

As quickly as it had begun, the slaughter was over. The strange warriors circled the remnants of the caravan, bows at the ready. Estienne counted at least a dozen of them, their expressions blank as they surveyed the carnage. Then one of them, eyes piercing with a long dark moustache that dropped below his chin, urged his horse forward. He barked out a command in a harsh, guttural language unlike anything Estienne had ever heard, and the other riders dismounted, moving with an eerie silence as they began to ransack the cart and strip the dead of anything valuable. Estienne watched, part of his mind marvelling at their efficiency while at the same time wondering what would happen next.

The leader's gaze fell upon the huddled group of slaves. There was a keen intelligence behind those eyes, a calculating coldness that sent a shiver down Estienne's spine despite the heat. For a long moment, no one moved.

Then the leader dismounted, his boots crunching in the blood-soaked sand. As he approached, Estienne saw his legs were slightly bowed from a lifetime ahorse. Up close, he could see the intricate patterns worked into his leather armour, the gleam of the well-oiled steel at his hip. This was no mere bandit, but a warrior of skill and means.

He spoke, the words harsh and clipped. When no one responded, he frowned, trying again in a different tongue. Estienne shook his head, frustration mounting. If only he could communicate, could somehow convey their desperate situation...

To his surprise, a voice spoke up from behind him. Isaac, his words halting but clear, addressed the warrior in what sounded like his own language. The leader's eyebrows rose, a flicker of surprise crossing his impassive features. A rapid exchange followed, Isaac's frail voice a stark contrast to the warrior's guttural, authoritative tone. Estienne watched, hardly daring to breathe, as the fate of their little band hung in the balance.

Finally, the leader nodded. He barked out another order, and one of his men approached with a waterskin. Estienne's eyes widened as the warriors began cutting the ropes that bound them, freeing them from the bonds of their captivity. The waterskin was pressed into Estienne's hands, and he nearly wept at the feel of it. Cool and heavy, with the promise of life sloshing within. But he didn't drink. Instead, he turned to Isaac, pressing it to the old man's cracked lips. Isaac drank greedily, water spilling down his chin. Only when he had slaked his thirst did Estienne allow himself a swallow, the liquid tasting like the finest wine on his parched tongue.

He sighed when he had finished, feeling some relief.

Turning back to Isaac, Estienne could not quell a grin. 'See, I told you, my friend. Opportunity would present itself.'

Isaac did not look so convinced. 'Don't be too hasty, Estienne. We are not out of this yet. Not by a long way.'

Estienne turned back toward their saviours to see the horsemen had finished their plundering and were tending their steeds and striking up a camp. As they began to drag the arrow-strewn corpses to one side, Estienne wondered if they had been so lucky after all. But they were alive, for now. It would have to be enough.

24

Night wrapped the desert in a black cloak, broken only by the flickering light of the campfire. Estienne sat cross-legged on the cooling sand, his back rigid with tension as he surveyed the scene before him.

One of their liberators tore into a strip of dried meat with his teeth, the tendons in his neck standing out like cords. Another passed around a skin of what smelled like fermented mare's milk, each man taking a long pull before handing it to his neighbour. Their raucous laughter and guttural speech cut the night air, but Estienne could take no solace in their levity. He felt such a hollow ache in his chest for green fields and forests, for the comforting rhythms of life in Christendom. It was as though he might never see those things again, and be consigned to this hell for eternity.

One of the horsemen suddenly thrust a wooden bowl into his hands, filled with some kind of stew. Estienne nodded his thanks before staring at it for a moment, hardly daring to believe it was real, before digging in with his fingers. The meat was tough and gamey, but to his famished body it was like the tenderest cut of venison.

A particularly loud burst of laughter drew his attention back to their rescuers. Two of them were now engaged in what appeared to be a contest of strength, arm-wrestling as their fellows cheered them on. These men were clearly born warriors bred to the saddle; their bodies honed by a lifetime of conflict. Estienne's eyes drifted to their curved bows, propped carefully against their wooden saddles, and he recalled the deadly accuracy with which they had cut down Alzeshi and his men. It was a very real prospect that they may well have given up one form of bondage for another, but for now they were safe.

Isaac sat hunched near the fire, deep in conversation with their leader. The horseman's face was impassive, but his eyes glittered with interest as Isaac spoke, his gnarled hands gesticulating to emphasise whatever point he was making.

As Estienne watched, the horse lord's eyes flicked toward him, flashing in the firelight. Estienne fought the urge to look away, meeting that gaze with what he hoped was a show of strength, but inside, his stomach churned with uncertainty as he wondered what plans this fierce warrior had for them.

The night wore on, the fire burning low, and one by one the horsemen retired to their felt-covered tents, until only a few remained on watch. Estienne fought against his exhaustion, determined to stay alert, to watch for any danger, but his eyelids grew heavy.

Just as he was about to succumb to sleep, Isaac's weathered hand touched his shoulder. 'Come. We must talk.'

Estienne nodded, rising gingerly and following the old man to a spot just beyond the circle of firelight. As they settled onto the cool sand, Estienne couldn't shake the feeling that whatever Isaac had learned would not be good news.

'Their leader is a man named Chatagai,' Isaac began. 'He leads this group of horse lords from the far-off Eastern Steppes, as I suspected. I have had dealings with their kind before along the Silk Road. They are warriors, followers of a great khan named Chingis. This group is part of a larger army serving under a warlord called Subetei. They're on a mission of vengeance against a sultan named Kwarazmshah, who defied their khan. Subetei pursues this sultan relentlessly, and Chatagai is one of his most trusted scouts.'

Estienne's mind reeled. 'So why help us? Surely they have more important concerns than a band of lost slaves. Why take the time to free us?'

Isaac's expression grew grim. 'That's the thing, my friend. We're not free. Not really.'

'What do you mean?'

'Chatagai's group became separated from the main force during the storm. He has failed in his pursuit of the Kwarazmshah and he fears the wrath of his lord, Subetei. Chatagai sees us as... a way to make amends for his error. Slaves to present to his lord to show that his detour wasn't a complete waste.'

Estienne looked around the camp with new eyes, seeing the way the horse lords regarded them, their calculating glances. They weren't saviours. They were just new masters.

'So we've swapped one form of captivity for another.'

Isaac nodded. 'It seems that way. Though I fear these warriors may prove far more dangerous masters than Alzeshi ever was.'

'So what do we do now?' Estienne asked, hating how lost he sounded.

Isaac's hand found his shoulder. 'We survive, my friend. As we have done thus far. We watch, we learn, and we wait. It may not come today, or tomorrow, but our chance will come. You said it once before.'

A heavy silence fell between them as Estienne processed Isaac's words. The old man's face was etched with tension, but there was a steely resolve in his eyes that spoke volumes. They were far from beaten.

Estienne's gaze drifted back to the camp. The fire had burned low, casting long shadows across the sleeping forms of their captors. He had railed under captivity at Alzeshi's hands. This time though, in bondage to a real warrior, he knew he had to be more cautious. He doubted Chatagai would offer him any mercy if he tried and failed to escape, where at least Alzeshi had allowed him to live.

For now, at least, freedom seemed further away than ever.

25

The desert was truly a merciless mistress, her scorching embrace threatening to consume Kashta with each laboured step. The sun's baleful eye glared at him as he trudged onward, legs trembling beneath him after days of relentless pursuit.

The sandstorm had very nearly claimed him. For hours, he had huddled against the fury of the elements, his body curled tight around itself as the wind howled and tore at his cloak. Sand had found its way into every crevice, every fold of skin, tormenting him like a nest of ants, determined to devour him whole. But even as the tempest blew, Kashta's mind had remained focused on his goal. His hate the only thing keeping him alive throughout the desert's raging. The prospect that he would find the man he had pursued across a hundred miles of sand.

When at last the storm had passed, leaving him half-buried in a dune, Kashta had clawed his way free. His water was gone, his provisions scattered to the four winds, but none of that mattered. He would crawl across this wasteland on his hands and knees if he had to, so long as it brought him closer to his quarry.

Now, as the last vestiges of daylight bled from the sky, Kashta paused atop a low rise and scanned the terrain. The storm had reshaped the landscape, erasing familiar landmarks and obliterating the well-worn path of the Silk Road, but Kashta was no mere warrior – he was a son of the desert, born with the whisper of dunes in his ears.

He knelt, fingers brushing the cooling sand. There, the faintest impression of a wheel track. There, a scattering of dung, not yet completely buried by the shifting sands. Signs invisible to most, but to Kashta, they were a map drawn in bold strokes across the earth.

'Not far now,' he murmured, feeling the beat of his heart quicken.

Rising, he pressed on, ignoring the protests of his battered body. He walked until the last rays of sunlight painted the desert in shades of blood, a sight that might have been beautiful were it not for his grim purpose. When night fell, bringing with it a chill that cut to the bone, Kashta's steps began to falter. His vision swam, dark spots dancing at the edges.

Perhaps this was it. Perhaps Allah had decreed that this was to be his final resting place, his bones left to bleach beneath the unforgiving sun. But before despair threatened to overwhelm him, he saw it. A faint glow on the horizon, barely visible. Kashta blinked, certain it must be some cruel trick of his failing senses, but no – it remained, steady and unwavering. A campfire.

His heart began to race, fatigue falling away to be replaced by determination. After so many days of pursuit, after so much hardship, could it truly be that his quest was nearing its end? Kashta's hand moved to the hilt of his sayf, fingers curling around the familiar grip, and a grim smile tugged at his cracked lips as, with renewed purpose, he began to move towards the distant light.

Each step brought him closer to his sworn enemy, closer to the reckoning he had crossed a sea of sand to claim. As he drew nearer, he altered his gait and moved with the silent grace of a desert predator. Using the terrain to mask his approach, he slithered on his belly over the crest of a dune, until he found a vantage point that offered both concealment and a clear view of the encampment beyond.

Squinting through the night, he frowned in confusion. This was not the ragtag group of slavers he had expected to find. Instead, the firelight illuminated warriors whose like he had never seen before. The men who moved about the camp were short and stocky, their high cheekbones and narrow eyes speaking of lands far to the east, beyond even the reaches of the great Silk Road. They wore leather adorned with intricate designs, and their heads were shaved but for long black tails. Curved bows hung from the saddles of their horses, steeds that looked swift yet sturdy.

Kashta's mind raced as he tried to make sense of what he was seeing. He had heard whispers, carried along the trade routes like so much spice and silk. Tales of fierce horsemen from the steppes, of a great warlord who had united the nomad tribes and now turned his gaze westward. But surely those were just stories, the fevered imaginings of merchants and travellers?

Yet the evidence was here before his eyes, as real as the sand beneath his palms. Somehow, in this vast emptiness, he had stumbled upon something far more dangerous than he could have imagined.

For a moment, Kashta's single-minded focus on vengeance wavered. He should turn back, he knew. Return to al-Mansurah and report what he had seen. Surely al-Kamil would want to know of foreign warriors in his lands. It was the sensible thing to do, the dutiful thing.

But then, as his gaze swept over the huddled forms of the captives gathered near the fire, he saw him.

Estienne.

The man he had come so far to kill.

In that instant, all other concerns fell away. The eastern warriors, the threat they posed – none of it mattered. Only his vengeance.

Estienne sat apart from the other prisoners, his bearing still proud despite the obvious signs of hardship etched into his frame. His hair was longer now, tangled and matted with sand and sweat, a bush of beard on his chin, but there was no mistaking that face. The scar that split his cheek seemed more prominent in the firelight, a badge of honour that this foreign knight wore with pride. Well, Kashta would grant him yet more honour. A scar that would not heal.

His fingers tightened on the hilt of his sayf, the familiar feel of it fuelling him like oil to a flame. With a final steadying breath, Kashta rose from his hiding place. The time for stealth was past. Now, there would be retribution… or death.

He strode into the circle of firelight. The camp fell silent, conversations dying mid-sentence as all eyes turned to this unexpected intruder. Warriors reached for weapons, muscles tensing in anticipation of violence, but Kashta paid them no heed. His gaze was fixed solely on Estienne.

'You,' Kashta snarled, that single word laden with hate.

Estienne's eyes widened in disbelief as he scrambled to his feet.

'Kashta,' Estienne breathed, the name barely audible over the crackling of the fire.

Before either man could say more, the warriors around the campfire rose, some grabbing their bows and nocking, others drawing swords. Kashta kept his eyes on Estienne. He would not be cowed, not when he was so close to his goal.

'I demand my reckoning,' he shouted. 'This man, this Frank, took my brother from me. Now I have come to claim the right of vengeance.'

His words were met with stunned silence. The warriors looked to one another, clearly unable to understand his impassioned plea. Then one drew back his bowstring, the arrow aimed at Kashta's heart.

'Wait.' A frail voice cut through the night, halting the warrior before he could loose. Kashta saw a wizened little man step forward into the campfire light. 'Let me speak to them. I can translate.'

Kashta's brow furrowed as he regarded the old man. He was clearly no warrior, his frame frail and bent with age, yet there was a sharpness to his gaze that spoke of keen intelligence.

The old man turned to one of the warriors, the tallest of their number, with a drooping moustache and stark eyes, who was clearly their leader. Words flowed between them in a harsh, guttural language unlike anything Kashta had ever heard. He watched, frustration mounting, as the two conversed, gesturing occasionally towards him and Estienne. Finally, when their talking was done, the leader stepped forward. He regarded Kashta with a mix of curiosity and wariness, as one might regard an exotic animal. Then he spoke directly to him, his words casual, as thought they were old friends.

'He says his name is Chatagai,' the old man translated. 'And you, desert warrior, have impressed him with your courage and resolve. To track one man across the sands, alone and unaided – that speaks of great strength and greater will.'

Kashta inclined his head slightly, acknowledging the words. 'Then he should understand why I must have my vengeance. If he gives me the Frank, I will trouble him no further.'

As the old man translated, Chatagai's lips curved in a humourless smile. Then he replied, shrugging his shoulders as though he had no choice in the matter.

'Chatagai says he cannot do that. This one' – the old man gestured towards Estienne – 'and the others are his property now. Slaves to be presented to his lord Subetei as a gift.'

Kashta's hand tightened on the hilt of his sayf, rage threatening to overwhelm his reason. 'Then I'll take him by force.'

A ripple of amusement passed through the gathered warriors as the old man translated his words, and Kashta realised with a sinking feeling just how hopeless his situation truly was. He might be able to reach Estienne, might even land a killing blow, but he would not survive long enough to savour his victory. Before he could make up his mind, the leader held up a hand, silencing his men, then spoke to his translator.

'Chatagai has a better solution,' the old man said. 'You wish to face Estienne in combat? He is happy to oblige you, and proposes a duel. You against the Frank. The victor will become his slave, to do with as he sees fit. The loser...'

It was obvious what would happen to the loser.

Kashta's mind reeled. This was his chance, the opportunity he had crossed a sea of sand to claim. But the price of victory would be his freedom exchanged for Estienne's life. And defeat... defeat meant death.

He looked to Estienne, saw the determination written across the Frank's face. He could not know yet what was being decided for him, but Kashta somehow knew he would not refuse the challenge.

'I would ask,' the old man said, before a decision could be

made, 'that you reconsider. This man is my friend. I would have died on the Silk Road without him. He is a man of honour. Please, just turn back. Forget this—'

'I accept the terms,' Kashta said, ignoring the plea.

The old man turned to Estienne, speaking in the Frankish tongue so he would understand what had been decided for him. To his credit, Estienne merely raised his chin and nodded his acceptance.

Chatagai clapped his hands, a predatory grin spreading across his face. As the camp erupted into a flurry of activity, Kashta's hand moved to the hilt of his sayf, fingers tracing the intricate patterns worked into the guard.

'May Allah guide my hand,' he whispered to the dark...

26

Night pressed in around them, held at bay only by the flickering light of the campfire. Estienne stood rigid, every muscle taut as he faced the towering figure of Kashta, his eyes burning with a hatred so intense they rivalled the flames that danced between them.

Estienne glanced to the ring of warriors that had surrounded them. Their faces were keen, almost hungry for the bloodshed to come, and it filled him with a strange kind of dread. He looked to Isaac, the old trader's weathered face a mask of concern. The little man who had become an unlikely friend on this hellish journey now stood powerless to intervene. Estienne offered a tight nod, hoping to convey some measure of reassurance, though he felt none himself.

'A weapon,' he said. 'I need a weapon.'

Isaac translated in the horsemen's guttural tongue. Chatagai stepped forward, an eager grin splitting his face, and with a flourish he drew his own sword and held it out, hilt-first.

Estienne hesitated for a heartbeat before grasping the unfamiliar weapon. It was lighter than he expected, the blade curved like the Saracen sabres he had faced in battle. The hilt was wrapped in some kind of hide, providing a secure grip despite the sweat that slicked his palms, and he tested its weight, finding it surprisingly well-balanced.

'Thank you,' he murmured, though he doubted Chatagai understood.

Estienne raised the blade, firelight dancing along its length, and for a moment he caught his own distorted reflection in the polished steel. His face was gaunt and bruised, eyes sunken, beard wild and unkempt. He barely recognised himself. A ragged, desperate man, about to fight for his life in some Godforsaken corner of the desert.

He pushed the thought aside, forcing himself to focus on the task at hand. Across the fire, Kashta flexed his massive arms, his own blade glinting wickedly. Estienne took a deep breath, centring himself as best he could. He had not come so far, survived siege and storm and slavery, only to fall here.

The fire crackled, sending sparks spiralling into the night sky. For a moment, all was still. Then Chatagai barked a command for the duel to begin.

Kashta came at him like a storm given flesh, all raw power and unrelenting fury. His massive sword cleaved the air with a sound like tearing silk, and Estienne barely managed to bring his borrowed blade up in time. The impact thundered through his arms, threatening to numb his fingers, and he stumbled back, narrowly avoiding another swing that would have opened him from shoulder to hip. The curved sword felt alien in his grip, its balance unlike anything he'd trained with, but Estienne forced himself to adapt. He had to, or he'd be dead before the next heartbeat.

The horsemen's eager shouts became a distant roar as he focused on his foe. Kashta charged forward again, sword swinging, and Estienne darted to the side, hoping his agility would allow him to avoid the earth-shaking blow. The blade passed by him, but only barely, and Estienne's bare feet danced across the sand before he regained his fighting stance.

Kashta came at him again, frustration making him launch one wild swing after another, and Estienne read each one before it struck. The big Moor's attacks were powerful but slow, each one committing fully, making him a dangerous but predictable opponent. It was almost too easy for Estienne to parry or move just subtly enough to avoid being struck.

Eventually he saw his opening and lunged, the curved blade singing through the air. There was a moment of resistance, then warmth on his hand as blood spattered from a shallow cut along Kashta's forearm.

The Moor bellowed, more in rage than pain, and redoubled his assault. His blade became a whirl of steel, and it was all Estienne could do to parry and dodge. Metal rang as their swords clashed again and again, the sound echoing out across the desert night.

A white-hot line of pain blazed across Estienne's bicep, and he realised Kashta had broken his guard. Blood trickled down his arm, but the wound wasn't deep. Just a stark reminder of how quickly this fight might turn.

They paused for a moment to regard one another. Estienne's chest heaved as he gulped in a breath. The long march along the Silk Road had taken its toll, leaving him weaker than he'd ever felt, but as he met Kashta's burning gaze, he saw a glimmer of fatigue there as well. The Moor had driven himself to exhaustion in his relentless pursuit, and now that weariness was beginning to show.

They circled each other warily, neither willing to commit to another all-out charge. Estienne's arms burned from the effort of deflecting Kashta's crushing blows, while sweat and blood made his grip on the sword's hilt treacherously slick.

'Is this what you wanted?' Estienne panted, though he knew Kashta couldn't understand him. 'To die in the sand in the middle of nowhere?'

Kashta snarled something in Arabic, the words alien but their meaning clear enough. He was happy to die here. He would face it gladly if it meant Estienne's end.

Eyes wide with hate, the Moor came at him, sword lancing down, a swooping eagle ready to pounce on its prey. This time when Estienne raised his blade to parry, the blow was not so powerful, but neither was his defence so strong.

Wearily they went at one another in the light of the single fire, as strangers whooped and cajoled them. The duel devolved into a brutal test of endurance, both men bleeding from multiple wounds, their ragged breathing punctuated by grunts of pain and exertion. Estienne's arms felt like lead, each strike a monumental effort, but he forced himself to stay focused, knowing that a single moment of inattention could be fatal.

Kashta's attacks, once brutal and strong, had become increasingly wild. Frustration and exhaustion fuelled his swings, each one enough to cleave a man in two, but lacking the accuracy of his earlier assault. Estienne recognised the change, his mind racing even through the fog of fatigue and pain.

There was a way to end this. He just needed to find it.

As Kashta lumbered in again, Estienne feinted left, then quickly stepped right, his curved blade whistling through the air. Kashta barely managed to block, and Estienne pressed his advantage, raining down a flurry of quick strikes that forced the larger man back a step.

Surprise flickered in Kashta's eyes, quickly replaced by a renewed fury, and he roared as he launched a devastating counterattack. Estienne retreated, deflecting what blows he could and dodging the rest. A glancing hit opened a gash along his ribs, but he barely felt it through the mist of his battle ardour.

There was no audience any longer, no desert, no past or future. Only the next breath, the next strike, the desperate struggle to survive...

There, Kashta overextended, and Estienne saw his chance. He feinted left once more, watching Kashta's eyes track the movement. Then, with every ounce of strength left in his battered body, Estienne spun to the right.

The curved blade sang through the air, its arc beautiful and terrible. Estienne felt the impact reverberate up his arm as the sword's cross-guard connected solidly with Kashta's temple. There was a sickening crack, like a branch snapping underfoot.

Kashta's eyes went blank, his massive frame swaying for a moment. Then, like a felled oak, he toppled backwards and crashed to the ground, sending up a small cloud of sand.

Silence descended, broken only by the crackling of the fire and Estienne's own heaving breathing. He stared down at Kashta's prone form, scarcely able to believe what had just happened. The Moor lay still but his chest rose and fell, beaten but alive at least.

The watching horsemen stepped closer, their earlier bloodlust replaced by a muted hush. Estienne tightened his grip on the sword, unsure of what would happen next, and his gaze found Isaac in the crowd, the old man's face a mixture of relief and awe.

For a long moment, no one moved, the fate of both victor and vanquished hanging in the balance, to be decided by the whim of their captors. Then he remembered – he was supposed to finish this. For the loser only death, for the victor… slavery.

Estienne loomed over Kashta's unconscious form and raised the curved sword for what should have been the killing blow. His arms trembled with exhaustion, blood from a half dozen minor wounds mixing with sweat to run in rivulets down his skin. One strike. That's all it would take to end this, to finish the warrior who had pursued him across an ocean of sand. But as he looked down at his fallen enemy, he hesitated. Kashta lay still and defenceless. This was no longer a fight for survival, but an execution. And despite everything – the hatred in Kashta's eyes, the relentless pursuit, the knowledge that the Moor would have shown him no such mercy – Estienne couldn't bring himself to do it.

He was a knight, trained in the arts of war but still bound by a code, no matter how far he was from home. To strike down a helpless foe, even one who had sworn to kill him, felt like a betrayal of everything he had once stood for. Of everything he still wanted to believe he was.

The moment stretched on as Estienne wrestled with his decision. Then, breaking the tension like a thunderclap, came the sound of laughter. Chatagai's deep, rumbling chuckle caught Estienne off guard. He turned to see the horse lord applaud him, a wide grin splitting his face. Then the other warriors joined in, their earlier bloodlust transformed into appreciation for the spectacle they had witnessed.

Chatagai moved closer, slapping Estienne on the shoulder before speaking words of congratulation, as Isaac hurried forward, his wrinkled face alight with nervous energy.

'He says you've impressed him. Your skill in combat, and your mercy. He grants you… your freedom.'

Estienne blinked, certain he had misheard. 'Freedom?'

Isaac nodded vigorously. 'Yes, yes. He says a warrior of your calibre deserves to choose his own path.'

Still in a daze, Estienne lowered the sword. Chatagai held out his hand, and Estienne realised the horseman wanted his weapon back. He handed it over, noting the approving nod Chatagai gave as he examined the blade for damage.

'What about Kashta?' Estienne asked, glancing at the still-unconscious Moor.

Isaac conferred briefly with Chatagai before turning back to Estienne, his expression grim. 'He says he'll take Kashta as his slave instead. A suitable substitute for his master Subetei.'

Estienne watched as some of Chatagai's warriors moved to bind Kashta's limp form. The big Moor stirred but didn't wake, a nasty bruise already forming where Estienne's blow had connected with his skull.

'You did it,' Isaac said softly, placing a gnarled hand on Estienne's arm. 'You won your freedom.'

Freedom. The word seemed almost foreign after so long. For weeks, his entire world had been nothing but the next step, the next beating to endure, the next impossible mile to cross. Now, suddenly, his world had opened up again, and he found himself at a loss.

'So what... what do I do now?'

As the thrill of combat began to ebb, leaving Estienne light-headed and weak-kneed, he swayed slightly, and Isaac steadied him with surprising strength for such a frail-looking man.

'Come. First let's see to your wounds. There will be time to ponder the future once you've rested.'

As Isaac led him away from the fire, Estienne cast one last glance over his shoulder. Kashta was being roughly hauled to his feet, still only half-conscious. Their eyes met for the briefest moment, and Estienne saw confusion there, and something that might have been grudging respect. Then the moment passed, and Estienne allowed himself to be guided towards the promise of rest.

He was free, yes. But as the weight of that fact settled over him like a heavy cloak, he couldn't shake the feeling that his trials were far from over.

27

Estienne stirred, each movement a stark reminder of the previous night's brutal duel, and his hand instinctively went to his side, probing the crude bandages Isaac had applied. The old man's gentle ministrations had made a welcome change from his mistreatment at the hands of Alzeshi and his men. To his shame Estienne couldn't remember thanking him.

His eyes scanned the camp, seeking out his friend. Instead, they fell upon Kashta.

The Moor sat apart from the others, his massive frame hunched. Thick ropes bound his wrists, but despite his bonds, despite the bruises that mottled his face, those eyes burned. There was no mistaking the hatred that smouldered there, a fire unquenched by defeat.

Estienne pushed himself to his feet, muscles protesting, and made his way towards the centre of the camp. The horsemen moved with practised efficiency, breaking down tents and readying their mounts for the day's journey.

'Estienne.' Isaac sat huddled near the remnants of last

night's fire, his face ashen in the early morning light. 'How do you fare, my friend?'

'I've felt better,' he replied.

Isaac opened his mouth to reply, but whatever he was about to say was drowned out by the sudden sound of a lone rider thundering into the camp, his horse lathered and heaving. The man practically fell from his saddle, stumbling towards Chatagai with an urgency that set Estienne's nerves on edge.

The two men conferred, and Estienne watched as Chatagai's expression hardened before he barked out a series of commands to his men. The camp erupted into frenzied activity, the warriors' earlier efficiency giving way to panicked haste.

'Isaac,' Estienne said, turning to the old man. 'What's happening? What did that rider say?'

But before Isaac could answer, one of the horsemen seized him and he was dragged towards the centre of the camp, where other prisoners were being gathered. Estienne moved to intervene, but was nudged aside, as the prisoners were made to stand in a line.

'What's going on?' he demanded.

No one answered as Chatagai stood before the bound men, his face an emotionless mask. Then he spoke rapidly, gesturing towards the north with sharp, decisive movements. Estienne's eyes darted between him and Isaac, desperate for some explanation, some hint of what was to come.

As Isaac listened, his face grew increasingly grave. When at last Chatagai fell silent, the old man turned to Estienne, his eyes filled with a sorrow that made Estienne's blood run cold.

'What is it?' Estienne demanded. 'For God's sake, Isaac, tell me what's happening.'

Isaac opened his mouth to speak, but before he could utter a word, Chatagai barked another order. The prisoners were suddenly being separated, roughly shoved into two groups. Estienne could see the bigger and stronger men were herded on one side, the smaller and weaker on the other. Isaac was among the weaker men, four in all, cowering in fear.

'Estienne, listen to me,' Isaac said, his voice cracking. 'There isn't much time.'

'What's happening, man? Tell me.'

'Subetei, Chatagai's lord, has been spotted to the north. They mean to rejoin him, but… they must be swift and can only take the strongest prisoners with them.'

A sudden cry rang out. Estienne turned to see one of Chatagai's men standing over a kneeling prisoner, a slight man with hollow cheeks and trembling hands. The horseman's sword flashed in the morning sun, a single, brutal arc. There was a dull thud, and the prisoner crumpled to the ground, his head rolling away in a spray of crimson.

'God in heaven,' Estienne breathed. 'We have to do something. We have to stop this.'

'There's nothing we can do, my friend,' Isaac replied, sounding resigned to his fate. 'We are Chatagai's property. He would rather leave us dead in the sand than abandon us to our fate so we might tell of his passing.'

'No,' Estienne growled. 'I won't let this happen. I won't stand by while they murder innocent men.'

He took a step forward, ready to throw himself at these animals, but Isaac's hand on his arm stopped him short.

'Estienne, please,' the old man begged. 'Don't throw your life away. Not for this. Not for me.'

'Wait,' Estienne shouted, ignoring Isaac's plea. He stumbled toward Chatagai, ignoring the growls the horse lord directed at his men. 'Isaac, tell him I need to speak. Tell him now.'

Another sword rang from its sheath as one of Chatagai's men moved to bar Estienne's path. Estienne grabbed the man's wrist, but he was strong, twisting free and raising that blade. Before he could strike, a snarled order from Chatagai stayed his hand.

'Tell him, Isaac,' Estienne spat. 'Tell him I would speak, as a free man.'

Isaac turned to Chatagai, relaying the instruction in that guttural tongue. The horse lord's eyes narrowed as he regarded Estienne. Then he replied slowly, those foreign words dripping with threat.

Isaac swallowed. 'He wants to know—'

'Yes, I understand. Tell him that he has to spare your life.'

Isaac did as he was told, listening intently to Chatagai's snarled reply.

'He asks why he should spare me, when I will only slow him down,' Isaac translated, his voice trembling slightly.

Estienne's mind raced. There had to be something. Had to be a way.

'Tell him you're invaluable,' Estienne said, his words coming in a rush. 'Tell him you're a master of languages, that you can be his lord's voice in foreign lands. That you would be of much use to this Subetei, worth more than any amount of gold... any horse.'

Isaac nodded, turning back to Chatagai. As the old man spoke, Estienne watched Chatagai's face, searching for any sign he might relent. The warlord's expression remained impassive, but there was a glimmer of interest in his dark eyes before he spoke again, his tone sharp.

'He wants to know how he can be sure I won't slow them down,' Isaac said.

Estienne swallowed hard, knowing his next words could seal their fate. 'Tell him I give my word as a knight. I will come with you and make sure you do not. If we become a burden, he can kill us both.'

Isaac hesitated for a moment before translating. For a long moment, silence stretched between them, broken only by the whisper of wind over sand and the nervous shuffling of horses.

Finally, Chatagai nodded, a single sharp movement. He spoke, his words curt but no longer filled with murderous intent.

'He says we may live,' Isaac translated, relief evident in his voice. 'For now.'

Before Estienne could respond, Chatagai turned back to his men. There was another noise of swift steel, another thud as one more prisoner was beheaded. Estienne could not bear to look, to see that worthless slaughter. He had managed to save Isaac, but what could he have done for those other men? Perhaps argued harder? Or might that have simply stirred Chatagai to even greater slaughter?

By the time the camp was broken, three corpses lay separated from their heads. The killing was done, the sand dark and sodden. A hand gripped Estienne's shoulder, and he turned to see one of Chatagai's men, face blank as he gestured toward a group of horses being readied nearby. Time to leave.

Estienne nodded, grabbing Isaac by the arm and helping him mount the beast. The other survivors – those deemed strong enough to be of use – were already mounting up. Among them, Estienne spotted Kashta, the Moor's massive frame dwarfing his mount. Their eyes met briefly, and Estienne saw a flicker of something in those dark depths. Understanding, perhaps. Or a shared sorrow for the senseless waste of life. Whatever it was, it was gone in an instant.

As Estienne climbed up in front of Isaac, the horse shifted beneath him, sensing his unease, and he gripped the reins tightly, fighting to maintain control of both the animal and his own rising anger. Then with a thunder of hooves, the horsemen began to move out.

'It seems I owe you my life once again, friend,' Isaac said above the drumming sound.

Estienne didn't have the heart to reply. He had saved no one yet.

28

Estienne's thighs burned from hours in the saddle, his hands raw and blistered from gripping the reins. The horsemen set a punishing pace, driving their mounts and prisoners alike to the brink of exhaustion. All the while Isaac gripped tight to his waist, clinging on for dear life as miles of desert raced by.

Sand stretched endlessly in every direction, dunes rising and falling like waves on a golden sea. Estienne's eyes stung, his throat parched after only tasting the tepid water they'd been allowed at dawn.

A strangled cry from behind drew his attention. One of the other prisoners swayed dangerously in his saddle, eyes rolling back in his head, before he toppled sideways, hitting the sand with a sickening thud.

'Wait!' Estienne called out. 'He's fallen—'

One of Chatagai's horsemen wheeled about. For a moment Estienne thought he might help the man, but instead he took up the reins of the abandoned mount, before urging his own steed after the others. The column continued its relentless advance, leaving the fallen man to his fate. Estienne twisted in his saddle, watching as the prisoner's form grew smaller and smaller, until it was swallowed by the shimmering heat haze.

He faced front once more, his jaw clenched tight against the surge of helpless rage. How many more would they lose before this hellish journey was done? How long before he, too, succumbed to the brutal pace?

Before despair could set in, a rider drew up alongside him, and Estienne recognised the massive frame of Kashta. The Moor's face was a mask of determination, sweat cutting clean tracks through the dust caked on his dark skin. His clothes hung in bloody shreds, a testament to their recent battle, yet he sat tall in the saddle, matching the horsemen stride for stride.

Their eyes met briefly, and Estienne felt a grudging spark of admiration. Despite the wounds he'd suffered, despite the bonds that chafed his wrists, Kashta endured. There was steel in the man, a will that refused to bend even in the face of certain death.

'Do you think he still wants to kill me?' Estienne cast over his shoulder, as the Moor rode on past them.

'I would not bet against it,' Isaac replied, still gripping on to Estienne for dear life.

As the sun began its slow descent towards the western horizon, and the heat of the day gave way to the chill of night, Chatagai barked an order. The column gradually slowed, then came to a halt in the lee of a towering dune. Estienne all but fell from his saddle, his legs trembling as they took his weight. Still, he managed to help Isaac dismount as all around them, prisoners and captors alike began the business of making camp. Tents were erected with practised efficiency, and a fire was started in their midst.

As he helped set up one of the felt-covered shelters, Estienne's mind raced. The coming darkness would offer cover, a chance to slip away unnoticed. But even if he managed to steal a horse and supplies, how far could he get with Isaac before these warriors ran him to ground? And what of the other prisoners? He could not simply leave them to their fate.

His gaze drifted to where Kashta sat, hands bound before him, glaring into the fire. The Moor had sworn to kill him, had pursued him across an ocean of sand to exact his vengeance. Yet now, in the face of a common enemy, Estienne could only wonder how much hate he still harboured.

Clenching his fists, he began to formulate a mad idea that set his heart to racing. But as the last light faded from the sky and the stars began to wink overhead, he knew with certainty that it was their only chance.

'Tonight,' he whispered to Isaac, once they had all eaten of their meagre rations.

'Tonight?' the old man replied.

'Just be ready.'

Isaac nodded his understanding. Not that there was much to understand, it was barely even a plan, but Estienne had to try, nonetheless.

He waited until night had wrapped the desert in blackness, broken only by the guttering light of the dying campfire. A chill wind whispered across the dunes, carrying with it the acrid tang of woodsmoke and the muffled snores of exhausted men. But Estienne lay awake, every muscle coiled tight, waiting for his moment.

When the last of the horse lords looked to be dozing, Estienne rose and shook Isaac from his slumber. A finger to his lips, signalling for silence, before he led the way across camp, each step placed with the intent of a stalking cat, heart thundering in his chest. As they neared the tethered horses, he saw a cooking fire smouldering. Beside it lay the detritus of the evening meal –

scraps of meat, bits of gristle, and there, glinting dully in the fading light, a knife. As Estienne's fingers closed around the hilt, he realised this was it. There would be no going back now.

After freeing Isaac's wrists, Estienne gestured for him to make his way toward the waiting horses, then crept into the area where the prisoners were kept, a collection of a half dozen sorry souls huddled together for warmth. With trembling hands, he began to saw through their bonds, signalling for silence when their startled eyes met his in the gloom. One by one, the captives were freed, a couple staring at him in mute gratitude, while one began to weep silently, overcome by this unexpected chance at freedom. Estienne worked quickly, all too aware of how little time they had.

At last, he came to Kashta. The Moor's massive frame was unmistakable, even in the darkness, and Estienne hesitated, the knife still poised in his grip. This man had sworn to kill him, had pursued him across a hundred miles of desolate land with murder in his heart. To free him now might well seal his own doom.

Kashta merely stared, not willing to beg for his liberty, and for a heartbeat they regarded one another. Then, with a barely perceptible nod, Kashta extended his bound wrists.

The moment Estienne's blade touched the ropes, a shout split the night.

They had been discovered.

Chaos erupted as their captors exploded from their tents, fumbling for weapons. The freed captives scattered, some making a mad dash for the horses while others simply ran, heedless of direction in their desperation to escape.

Estienne's knife flashed, severing Kashta's bonds even as an arrow whistled past his ear. He grabbed the Moor's arm, hauling him to his feet.

'Come on, we have to—'

His words were cut short as one of the horse warriors barrelled into him, and they went sprawling in the sand. Estienne's knife went spinning away into the darkness as meaty hands closed around his throat. He grabbed the man's wrists, spots dancing at the edges of his vision as he fought to free himself, but the stocky horseman was simply too strong.

Then suddenly the pressure was gone, the easterner collapsing limply to one side. Kashta stood over him, a rock held in his massive hands. With a snarl, the Moor hurled the rock aside and reached down to haul Estienne to his feet.

He snarled something in Estienne's face that he couldn't understand. Then as quick as he'd grabbed him, the Moor let him go, and turned to find a way of escape. All around them, the night had become a storm of violence and confusion. The flickering light of the dying fire cast writhing shadows across the sand as men fought and died, the air thick with the metallic ring of steel and the hiss of arrows. Estienne ducked as one whistled close enough for him to feel the breath of its passage. Beside him, Kashta's eyes blazed with a terrible fury, his lips peeled back in a feral snarl as he dashed for the safety of darkness.

Estienne could only follow, lurching after the hulking figure as he bounded through the violence.

A figure ran at them, blade raised high.

'Watch out,' Estienne cried, as the swordsman headed straight at the Moor.

Kashta ducked a swipe of the sword, rolling in the sand to snatch up a fallen spear, before rising in one fluid motion. With a roar, he hurled it, the weapon taking the horseman square in the chest, the force of it sending him tumbling back.

Estienne scrambled towards the man's fallen weapon, fingers closing around the grip. He brought it up just in time to parry a vicious overhand strike from another charging warrior, and steel rang against steel. Estienne gave ground as his opponent pressed forward, his attacks savage, a sneer twisting his features. Their exchange was all too brief before Estienne's blade found the man's throat and hot blood spattered his arm. His enemy fell gurgling to the sand, but there was no time to dwell on it. More warriors had burst from their tents to join the fray, as Chatagai's voice boomed through the night.

An arrow thudded into the ground at Estienne's feet, as he and Kashta ran in opposite directions. In the waning light of the fire Estienne could still see the battle raging, but the men he had freed could not fight all night. Kashta was gone, and he was left weak and alone with but a single blade to fight a group of skilled warriors. No hope left.

The sound of hooves pounding the earth, and he turned, seeing Isaac astride one of the squat mounts, leading a second horse by its reins. The old man's eyes were wide with fear, sitting uneasily astride that mount, and Estienne almost shouted his relief.

Instead, he launched himself into the vacant saddle, still gripping tight to the sword. His fingers had barely closed around the reins before another horse bolted past them – Kashta, spurring his own stolen mount forward and into the night.

'Come on, old man,' Estienne snarled, kicking his horse as viciously as he could manage.

Wind whipped at Estienne's face as he galloped headlong into the dark. Isaac was right at his side, clinging to reins and mane for dear life, as behind them war cries split the night. An arrow whistled between them, so close Estienne felt it brush his sleeve. Then they let the night take them, driving their steeds into the dark and leaving all else in their wake.

29

He hunched over the neck of his mount, exhaustion pulling at every sinew. Still he fought against it, desperate to stay awake, stay aware as the sunrise began to light their way. A glance to his right and Isaac was still there, looking even more weary than Estienne felt. When the old man offered a tired nod, Estienne felt some relief that he was still alive, but they were not out of this yet. Not by a long way.

The desert was filled with dangers, and perhaps the greatest one was the man that rode to his left. The Moor who had been his enemy, his pursuer, and now... what? Ally seemed far too generous a term for this fragile accord born of necessity.

For his part, Kashta had ridden in silence, and made no move to exact his promise of vengeance. Estienne could only think the Moor was given pause by the blade Estienne still clutched in his hand. Whatever it was, he was glad of the reassurance the sword gave him, even if he felt too weak to wield it.

On they rode in a seemingly aimless slog until the sun had reached its zenith, and Kashta suddenly reined his horse to a halt. Estienne followed the man's keen gaze to a patch of scrubby vegetation and weathered rock jutting from the endless sand. There, nestled in its midst, was what looked like a well, barely more than a circle of stones, but achingly welcome to Estienne's eyes.

Kashta urged his horse closer, and they drew rein at the edge of the scrub. Isaac was quick to follow, almost toppling from the saddle in his haste. As Estienne dismounted beside them, his legs trembled under him as they took his full weight. Pain flared from days of travel, from combat, but it was all distant, subsumed by the desperate need for water that clawed at his throat.

He watched and waited as Kashta knelt by the makeshift well, pulling up a rope. At the end of it was a cup, which the Moor examined for a moment, before placing it to his lips, tentative at first, then he gulped down whatever was within. When he was done, he offered the cup to Isaac, who knelt like he was praying at an altar before drinking deep. After he had drunk his fill, he moved aside, allowing Estienne his turn.

He fell to his knees, dropping the cup back into its sinkhole and drinking the brown water it caught. He didn't care about how it tasted, about the grit that crunched between his teeth. It could have been poisoned for all he cared, he would still have quaffed it down like sweet wine.

'More miracles,' Isaac breathed, a crooked smile on his weathered face.

'Keep praying for them, old man,' Estienne croaked in return. 'We will need many more if we're to get out of this.'

As Estienne dragged himself to his feet, he turned to regard his unlikely travelling companion, who drew more water to offer their horses. Kashta had made no move to harm him during their headlong flight, but Estienne knew well how much danger he was in. The silence stretched taut between them, broken only by the gentle wicker of the horses and the hiss of the desert wind. Estienne found himself suddenly desperate to speak with this man. Perhaps to make things right between them.

'Isaac,' he said, gesturing to the Moor. 'Ask him...'

What? Whether he had forgiven his debt of vengeance yet? Whether he had decided the death of his sworn brother did not matter any longer? Estienne knew the answer to that well enough. Had he been in Kashta's position; he doubted there would have been much room for forgiveness, even after the trial they had just shared.

'You want me to ask if he still intends to kill you?' Isaac asked. 'Because I'm pretty sure I already know the answer. The al-Sudan are loyal unto death. If he has a blood debt to pay, then it will be paid no matter what.'

Kashta turned as they spoke, eyes flitting from one, then the other. He said something to Isaac, his words fast and harsh.

Isaac turned, looking sheepish. 'He demands to know what we are saying. Whether you are plotting to kill him.'

'Tell him I have no intention of killing him, as long as he offers the same courtesy.'

Isaac relayed the terms. Kashta glared at Estienne, before speaking his reply through gritted teeth.

Isaac sighed. 'I'm afraid he still intends to kill you. Once the current danger we face has passed.'

Estienne felt his anger bristle. Damn this Moor and his fanatic quest. Had Estienne not done enough to make amends?

Teeth gritted in frustration, he stalked toward Kashta, brandishing the sword he had stolen. Kashta stood tall, ready to absorb Estienne's attack, as though he were armoured in an impregnable coat of mail. But Estienne did not make to strike him. Instead, he grasped the blade, holding out the hilt.

'Here. You want your vengeance so badly? Then take it. Go

ahead. Take my head and leave the body for the fucking vultures. Or is that too easy? Maybe you want to gut me slow, watch me bleed my last drop at your feet. Is that it?'

Kashta regarded the blade, hand still gripping the rein of his horse. For a moment, his face remained that same mask, eyes glaring at Estienne with utter disregard. Then, in a single fluid motion, he reached out, fingers closing around the sword's hilt. Estienne loosed his grip on the blade lest it slice his fingers, and Kashta held it between them.

For a moment, Estienne regretted his rash action. Regretted allowing his anger to get the better of him. The sword wavered in Kashta's hand, the tip dipping low until it hovered a bare handspan from Estienne's heart. He stared with those fathomless eyes, and Estienne did his best to glare back, seeking some hint of intent. Was this it? Had he just handed his mortal enemy the means to exact his vengeance?

Estienne waited for the bite of steel, but it never came. Instead, Kashta hurled the sword aside, where it hit the sand with a dull thump. Then he turned back to his steed, dismissing Estienne with the finality of a door slamming shut.

Isaac let out his sigh of relief in a long gust. 'That was hot-blooded of you, my young friend.'

Feeling not a little foolish, Estienne walked to where Kashta had flung the sword and picked it up. When he turned back, Kashta had mounted his horse once more.

'It was,' Estienne admitted. 'It's a habit of mine I've been working to break. Come, it looks like we are done here.'

Estienne turned towards his own mount, but before he'd taken more than a step, Kashta's arm shot out, finger pointing at the distant horizon.

Following the line of Kashta's gesture, Estienne squinted against the sun, searching for whatever he was pointing at. At first, he saw nothing but endless sand, the shimmering haze of heat distorting the horizon. But as he looked harder, a flicker of movement caught his eye. Out there, little more than a smudge against the endless blue of the sky, a dark shape danced. No, not one shape. Many. And as he watched, the smudge grew, resolving into a haze of billowing dust, the unmistakable sign of hard-ridden horses.

A surge of dread rose to choke the breath from his lungs. Beside him, Kashta let out a low hiss. Even at this distance, Estienne knew it could be no other. The horsemen had managed to track them through the waste. Chatagai was coming, for vengeance or to reclaim what he saw as rightfully his.

The petty resentments that had seemed so vast mere moments ago suddenly shrank to insignificance. There was no time for pride or the nursing of old wounds, not with the spectre of death breathing down their necks once more.

'I thought they were riding hard to meet with their master, Subetei,' Estienne snarled in frustration.

Isaac shook his head in disbelief. 'It seems the Moor is not the only one willing to abandon all else so he might kill you, Wace.'

He was already scrambling into his saddle, and Estienne shoved him onto his horse before swinging atop his own. With a thunder of hooves, the three men spurred their horses to a gallop, leaving the shelter of the oasis behind.

The time for talk was done. Now they had to ride like they never had before.

30

Their horses thundered across the sand, each impact of hooves sending jolts of pain through Estienne's battered body. The leather of the reins had long since burned blisters into his palms, but he barely noticed the sting, his focus now on the horizon ahead.

He risked a glance over his shoulder, his heart sinking as he saw the dust cloud of their pursuers. It had grown larger, a billowing mass that dogged their trail relentlessly. The horsemen were slowly gaining ground, their mounts tireless despite the unforgiving landscape.

Beside him, Kashta and Isaac rode in grim silence, the Moor's massive frame hunched low over his mount's neck, the old trader looking as though he might topple from the saddle at any moment.

As the sun climbed higher, baking the air, each breath felt like inhaling fire. Sweat plastered Estienne's tattered shirt to his skin, and he could feel the chafing rawness of flesh where his legs gripped the saddle. He had lost track of how long they had been riding. Had it been hours? Days? Time seemed to lose all meaning in this endless expanse of sand and sky.

Just as the sun began to fall toward the distant horizon, he caught a glimpse of something, some obstacle in their path. The closer they got, the more it resolved itself into a definite structure.

Estienne pointed ahead. 'Look.'

Kashta's eyes followed his gesture. There, spanning a deep ravine that cut through the desert like a scar, stood an ancient bridge. Its wooden planks were weathered and warped, the supporting beams looking as though they might crumble at the slightest touch. But it was their only way forward. If they did not cross they would have to veer off one direction or the other and then surely their pursuers would catch them.

'Are we saved?' Isaac gasped wearily. 'Is this yet one more miracle?'

'Don't stop praying yet, old man,' was all Estienne could reply as they covered the remaining yards to the bridge.

He reined in his horse at the edge of the ravine, doubt gnawing at him as he surveyed the rickety structure that spanned it. Could it even support the weight of their horses if they tried to cross? But the alternative was to turn and face certain death at the hands of Chatagai and his men...

He turned to Kashta, seeking some sign of what he thought they should do. As if in answer, Kashta didn't hesitate, spurring his mount forward and advancing on the bridge without a backward glance.

For a moment, Estienne could only admire Kashta's boldness. Then, with a muttered curse, he dug his heels into his horse's flanks and followed. It might well be safer to cross one after the other, but a glance over his shoulder told him they had run out of time for such caution. If they were to die, better it be on their own terms than at the mercy of their pursuers.

The first step onto the bridge sent a shudder through the entire structure. Estienne's mount shied nervously as it sensed the danger beneath its hooves. He leaned forward, murmuring soothing nonsense as he goaded the frightened animal forward. Ahead, Kashta had already reached the midpoint of the bridge, his steed moving with a surety that Estienne could only envy. Behind, Isaac was urging his horse after them both, holding up the reins as though they might bite him as he cooed and shooed.

Estienne forced himself to focus on Kashta's back, trying to ignore the groaning of the wood beneath him. Each step made the bridge creak alarmingly, and he didn't dare look down, knowing that the sight of the ravine's depths would likely unman him entirely.

A crack of wood and Estienne's blood ran cold. He froze, certain that this was the moment the bridge would give way, but the planks held, if only barely. Swallowing hard, he pressed on, aware that to hesitate now would only mean certain death.

As they neared the far side, a chorus of shouts erupted behind them. Estienne chanced a glance over his shoulder to see the horsemen nearing the edge of the ravine, their mounts rearing and snorting as their riders urged them forward.

'Get a move on,' Estienne called out, knowing the words would be meaningless to Kashta but feeling the need to say them, nonetheless.

The Moor didn't offer a reply, but Estienne saw him nudge his horse to greater effort. They were so close now, the solid ground on the far side tantalisingly near.

With a final clatter of hooves, Kashta's mount cleared the bridge. Estienne's followed a heartbeat later, and he felt a rush of relief to be on firm earth once more. Isaac brought up the rear, gasping as his own horse clattered onto solid ground. But no time for celebrations. Estienne knew they had only moments before Chatagai and his men would be upon them.

He wheeled his horse around, gripping the sword he had carried so far through the desert. It might not be enough to take on a dozen killers, but what else did he have?

Kashta quickly urged his horse alongside Estienne's, and held out his hand for the weapon. Estienne hesitated for only a heartbeat, wondering whether it was wise to hand over the sword for a second time, before the Moor spoke in urgent tones.

'He has a plan,' Isaac said.

'Whatever it is,' Estienne replied, handing Kashta the blade, 'he'd best do it fast.'

Kashta's fingers closed around the hilt and Estienne saw a glimmer of grim satisfaction in the man's eyes. As the first of their pursuers urged his horse onto the bridge, Estienne thought Kashta might go charging to meet him, but the Moor had other ideas. With a speed belying his size, he dismounted, striding purposefully towards the bridge's support struts. Realisation dawned on Estienne as Kashta raised the sword high, then grunted as he brought it down on the weathered wooden post. The impact sent splinters flying, but the ancient wood proved stubborn. Kashta snarled, redoubling his efforts as he hacked at the beam with all his strength.

A whistle cut through the air, followed by a dull thud as an arrow embedded itself in the ground mere inches from Kashta's foot. Estienne looked around, searching for something, anything he could use to help. His gaze fell upon a long piece of wood, likely part of the bridge's original railing, now lying discarded on the ground. Without hesitation, he leapt from the saddle, snatched it up and hefted it like a shield.

Scrambling forward, Estienne positioned himself between

Kashta and the oncoming hail of arrows. The first struck the makeshift shield, arrowhead slamming through the rotted wood an inch from Estienne's face. He gritted his teeth, adjusting his stance to better protect both himself and Kashta, as more arrows struck.

Kashta went at the support with abandon. It was already a mess of splinters and gouges, but still held. Risking a look from behind his wooden shield, Estienne could see the first of the riders reaching the near side of the bridge. They were out of time.

'Faster,' Estienne bellowed, as another arrow hammered into the shield.

Whether he understood or not, Kashta redoubled his efforts, hacking at the wooden prop, each vicious swing sending a shower of wood into the air.

Then an ominous groan, as the entire structure shuddered.

Kashta bellowed triumphantly, scrambling away from the bridge. Estienne didn't need to be told twice, dropping his improvised shield before moving after him to where Isaac sat holding the reins of their steeds.

A deafening crack split the air before the bridge gave a final, mournful groan and collapsed in on itself, taking two of the riders with it as it plummeted into the ravine below. Both men cried out in panic, joined by the fearful whinnies of their terrified steeds, as they fell to their deaths. A thunderous crash echoed across the desert.

Estienne stood motionless, staring at the yawning chasm where the bridge had been just moments before. The dust that had billowed up from the ravine was settling as he turned to Kashta, and their eyes met. Estienne offered a small smile, nodding his appreciation. The Moor's usual stoic expression cracked just enough to reveal a glimmer of acceptance, but the moment was short-lived.

Angry shouts drifted across the span, drawing their attention back to the immediate danger. Chatagai began barking orders to his men, and the riders immediately began to head along the edge of the ravine. Estienne's heart sank as he realised what they were doing – looking for another crossing. This was not over by far. Kashta had bought them time, but nothing more. Soon enough, Chatagai and his men would find a way across, and the chase would resume.

'We have to move,' he said, taking the reins from Isaac's grasp. 'There could be another crossing only a few miles along that ravine. Who knows how long we have.'

'But surely...' Isaac said, then thought better of it. There was no room for hope, not yet.

Without another word, they all turned their mounts away from the ravine and urged them into motion once again.

31

The relentless rhythm of hoofbeats had long since faded to dull noise as they cantered ever southward. Or as southward as Estienne could discern, from the passage of the sun. After a full night and day on the run the direction had become irrelevant. Estienne had only hoped their trail would be lost to their pursuers and that they found signs of life soon, before the thirst got to them.

Their mounts, once stout and strong, now moved with the sluggish gait of animals pushed far beyond their limits. Foam flecked their flanks, and their breath came in ragged gasps. Estienne knew they couldn't go on like this much longer. Man and beast alike would soon reach breaking point.

As the sun once more began its slow descent towards the western horizon, the quality of light changed, softening from the harsh glare of day to something softer. The dunes cast long shadows across the sand, their crests blazing with amber fire. Despite his exhaustion, Estienne found himself marvelling at the sight. The desert sunset was a spectacle unlike anything he'd witnessed in his homeland, a riot of colour that seemed to set the very air ablaze. Beautiful, yes, but right now Estienne would gladly have forfeited it for the green of England. For the cold, and most certainly for the rain.

Kashta looked almost unaffected by the conditions, though it was doubtful he would have complained even if he were. He sat as upright as he could manage, eyes always fixed on the way ahead. In contrast, Isaac sat slumped across the neck of his horse, and more than once Estienne had been forced to grasp him before the old man fell. There was no way he could carry on like this for much longer, but Estienne would not abandon him. Not after they had come so far together.

As the last rays of sunlight bled from the sky giving way to twilight, Estienne's eyes caught a flicker of movement in the distance. At first, he thought it might be a trick of the fading light, but as he squinted against the gloom, he saw it again – pinpricks of fire, dancing on the horizon.

His heart quickened. Those lights could only mean hope. Shelter, perhaps. Maybe even water and food. But with that tantalising prospect also came danger. Who knew what welcome three ragged strangers might receive in the heart of the desert?

'Isaac,' he croaked.

No answer, and he looked to see the old man had passed out across the back of his horse. Or at least Estienne hoped he was passed out.

He cast a sidelong glance at Kashta, seeing the Moor had also spotted the distant lights. Kashta's eyes met his, and Estienne saw his own wariness reflected there. For a moment, neither man spoke, then Kashta offered a slight nod. There was no choice but to approach, and they both knew it.

The lights of the camp beckoned, and they urged their plodding mounts closer, Estienne leading Isaac's horse by the loose rein. Eventually they came to a halt atop a low rise, both men gazing toward the flickering torchlight that illuminated a half dozen fluttering tents. A trio of camels sat nearby, reclining in the evening breeze, and Estienne spied children among the robed nomads. A family perhaps, but still, it did not mean there would be no danger. Nevertheless, Kashta did not seem to fear as he kicked his horse's flanks and led the way closer.

As they drew nearer to the encampment, Estienne felt his nerves stretched taut. The faint sounds of voices carried on the night air and it all seemed so peaceful, so utterly removed from the danger that pursued them. For a moment, Estienne was struck by a pang of guilt. They were about to shatter that peace. What followed them through the desert would not relent. If Chatagai and his horsemen found these travellers, they would offer no mercy. Estienne and Kashta had brought death to these people's doorstep, as surely as if they attacked themselves.

Kashta raised a hand, signalling for them to slow their approach. Estienne followed his lead as he dismounted at the edge of the firelight, movements slow and deliberate. No sense in spooking these people who would hardly be expecting visitors out here in the desert.

Estienne nudged Isaac, who stirred sluggishly. With no little effort he helped the old man down from his horse, holding him steady as they followed Kashta toward the nomads.

A shout rang out from the camp – a challenge in Arabic that made Estienne's hand instinctively go to his sword hilt. Kashta stepped forward, hands held out in a gesture of peace. His voice, when he called back, was steady and clear, carrying an authority that seemed to still the very air around them. From the shadows of the camp came two men, perhaps the leaders of this travelling band, or the patriarchs of the family. Either way, they conversed briefly with Kashta, and for all Estienne could tell the greeting was cordial enough.

A small crowd began to gather around them, women and children allowing curiosity to overcome their fear, their faces a mix of suspicion and growing alarm. Estienne stood silent, acutely aware of the many eyes upon him.

As he watched, a young boy came forward. He held out what Estienne could only hope was water in the unmistakable bladder of a goat. Estienne didn't wait to find out, placing it to his lips and drinking deep, before he remembered his companion. Isaac took the skin gratefully, drinking with no less gusto, some light returning to his hooded eyes.

Then one man stepped forward – older than the rest, with a beard streaked grey and eyes that seemed to pierce the darkness. He spoke rapidly to Kashta, his tone sharp with questions. Kashta answered just as quickly, his words tumbling out in a torrent of explanation. Estienne watched in fascination as the Arabic flowed. He couldn't understand a word, but the urgency in Kashta's tone was unmistakable. The Moor's hands moved in expansive gestures, painting pictures in the air of riders on swift horses, of danger sweeping across the desert like a sandstorm. Estienne might not have grasped the words, but he recognised the moment when understanding took hold. The old man's eyes widened, his face paling visibly even in the dim firelight. He barked out a series of commands, and suddenly the camp was a flurry of activity.

Women began gathering children and belongings, while men rushed to ready their camels and douse fires. The atmosphere crackled with a sense of urgency, fear rippling through the crowd like wind through tall grass. They had succeeded in warning these people of what was coming, but now what? Where would they go? How long could they stay ahead of Chatagai and his relentless hunters?

As the last of the camp disappeared into tightly bound bundles, the old man who had first listened to their warning approached. He spoke briefly to Kashta, then turned to Estienne with eyes that seemed to see right through him. With a gesture that needed no translation, he beckoned for them to join the tribe's flight.

'They want us to travel with them?' he asked, knowing they could not possibly understand.

Despite that, Kashta offered a nod. Two of the nomads came forward, taking Isaac from where he leaned against Estienne's shoulder, with gentle ease. He was conveyed to a makeshift litter dragged behind one of the camels, where two women began ministering to him. Even as they did so, they spared Estienne more water, the eyes of the boy who offered it looking friendly, as though they had come from the desert bearing gifts, rather than the grim news of what pursued them.

Estienne could only marvel at their generosity. These people had no wealth. The most valuable thing they carried was water, and yet they gave it freely. These men from the desert had brought doom upon them, and yet they treated them as family.

Under the cover of darkness, they set out. The silence was eerie – no jingle of harness or creak of wagon wheel, just the soft padding of feet and hooves on sand. Estienne found it hard to comprehend how a group this size could move so quietly, but it was as if the desert itself was conspiring to hide their passage. He fell into step beside the nomads, casting a glance toward where Isaac lay, hoping the old man could hold on long enough for them to find some semblance of civilisation.

Then, glancing back the way they had travelled, he was

reminded that any moment Chatagai and his men might crest the horizon and fall upon them like a storm. Finding civilisation might be the least of their troubles.

32

The desert wind keened a mournful dirge as Estienne trudged alongside the caravan. Sand was listless beneath his feet, a reminder of how far he was from the verdant fields of home. The sun hung low on the horizon – a sight that might have been beautiful were it not for the constant dread that gnawed at his gut.

He cast a wary glance over his shoulder, half-expecting to see the dust cloud of Chatagai's riders, but there was nothing save the endless expanse of sand, stretching as far as the eye could see. Perhaps they had given up the chase. Maybe he feared only phantoms and memories. But perhaps the danger was still real. He had to assume Chatagai was as relentless as he feared, and carry on until he had reached safety.

Over the past two days, he, Isaac and Kashta had been treated like family among these nomads. They had all recovered quickly from their ordeal, and though far from the man he had been, Estienne was beginning to feel stronger already. He could only hope he would be strong enough to fight if Chatagai finally caught them.

The call went up from ahead for the caravan to halt. Time to rest for the night, to give their animals a chance to recover, and prepare for the journey to come. Estienne and Kashta helped erect the tents as they'd be shown over the previous nights while Isaac conversed with one of the clucking old women in their strange dialect. It had come as a relief to see how the old man had recovered. How the smile had returned to his face. Estienne could only hope that wasn't all ripped away by the men that pursued them.

A burst of laughter pulled him from his dark musings. At the edge of the camp, a group of children chased each other, their bare feet kicking up small clouds of sand. Their shrieks of delight carried on the wind, a stark contrast to the grim silence and snarled orders that had been Estienne's constant companion these past weeks as he was driven through the desert.

As he watched, one of the boys – no more than six or seven years old – stumbled and fell. Before Estienne could even think to move, an older girl was there, helping the lad to his feet. She brushed the sand from his robes with gentle hands, murmuring words of comfort that Estienne couldn't understand. The tenderness of the gesture struck him harder than he would expect. How long had it been since he'd witnessed such simple kindness? On the walls of Damietta, on the merciless Silk Road, in their flight across the desert – there had been no room for gentleness. Yet here, among this nomadic band, it flourished.

A shadow fell across him, and Estienne looked up to see Kashta towering over him. The Moor's eyes were fixed on the horizon behind them, his brow furrowed. Estienne opened his mouth to speak, then closed it again. Even after their shared ordeal, the barrier of language still stood between them, as vast as the walls of the city he had come to besiege. With Isaac otherwise engaged, that barrier was all but impassable, but when Kashta gestured back along their path, Estienne could not remain silent.

'Yes. We have to assume they are coming. And if they are, they'll catch up with us eventually.'

Kashta looked back at him for a moment, then placed a hand over his heart, gesturing towards the nomads with his other hand. Then he repeated the gesture, adding a sweep of his arm that seemed to encompass not just the nomads, but Estienne as well.

'We must protect them,' Estienne said. 'I know. I follow a code, Kashta. I am bound to it. I will give my life to protect these people, as they have risked theirs to save us.'

Kashta looked as though he might reply, but before he could a woman's voice rang out – a lilting call in Arabic that Estienne didn't understand. The children immediately ceased their play, scampering towards one of the tents that had been erected for the night's rest.

Kashta touched Estienne's arm, jerking his chin towards the gathering nomads. It was time for them to take their rest. He looked back at Kashta as he made his way to his own shelter and realised that despite all that had gone between them, they were united now, not by common tongue or creed, but by the simple, brutal fact of survival.

In his own hide tent, he sat on the mat given him by the nomads and listened to the silence of the desert. It was rudely interrupted by the shuffling feet of Isaac, as he squeezed inside and lay down opposite.

'Oh, I think that woman likes me,' he said, a wicked grin on his face.

'Does she like you enough to tell you where we are headed yet?' Estienne replied.

'From what I could glean, we are heading south through the desert of al-Nafūd. There is a port not too many miles away to the southwest. From there we should be able to find passage on a ship across the Red Sea, and take the road back to Damietta and safety.'

'So you have managed to unravel the tongue of these nomads at last?'

Isaac shrugged. 'Some of it. But other things you can just tell, my friend. Though she has not said it in so many words, I know that woman is smitten with me.'

'I am sure she is,' Estienne said, unable to disguise the note of scepticism in his voice. 'Especially when there's such a shortage of scrawny old men for her to take her pick from.'

Isaac struggled up onto his elbows, looking not a little hurt in the light of the flickering torch they shared. 'I have been around for many years, young Wace. Was married for thirty-three of those. Trust me, a man can tell.'

'I bow to your superior knowledge of such things.' Estienne lay on his back, closing his eyes in the hope that would be an end to it.

'Good that you... wait a moment... are you mocking me, Wace?'

'Not at all.'

'I may look old, but there is still plenty of life in this dog yet.'

'I have no doubt.'

'I think you do, Wace. I think you question my prowess.'

Estienne held his hands up in surrender. 'Forgive me. I yield. Isaac ben Berachiyah is unquestionably the most vigorous swordsman in the Levant.'

'There. Mocking again. I'd like to know exactly what you've done by comparison, Wace. How many women you have wooed.'

'Trust me, it is not many.'

'Exactly. And I'm sure you are too young to have ever known the true love of a woman. To have felt her in your arms. To have breathed in the scent of her hair as she slept at your side.'

A memory of Eva suddenly flashed, her dark locks, her eyes so intent on him, filled with hurt as he stood at the dock. The last time he had ever seen her. How he would have loved to have taken her in his arms that day. To abandon his duty, his thirst for a cause, and spend every night until his final night beside her. It was a dream shattered. One whose shards could never be put back together. By now she was most likely married to her Marcher lord. Lady of a powerful house. Perhaps even about to bear him a child...

'Apologies, my friend,' Isaac said, after the silence had stretched on. 'It was merely a jest. I did not mean to stir a hurtful memory.'

Estienne quashed the thought as best he could. He had tried to forget Eva. Fought to put that part of his life away, as he strove to build himself anew. It seemed that even a holy crusade and five hundred miles of desert could not erase her from his mind.

'It is nothing, old man. Go to sleep,' he whispered.

'Of course, my friend. Sleep well.'

In the dark he heard Isaac shuffle, making himself more comfortable. Guilt then, that he had responded so curtly, but her memory had cut like a knife. A memory that would not help him out here, when already faced with such peril. Best he lock it away. Bury it deep. It could do him no good any more.

* * *

He blinked away the remnants of a fitful sleep as he felt a gentle tug at his sleeve. At first he thought it might be Isaac, easing him awake, but as his bleary eyes focused he saw a young girl, no more than seven or eight years old, sitting beside him. Her dark eyes were wide with curiosity, fascination playing across her features as she regarded the strange man in their midst. For a moment, they simply stared at one another, before Estienne managed a small smile, hoping it looked friendlier than he felt.

'Hello, little one,' he said softly, knowing full well she couldn't understand a word.

The girl cocked her head to one side, studying him intently. Then, to Estienne's surprise, she broke into a wide grin and held out her hand. Nestled in her small palm was a stone – nothing remarkable at first glance, just another piece of the desert. But as Estienne leaned closer, he saw that it was shot through with veins of some pale mineral, creating a pattern that looked uncannily like a blooming flower.

'It's beautiful,' he murmured, reaching out to touch the stone.

The girl placed it in his hand with a solemnity that belied her years. Estienne turned it over, appreciating the beauty of it. Before he could thank her for the gift, she held out her other hand, this time clutching something that moved. Estienne leaned in, curious despite himself, and found himself face-to-face with a beetle. Its carapace shimmered with iridescent blues and greens, a riot of colour in this monotone land.

She giggled something in her native tongue. Though Estienne couldn't understand the words, her meaning was clear: *Look at this wonder I've found.*

For a moment, he was transported back to his own childhood. How many times had he brought some small treasure to his Aunt Marion? A flower from the farm, a bird's feather – each precious to his child's eyes. He'd thought those days long behind him, buried beneath the weight of duty and the brutality he'd witnessed. Yet here, in the heart of the desert, with killers nipping at their heels, this girl had still offered him something to smile about.

A shout from across the camp made them both start. The girl's mother was calling, her voice tinged with worry. The spell broken, the child scrambled from the shelter before scampering off toward her family's tent. Estienne watched her go, a strange ache in his chest. He looked down at the gifts she'd left him – the stone and the beetle, now crawling across his palm. Such simple things, yet they seemed to carry such weight. How blind he'd been to the beauty that flourished here, to the people who called this harsh land home. All he had come to do was conquer in the name of Christ, never thinking of the people who lived here. Estienne had been so consumed by his search for purpose, for meaning, that he had ignored what was right in front of him. Had forgotten the code he had been raised to follow.

He pocketed the stone and gently set the beetle down in the sand. As he did so, he caught sight of Kashta through the opening of his tent, watching him from across the camp. The Moor's expression was unreadable, but there was something in his eyes – a glimmer of understanding, perhaps.

Estienne stood, stretching his aching limbs, as the camp stirred to life around him. Already the camels were being loaded, tents broken, a new sense of urgency about the place. Another dawn, another relentless trek towards God knew where. He could only hope their deliverance would come soon.

* * *

The coastal port materialised from the shimmering haze like a mirage, its crumbling walls and leaning towers stark against the endless blue-green of the sea beyond. Estienne felt a surge of hope as he tasted the tang of salt carried on the breeze, a promise of salvation after days of relentless pursuit across the burning sands.

'We are saved,' Isaac breathed, unable to take his eyes off the place.

But as they drew nearer, that hope was replaced by a creeping dread that spread through Estienne like poison. When they were within a hundred yards, he could hear the port was silent. Empty. Abandoned.

The caravan picked its way through the debris-strewn streets, hooves clopping hollowly against sun-bleached cobblestones. The wind whispered through empty doorways and shuttered windows, carrying with it the ghosts of a town long silenced.

'What do we do now?' Isaac asked mournfully. 'Without passage across the sea we are trapped here.'

There was no way to answer. Estienne glanced at Kashta, seeing his own dismay mirrored in the Moor's eyes. They had pinned their hopes on finding a vessel when they reached the coast, some means of putting the vastness of the sea between them and their relentless pursuers, but the harbour lay as empty as the town, save for a few listing hulks half-buried in the sand, their timbers rotted by sun and salt.

The nomads spread out behind them, their initial relief at reaching the coast giving way to confusion and fear. Children clung to their mothers' robes, eyes wide as they took in the desolation. The old man who had first welcomed the three of them to their band shuffled forward, his weathered face a mask of despair as he surveyed what should have been their salvation.

Estienne led the way towards the dock, desperate for some sign of hope, some glimpse of a sail on the horizon. But there was nothing save the endless expanse of water, stretching away to meet the sky.

'God's wounds,' he breathed, the enormity of their situation weighing him down like armour. They had run out of land. Out of options. There was every chance Chatagai would be upon them soon. And then...

As the last vestige of hope threatened to abandon him, he heard Kashta speak. Looking up, he saw the Moor gesturing at something half-buried in the dunes near the dilapidated pier. He strode towards it with purpose, and Estienne followed, allowing hope to stir him just a little.

At the edge of the shore was a boat – battered and worn, its planks cracked, but unmistakably a vessel that might bear them across the merciless sea. Kashta turned to Estienne, a fierce light in his eyes. He gestured emphatically towards the boat, then out to sea, his meaning clear, even without words.

Estienne nodded, hope rekindling. But as he surveyed the damage – the gaping hole in the hull, the missing planks, the rotted rigging – he couldn't help but wonder if this was merely delaying the inevitable. Could they truly make this wreck seaworthy before Chatagai and his riders descended upon them?

Kashta, it seemed, harboured no such doubts. He was already striding back towards the nomads, gesturing and speaking rapidly in their tongue. Estienne watched as understanding dawned on the nomads' faces, and within moments, the beach was a flurry of activity. Men and women alike set to work, some digging the boat free of its sandy prison while others scavenged the abandoned port for anything that might aid in repairs. Children were set to gathering palm fronds and seaweed, to be used for caulking the leaks. Kashta directed the efforts with the authority of a ship's captain, his meaty hands gesturing as he assigned tasks.

'What do I do?' Isaac asked, looking more pitiful that ever as he stood at the end of the beach.

'Those eyes still work, don't they?' Estienne asked. 'Watch to the northeast. Any sign of horses, any sign of anything, you shout till your lungs burst.'

Isaac nodded, turning and shambling off as fast as he could back through the abandoned town.

For his part, Estienne pitched in with the boat where he could, hauling planks and helping to brace the hull as others worked to patch the gaping holes. As he laboured alongside the nomads he felt a growing sense of kinship with these strangers. They worked without complaint, their faces set with grim determination, and there was something to be admired about their stoic aspect.

He caught the eye of the young girl who had shown him the beetle, now busily weaving palm fronds into rope. She flashed him a quick smile before returning to her task, and Estienne felt a surge of affection for these people who had accepted him without question.

As the sun climbed higher, and sweat poured down Estienne's face, he pushed through the fatigue. Every moment they delayed brought Chatagai and his riders closer. Estienne could only pray their labours would be the swifter.

33

Dawn's light crept across the abandoned port, painting the crumbling buildings in bone-coloured hues. Estienne stood at the water's edge, eyes fixed on the battered vessel that was their last hope. The boat was frustratingly close to seaworthy, yet maddeningly incomplete. Each hammer on wood, each grunt of effort from the labouring nomads, seemed to echo his frustrations.

A noise rose above the sound of gulls, a distant shout that echoed over the crumbling rooftops. Estienne's gaze turned from the boat to the edge of the town, seeing Isaac in the distance, arms waving above his head. When he saw he had Estienne's attention he gestured to the northern horizon. Estienne scanned the desert for any sign of movement. What he saw made the breath catch in his throat.

There, in the distance, a smudge of darkness marred the pale morning sky. At first, he prayed it was merely a trick of the light, a mirage born of fear and exhaustion, but as he watched, the smudge grew, resolving into an all-too-familiar billowing cloud of dust.

'Shit,' Estienne breathed. Then, louder, the words bellowing across the seafront, 'They're coming!'

All around him, activity ceased for a heartbeat. Then, chaos erupted.

Kashta sprang into action, his deep voice booming across the beach. The nomads redoubled their efforts, their activity taking on a desperate urgency. Children who had been gathering seaweed now scrambled to load supplies onto the boat, their faces etched with terror.

Estienne's eyes met Kashta's across the throng of bodies. The Moor's face was set in grim determination, a mirror of Estienne's own resolve. Both knew they had run out of time. The boat was so close to being ready, but not ready enough. Now they knew what had to be done.

With a deep breath, Estienne hefted his sword. As the nomads continued their frantic repairs under Kashta's watchful eye, he turned toward the north and made his way along the path between those dilapidated buildings. As he did so, he saw Isaac, half running half stumbling toward him.

'They are coming,' he gasped. 'We must away.'

Estienne grabbed him by his frayed tunic. 'Listen to me. The boat is almost readied. Once it is launched, do not wait. Hoist the sail and row it as far out to sea as you can. Do you understand?'

Isaac eyes were wide with confusion. 'What... what are you going to...'

He stopped when he saw the blade in Estienne's hand and shook his head.

'It is what I have to do,' Estienne said, a strange calm falling over him. 'What I am meant to do.'

'But—'

'No time, old man. Get to the boat.'

Then he shoved Isaac toward the dock and carried on to the edge of town. With every step he steeled himself for what was coming, as that dust cloud grew larger with each passing moment. Estienne could just hear the thunder of hooves now, the whooping cries of their pursuers carried on the breeze. They had spied their quarry.

'God hear me,' Estienne murmured, reaching the eastern edge of the port and raising his blade. 'You have watched over me so far. Now grant me the strength to see those people safe.'

The thunder of hooves grew deafening as Chatagai and his riders crested the final dune. Their war cries carried on the wind, a chilling chorus that sent shivers down Estienne's spine. He tightened his grip on his sword, jaw clenched as he watched those ten riders bear down on the town like a sandstorm given flesh.

'Here,' Estienne bellowed, raising his arm to hail the coming riders. 'I am here, bastards.'

Chatagai, riding at the fore, reined in his steed, the others drawing to a stop behind him. His eyes glared with fury as he regarded his prey. Estienne felt a glimmer of satisfaction at that. He had intended to offer himself as a lure, and it was clear the horse lord could not resist the bait.

Bows were unstrung at Chatagai's spat his order, but Estienne darted towards the nearest building before they could loose. Its crumbling walls and empty windows offered scant cover, but it was better than facing the mounted warriors in the open.

The first volley of arrows hissed toward him as he ducked low. Estienne pressed himself against the weathered stone, feeling the impact of shafts striking the wall mere inches from his head. Dust and chips of masonry stung his face, and he allowed himself a heartbeat to steady his breathing before sprinting to the next piece of cover.

An arrow whistled past his ear, so close he felt it whip his hair. Another grazed his arm, opening a shallow cut that he barely registered in the heat of the moment. He weaved between the abandoned buildings, using every scrap of cover the ghost town offered. The frustrated cries of the pursuing warriors echoed off stone walls as they wheeled their horses along the tight streets, their prey eluding them. Estienne's legs burned with the effort, his lungs heaving as he pushed himself beyond exhaustion, managing to stay one step ahead...

A rider appeared suddenly around a corner, his mount's hooves clattering against the cobblestones. Estienne ducked and rolled, feeling the rush of air as the warrior's blade sliced through the space where his head had been a moment before. He came up in a crouch, sword at the ready, but the narrow alley worked against the mounted attacker. Before the rider could wheel his horse around, Estienne had sprinted into the maze of ruins once more.

The game continued – Estienne darting from shadow to shadow, the riders howling their frustrations, but they were relentless. Still, he led them on a merry chase through the abandoned port, drawing them away from the beach, hoping that Kashta, Isaac and the others would have enough time to launch the boat.

But he couldn't keep this up forever. Already his breath came in laboured gasps, a stitch burning in his side. It was only a matter of time before exhaustion or ill luck caught up with him.

Suddenly he heard the sound of boots on stone. Peering around the edge of one hovel he saw one of the riders had dismounted, abandoning his horse to pursue on foot through the narrow streets. Estienne's heart hammered – these hunters were closing in, and he was running out of options.

He rounded a corner and found himself in a small courtyard, the dried-up remains of a fountain at its centre. Three paths led away from the open space, but before he could choose which, a figure loomed from one of them.

The warrior's blade was drawn, eyes glinting with a predatory edge. Estienne raised his sword, muscles trembling with fatigue. He opened his mouth, whether to utter a challenge or a curse he wasn't sure which, but before he could, the warrior charged.

His blade sang as it came down in a lethal arc at Estienne's skull. He brought his own sword up in a desperate parry, the clash of metal-on-metal ringing all too loud in the cramped courtyard. The force of the blow drove Estienne back a step, his bare feet scraping on loose stones.

He recovered quickly, muscle memory taking over as he countered with a swift stab at the warrior's belly. His sword sliced through leather, sinking deep into armour and flesh, before he withdrew the blade as quickly as he had struck. The warrior's eyes widened in shock, a gurgling cry escaping his lips as his knees gave way.

Estienne had no time to catch his breath as he heard footsteps approaching along the other paths. Before he could even think to flee, two more warriors came stalking toward him from different directions. No way to escape even if he wanted to.

He brought his sword up in a guard position, sweat stinging his eyes as he prepared to face this new onslaught. The horsemen began to circle, looking to flank him, and he knew with grim certainty that he couldn't hope to fend them both off, not with his muscles screaming with fatigue, each breath an effort...

A blur of motion erupted from the shadows as a mountain of a man crashed into one of the warriors like a battering ram. Kashta, his massive hands closing around the horseman's throat and bearing him to the ground.

Estienne had no time to think on his sudden good fortune, as he darted at the remaining warrior. Steel clashed all too briefly, before Estienne scored a strike against the warrior's arm. The blade fell from his hand, his eyes widening with panic, before Estienne's backswing cut out his throat.

The man fell gurgling, the sound punctuated by a rhythmic clack of stone. Estienne turned to see Kashta astride the last warrior, a rock in his hand pounding the man's skull with bone-crushing force. The sickening impact and the spray of crimson was somehow satisfying, but Estienne fought down any sense of victory. They were not out of this yet.

'Come on,' Estienne urged. 'I think he's dead.'

Kashta froze, realising his enemy was defeated, before casting the rock aside and rising to his feet. For a moment they stood amid the carnage, chests heaving, eyes locked in a moment of understanding. They had been enemies once, sworn to kill one another. Now, improbably, they had to fight alongside one another, or they would surely die.

Kashta growled something in Arabic, the words meaningless to Estienne, but their urgency clear. Estienne nodded, and together they sprinted from the courtyard and through the narrow streets.

Estienne could still hear the sound of hooves, the whoop of the enemy. He ran in Kashta's wake, all thought of combat forgotten, hoping that the Moor had come to his aid because the boat was ready to leave.

Their mad dash brought them back to the waterfront, where the vessel bobbed at the edge of the surf. Nomads strained at the mooring ropes, the sail full, ready to carry the boat toward the open sea. Women and children huddled aboard, their eyes wide with fear as they watched Estienne and Kashta's approach. At the prow stood Isaac, gripping the rigging, eyes desperate.

Arrows hissed through the air as Estienne and Kashta sprinted across the beach. The boat was so close now, salvation within reach. Kashta leapt aboard first, his powerful frame landing with a thud that made the rickety vessel creak. He whirled around, arm outstretched, ready to haul Estienne to safety... but the sound of pounding hooves stopped him in his tracks.

Estienne turned, gripping his sword, seeing Chatagai astride his horse. The war leader's face was a mask of fury, his eyes burning with a rage that bordered on madness.

'Go,' Estienne said, still holding Chatagai's gaze. 'Get them to safety.'

Without waiting to see if Kashta heard or understood, Estienne strode to face his enemy, as Chatagai leapt from the saddle, sabre in hand. No salute. No word of acknowledgment. Their blades met with a sound like thunder, the force of it threatening to tear the sword from Estienne's grasp. He stumbled back, bare feet sinking into the wet sand at the water's edge.

Chatagai pressed his advantage, raining down blow after punishing blow. Each strike felt like it might shatter Estienne's sword, and he was dimly aware of the boat pushing off behind him.

With every swing, Chatagai snarled something in his language, spittle flying from his lips. Each word a curse on the man who had defied him. In reply, Estienne said nothing, saving his breath for the fight.

As Chatagai raised his sword for another crushing blow, Estienne saw his opening. With the last reserves of his strength, he feinted left. Chatagai, caught off guard, swung wide, and Estienne pivoted, bringing his blade up in a desperate arc.

Steel met flesh with a wet sound. Chatagai howled in shock as blood fountained from the ruin of his face, sword falling from his grip as he staggered back, landing in the surf with a splash.

For a moment, all was still. Estienne stood over his fallen foe, chest heaving, sword dripping crimson into the frothy water. Chatagai foundered as the waves lapped against his prone form, hand clamped to his face as blood spewed between his fingers. He glared with one hateful eye, defiant to the last, facing his end like a true warrior.

Estienne became aware of the shouts from across the beach, the whistle of arrows, the pounding of approaching hooves. With a final glance at Chatagai's beaten form, he turned and ran. The boat was a dozen yards from shore now, Kashta standing at its stern, arm outstretched. Estienne plunged into the water, exhaustion and his sodden clothes dragging at him with every step. He fought to swim against the waves, each stroke a battle, but just as his strength began to fail, Kashta's strong hands closed around his wrist. With a mighty heave, the Moor pulled him aboard, and Estienne collapsed on the deck, gasping for breath.

As arrows continued to splash into the water around them, Estienne raised his head. Through salt-stung eyes, he watched the shore recede, saw Chatagai's diminishing figure now standing at the water's edge, and even at this distance he could feel the weight of that hateful stare.

The makeshift vessel creaked and groaned as it cut through the waves, each swell threatening to overwhelm its patchwork hull, but he didn't care any more. As he gulped in great lungfuls of salt-laden air, every muscle in his body crying for mercy, he closed his eyes and succumbed to exhaustion.

34

The boat creaked and groaned as it approached the weathered docks of the small fishing port. Their journey across the Red Sea had been long, but against the odds, they had made it. The hull was starting to leak profusely, but between them they had managed to bail with enough effort to avoid sinking. It was not until the boat bumped against the worn timbers of the dock, that Kashta allowed himself a moment of relief. The air was thick with the stench of fish, a far cry from the desert winds they were accustomed to, but to Kashta, it smelled of salvation.

Leaping ashore, he watched as the Bedouins began to disembark, their faces etched with a mix of exhaustion and relief. One by one, the nomads stepped onto solid ground, their legs unsteady after days at sea. Children clung to their mothers, wide-eyed at the unfamiliar sights and sounds of the port. As they gathered their meagre belongings, many turned to Kashta, gratitude shining in their eyes. The elder, who had first greeted them those days ago in the desert, clasped Kashta's thick hand between his own.

'Blessings of the Prophet be upon you,' he said, his voice thick with emotion.

Kashta nodded, appreciating the sentiment. He watched as the old man turned to Estienne, repeating his thanks. The Frank stood awkwardly, clearly not comprehending the words, but the warmth in the old man's tone needed no translation. The trader, Isaac, received his own share of thanks, though he had contributed little to their survival. One of the older women showed him particular attention, which he appeared in no hurry to rebuff.

More of the Bedouins approached, offering their thanks in a flurry of words and gestures. Women pressed tokens into their hands – a woven bracelet, a tiny pouch of spices – small offerings that spoke the weight of their gratitude. Children darted forward to touch the tattered cloth of Estienne's shirt before being pulled back by their mothers, giggling at their own daring.

As Kashta observed this outpouring of thanks, he felt a sudden swelling of pride. These people, who had welcomed the trio despite the danger, were safe now. They would live to see another sunrise, to feel the desert wind on their faces once more. And he, Kashta ibn Assad, had played a part in their deliverance.

His gaze drifted to Estienne, who was awkwardly patting the head of a little girl who had latched on to his leg. The Frank's face was a mix of embarrassment and genuine warmth, his lack of understanding of their words not diminishing the impact of their thanks.

For a moment, Kashta allowed himself to see Estienne not as the enemy who had slain his brother, Wasim, but as the man who had fought beside him, and risked his life to save these innocent souls. It was a disconcerting thought, one that sent a ripple of unease through him. But as he watched Estienne crouch down to the girl's level, offering a gentle smile, Kashta couldn't deny the nobility he saw in the act.

The last of the nomads finally disembarked, leaving the three of them alone on the dock. The sounds of the port – the cry of gulls, the shouts of fishermen, the creaking of boats – washed over them. It was a moment of quiet amidst the chaos, a breath of relief between one challenge and the next.

Estienne turned to Kashta, his blue-grey eyes keen, despite the fatigue writ on his bearded face. For a heartbeat, they simply looked at each other, two warriors who had traversed a sea of sand and salt together, who had faced death and emerged victorious. Then Estienne spoke, his words incomprehensible to Kashta, but his tone friendly, almost warm.

'He wants to thank you,' Isaac said. 'He says without you, none of us would have survived.'

The weight of Kashta's vow to Wasim hung heavy in the air between them, a barrier as tangible as the language that separated them. He should kill this man, this Frankish knight who had taken his brother in arms from him. Honour demanded it. And yet, as Kashta looked at Estienne, he saw not just an enemy, but a man who had shown nobility and bravery in the face of overwhelming odds.

'Then I thank him in return,' Kashta said. 'He showed courage. Selflessness I did not expect his people capable of.'

Isaac relayed the words in the Frankish tongue. Estienne replied, eyes solemn, tone serious, before Isaac turned back to Kashta.

'He hopes, then, that his actions have made amends for the grievous wounds he has caused you. He is sorry for your brother and says he will pray for his eternal soul.'

Amends. Prayers.

All they had been through. All they had faced together, and yet… no. It still was not enough.

In that moment, Kashta realised he could not forsake his vow to Wasim – the debt of blood still stood. But neither could he strike down this man who had fought beside him, who had shown honour and courage in equal measure. Not here, not now, when the echoes of their shared trials still hung heavy.

'No,' Kashta said. 'He has not made amends. For now, I will honour the bond forged during our journey. I will allow him to return to his own people. But if Allah decrees that we should meet again on the field of battle, I will kill him.'

Isaac relayed the message. On hearing it, Estienne merely nodded his acknowledgment. Almost as though he had expected such an answer.

Kashta turned, eyes scanning the bustling port. Somewhere in this teeming mass, there must be someone who could guide Estienne and Isaac back to Damietta, back to the Frankish armies that still lingered on Egypt's shores.

His gaze fell upon a merchant. The man stood near a stack of crates, overseeing the loading of goods onto a merchant caravan. His rich robes and the deference shown to him by the workers marked him as a man of influence. Perfect.

'Wait here,' Kashta ordered, before approaching the merchant. The man looked up as Kashta drew near, wariness flickering across his features at the sight of the imposing Moor.

'Peace be upon you,' Kashta said, offering a slight bow. 'I have a proposition that may be of interest – were you to grant me the time to speak it.'

The merchant's eyebrow arched. 'Oh? And what might that be?'

'Your caravan is heavily laden. Are you by any chance headed to the city of Damietta?'

The merchant screwed up one eye and spat on the ground. 'As if I would trade among the Franks. They are a curse upon our lands.'

'Because if you were, I might be able to offer you a rich reward for a small service.'

That piqued the man's interest, and he rubbed his stubbly chin thoughtfully. 'Well... if I was headed to Damietta, what might I have to do for such a reward?'

Kashta gestured back towards Estienne. 'You see that man? He is a Frankish knight, one of great importance to the Christian armies.'

The merchant's eyes narrowed as he studied Estienne. 'He looks more like a beggar to me.'

'Appearances can be deceiving. He has endured great hardships, but I assure you, he is a warrior of renown among his people.'

The merchant stroked his beard thoughtfully. 'And what is it you propose?'

'I ask that you return him, and his companion, to Damietta. The Franks would reward you handsomely for the safe return of one of their own.'

The merchant scoffed. 'And risk the ire of the sultan for aiding his enemies? I think not.'

Kashta leaned in closer, his voice dropping to a conspiratorial whisper. 'Think, my friend. The Franks now control the flow of trade through the mouth of the Nile. A man in your position could benefit greatly from their gratitude.' He could see the wheels turning in the merchant's mind, greed warring with caution, and pressed his advantage. 'Besides, is it not written that kindness to a stranger is a virtue in the eyes of Allah?'

'Very well,' the merchant said with a sigh. 'I will see your Frank and his old man safely to Damietta. But if this brings trouble upon my head, it will be on your conscience.'

'You have my thanks. May Allah guide your journey.'

The deal struck, Kashta returned to Estienne and Isaac, who had been watching the exchange with curiosity. 'The merchant has agreed to take you both back to Damietta. For a price I am sure you would be more than happy to pay.'

A crooked smile crossed Isaac's face. 'I am confident we're good for it.'

'Then go swiftly. I doubt this place will remain safe for either of you much longer.'

Isaac bowed his gratitude, speaking quick words to Estienne, before he approached the merchant himself. Kashta was left alone with Estienne, his sworn enemy. A man he had fled across the desert with. Fought beside. Bled beside.

They regarded one another for one final time, a silent mark of respect between warriors on opposite sides of a conflict neither of them had started. Then, with a final nod of acknowledgment, Estienne turned and made his way towards the caravan.

Kashta watched as they were both greeted with some warmth, the promise of wealth cooling the merchant's temperament toward the foreign invader. It was not long before that caravan began to trundle its way from the port, making its way northward, Isaac offering one last wave farewell. The Frank did not offer Kashta so much as a backward glance.

As the caravan dwindled to a speck on the horizon, Kashta felt a curious mix of emotions. Pride, that he had honoured his debt to Estienne. Regret, that circumstances had cast them as enemies when they could have been brothers in arms. And beneath it all, Kashta knew that their paths may well cross again, and when they did, there would be no room for brotherhood between them.

For now, his own path was clear. He needed to return to al-Kamil, to rejoin the fight against the invaders. The sultan would need every warrior in the battles to come... and Kashta would prove his worth once more.

PART THREE: THE ROAD TO CAIRO

EGYPT – 1221 AD

35

The merchant caravan ground to a halt just beyond the gates of Damietta, the groan of wooden wheels giving way to the cacophony of a bustling city. Estienne's journey had been interminable, days bleeding together until time itself lost all meaning. But he was here. He had made it.

As the merchant, who had already revealed himself to be of distinctly uneven temper, began barking orders at his men to unload, Estienne took in the scene before him. The relief he had expected to feel at the sight of Damietta's walls crumbled like brittle wood, replaced by a growing dismay.

The streets beyond the gate seethed with chaos. Drunken men staggered between market stalls, their raucous laughter mingling with the angry shouts of vendors. A fight broke out near a tavern, fists flying as onlookers cheered. The stench of unwashed bodies, rotting food and human waste assaulted Estienne's nostrils, making him gag.

This was not the righteous Christian stronghold he had envisioned returning to. This was Sodom reborn.

'Good to be back?' Isaac asked.

'Good that the journey is over,' Estienne replied. 'But the destination leaves a lot to be desired.'

Both men climbed down from the cart as the merchant's voice cut through the clangour, his Arabic loud and urgent. Estienne turned to him, and saw his face twisted in a scowl of impatience.

'He demands the payment he was promised for bringing you here,' Isaac said. 'In gold.'

'I have no coin,' Estienne admitted. 'But tell him I can get it. I just need time to—'

'No need,' Isaac said with a grin.

'What do you mean?'

There was a sudden twinkle to the old man's eyes. 'On the way here, I have watched as this man has done business. I think there is a gap in his mercantile dealings that I can fill. There is a way he and I may profit much more than a single payment of gold. I have worked the streets of Damietta for many years. I know many contacts. Routes of trade. Officials prepared to turn a blind eye for the right rewards. This man shouts and spits, but he is reasonable beneath it all. I am sure I can persuade him to partner with me in a new endeavour based in this very city. So just leave the payment to me.'

'But I—'

'Trust me on this. It is sound business.'

Estienne took the old man by the shoulders. 'I don't know how to thank you.'

Isaac took his hand. 'You already have, Estienne Wace. My bones would be bleaching in the desert were it not for your courage. Now go, before I begin to get sentimental.'

'Good luck, Isaac,' Estienne whispered.

'Shalom, my friend.'

As he walked away, leaving Isaac to his dealings, the weight of circumstance began to bear down. He was alone now, in a city gone mad, without a coin to his name. His only chance was to return to the church of the Templars and throw himself upon their generosity once more. He could only hope Hoston would be pleased to see him after so long.

As he pushed his way through the teeming streets, his eyes fixed on the distant spire of the Temple church. Surely there, among his brothers in faith, he would find some semblance of order in this madness. Some reminder of the holy purpose that had driven him to these shores.

A drunkard stumbled into his path, reeking of cheap wine and puke. Estienne sidestepped past him, ignoring the man's slurred curses. All around, the city pulsed with a feverish energy as crusaders and locals alike cavorted in the streets, their revelry a mockery of the pious devotion Estienne had once imagined would fill this place.

When at last he reached the temple, its imposing facade was a stark contrast to the tumult surrounding it, but as he pushed open the heavy wooden doors, that spark of hope was quickly extinguished. The building stood empty, its vast hall echoing with nothing but the sound of his footsteps. The quiet was oppressive, broken only by the muffled sounds of the city beyond.

'Shite,' Estienne breathed, instantly regretting cursing in such a holy place.

He walked back out into the street, his mind reeling. When he saw a passerby, who looked to be a celebrant of some sort, Estienne hailed him with a raised hand.

'The Templars,' he said, gesturing towards the empty church. 'Where are they?'

'Gone,' the man replied with a shrug. 'Left to defend their

fortress of Athlit from al-Mu'azzam, the emir of Damascus. Been gone for weeks now.'

Estienne felt his last hope crumble. Weeks. He had missed them by weeks. Now he was truly alone, adrift in a sea of strangers, with no idea where to turn or what to do next.

As he stood there in nothing but rags, with no friends left in this alien land, he could only wonder what was left for him. This crusade, that had seemed so righteous, so clear in its purpose, now felt lost. He had seen the face of the enemy, had broken bread with them, had fought alongside them against a common foe. How could he raise a sword against men who were, in the end, not so different from himself? Not that he had a sword to raise any more.

The actions of Francesco, that idealistic monk who had sought peace through understanding, echoed in his mind. Had the man been right all along? Was there another path, one that didn't end in blood and sorrow?

He closed his eyes, feeling the warmth of the sun on his face. When he had set out on this journey, he had been so certain of his path, so sure of the righteousness of his cause. Now, standing amidst the wreckage of those lofty ideals, he felt more lost than he had in the trackless wastes of the desert.

'Estienne? By God, can it be?'

The voice, achingly familiar, cut through his despair like a knife. Estienne opened his eyes and there, pushing through the crowd with a look of utter disbelief, was a face he had thought he might never see again.

'Amalric?' Estienne breathed, scarcely daring to believe it.

The knight closed the distance between them in a few long strides, his handsome face breaking into a wide grin. Without hesitation, he enveloped Estienne in a tight embrace.

'We thought you dead,' Amalric said. 'When your ship was lost... Christ's bones, man, where have you been?'

Estienne felt the first glimmer of hope he'd felt since returning to Damietta. 'It's... it's a long story, my friend. One you might not believe even if I told you.'

Amalric clapped him on the shoulder, steering him away from the abandoned temple. 'Well, you look like you could use a drink. Come, tell me everything.'

Amalric led him to a makeshift tavern at the end of the road. As they settled at a rough-hewn table and Amalric ordered wine, Estienne began to recount his harrowing journey. He spoke of the shipwreck, of his capture by slavers, of the brutal march across the desert, of Isaac. He told of Kashta's relentless pursuit, of their unlikely alliance against the eastern horse warriors. All the while Amalric listened in rapt attention, his eyes widening with each new part of the tale. When Estienne finally fell silent, drained by the recounting, Amalric shook his head in wonder.

'It truly sounds like a journey beyond endurance. Yet you have endured it. And now, returned to us as if by miracle. Surely this is a sign from God, my friend. He has preserved you through these trials for a purpose.'

'Perhaps you're right,' Estienne said, managing a small smile. 'Though I'm not sure I'm the same man who left these shores those months ago.'

'No,' Amalric smiled. 'By the sounds of it, you are even more courageous. But there are things you should also know. In your absence, the crusade has stalled, mired in political infighting. However, rumours of a push southward are circulating, whispers of a grand offensive that would strike at the very heart of al-Kamil's territory. Not that you should be concerned. I imagine you would want to return home after what you've been through?'

Estienne thought on that for a moment. Fact was, he had no home. Not any more. As far as he could surmise, he had three paths before him: seek out the Templars at Athlit, abandon the crusade entirely and return to Europe, or stay and continue the fight alongside Amalric and the Order of Saint Mary.

His gaze drifted to the bustling street outside the tavern. To the degradation that had seized the city they had fought so hard for in God's name. For a moment, the temptation to flee, to wash his hands of this whole bloody affair, was almost overwhelming. Why should he continue the fight when he had seen so much more now? The fierce dignity of Kashta, the quiet strength of the nomads they'd saved, the unexpected generosity of al-Kamil. The Saracens were no longer faceless enemies to be cut down in the name of God. They were people, as complex and contradictory as any he'd known.

'I… I don't know what I should do, Amalric,' Estienne admitted. 'How can I raise my sword against men I've broken bread with? Men who showed me mercy when they could have left me to die? Am I to believe God still wishes for me to fight these people?'

Amalric leaned forward, his face earnest. 'Don't you see, Estienne? The fact that you're here, that you survived such adversity, it must be a sign. He has tested you in a trial of the desert and found you worthy. You've been delivered from slavery and returned to us. Surely that means something.'

Estienne's brow furrowed as he considered that notion. Was it truly divine providence that had seen him through his ordeal? Or merely blind luck?

'Maybe you're right,' Estienne said at last. 'God has delivered me back to Damietta. I cannot refuse him. But look at me, I am in no condition to—'

'Details, Wace. Once you are fed, rested, you will be a warrior of God once again.'

'You paint a hopeful picture, Amalric.'

'Then it's decided. You will return with me to the garrison of Saint Mary. You will feast, recover. And then we shall see what God has in store for you.'

Estienne glanced down at his rags. 'I pray he has a bath in store, before anything else.'

Amalric barked a laugh, clapping Estienne on the shoulder and they made their way from the tavern. As he followed his friend, Estienne still knew the path ahead was far from clear, and the doubts that had taken root during his long exile still gnawed at his resolve. But at least he was no longer alone.

36

Kashta crested the final rise, eyes weary after days of relentless travel, but they widened at the sudden sight before him. Al-Mansurah, that walled city on the banks of the Nile, had undergone a transformation so profound it took his breath away.

Where once stood humble mud-brick dwellings and simple marketplaces, now loomed walls of sun-baked stone, their imposing height punctuated by watchtowers that thrust skyward. The city had become a fortress, a bulwark against the tide of invaders that threatened to sweep down from the north.

As Kashta approached, the distant clamour of the city grew louder, shouted orders, hammering, and the clash of steel on steel. Preparations for war. The notion was enough to set his heart racing. In all the time he had been away, it seemed that the conflict still raged between his people and the Franks.

The gates of al-Mansurah yawned before him, a maw of weathered wood and iron-studded beams. Guards in polished lamellar stood sentinel, their eyes sharp beneath the rims of their baydahs. Kashta felt their gazes upon him as he approached, assessing, wary, but they made no move to stop him.

As he strode beneath the shadow of the gate, the full scope of al-Mansurah's transformation revealed itself. The streets teemed with soldiers, their spearheads glinting in the fading light. Everywhere he looked, Kashta saw signs of a city girding itself for war. Blacksmiths hammered at white-hot metal, the ring of their work echoing across the rooftops. Fletchers sat in doorways, nimble fingers affixing feathers to arrow shafts with practised ease.

In the time since he'd left to pursue his vendetta, al-Kamil had clearly been far from idle. The sultan had gathered his strength here, transforming al-Mansurah into a bastion of Saracen might. It was a city that breathed war, every stone and timber infused with it.

Kashta shouldered his way through the press of bodies, his eyes constantly moving, taking in every detail. He passed a group of men struggling to manoeuvre a massive trebuchet into position atop the city walls, its wooden frame creaking ominously. Nearby, a cluster of boys no older than twelve listened intently as a grizzled veteran demonstrated the proper grip for a spear. The sight of boys so young being instructed in the ways of war sent a chill down Kashta's spine. But then, he had been such a boy once.

As he made his way deeper into the heart of the city, he couldn't shake the feeling that he had stepped into a world utterly changed. The air thrummed with a palpable sense of anticipation that set his nerves on edge. Whatever storm was brewing on the horizon, it was clear that al-Kamil meant to weather it here. And now Kashta had returned to offer his blade once more to al-Kamil's service... but would the sultan even have use for one more warrior in this sea of might?

As Kashta began to wonder where he might find his former master, a familiar voice cut through the din. 'By Allah's grace, can it be? Kashta ibn Assad, returned from the dead.'

Kashta turned, a smile breaking across his face as he recognised Hijaz, a mamluk in service to the sultan, pushing his way through the crowd. The two men embraced, clapping each other on the back with the familiarity of warriors who had shared both triumph and hardship.

'Hijaz, you old jackal,' Kashta said, holding the man at arm's length to study him. 'It is good to see you. I'd have thought some Frankish blade would have found your throat by now.'

Hijaz laughed, a booming sound that drew curious glances from passersby. 'Let myself be slaughtered by foreign dogs, and miss the chance to see your ugly face again? Never.' His expression sobered as he took in Kashta's travel-worn appearance. 'But where have you been, brother? We thought you lost. You just disappeared.'

'It's... a long tale, my friend. One best told when I have rested.'

'I've no doubt,' Hijaz replied, his eyes narrowing shrewdly. 'But you are back now. And you intend to fight beside your brothers once again?'

Kashta nodded. 'Aye. I will offer my blade once more in service to the sultan and our people.'

Hijaz's expression grew grave. 'Then be warned, brother. The sultan may not look kindly upon your long absence. Much has changed since you left, and al-Kamil's mood has grown... intemperate.'

'I must try, Hijaz. I've not given up on what was promised to me. Land of my own. Serving al-Kamil is the surest path to that end. If I can persuade him I am still loyal, still willing to fight in his name with courage, then I may yet see that reward made real.'

Hijaz studied him for a long moment, then clapped him on the shoulder. 'Your courage was never in question, my friend. I pray Allah grants you favour in the sultan's eyes. But tread carefully. The Franks gather their strength to the north, and tensions run high within these walls. One wrong word, one misstep...'

'Fear not, Hijaz.' He grasped his friend's shoulder in return. 'I've not come this far to falter now.'

With a final embrace, the two men parted ways. As Kashta continued towards the sultan's palace, Hijaz's words echoed in his mind. The path ahead was fraught with danger, but he had crossed deserts and faced death to return here. Whatever al-Kamil's judgement might be, Kashta would face it with the same iron resolve that had seen him through so many trials.

It was with no small amount of trepidation that he reached the palace gates. Men stood guard, barring his path, but it took only a few words for them to recognise the great Kashta ibn Assad, and grant him entry. Those same guards guided him across the gardens to the palace proper and shadowed him as he entered.

Within, the sultan's audience chamber was a study in opulence. Intricate mosaics adorned the walls, their jewel-toned tiles catching the light of a hundred oil lamps. The air was thick with the cloying scent of incense, mingling with the distant aroma of spiced meat over open flame that made his empty stomach grumble.

And there, upon a pile of cushions, al-Kamil himself, surrounded by courtiers and his jandariyah – men more than willing to die in the service of their sultan. Kashta stood before him, head bowed in deference, every muscle taut. He could feel the weight of the sultan's gaze upon him, keen as a razor against his neck. The silence stretched, pregnant with unspoken judgement.

'Kashta ibn Assad.' When al-Kamil spoke, his voice was as sharp as a sayf. 'The prodigal warrior returns after disappearing like water under the high sun. Tell me, what brings you back to us after so long an absence? Surely not loyalty to your master.'

Kashta knew he danced on a knife's edge, but he kept his tone measured. 'Great Sultan, I come to offer my blade once more in service to you and to Allah. I have wandered far, but my heart has always remained true to your cause.'

Al-Kamil's eyes narrowed, his bejewelled fingers drumming a staccato rhythm on his knee. 'Your heart? Your heart led you to abandon us, to forsake your duty in pursuit of... what?'

Only the truth would do now. Al-Kamil would see through a lie as easily as looking through glass. 'I followed the man who slew my brother, a Frank who was taken along the Silk Road, so that I might kill him.'

'A personal vendetta? And while you chased shadows across the desert, your brothers in arms bled and died defending our lands from the Frankish dogs.'

The rebuke stung, but Kashta accepted it without flinching. 'You speak truly, my Sultan. I have no excuse to offer, save that I believed my actions were the right ones. I was wrong, and I accept whatever punishment you deem fit for my transgression.'

A murmur rippled through the assembled courtiers, but al-Kamil silenced them with a sharp gesture. He leaned forward, his gaze boring into Kashta.

'Let us not talk of punishment. Let us instead talk of forgiveness, and its price.'

'Anything. I would offer anything.'

'What about loyalty? Devotion?'

'You have it, my Sultan.'

'But what assurance can you give that you will not abandon us again when the whim takes you?'

Kashta raised his head, meeting the sultan's eyes with unwavering resolve. 'From this day forward, my life is yours to command, great al-Kamil. My blade, my blood, my very breath – all are pledged in service to you and to Allah. I swear by all that is holy, I will not falter again.'

Al-Kamil's expression remained impassive, giving no hint of his thoughts. The tension in the chamber was palpable, as Kashta stood tall under the weight of that scrutiny. He had laid bare his soul, offered everything he had. Now, his fate rested in the hands of the man before him, a sultan who held the power of life and death with the merest flick of a finger.

Al-Kamil leaned forward, and the ghost of a smile played at the corners of his mouth. 'Very well, Kashta ibn Assad. I accept your pledge. It gladdens my heart to have my lion returned to the pride.'

A wave of relief washed over Kashta, so powerful it nearly brought him to his knees. My lion. The term spoken with such authority, it filled him with a fierce pride.

He was home at last.

'You have my eternal gratitude, Great Sultan,' Kashta said, bowing low. 'I swear, I will not disappoint you.'

Al-Kamil's eyes glinted in the lamplight, a hint of steel beneath the warmth. 'See that you don't. A storm is coming, and when it breaks, I intend to unleash you upon our enemies.'

With a final nod of dismissal from his sultan, Kashta backed away. As he strode from the audience chamber, his mind whirled. Relief at his acceptance warred with anticipation of what was to come. He had dreamed of peace, of a plot of land to call his own, but it seemed Allah had other plans before that could happen.

All he had been through, all he had sacrificed, would now have to be forgotten. For he was Kashta ibn Assad, the sultan's own lion. And when the Franks came once more, his roar would shake the earth beneath their feet.

37

The clash of steel rang out across the sun-splashed courtyard, a staccato rhythm punctuated by grunts of exertion and the scuff of boots on stone. Estienne's muscles burned as he raised his shield to catch Amalric's blow, and he revelled in it. Sweat stung his eyes, but he blinked it away, focused entirely on his opponent's next move.

Amalric pressed forward, his practice sword a blur of motion. '*Komm schon, mein freund. Zeig mir, was du kannst.*'

Estienne's brow furrowed as he parsed the words. Almost five months among the German-speaking knights of the Order of Saint Mary had gifted him a rudimentary grasp of their tongue, but Amalric's fast-paced speech still often left him struggling.

'Slower, if you please,' he replied in Latin, their common tongue when the barriers of language proved too much.

Amalric laughed. 'I said, come on, my friend. Show me what you can do.'

A smile tugged at Estienne's lips. 'As you wish.'

He lunged forward, his practice blade singing. Amalric

parried, but Estienne had anticipated it and feinted left, then spun right, bringing his sword up in a swift arc that caught Amalric's weapon near the hilt. With a deft twist, he sent the sword clattering to the stones.

'*Sehr gut*,' Amalric said, rubbing his sword hand.

Estienne lowered his blade, chest heaving as he caught his breath. The exertion felt good, a reminder of how far he'd come since his ordeal in the desert. When he'd first arrived at the Order's compound, weak and wasted, he could barely lift a sword. Now, after months of training, he felt almost whole again.

Almost.

'*Dank dir geht es mir von tag zu tag besse*,' Estienne said. *I get better every day, thanks to you.*

'And your Deutsch improves,' Amalric said as he retrieved his fallen sword. 'Soon you'll be talking like a true Teuton.'

Estienne chuckled. 'God willing, though I fear my accent will always betray me.'

They made their way to a stone bench beneath the spreading branches of a fig tree. As they sat in its shade, Estienne's gaze wandered over the peaceful courtyard. Palm fronds rustled in the warm breeze, a far cry from the cold, damp halls of Pembroke Castle, yet in the months since his return, it had become a sort of home.

'It gladdens my heart to see you whole again,' Amalric said. 'The Order is stronger for your presence.'

'It wouldn't have been possible without the generosity of the grand master,' Estienne replied, his hand drifting to the hilt of the fine sword he'd been gifted, that leant beside the bench.

He'd pledged it to the service of the Order, to the grand cause that had brought them all to this sun-baked land. But as he sat in the peaceful courtyard, the riotous sounds of the city beyond the walls a constant reminder of the world they sought to conquer, he couldn't help but wonder if he had made the right decision. It might have been better if he had abandoned this crusade altogether and returned... where? There was nowhere he could call home now, and in the past months he had become as brothers to the men of this Order. Without them, he would have been nothing but a vagabond on the streets of a foreign city.

The tramp of feet on stone pulled Estienne from his thoughts. He looked up to see a young squire hurrying across the courtyard, his face flushed with exertion.

'Sirs,' the boy called out. 'The grand master summons all knights to the great hall. At once.'

Estienne exchanged a glance with Amalric, seeing his own bemusement mirrored in his friend's eyes.

'Come,' Amalric said, rising to his feet. 'It seems our day of leisure is at an end.'

As they followed the squire towards the great hall, Estienne felt a flutter of anticipation in his gut. There had been no movement among the crusading factions for months. Now it appeared something might be afoot.

The great hall of the Order of Saint Mary thrummed with noise as knights filed in, their whispered conversations creating a low, expectant hum. Estienne followed Amalric through the press of bodies, and as they found a place near the back of the hall, his eyes swept over the assembled knights. He recognised the brothers he'd trained with, men who had become, if not quite friends, then at least comrades in this strange land.

'What do you think this is about?' Estienne asked, keeping his voice low.

Amalric shrugged. 'Who can say? The grand master has been locked in talks with the other leaders for weeks. Perhaps they've finally reached some sort of agreement.'

Before they could speculate further, a hush fell over the assembled knights. Estienne craned his neck to see Hermann of Salza stride onto the dais at the front of the hall, his bearded face grave as he surveyed the crowd. The grand master's presence commanded the attention of all convened, without a word spoken.

'Brothers,' Hermann began, his voice carrying easily to the farthest corners of the room. 'I have summoned you here to share news of great import. Our long wait may finally be at an end. Duke Ludwig of Wittelsbach has arrived in port, bringing with him a sizeable fleet and fresh troops.'

A murmur of excitement rippled through the crowd, but Hermann raised a hand for silence.

'But that is not all,' he said, his eyes gleaming. 'The Duke brings word from the Holy Roman Emperor himself. Frederick is to join us, and soon, but he requests that we do not wait. We are to press south, take Cairo in his name and reclaim the True Cross.'

Estienne felt Amalric tense beside him. This was it. The moment they'd all been waiting for.

'Brothers,' Hermann declared, his voice ringing with conviction, 'prepare yourselves. The time has come to carry Christ's banner into the very heart of Saracen lands.'

The hall erupted in a chorus of cheers and shouts. Knights clapped each other on the back, faces alight with fervour. But as Estienne stood amid their celebration, he couldn't shake a nagging sense of unease. The notion that the enemy they faced, the heathen Saracens, were not the monsters they had been made out to be, but merely men defending their own faith.

He pushed the thought aside, focusing instead on Amalric's beaming face. This was what they'd come for, after all. A chance to strike a decisive blow for Christendom.

'Grand Master,' a voice called out through the din, 'what of John of Brienne? What says the King of Jerusalem to this plan?'

Hermann's face remained impassive, but Estienne thought he detected a hint of tension. 'King John's counsel has been... cautious. He urges restraint, argues that we should consolidate our hold on Damietta before pressing further inland.'

Murmurs of discontent cut through the room. It seemed that despite an edict from the Holy Roman Emperor himself, there was still disharmony among the leaders of this venture.

'Brothers, I will not deceive you,' the grand master said, clearly sensing the doubts forming. 'The path ahead is fraught with danger. The Saracens are weakened, yes, but far from broken. Cairo lies over a hundred miles to the south, beyond the limit of our ships and supply lines. But it is for this very purpose that we have come to the Holy Land. To carry the light of Christ into the darkness, to reclaim Outremer from the infidel. Will we falter now, when victory lies within our grasp?'

'*Deus vult*!' someone cried in answer.

It provoked a roar of approval from the assembled knights, a thunderous affirmation that shook the rafters of the hall.

Hermann of Salza raised his arms, his voice rising above the clamour. 'Prepare yourselves, brothers. In the days to come, we will march south, towards Cairo and glory. May God guide our swords and shield us from harm.'

The hall erupted once more, knights drawing their swords and raising them high, their voices united in a thunderous cry: '*Deus vult*! God wills it!'

Amid that tumult, Estienne could only stand rigid, unmoved by their zeal. As they filed from the hall, Amalric clapped a hand to his shoulder.

'Well, brother, it looks as though we will have our chance to fight side by side once more.'

Estienne gritted his teeth, looking out across the courtyard, past the trees to the blue sky beyond. It was so peaceful now. A calm before the storm they were about to inflict.

'I… I don't think I can, my friend.'

He spoke the words without thought, but meant them just the same. Despite how craven he felt for admitting it, Estienne knew he could not join the Knights of Saint Mary in their fight. This crusade, this invasion, was over for him.

'What do you mean?' Amalric said, brow furrowing in confusion. 'You are stronger than ever. More than a match for any man among the Order. The great Black Lion will roar—'

'It's not that, Amalric. It's…' What was it? A loss of faith? A loss of nerve? No, it was nothing he had lost, but rather something he had gained. 'A have met these Saracens. I have seen them for who they are, with all their faults and virtues. They are not our enemy, Amalric. And I cannot make war against them. Not now.'

He expected his friend to rage, to demand a real reason, to call him a coward. Instead Amalric's expression softened.

'I am sorry, Estienne. After all these weeks we have been together I never once saw the pain you have suffered. What you endured. Of course I understand, my friend. You will need time.'

Estienne wanted to tell him that wasn't it. That no amount of time or healing would restore his fervour for this crusade. Instead he placed a gentle hand on Amalric's shoulder.

'Thank you. I will explain myself to the grand master. I will thank him for his hospitality and leave this place on the morrow.'

Amalric shook his head. 'You will not. You will remain here. You will grow strong again. And when we return victorious from Cairo you can greet us as the brother you are.'

The notion brought a smile to Estienne's face. The

generosity almost overwhelmed him, and he clasped Amalric's arms tight.

'Then you'd best make sure you come back in one piece, *mein freund*.'

'Oh, I intend to,' Amalric replied.

Estienne clapped him on the back, as they made their way back to the garrison. Though it pained him to abandon these men who had become as brothers, he knew it was the only thing he could do. His fine sword, that gift to him, would remain in its scabbard until there was a fight worthy enough for him to draw it.

38

Estienne leaned against the rough stone of an arched window, his eyes fixed on the bustling streets below. The clamour of the city – shouts of merchants, braying of donkeys, the constant hum of a thousand voices – seemed muted within these walls, as if the very air conspired to maintain the sanctity of this place.

With the Order of Saint Mary gone south alongside the rest of the crusader army, Damietta had become a place of peace. Gone were the preachers and the rowdy mercenaries, and with them the sense of righteous purpose that had pervaded the streets. Without it, Estienne's decision to remain behind had seemed more rational with every passing day. The zeal with which he had sailed to these shores, and faced death upon the city walls, had all but vanished. Now it felt as though his mind was his own once again. If God truly intended his servants to retake the Holy Land, then Estienne was not part of that plan.

A knock at the door of his chamber pulled Estienne from his musing. After he beckoned them enter, a novice of the Order of Saint Mary came in, a sealed parchment clutched in his hand.

'A letter for you, Ser Estienne,' the boy said, offering the missive with a slight bow. 'From Grand Marshal Hermann von Salza himself.'

Estienne's brow furrowed as he took the letter. News from Hermann could only mean tidings of great import, and the weight of the parchment in his hand felt suddenly ominous. With a murmured word of thanks, he dismissed the novice and broke the seal.

Ser Estienne Wace,

I write to you with a heavy heart and grave tidings. Three days past, as our column traversed the arid lands north of the town of Sharamsah, we were set upon by Saracen horse archers. They struck without warning, their arrows sowing chaos and death among our ranks. Though we were better prepared than our last sojourn into enemy territory, bearing tall shields to defend against such attacks from mounted archers, we were still surprised by the suddenness of their ambush.

In this moment of crisis, it grieves me to report that your brother in arms, Amalric von Regensburg, distinguished himself with valour befitting a true knight of our Order. Witnessing the disarray of our forces, he took it upon himself to rally a counterattack, and with lance in hand, he led a charge against our attackers.

Amalric's bravery was beyond question, his skill in battle a testament to his courage and faith. Yet, even the mightiest warrior can fall prey to overwhelming odds, and in the heat of the melee, Amalric found himself cut off from our main force. Though he fought with strength and valour, he was ultimately overwhelmed.

It pains me deeply to inform you that Amalric was taken captive by the Saracen forces. We attempted to reach him and bring him back to our lines, but the tide of battle turned against us and we were forced to retreat, lest we lose more brave souls to the desert sands.

I know you and Amalric shared a bond forged in the fire of our holy mission. His loss is felt keenly by all who knew him, and I can only imagine the depth of your grief. Take solace, if you can, in knowing that Amalric comported himself with honour to the last, embodying the highest ideals of our Order.

We continue south, burdened by this loss but resolute in our purpose. Pray for us, Ser Estienne, as we shall pray for Amalric's deliverance. May God guide our swords and shield us from harm.

With heavy heart,
Hermann von Salza
Hochmeister of the Order of Saint Mary

The parchment slipped from Estienne's numb fingers, falling to the floor with a soft rustle. The room seemed to spin around him, the walls closing in as the full weight of the news crashed over him.

Amalric. His friend, and brother in arms. The man who had saved his life, more than once, now lost, at the mercy of an enemy who had little cause to show him any.

A wave of guilt and grief washed over him. He should have been there. Should have been fighting alongside Amalric, watching his friend's back. Instead, he had been here, safe within these walls, while Amalric faced the Saracens alone.

For long moments he sat there, as the bright of day darkened, and with each passing moment a fierce resolve took root within him. He could not abandon Amalric to his fate. Whatever it took, whatever the cost, Estienne would find a way to save his friend.

Twilight cast ominous shadows across the city, as he left the sanctuary of the garrison and made his way into the streets of Damietta. Eventually he reached his goal – the marketplace, teeming with life, a riot of colour and sound that assaulted his senses as he pushed his way through the crowds. Merchants hawked their wares, competing with one another for the loudness of their cries, the air thick with the mingled scents of spices, animals and roasting meat. On any other day, the vibrant energy of the place might have lifted Estienne's spirits. Now, it only served to underscore the urgency of his task.

His eyes scanned the sea of faces, searching for one in particular. Isaac had to be here somewhere, among the tangle of stalls and awnings. The old trader might be Estienne's best hope – perhaps his only hope – of finding a way to reach Amalric.

A familiar voice caught his ear. There, near a stall piled high with bolts of brightly coloured silk, stood a familiar figure. Isaac's weathered face was creased in concentration as he haggled with a merchant, his gnarled hands gesticulating as he argued his price. He looked to have recovered almost entirely from their ordeal in the desert, becoming weightier in the face and belly, and it appeared business was back to booming.

Estienne shouldered his way through the press of bodies, heedless of the angry mutters that followed in his wake. 'Isaac,' he called out, not bothering to hide the urgency in his voice. 'Isaac, I need to speak with you.'

The old man turned, surprise writ in the deep lines of his face. Whatever deal he had been negotiating was forgotten as he moved from behind his stall and spread his arms in greeting.

'Estienne? It has been too long since we saw one another.' He took in Estienne's worried features. 'What's wrong, my friend? You look troubled.'

'Is there somewhere we can talk privately?' Estienne replied, glancing around at the curious onlookers.

Isaac nodded, gesturing to a boy nearby to watch his stall, before leading Estienne away from the bustle of the main square. They ducked into a narrow alley, the sounds of the marketplace fading to a distant murmur. Here, in the relative quiet, Estienne felt he could breathe again.

'Now,' Isaac said. 'Tell me what's happened.'

The story relayed in Hermann's letter poured out of Estienne in a torrent, his voice tight with emotion as he recounted its contents. He spoke of the Saracen ambush, of Amalric's capture, of his own guilt at allowing his friend to ride off into danger alone.

'I have to do something, Isaac,' Estienne said, finally. 'I can't just sit here while Amalric lies imprisoned by the Saracens. But I don't know where to begin. I don't even know where they're holding him.'

Isaac let out a long, weary sigh. 'This is no small task you set yourself, my friend. To seek a single man captured by the forces of al-Kamil… it would be like searching for a grain of sand in the sea.'

'I don't care,' Estienne growled. 'I'll scour every inch of this cursed land if I have to. Amalric would do no less for me.'

Isaac looked at the ground, deep in thought. 'Perhaps there might be a way. I have… connections. Friends among the merchants who travel the roads and river from Damietta to Cairo. Men who keep their ears to the ground and their eyes open. If anyone knows where your friend is being held, it will be them. I will travel with you, and together we may be able to find your lost friend.'

Estienne felt a sudden surge of hope. 'Isaac, I… thank you. I know I have no right to ask this of you, after everything you've done for me already.'

'You saved my life, Estienne. More than once. Consider this a repayment of that debt. But you must understand, the lands south of Damietta are fraught with danger, even in times of peace. And these are far from peaceful times.'

'I understand, Isaac. But I must try. Amalric... he's more than just a fellow knight. He's my friend. My brother. I can't abandon him.'

'Very well. Then we shall go. God knows we've seen enough suffering in recent times. If there's a chance to save even one life...'

Estienne reached out, clasping Isaac's shoulder with a grip that spoke volumes. 'Thank you. I will have horses secured for our journey. We can leave at first light.'

Isaac shook his head. 'No. The road is too dangerous, as your friend has already proven.'

'Then by ship?'

'Of course. Supply vessels ply the Nile daily. All we need do is secure passage on one of them. It's the swiftest way to Sharamsah – far quicker than travelling by land.'

'But not without risks of its own.'

'Indeed,' Isaac replied, sucking a breath through his teeth. 'But it's a risk we must take. The river is our best chance.'

Estienne nodded, his hand unconsciously drifting to the hilt of his sword. 'You're right, of course. If you can secure us passage, I will gather my arms and meet you at the dock by sunrise.'

'Very well,' Isaac said with a bow. 'I will head to the dock and arrange our passage. Try not to be late.'

As he watched Isaac scurry off into the crowd of the market,

Estienne knew he would not be late. A life depended on it. One he might have to give his own to see spared.

39

The Nile stretched before them like a great black serpent, its waters reflecting the fading light of day. Estienne stood at the prow of their small vessel, his eyes scanning the shoreline for any sign of movement. Behind him, the creaking of worn timbers and the soft splash of oars cutting through water were the only sounds that broke the eerie silence.

Three ships made up their scanty convoy, each one barely seaworthy. Estienne's gaze drifted to the vessel directly behind them, its hull patched with planks of mismatched wood, the sails little more than tattered rags. The one in front was no better as it plied the way ahead.

'I must apologise again for the state of our transportation,' Isaac's voice came from behind him, tinged with embarrassment. 'It was the best I could secure on such short notice.'

Estienne turned, offering a smile of conciliation. 'No need for apologies, my friend. I am thankful you managed to find us passage on anything so quickly.'

Isaac nodded, his weathered face etched with concern. 'Still,

I fear we may be inviting disaster. These waters are treacherous enough on a sturdy ship. On this…' He gestured at the worn planks beneath their feet.

'We'll make do,' Estienne said. 'We have to.'

As night began to fall, casting long shadows across the water, the air grew increasingly tense. A rustle in the reeds along the bank caught his attention, but it was only a water bird taking flight, its wings beating a frantic rhythm as it disappeared into the gathering gloom.

With a relieved sigh, he made his way below deck. There were no berths within the supply ship, but a makeshift bed of straw had been laid out on the sacks of grain bound for the crusader camp to the south.

Estienne lay himself upon it, listening to Isaac's gentle snoring and the lap of oars beyond the hull. It was just as he was drifting towards sleep that the night exploded into chaos.

His eyes snapped open at the sound of panicked screams, and he lurched to his feet. Bolting across the darkness of the hold he took the stairs to the deck in two bounds. Arrows hissed through the air to greet him, thudding into wood and lashing through sail. He just caught sight of the captain hauling on the tiller in panic, and nearly lost his balance as the ship lurched beneath him.

'We're under attack!' The cry went up, followed by shrieks of pain and terror as more arrows whipped from the dark.

A sickening orange glow illuminated the river behind them. Estienne turned to see the rearmost ship engulfed in flames, Greek fire coating its deck in a hellish blaze. Men writhed in agony, their flesh melting as they threw themselves into the Nile, desperate to escape the inferno.

Another volley of arrows arced overhead. One struck the

helmsman squarely in the throat, and he crumpled to the deck, blood spurting between his fingers as he clawed at the shaft. The tiller, suddenly free, began to lurch wildly.

Without hesitation, Estienne lunged for it, his fingers closing around the smooth wood just as the ship began to veer dangerously towards the shore. He threw his weight against it, muscles straining as he fought to bring them back on course.

'Row, damn you,' he roared at the oarsmen below, some of whom had abandoned their posts in panic and leapt overboard. 'Row or we're all dead.'

Fire bloomed along the larboard gunwale as a pot of naphtha smashed against the hull. The acrid stench of smoke filled Estienne's nostrils as he struggled with the tiller, before another pot of Greek fire sailed over their heads, missing the deck by mere inches to splash into the water beside them.

'Estienne.' Isaac's voice cut through the din, and the old man appeared at his side. 'What can I do?'

'Keep the men rowing,' Estienne grunted, teeth gritted with effort. 'And pray to God that the sail doesn't go up in flames.'

He spared a glance up at the sail, billowing dangerously close to the fire that raged to larboard. Two men were doing their best to douse it with buckets, but they were hampered by the incessant rain of arrows that lashed across the deck.

A scream of splitting timber drew his attention up ahead, to where the lead ship was foundering. It had been rammed by another Saracen vessel and now warriors swarmed its deck, their sabres flashing in the firelight as they cut down the crew.

'Faster,' he urged the rowers, his voice almost hoarse. 'Put your backs into it.'

As if in answer to his command, the oars ploughed the water with renewed haste. Estienne's eyes scanned the river ahead, searching desperately for some way past the two ships that were locked together.

There, in the gloom – a narrow gap between those vessels and the shore. It was their only chance.

'Hold fast,' he called out, setting his jaw as he angled the tiller toward the tight passage. 'This is going to be close.'

The narrow gap loomed before them, a maw of jagged rock on one side, ready to tear their fragile vessel to splinters. Estienne's knuckles whitened on the tiller as he guided them towards it, every muscle in his body taut with concentration.

'Oars up!' he bellowed, just before they entered the passage.

The rowers complied, those oars rising as one. More arrows whipped over the deck and one of the crew fell screaming, but Estienne held firm, eyes fixed ahead, as the rock wall seemed to loom over them. A scraping sound from the starboard side sent a shudder through the hull. Splinters flew. Men cried out in alarm.

'Hold fucking steady,' Estienne growled through gritted teeth.

To larboard, the sounds of battle raged on. The lead ship was now fully overrun, Saracen warriors swarming its deck like rats on a carcass, and the screams of the dying carried across the water, punctuated by a clash of steel. Estienne's jaw clenched, knowing there was nothing he could do for them now.

An arrow whistled past his ear. Another thudded into the deck near his feet. The Saracens had noticed their escape attempt.

'Archers,' Isaac's voice rang out in warning.

Estienne looked up to see another pot of Greek fire arcing through the air towards them. Time seemed to slow as he watched its trajectory, knowing that if it struck, they were finished, and he threw his weight against the tiller. The ship heeled hard to starboard, timbers groaning in protest. The pot of fire splashed into the water mere inches from their rail, sending up a geyser of flame that licked at the side of the ship, but there was no time for relief. Their starboard side veered dangerously close to the rock wall, and Estienne dragged back on the tiller to right them.

A scrape like nails across granite. The crack and splinter of wood, as the hull shrieked and rock tore into it. Then, suddenly, they were through, the passage opening up to reveal a wider stretch of river beyond.

Estienne's legs nearly gave out beneath him as the tension drained from his body.

'We made it,' someone yelled, stating the bloody obvious.

Estienne realised his hands were shaking as he released his grip on the tiller. Behind them, the sounds of battle were already growing fainter, the narrow passage they'd navigated acting as a barrier between them and their pursuers. But there was no time for celebration. They had survived, yes, but at what cost? Two ships lost, all those lives snuffed out in the blink of an eye.

'Check for damage,' Estienne ordered, now there was no captain to speak of. 'And tend to the wounded. We're not safe yet.'

As the crew scrambled to obey, he shot a last glance behind them. The orange glow of fire still lit the night sky, but the sounds of battle had faded into the night, leaving an eerie silence. Estienne allowed one of the crew to take the tiller and moved to the rail. The blood that had coursed through his veins during the ambush was ebbing now, leaving him feeling hollow.

'A miracle,' Isaac murmured, coming to stand beside him. 'By all rights, we should be dead.'

'God smiles on us again,' Estienne replied.

'Aye, that he does. And he seems to hold you in particular

favour, Estienne. All the more reason for me to stay close at your side.'

Isaac flashed him a wink, before making his way across deck to help the other crewmen with their hasty repairs. Estienne watched him go, wondering if he was right – if God truly was watching over him... or if he was just one lucky bastard.

40

The ship groaned like a dying beast as it limped into the harbour of Sharamsah. Estienne surveyed the town, once a quiet Saracen settlement, now a supply point from which the crusaders could strike further south toward Cairo. Ships of all sizes jostled for position, their decks swarming with men loading supplies and readying rigging. The air thrummed with a disharmony of shouted orders, all blending into a discordant symphony of martial fervour.

'Barukh Hashem, we have made it,' Isaac whispered at his side.

'We haven't made it yet, my friend,' Estienne replied, as their ship bumped against the weathered planks of the dock.

'Can we not revel in but one victory, before you blunder toward the next?'

That brought a smile to Estienne's face he hadn't expected. 'Revel all you like. But let's do it on the move.'

The gangplank was lowered, and as he and Isaac made their way ashore the clamour of the harbour washed over them – the grind of weapons being sharpened, the nickering of horses, the shouts of men preparing for war.

As they made their way along the bustling quayside, Isaac laid a gnarled hand on Estienne's arm. 'I'll seek out my contacts, see what I can learn of your friend's fate. If any of them are still here, that is.'

Estienne nodded. 'And I'll see if I can find Hermann of Salza. Discover if he knows any more of what happened to Amalric on the road south. We'll meet back here at the dock when the bells chime for nones.'

With a nod, they parted ways, each disappearing into the press of bodies that thronged the harbour. Estienne threaded his way through the narrow streets of Sharamsah, each step revealing how thoroughly the crusaders had stamped their presence upon the town. As he passed abandoned market stalls the calls of local merchants were silent. In their place stood makeshift forges, the rhythmic clang of hammers on anvils punctuating the air as mail was mended and weapons sharpened.

The scent of roasting meat wafted from impromptu cookfires, mingling uneasily with the stench of unwashed bodies. Estienne's hand instinctively went to the hilt of his sword as he passed a group of mercenaries, their eyes hard and calculating as they appraised him. Suddenly spurred by a newfound sense of urgency, he asked a passerby where he might find the Order of Saint Mary and was directed toward the town's central square.

There he found Hermann of Salza in what had been transformed into a command post for the Order. The black cross on white fluttered from a dozen banners, as men he recognised prepared for war in their own way – muttering prayers, oiling weapons, brushing down steeds. The grand master stood to one side, reading a missive, his brow furrowed in concentration. As

Estienne approached, Hermann looked up, surprise flashing across his bearded features.

'Estienne Wace,' he said. 'I did not expect to see you here.'

Estienne inclined his head in respect. 'After receiving your letter, I came with all haste, Grand Master.'

'To what end?'

'To find Amalric and see him liberated.'

Hermann shook his head almost imperceptibly. 'That... may be a trial too far, Estienne.'

'Perhaps. Perhaps not.'

A shadow passed over Hermann's face. 'I will admit, when I saw you I had hoped you had come to join our cause. To take Amalric's place and march south with us to Cairo.'

Estienne shook his head. 'That is no longer my cause. And neither do I think it God's will.'

Hermann's eyes flashed with annoyance. 'So you have lost faith?'

The accusation stung, but Estienne held firm. 'My faith remains, Grand Master. But perhaps not in the righteousness of our deeds here. I've seen too much blood spilled, too many lives shattered in the name of Christ. At what point do we ask ourselves if this is truly God's will, or merely the ambitions of men?'

A heavy silence fell between them, broken only by the routine sounds of the camp. Hermann's face was unreadable, a mask of stone that betrayed nothing of the thoughts churning behind those piercing eyes.

'Such doubts are... understandable,' he said at last, his voice softer now. 'But I cannot afford to entertain them, Estienne. Not when so many look to me for guidance, for certainty in this uncertain endeavour. I do not have the luxury of being able to question the Pope's wishes, or those of the Holy Roman Emperor.'

Estienne nodded, feeling the weight of the grand master's burden as if it were his own. 'I understand. And I do not judge you for what you must do. I only came to ask if there was anything further you could tell me about Amalric's capture? Anything that might offer an answer to where he was taken?'

'I wish there was. But all I know, I wrote in the letter I sent you.' Hermann stepped forward, clasping Estienne's shoulder. 'Your loyalty to your friend does you credit, Wace. Would that all men showed such steadfastness in these dark times.'

'I thank you, Grand Master. And hope to return your brother to your side, if I can.'

'And for that, you do yourself credit, my young friend. May God go with you.'

With a final nod of respect, Estienne turned to leave. As he made his way back through Sharamsah's streets, he passed a building that had once been a mosque, its graceful minaret now overshadowed by a hastily erected wooden cross. The incongruity of it struck Estienne hard. Was this truly God's will? To strip away the beauty and tradition of one faith, only to replace it with the trappings of another?

As he neared the docks, the crush of bodies grew denser, the air thick with the mingled stink of men and beast. Eventually he found himself at the water's edge, the lapping of waves against weathered pilings a soothing contrast to the chaos of the port.

The sun hung low on the horizon by the time he finally spotted Isaac. The old merchant made his way closer, cloak wrapped tight about him, despite the balminess of the evening.

'What news?' Estienne asked as Isaac drew close.

'My contact believes the prisoners have been taken to Baramun, before they are sent on to al-Mansurah. Little over ten miles upriver from here. Your friend, if he lives, would likely be among them. But we must act swiftly, the town will likely be abandoned once your Frankish friends continue their move south.'

'Then that's where I must go,' Estienne said, wondering how he would even start such a journey.

'I?' Isaac said, incredulity dripping from the word. 'Surely you mean we?'

Estienne shook his head. 'No. This will be dangerous enough for me alone. I can't ask you to take such a risk. Besides, you have done enough already.'

The old man's eyes flashed with determination. 'You ask nothing, my friend. I offer freely. Have you forgotten the debt I owe you? My life, saved more than once by your hand. I may be an old merchant, hard-bitten by life, but I have not forgotten the meaning of friendship... or of honour.'

Estienne opened his mouth to argue further, but he could see the steel settling behind Isaac's eyes. He had seen it before, in the eyes of stronger and more dangerous men, but it was steel just the same.

'Very well. How do you think we should proceed?' he asked. 'I take it we can't just stroll through the gates of this town?'

A glimmer of mischief replaced the hard edge in Isaac's eyes. 'I have some tricks up my sleeve, young Wace. I can play the part of a slaver easily enough – it's a role I've had to adopt more than once in my travels. And you' – he gestured to Estienne's imposing frame – 'you can be my silent, menacing bodyguard. Who would question such a pair come to trade in captured prisoners?'

For a long moment, Estienne weighed the proposal. It was mad, fraught with danger, and yet, what other choice did he have?

'That might well see us through the gates, but what then?'

'Then we'll face that bridge when we come to it,' Isaac finished for him, a wry smile tugging at the corners of his mouth.

Estienne couldn't help but chuckle, feeling some of the tension drain from his shoulders. 'Very well. We'll enter Baramun together and... we'll work out the rest as we go.'

Isaac's smile widened. 'Now you're thinking like a true merchant, Estienne. Sometimes the best plans are those that leave breadth for invention.'

'Let's hope you're right,' Estienne replied, turning back toward the dock. 'But first, we need another boat.'

41

Oars sliced through the black waters of the Nile, each stroke sending ripples across the river's surface. Estienne's muscles burned with the effort, but he dared not slow his pace.

Isaac sat hunched at the prow, his wrinkled face a mask of concentration as he scanned the shoreline. As they neared it, Estienne could make out the looming silhouette of Baramun's walls against the star-strewn sky, the town crouching on the riverbank like some hungry reptile, patient and watchful.

'Easy now,' Isaac whispered, his voice barely audible above the gentle lapping of water. 'Bring us in slow and quiet.'

'What do you think I'm going to do, old man?' Estienne shot back. 'Bang a drum and herald our arrival?'

Isaac shrugged his apology as Estienne pulled in the oars. The boat's momentum carried them the last few yards to the shore, where they ground to a halt on the muddy bank with a soft scrape that sounded deafening in the stillness of the night.

As they clambered out of the boat, Estienne scanned the shore for any sign of waiting Saracens. There was nothing but the distant keen of chirruping insects, and the lap of the river against the bank.

'Remember,' Isaac said as they began to make their way towards the city, 'you're my silent bodyguard. Not a word, no matter what happens. Understood?'

Estienne grunted in acknowledgment as he began to wrap a length of cloth around his head and face to hide his western features. The disguise was flimsy at best, but it would have to do.

As they drew closer to the gates, he could make out warriors patrolling the walls, their silhouettes stark against the night sky. The path into the city lay open, but armoured spearmen stood barring the way. Isaac stepped forward without hesitation, his bearing suddenly transformed. Gone was the stooped old man Estienne had come to know. In his place stood a bold character, his voice ringing out in confident Arabic as he hailed the guards.

Estienne held his breath as the guards responded, their voices sharp with suspicion. He caught Isaac announcing his name amidst the flurry of foreign syllables, answered by what he could only assume were demands for explanation. Isaac gestured expansively, his tone by turns cajoling and imperious. The exchange seemed to stretch on for an eternity, each moment pregnant with the possibility of violence. Estienne's palms grew clammy with sweat, every instinct screaming at him to draw his sword, to fight his way through, but he held himself in check, trusting in Isaac's quick tongue.

Finally, one of the guards laughed and they stood aside, allowing Isaac and Estienne to pass. One of them even offered a bow of respect. Isaac turned, a triumphant gleam in his eye, and jerked his head towards the narrow opening.

As they passed through the gates, Estienne felt the weight of a dozen suspicious gazes upon him. He kept his eyes fixed straight ahead, praying that his wariness didn't show through his disguise, and with each step deeper into Baramun he felt as though he were walking into the belly of the beast itself.

The streets unfolded before them, a labyrinth of shadow. Estienne's eyes darted from darkened doorway to shuttered window, every nerve straining for some sign of imminent threat. The town seemed to hold its breath, the usual bustle of life muted by the lateness of the hour and the heat that still hung in the air like a sodden blanket.

Isaac moved with surprising sureness, his steps quick and purposeful. Estienne found himself struggling to keep pace, acutely aware of how conspicuous they must look – a hulking figure, his face hidden, trailing in the wake of a wizened old man.

'We head towards the barracks,' Isaac said in a hushed voice. 'If Amalric is here, that's where they'll be keeping him.'

Estienne nodded, not trusting himself to speak. If they were caught, there would be no mercy, no chance for explanation or appeal, and he kept his jaw clamped tight to remove any risk he might give them away.

As they rounded another corner, the barracks came into view. The building loomed before them, a squat, fortress-like structure that seemed to radiate menace. A pair of guards stood to attention before the main entrance, their spears glinting dully in the moonlight.

Isaac didn't hesitate, striding forward with the confidence of a man who belonged here, as Estienne hung back, his hand once again straying to his sword hilt as he watched the old trader approach the guards.

The following staccato exchange of Arabic washed over Estienne. He watched the guards' faces, searching for some hint of their intentions, but their expressions remained impassive. After a brief back and forth that ended with Isaac rubbing finger and thumb together in the universal gesture for coin, one of the guards nodded curtly and led the way inside. Isaac turned, beckoning Estienne forward with another slight jerk of his head.

All he could do was follow, trusting to the deftness of the old man's subterfuge.

Inside, the courtyard beyond was dimly lit, the air thick with the mingled scents of sweaty bodies and burning lamp oil. Isaac paused, exchanging a few quiet words with their guide before turning to Estienne.

'Wait here,' he whispered. 'I'll go with the guard to... negotiate. Remember, not a word.'

Before Estienne could protest, Isaac was gone, disappearing into the depths of the barrack building with their host. Left alone in the unfamiliar surroundings, Estienne felt suddenly exposed. He pressed himself against the wall, trying to make his bulk as inconspicuous as possible, and settled in to wait.

Time crawled by with agonising slowness. Estienne's every sense strained for some sign of Isaac's return, or any hint of danger. The distant murmur of voices echoed from within the building, and with every passing moment he willed Isaac to cease his wittering and get to the end of the negotiation.

Footsteps approached from across the courtyard.

Estienne tensed, pressing himself further into the shadows. A figure rounded the corner – another guard, his hand resting casually on the hilt of his sword. The man's eyes widened slightly as they fell upon Estienne, then narrowed with sudden suspicion.

'*Man 'ant*?' The guard's voice was sharp, demanding.

Estienne's mind raced. He opened his mouth, but no words came. What could he say? How could he explain his presence without giving everything away?

The guard's hand tightened on his sword hilt. '*Yujibuni*.'

Panic surged through Estienne. He had to act. Do something. Anything.

He lunged forward, hand grasping the back of the guard's head, fist connecting with his jaw, once twice, three times until he sagged. As the man's eyes rolled back in his head, his body going limp, Estienne caught him before he could fall, the sudden dead weight nearly pulling them both to the ground. Heart pounding, he dragged the unconscious guard into a nearby alcove, praying that no one had heard the commotion.

No time for regrets. He had to find Isaac before the unconscious man was discovered. Had to get them out of here before everything fell apart.

Estienne moved swiftly toward the barrack building and grasped the handle of the door. Gritting his teeth he turned it, pushing the door open to reveal a small chamber within. Isaac sat laughing, a cup of wine in his hand, deep in animated conversation with the guard who had led him away. For a moment, Estienne could only stare.

The laughing stopped as Isaac regarded him, panic slowly spreading across his face. The guard looked at Estienne, then back at Isaac, then Estienne again. His hand flew to his weapon but Estienne was faster. A quick, brutal strike, knuckles smashing against a second jaw, and the man crumpled to the floor.

Isaac blinked up at him, alarm on his weathered face. 'Could you not have waited but a little longer? I was starting to get somewhere with my negotiations.'

'Change of plans,' Estienne growled, hauling the old man to his feet. 'Negotiations are over. We need to move. Now.'

Isaac nodded. 'The prisoners. I know where they're kept.'

He bent, fumbling at the unconscious guard's belt. A soft

jingle of metal and Isaac straightened, a ring of keys clutched in his gnarled hand.

'This way,' he hissed, pushing past Estienne and into a corridor.

They moved swiftly, as Isaac led them deeper into the barracks, down twisting corridors that all looked the same to Estienne's eyes. A final turn brought them to a heavy wooden door, and Isaac's hands shook as he tried key after key, each failure sending a fresh spike of fear through Estienne's gut.

A click. The door swung open with a groan that seemed to echo through the entire building.

The stench hit them first – the reek of unwashed bodies mixed with the tang of piss. As Estienne's eyes adjusted to the gloom, he made out a row of iron-barred cells. And there, huddled in the furthest corner...

'Amalric,' Estienne breathed.

His friend's head snapped up at the sound of his name. Amalric's face was gaunt, his once-proud bearing now sallow, but his eyes lit up with recognition.

'Estienne? By God's grace, what are you—?'

No time for reunions. Estienne snatched the keys from Isaac, fumbling with the cell's lock as Amalric struggled to his feet. In the other cells, more figures stirred – half a dozen knights, their faces a mix of hope and disbelief.

The lock clicked and Estienne hauled the cell door open, enveloping Amalric in a brief embrace before turning to the other prisoners.

'Quickly,' he urged, moving from cell to cell. 'We don't have much time.'

As the last lock fell away, Estienne turned to Isaac. The question he'd been avoiding could no longer be ignored.

'What now? How do we get out of here?'

Isaac's face fell, the reverie of their success giving way to dawning horror. 'I... I don't know. I never thought we'd get this far.'

'All right then,' Estienne replied. 'One thing at a time. Let's just get out of this building.'

Isaac nodded, leading them back along the maze of corridors and out into the night. The half dozen knights followed in silence, their bare feet making no sound on the rough stone floor. Isaac paused, glancing about the courtyard, and Estienne squinted through the dark, seeing the way they had entered now stood unguarded. A rare beam of fortune shining upon them.

He led the way, darting across the open ground, drawing his sword in case of an unwelcome surprise. Then they were out on the street once more.

'Which way?' Estienne hissed.

Isaac opened his mouth to answer, when the clang of a bell shattered the night's silence. Estienne's blood ran cold.

'The docks,' Isaac hissed. 'This way.'

He led them down a narrow alley, with more vigour than Estienne would have thought possible from those old limbs. Shouts echoed behind them. The thud of running feet. There was no sign of anyone yet, but it wouldn't be long before they were spotted.

Estienne spared a glance behind, seeing the knights keeping pace, Amalric helping one of his fellows who looked to have a wounded leg. When they finally emerged onto the riverfront there were boats bobbing at anchor, but the sound of voices raised in anger were still hounding them, not too far behind.

A solitary rowboat bobbed on the jetty, its lone occupant frozen in surprise at their sudden appearance. No time for niceties. Estienne barrelled forward, and at his aggressive advance, the man leapt into the water with a yelped curse.

'Get in,' Estienne ordered, already shoving the boat away from the dock.

The freed prisoners scrambled aboard, the small craft sitting dangerously low in the water under their combined weight. Estienne and Amalric seized the oars, straining against the current, and no sooner had they pulled off than a cry went up from the docks.

Torchlight flared as guards poured onto the waterfront.

'Faster,' Isaac yelped, his voice urgent with fear.

Estienne's muscles burned as he pulled at the oars. An arrow hissed past, all too close. Another splashed into the water beside them. Not long before one found its mark.

'Keep your heads down,' he growled.

The shouts from the shore grew fainter as they powered their way along the Nile. Estienne focused all his energy on the rhythmic pull of the oars, aided by the current, and before long the sounds of their pursuers faded in the distance.

Heaving in breath, he and Amalric slowed their frantic rowing and allowed themselves a satisfied smile.

'I think that went rather well,' Isaac grinned from the prow. 'There is no way they will pursue us toward the armies waiting to the north.'

'Sure,' Estienne replied, when he could breathe again. 'But next time we do this, maybe an actual plan, eh?'

'As you wish, my friend,' Isaac chuckled. 'As you wish.'

42

The first light of dawn crept across the sky as Estienne's weary arms pulled at the oars. Beside him, Amalric rowed in time, his movements sluggish but determined. In the stern, Isaac dozed among the other liberated men, the old man's face etched with exhaustion.

As they rounded a bend, the jetty of Sharamsah came into view. Even in the dim light of morning, Estienne could make out figures moving at the water's edge.

'We're nearly there,' he murmured, more to himself than his companions.

Amalric grunted in acknowledgment, his grip tightening on the oar as he put his back into one final push. The boat's prow cut through the water with more speed, and as they drew closer, shouts of recognition rang out from the shore.

'Look,' someone cried. 'Those men. Help them.'

The boat bumped gently against the jetty, and eager hands reached down to secure it. Estienne stumbled as he climbed onto the wooden planks, and a strong arm steadied him. He and the other knights were helped up onto solid ground, men crowding them, patting backs in welcome and uttering prayers of thanksgiving. Estienne watched as Isaac was helped ashore, the old trader's face creased in a weary smile as he nodded to those who greeted him.

'Come,' Amalric said, tugging at Estienne's sleeve. 'We should find the encampment of my Order. A warm meal and a proper rest are long overdue.'

Estienne hesitated, looking to where Isaac stood. 'I will, but... there's something I need to do first.'

Amalric nodded. 'Of course. Find me when you're done. We have much to discuss.'

As Amalric moved off to help the other returning knights, Estienne made his way towards Isaac. The old man looked up as he approached, a weary smile crossing his face.

'Walk with me?' Estienne asked softly.

Isaac nodded, falling into step beside him as they moved away from the bustle of the jetty. They walked to a quiet spot along the river's edge as, in the distance, the sounds of the crusader camp stirring drifted from the town.

'Isaac, I wanted to thank you. For everything.'

The old trader raised an eyebrow. 'Thank me? My friend, it is I who should be thanking you. You risked your life to save those men. Just as you did to save me.'

'And you risked yours to help me do it. I couldn't have saved them without you.'

'There is no need for thanks between us. I owe you a debt that can never be repaid. Should you need me again, I will be there.'

The old man's words were almost overwhelming, and Estienne had to swallow down a sudden lump in his throat. 'What will you do now?'

Isaac fixed his eyes on the northern horizon. 'I will return to

Damietta. I have begun to rebuild, thanks to you. Now I have the chance to regain some of what I lost.'

'Then I will see you again. Soon, my friend.'

Impulsively, Estienne pulled Isaac into an embrace. The older man stiffened for a moment, then returned the hug with surprising strength.

'Go well, Estienne Wace,' Isaac murmured. 'And may God watch over you.'

Estienne waited as Isaac made his way back towards the jetty. Then, with a deep breath, he turned back to the town. Men were rising as he made his way back through the streets towards the marketplace, and the camp of the Order of Saint Mary buzzed with activity as Estienne arrived, knights noisily welcoming their brothers so recently released from bondage.

'Estienne Wace.' The deep voice cut through sounds of chattering men, and he saw Hermann of Salza grinning at him. 'By God's grace, I thought you were mad when you told me what you intended to do. But it seems I underestimated the Black Lion.'

'Grand Master,' Estienne replied with a bow. 'I only did what was right.'

'What was right, and nigh-on impossible. Your deed will not soon be forgotten.'

Amalric pushed his way from the crowd, a cup in one hand, a strip of cured meat in the other. 'No, it will not. The name of Estienne Wace will be writ large in the histories of this crusade once we have retaken the Holy Land.'

Hermann clapped Estienne on the back. 'So it will. And we would be proud to have you ride with our Order when we take Cairo.'

Silence then. Were they expecting him to thank them for

such generosity? Was this his reward for risking his life to save an old friend – riding into a war he no longer believed in?

'You still harbour doubts?' Amalric asked, reading the look on Estienne's face.

Estienne sighed. 'It's not as simple as doubt, Amalric. I've seen things... done things... I'm not sure I can reconcile with the man I thought I was.'

'Then let me help you reconcile them,' Amalric replied. 'Estienne, you saved my life. You risked everything to bring me and the others back safely. If that's not the act of a true knight, a true servant of God, then I don't know what is.'

'But how can I continue to raise my sword in God's name when I'm no longer certain of the righteousness of our purpose?'

Hermann took a step closer, and when he spoke his voice was low and crisp with understanding. 'Perhaps that uncertainty is exactly why you must come. You've seen both sides of this crusade. Treated with the enemy, been shown mercy and shown it in return. If men like you abandon this cause, who will be left to question our actions? Who will remind us of our duty to protect the innocent, not just conquer in God's name?'

'I am no monk,' Estienne replied. 'No preacher. I cannot ensure we are on the right path, that is not my place. I have been bred for war. To serve. To protect.'

'And protect you shall,' Amalric replied. 'I for one need you here, my friend. You've saved me more than once already. Who knows what trouble I might get into without you to watch my back?'

Despite himself, Estienne chuckled. 'You do have a talent for finding mischief.'

'Then stay,' Amalric pressed, gripping Estienne's arm. 'Stay and help us.'

Estienne's mind whirled. The pull of home, the prospect of

leaving behind the blood and chaos of this crusade, was strong. But so too was the bond he shared with Amalric, the sense of purpose he'd found among these men.

Slowly, Estienne nodded. 'Very well, my friend. I'll stay. For now, at least.'

Amalric's face split in a wide grin. He pulled Estienne into a strong embrace, thumping him on the back. 'You won't regret this, I swear it.'

'Good to have you with us, Wace,' Hermann said, once Amalric released him.

All Estienne could do was bow as the revelry continued around him. Seeing such gladness made him think that perhaps this was the right path after all, and the right company in which to walk it. He could only hope the good nature of his fellow knights would endure the road to Cairo. Somehow, he doubted it would.

43

Raised voices tore through Estienne's fitful slumber, dragging him from a blood-soaked dream he could barely recollect. For a heartbeat, he lay still, disoriented, his hand instinctively seeking the hilt of his sword. The rough weave of his blanket scratched against his skin as he pushed himself upright, blinking away the last vestiges of sleep.

Pale light filtered through the cracks in the mud-brick walls of the billet, casting long shadows across the empty pallets that surrounded him. The absence of the Knights of Saint Mary was jarring, their usual morning routines of prayer and preparation conspicuously silent.

Estienne rose and donned his tunic, before buckling on his sword belt. The argument that had roused him continued to echo in the distance, the furore of angry voices reverberating through the streets. Curiosity warred with caution as Estienne stepped out into the narrow alley beyond the billet. The air was already thick with heat, the promise of another sweltering day hanging heavy over the abandoned dwellings.

He made his way through the winding streets, each turn bringing him closer to the source of the commotion. The usual bustle was absent, replaced by an eerie stillness that set Estienne's nerves on edge. As he rounded the final corner into Sharamsah's square, the scene that greeted him was one of barely contained chaos. The open space was packed with knights and men-at-arms, their faces a sea of anger. At the centre of it all stood the leaders of the crusade, locked in furious debate.

John of Brienne stood tall and defiant. Opposite him, Cardinal Pelagius quaked with righteous fury, his opulent robes a stark contrast to the dust and grime that clung to everyone else.

Estienne pushed his way through the crowd, his murmured apologies lost in the din of shouted arguments. He found a place near the edge of the gathering, close enough to hear the heated exchange between John and Pelagius, but far enough to avoid being drawn into the fray.

'We cannot continue this madness.' John of Brienne's voice cut through the clamour. 'Our supplies dwindle, our men weaken with each passing day. To press on towards Cairo is to march willingly into our graves.'

A murmur rippled through the gathering, some nodding in agreement, others shaking their heads in disbelief. Estienne felt some sympathy with John's words. How many times had similar thoughts plagued him?

Pelagius stepped forward, his face flushed with indignation. 'You speak of madness? The only madness here is your cowardice in the face of our holy mission.'

'Cowardice?' John spat, his voice low and dangerous. 'Is it cowardice to value the welfare of our men over your dreams of glory, Pelagius? We came to reclaim the Holy Land, not to throw away Christian lives in a foolhardy charge into the heart of Egypt.'

Pelagius's eyes blazed with righteous fury. 'Every step we take is guided by the hand of God Himself. To turn back now is not merely cowardice, it is sin. Would you have us abandon our sacred duty, forsake the very purpose that brought us to these shores? We cannot squander this opportunity. God has delivered the Saracens into our hands. Their sultan cowers to the south, his armies scattered before us. If we turn back now, we betray not only our cause but the very will of Almighty God.'

John's face hardened. 'And what of the will of our men, Pelagius? What of their lives, their families waiting for them across the sea? Are we to sacrifice them all on the altar of your ambition?'

The gathered crowd shifted uneasily. Sensing the wavering resolve of the gathered crusaders, Pelagius seized the moment. He stepped forward, arms spread wide, his voice taking on a honeyed tone that was a stark contrast to his earlier fury.

'My brothers in Christ, consider the prize that lies before us. Cairo – the crown of Egypt, the very heart of the Ayyubid realm. Imagine the riches that await us within those ancient walls. Gold beyond the counting, silks finer than any in Christendom, spices to make the markets of Venice weep.'

A hush fell over the crowd as Pelagius wove his tapestry of promises, each word carefully chosen to ignite the flames of desire in the hearts of his listeners. Estienne watched as the faces around him transformed, doubt giving way to a kind of hunger. He saw weathered veterans and fresh-faced recruits alike leaning forward, caught in the cardinal's spell.

'But more than mere treasure,' Pelagius pressed on, 'think of the glory. Your names will be etched in the annals of history, spoken of in the same breath as the *Coeur de Lion* himself. You would have the honour of reclaiming the Holy Land for Christendom. Imagine kneeling in prayer at the Church of the Holy Sepulchre, knowing that it was your hand, your sword, that made such an act possible.'

The square erupted in cheers, men raising their fists to the sky in mock triumph. Estienne remained still, a rock in a sea of surging exultation. He couldn't help but marvel at how easily some of his fellow crusaders were swayed, their earlier doubts swept away by the allure of wealth and glory.

As he scanned the faces around him, Estienne's gaze fell upon a young knight, barely more than a boy. His eyes shone with unshed tears, his expression a mix of awe and hope. In that moment, Estienne saw himself as he had been when he first arrived on these shores – full of righteous purpose, untouched by the harsh realities of war in this unforgiving land.

He had come driven by a sense of holy purpose, believing in the righteousness of their cause. But standing here, watching as men were so easily persuaded by promises of wealth and acclaim, he couldn't help but question whether this was really God's will. Or were they all merely pawns in a game played by men like Pelagius, their lives and souls bartered for land and gold?

But a palpable shift had come over the gathered crowd. The earlier division began to fade, replaced by a burgeoning consensus. Estienne watched as even some of John of Brienne's staunchest supporters began to waver, their expressions caught between lingering doubt and newfound hope.

John himself stood rigid, his face a mask of grim resignation, but there was something else in his eyes – a flicker of fear that he was fighting a losing battle. That the threat hanging over his head was far graver than mere disagreement. Railing against the will of the Holy See might be looked upon as sedition. And here, with tensions running high and faith being questioned, the consequences of his continued opposition could be fatal.

As if sensing the shift in mood, Pelagius moved in for the killing blow. 'So I ask you, brothers in Christ, are we to heed the counsel of doubt and fear? Or shall we press on, as God Himself commands, to claim the glory that is rightfully ours?'

The response was deafening. A thunderous chorus of approval echoed off the mud-brick walls of Sharamsah, drowning out any voices of dissent. In that moment, Estienne knew with crushing certainty that the decision had already been made. They would march on Cairo, regardless of the risks, regardless of the cost in blood and lives.

Having heard enough, Estienne pushed his way from the cry as its fervour only rose. Before he could make his way back to the billet he felt a hand on his shoulder, and turned to find Amalric grinning, his face flushed with excitement.

'So it is finally decided, my friend? Cairo awaits. We'll be the ones to plant the cross in the very heart of the Saracen realm.'

Estienne managed a weak smile. 'Yes. It seems our path is set.'

Amalric's brow furrowed, his excitement dimming as he took in Estienne's demeanour. 'You don't seem pleased. I know you have had your doubts, but surely you see the wisdom in pressing our advantage?'

'I'm just... concerned,' Estienne said carefully. 'The road ahead will not be easy.'

Amalric clapped him on the back, his smile returning. 'When has it ever been? But we face it together, brother. With God on our side, how can we fail?'

As Amalric moved off to join their fellow knights, already deep in discussion about the coming march, Estienne stood rigid in the emptying square. As they dispersed, his eyes drifted to where John of Brienne had stood, where he had pleaded for some semblance of sanity. The ease with which the crowd had been swayed, the willingness to gamble countless lives on grandiose promises, only served to deepen Estienne's growing uncertainty. But he had to quash it. Had to bury it beneath the belief that this was the right path. For doubt could see a man damned, just as readily as a blade.

44

The crash of stone echoed across the Nile, a thunderous din that made Estienne wince. He stood back from the riverbank, watching as another volley arced from the siege engines, boulders hurtling towards the walls of al-Mansurah. Even at this distance, he could see the impact, could almost feel the shudder of the earth as the artillery found its mark, but still the walls stood defiant.

'Again!' The cry went up, a hoarse voice carried on the hot wind.

The air was filled with the mayhem of battle – the creak and snap of ropes as the trebuchets were reset, a whoosh and groan as another volley arced across the water, the dull thud of stone against stone, the shouts of men straining to load the next boulder.

Around him, the crusader army seethed with activity, a hive of men and machines all bent to the singular purpose of breaking this Saracen stronghold. Crossbowmen lined the shore, their weapons thrumming a staccato beat as they loosed bolt after bolt towards the enemy lines. Across the water, Turkic archers answered in kind, their arrows hissing through the air like angry bees. Estienne watched the deadly exchange, transfixed by the macabre dance. Shafts and bolts crisscrossed the river, some finding flesh, most plunging into the murky waters.

Their progress toward Cairo had halted here. The temptation of taking al-Mansurah, the city of al-Kamil himself, too much for Pelagius to resist. And so here they were – attempting to breach the walls of a fortified city, separated from them by the vast expanse of the Nile. A feat that seemed to border on the impossible, a fact that was becoming clearer with each passing day.

Estienne's gaze drifted along the riverbank, taking in the teeming mass of humanity that made up the crusader force. Where once there had been order, a sense of shared purpose, now he saw only chaos. Their numbers had dwindled, thinned by desertions and disease, each man who slipped away in the night a testament to the wavering resolve that plagued their ranks. And despite it all, the trebuchets hurled their burdens, the crossbows sang their deadly song, and the walls of al-Mansurah stood firm against the onslaught.

This was the reality of their grand crusade, stripped of all its shining ideals and pious platitudes. A mire of blood and shit and suffering, all in the name of a God who seemed increasingly distant with each passing day. Where once there had been gleaming armour and bright banners, now Estienne saw only the tarnish of prolonged campaigning. Surcoats were stained and tattered, metal scored and dented. Even the horses seemed to droop beneath the weight of their burdens, their coats dull and matted with sweat. But more concerning than the physical toll was the fracturing of unity, the slow unravelling of the bonds that had once held this army together. Everywhere Estienne looked, he saw signs of it – men huddled in small groups, their whispers carrying an undercurrent of discontent, squires and serving-brothers moving about their duties with a listless, distracted air.

And at the heart of it all, the continuing squabble between Pelagius and John of Brienne. Their voices carried across the camp, the legate's strident and unyielding, the King of Jerusalem's increasingly desperate in its calls for reason.

'We have no choice but to retreat!' John's words echoed in Estienne's mind. 'To continue this folly is to condemn us all!'

But Pelagius, it seemed, would not be swayed. They would press on, regardless of the cost, heedless of the growing unrest among their own ranks.

'Estienne!'

The call of his name drew him from his dark musings. He turned to see Amalric approaching, the knight's face etched with weariness.

'Amalric,' Estienne replied as his friend came to stand beside him. 'Come to see the progress we have made?'

Amalric's gaze drifted to where the trebuchets continued their relentless work. 'Just watching us waste time throwing ourselves at these walls. Cairo was our aim, but it seems we are now mired here.'

Estienne turned to his friend, seeing the rings of fatigue that marred his handsome face. 'It is unlike you to voice such doubts.'

Amalric sighed. 'I joined this cause because I believed in it, Estienne. Believed in the righteousness of our purpose. But now... now, I fear our leaders' ambition has outstripped their reason. That they are so fixated on the prize of Cairo, they've lost sight of the cost.'

Estienne nodded, suddenly emboldened by their shared

feelings. 'And yet, here we stand, still a part of this war, heedless of the destruction it leaves in its wake.'

Amalric was silent for a long moment, his gaze fixed on the distant walls of al-Mansurah. When he finally spoke again, his voice was low, almost lost beneath the sounds of the siege.

'I fear we are but toys, Estienne. Toys in a game played by men who will never set foot on this blood-soaked ground, who will never know the true cost of their ambitions.'

There was a bitter truth to Amalric's words, one that Estienne could not refute. Pope Honorius had enforced the decree that they should take the Holy Land, but he was not here – only Pelagius, his representative, and he was no leader of armies. The Holy Roman Emperor himself had threatened to come, bringing a host of his own, and yet where was he? They were all of them pieces on a vast board, moved and sacrificed at the whims of those who styled themselves as leaders, and men of God.

'You're right,' Estienne said at last, his voice heavy with the weight of admission. 'It appears we are nothing more than instruments in the hands of ambitious men.'

'But even so,' Amalric breathed. 'I cannot bring myself to desert this cause.'

Estienne turned to him. 'Even now?'

Amalric nodded, his jaw tightening with resolve. 'Even now. We have come too far, sacrificed too much, to turn back. To abandon our oaths now would render all that suffering, all those lives lost, meaningless. No matter my reservations, I cannot forsake them.'

'Then I am with you,' Estienne replied, without thought or hesitation. 'For God. And for brotherhood.'

The moment was shattered by the boom of another volley launching from the siege engines, the stones arcing high over the river before plummeting towards al-Mansurah's walls. Estienne watched their flight, his heart heavy with the knowledge of the destruction they heralded.

But beneath that weight, he took solace in the knowledge he had made his choice, for good or ill. He would see this through to the end, for the sake of loyalty and the Almighty, whatever that end might be.

45

The makeshift watchtower swayed gently in the hot breeze, its rough-hewn timbers creaking beneath Estienne's feet. He gripped the railing and gazed out over the sprawling crusader camp towards the distant walls of al-Mansurah. Another volley of stones arced through the air, hurled from the massive trebuchets that lined the bank of the Nile, the great engines of war groaning and creaking, their frames trembling with each release. The impact came with a dull, distant boom that Estienne felt in his chest more than heard. Dust billowed up from the point of impact, obscuring the result for a long moment. As it cleared, he saw the walls stood firm, barely scathed by the assault that had cost them so dearly in time and resources.

He turned his gaze to the camp below, taking in the rows of tents now sagging and discoloured by the unrelenting sun. Men moved between them, their steps heavy with exhaustion and growing despair. The air hung thick with the stench of unwashed bodies, rotting food, and the sickly-sweet odour of festering wounds. Flies buzzed a monotone refrain, pestering them all relentlessly.

In one corner of the camp, a group of knights huddled around a small fire, their voices rising in argument. Estienne couldn't make out the words, but the tone was clear enough – frustration, fear and a growing sense that they had been led astray. He'd heard similar whispers throughout the camp, growing louder with each passing day. Pelagius's words on the righteousness of their campaign, of the promised riches that awaited them in Cairo, had all but been forgotten now. The confidence that had buoyed them as they'd set out from Sharamsah a distant memory. They had come to claim Cairo, to strike at the very heart of Egypt. Instead, they found themselves trapped here, beating themselves bloody against the unyielding walls of al-Mansurah.

A commotion from across the camp drew Estienne's attention. A small crowd had gathered, their voices raised in anger, and Estienne leaned forward, straining to hear the cause of the disturbance. It was no use; he could learn nothing from up here.

As he made his way down from the tower, passing other men lacklustre in their enthusiasm for the cause, he sensed a palpable shift in the air, a sudden increase in the volume of voices carried on the hot wind. He paused halfway down the rickety ladder, straining to catch the words that seemed to flutter just beyond his hearing.

'...supplies gone...'

'...Saracen dogs...'

'...all is lost...'

Fragments of conversation, each more ominous than the last. Estienne hurried down the remaining rungs and began to move through the camp. The deeper he went, the more the sense of woe grew. Hushed conversation was quickly replaced by urgent movement. Anger flashed on faces, as others hastily began to gather their meagre belongings. Ahead he caught sight of a young squire, barely more than a boy, sinking to his knees in the dust, tears cutting clean tracks down his grimy cheeks.

'What's happened?' Estienne demanded, grasping the arm of a passing knight.

'The last of our supply ships,' the knight snapped. 'Captured by the Saracens up-river. We're cut off. Cut off and doomed.'

'Doomed?'

'Aye,' the knight nodded. 'Reinforcements are coming to relieve al-Mansurah. Saracens marching from the south. Thousands of them, they say.'

Estienne released the man and he hurried on his way. Moving on, Estienne heard the increasing volume of panicked voices. The crowd that had gathered near the centre of the camp was larger now, men pressing close to hear the latest news, their faces twisted with fear and disbelief.

'We're finished.' someone shouted, his voice high with hysteria. 'The heathen hordes will be upon us, and we'll be slaughtered like lambs.'

'Silence, you fool.' Another voice cut through the din, thick with barely contained panic. 'Would you spread fear through the whole camp?'

'Brothers, we must not lose faith,' said another. 'God has not abandoned us. We must trust in His plan.'

A bitter laugh rose from the crowd. 'God's plan? Was it God's plan to lead us into this trap? To send us here to die in this Godforsaken desert?'

Estienne had heard enough, turning from the crowd, the sudden urge to find a familiar face spurring him to increase his stride. Before he could find Amalric or any of the other Knights of Saint Mary, he spied a further commotion around the main command tent. The leaders of the crusade had already gathered at the news, and as Estienne approached he spied John of

Brienne, along with Hermann of Salza. Men gathered in small clusters, their voices low and urgent, eyes darting towards the large pavilion where the fate of their crusade would be decided.

Estienne found a spot near the edge of the gathering. He watched as the leaders of their beleaguered host filed into the tent – knights and nobles, now looking as far from nobility as one could get. Last to enter was Pelagius himself, the papal legate's once-proud bearing now bent with the gravity of their situation.

'My lords,' Pelagius began, his voice carrying clearly to where Estienne stood. 'We find ourselves at a crossroads. Our situation grows more perilous with each passing hour.'

A murmur ran through the assembled leaders, a sound of grudging agreement tinged with fear. Estienne strained to hear more, acutely aware of the weight of the moment. This was the man who had driven them on, who had promised them glory and God's favour. Now, he seemed a pale shadow of that fiery orator, his words heavy with the weight of impending failure.

'The Saracens have cut our supply lines,' one of the knights spoke up. 'We have provisions for twenty days at most, and that's if we ration sparely.'

'And what of al-Kamil's reinforcements?' another demanded. 'How long before they're upon us?'

That provoked a sudden murmur of discontent, and Pelagius raised a hand for silence. 'Our scouts report a large force moving north from Cairo. They could be here within two days.'

The tent erupted into bedlam, each man shouting to be heard above the din. Estienne watched as Pelagius struggled to maintain order, his earlier confidence evaporating in the face of their collective fear.

'Silence.' The command cut through the noise, and Estienne recognised the voice of John of Brienne. 'We all know what must be done. There is only one choice left to us. Isn't that right, Cardinal?'

A heavy silence fell over the gathering, as the King of Jerusalem held Pelagius in a narrow stare. Pelagius seemed to deflate before that gaze, his shoulders sagging as he nodded slowly.

'You are right, of course. We must... we must retreat. Take the road back north to Damietta.'

The words hung in the air, a death knell for all their hopes of glory. Estienne felt a curious mix of emotions wash over him – relief that they were abandoning this doomed endeavour, disappointment at their failure, and a gnawing sense of guilt for those lost in pursuit of their ill-fated goal.

As the leaders filed out of the tent, their faces fixed in grim resolve, Estienne caught sight of Pelagius. The man who had once exhorted them to glory with such passion now looked lost, his eyes haunted by the weight of his decision. For a moment, Estienne felt some sympathy for the legate. To have come so far, to have believed so fervently, only to be forced to admit defeat – it was a burden he wouldn't wish on any man. But ultimately he had led them to this for no reason but his own zealotry. For that, he could never be forgiven.

With a heavy sigh, Estienne made his way back to his own tent. The retreat loomed before them, a journey as fraught with danger as their ill-fated advance had been. As he walked, the news spread quickly, a ripple of whispers that soon became a torrent of activity. Men rushed to and fro, packing what meagre possessions remained to them, preparing for the long march north. The air of defeat was palpable, but beneath it he sensed an undercurrent of relief. They were going home, or at least away from this place that had nearly become their tomb.

When he reached the encampment of the German Order,

the knights were already busying themselves with preparation. Without a word, Estienne moved to help, taking down tents and loading their horses for the journey. As they worked, Estienne found himself stealing glances at his companions, reading the mix of emotions that played across their faces.

Amalric caught his eye, offering a wry smile. 'Not quite the triumphal procession home we imagined, eh?'

Estienne couldn't help but chuckle. 'No, my friend. A long, ignoble walk north. But it beats the alternative.'

'The alternative being our bones bleaching in the sun outside Cairo's walls? Aye, I'll take a long walk over that fate any day.'

They worked in companionable silence for a time. Around them, the camp was slowly disappearing, tents collapsing, and wagons being loaded with what meagre supplies remained. As they paused to catch their breath, Estienne found himself gazing back towards al-Mansurah's distant walls. The city stood defiant, a stark reminder of their failure. Or perhaps a reminder of the lessons learned here. That zeal and faith were no armour against folly.

Estienne silently vowed to carry that lesson with him, whatever lay ahead.

46

The chamber buzzed with barely leashed joy, a stark contrast to the sombre mood that had permeated al-Mansurah's halls for so many days and nights as the city walls were pummelled. Kashta stood among the sultan's advisors and generals, his massive frame dwarfing the men around him. The air was thick with the scent of incense and sweat, the heat of so many bodies packed into the ornate room making the atmosphere almost suffocating.

His eyes swept across the assembled men, taking in their eager faces, the flush of victory already shining in their eyes. Or was it relief, that after such a protracted assault the siege had finally been broken? No matter. For now, they were delivered, Allah be praised, and all awaited the word of al-Kamil on what might happen next.

The sultan sat upon his ornate chair, fingers steepled before him, his face a mask of stern contemplation that stood in stark contrast to the jubilation surrounding him. A vizier stepped forward, his voice barely contained as he spoke.

'Great Sultan, the Franks are now in full retreat. They flee north like the dogs they are. Whipped curs, howling for their bitch mothers.'

A ripple of laughter swept through the room, but Kashta noticed al-Kamil did not share in their mirth. The sultan's gaze remained fixed on some distant point, his brow furrowed in thought. This was not a man content with a simple victory.

'What would you have us do, Great Sultan?' asked another vizier. 'Do we grant them safe passage?'

'No,' another bellowed. 'We must hunt them like the animals they are—'

More voices joined the fray, and immediately the chamber was consumed with the din of it. Al-Kamil raised a hand and the room fell silent. When he spoke, his voice was low, measured, each word carrying the weight of steel.

'They retreat, yes. But a wounded beast is often the most dangerous. We must not merely defeat them. We must break them.'

Kashta felt a chill run down his spine at the sultan's words. He recognised the look in al-Kamil's eyes now – it was the same hunger for vengeance that had driven Kashta across the desert after the Frankish knight, Estienne. The one that had seen him endure more than he could ever have thought possible in pursuit of his reckoning.

'My Sultan,' another advisor ventured, 'surely their humiliation is enough. We have defended al-Mansurah, protected Cairo—'

'Enough?' al-Kamil's voice was sharp, silencing the advisor like a razor to his throat. 'They still hold Damietta. Our people still suffer under their rule. No, this is not enough. We will not merely send them home in disgrace. We will crush them, destroy them, and liberate what is ours.'

The room erupted into murmurs, a mix of excitement and

trepidation. As the council began to discuss strategies for their pursuit, Kashta's mind raced. He had tasted defeat at the hands of the Franks, had seen the devastation they could wreak. But now, standing in this chamber, feeling the tide of war shift, he realised there was a real chance for redemption.

Before any plans could be formulated, the heavy doors of the council chamber swung open with a resounding boom, silencing the ongoing discussions. Kashta turned, his hand instinctively moving to the hilt of his sword, only to relax as he recognised the figures striding into the room.

Al-Mu'azzam, brother of al-Kamil, entered carrying an air of unquestionable power. Behind him came al-Ashraf, also a brother of al-Kamil, though cutting an altogether less imposing figure. Al-Mu'azzam moved with the fluid grace of a seasoned warrior, his weathered face set in lines of grim determination. In contrast, al-Ashraf's eyes darted about the room, keen and calculating, taking in every detail.

The assembled advisors parted before them, creating a path for the men to approach al-Kamil, and Kashta watched as the three came together. There was no embrace, no warm words of greeting. Instead, they regarded each other with a mixture of respect and wariness, like three lions circling before deciding whether to fight or hunt together.

Al-Kamil broke the silence first. 'Brothers, you have come at a crucial moment. The Franks retreat, but our victory is not yet complete.'

'Our forces are ready to fight at your command.' Al-Mu'azzam's voice was deep and resounding as a drum.

'Good,' al-Kamil nodded. 'We will need every sword, every horse, every arrow to crush these invaders once and for all.'

Al-Ashraf stepped forward, his voice smooth as silk. 'What of Damietta? It must be reclaimed.'

'Damietta will be ours again,' al-Kamil assured him. 'But first, we must ensure the Franks never return to threaten our lands.'

'They will be slowed by their baggage trains, their wounded,' al-Mu'azzam said. 'If we strike swiftly, we can cut them off before they reach safety.'

Al-Ashraf shook his head. 'But how? They are already on the road north. They will reach the haven of Sharamsah within days.'

Kashta watched as al-Kamil's eyes lit up, a smile spreading across his face. 'I believe I know a way.' The chamber fell silent as al-Kamil rose from his seat, and when he spoke, his voice was low and charged with purpose. 'We will open the sluice gates along the Nile.'

His words silenced the chamber with their brilliance. The Nile, the very lifeblood of Egypt, would become their greatest weapon against the invaders. Its waters, usually carefully controlled to nourish the fertile delta, would be unleashed. They would surge across the land, transforming the crusaders' path of retreat into a treacherous quagmire. The Frankish army, already weighed down by armour and supplies, would find the ground beneath its feet turn to mud. Its heavy warhorses would struggle to pull wagons through the rising waters. Men would flounder, their already fragile discipline giving way to panic as the flood rose around them. The crusaders would find themselves at the mercy of the very land they sought to conquer.

'My Sultan,' one of the advisors ventured, his voice trembling slightly, 'the damage to our own lands—'

'Will be nothing compared to the destruction the Franks will bring if we allow them to regroup. We are fighting for the soul of Egypt. No price is too high.'

Kashta felt a sudden surge of pride in his leader. This was a man who understood sacrifice, who was willing to wound his own land to deliver a killing blow to the enemy. It was the kind of decision that separated great rulers from mere men.

As the sultan's orders were relayed and men rushed to carry them out, Kashta pictured the crusaders' organised withdrawal descending into chaos. Proud knights flailing in the rising waters. Supply wagons entrenched in the muddy torrent. And through it all, he saw himself and his fellow warriors moving with the practised ease of those who had lived their lives along the Nile's banks. They would strike like crocodiles, swift and merciless, picking off the struggling invaders one by one.

Then Kashta caught the eye of the sultan. Al-Kamil's gaze was sharp, assessing, and Kashta felt as if his very soul was being weighed.

'Kashta ibn Assad,' al-Kamil's voice rang out, silencing the murmurs in the room. 'You will lead the vanguard against the retreating Franks.'

He felt his chest swell with pride and anticipation, even as the weight of responsibility settled on his broad shoulders. This felt like more than just an order – it was a testament to the sultan's faith in him, a chance to prove his worth beyond any doubt.

'Be among the lions that hunt, Kashta,' the sultan continued. 'Show these invaders the true fury of Egypt.'

'It will be done, my Sultan,' Kashta replied, before bowing low.

As the council dispersed, Kashta strode from the chamber, his mind drifting unexpectedly to the Frankish knight he had once fought alongside. Estienne, the man had called himself. Kashta wondered if he was among those they would soon engulf, and if fate would bring them face-to-face once more – this time as enemies on the battlefield.

There was still a debt between them, a score to settle. Yet, Kashta couldn't deny the grudging respect he held for the Frank's skill and courage. In another life, they might have been friends. But this was not that life. If they met again, it would be as foes, and this time, Kashta vowed, he would emerge victorious.

The Franks thought they were retreating to safety, but they were riding into a trap of water and steel. And Kashta ibn Assad, Lion of the Sudan, would be there to spring it.

47

The floodwaters lapped at Estienne's calves, each step a battle against the sucking mud that surrounded them like a sea. What had begun as an orderly withdrawal from al-Mansurah had devolved into a desperate struggle for survival, their army now little more than a bedraggled herd, stumbling northward along the river's swollen banks.

His muscles screamed with every movement, his heavy gambeson chafing against skin rubbed raw by days of ceaseless marching. The weight of his sword, once a comfort, now felt like an anchor dragging him down into the bog.

Ahead, a wagon laden with supplies lurched to a halt, its wheels mired in the thick mud. The desperate cries of its handlers cut through the air as they urged their straining horses forward.

'Come on, you bastards,' a knight bellowed, his face red with exertion as he shoved his shoulder against the wagon's rear. 'Push, damn you.'

Estienne slogged towards the stricken wagon, exhaustion

momentarily forgotten. He pressed his back against the rough wood, bracing his feet as best he could in the treacherous mud.

'On three,' he growled to the men around him. 'One... two... three.'

They heaved as one, muscles straining, teeth gritted against the effort. For a heart-stopping moment, nothing happened. Then, with a sickening squelch, it lurched forward, horses whinnying in protest, but their hooves found purchase, and the wagon began to roll once more.

Estienne stumbled back, gasping for breath. His gaze swept over the dismal scene. As far as the eye could see, the crusader column stretched like a great, wounded serpent. Men and beasts alike floundered in the rising waters, their progress painfully slow. Here and there, islands of relative dry land stood out amid the flood, oases of momentary respite in their gruelling march.

A hand clasped his shoulder and Estienne turned to find Amalric at his side, the knight's usually immaculate appearance a distant memory. His beard was matted with mud, hair unkempt, surcoat stained and torn.

'This is madness,' Amalric muttered. 'The Saracens need not lift a finger against us. This cursed land will claim us all.'

'And yet we've no choice but to press on,' Estienne replied.

Before they could lament further, a cry went up from somewhere near the rear of the column.

'What now?' Amalric's voice was taut with frustration.

'Come on,' Estienne said, already moving towards the commotion.

As they drew closer, they saw a horse, trapped in a deep section of the flood, thrashing wildly in the water. Its rider, a young squire by the look of him, clung desperately to the animal's neck.

'Help me.' The boy's voice was shrill with terror. 'Please, I can't swim.'

Estienne didn't hesitate, wading into the deeper water. The horse's panicked movements sent waves splashing over him, but he pressed on, reaching for the squire's outstretched hand.

'Let go of the horse,' he shouted over the animal's frantic whinnying. 'There's nothing you can do for it.'

The boy's eyes were wide with fear, but he nodded, releasing his death grip on the horse's mane. In that instant, Estienne lunged forward, seizing the squire's arm and hauling him towards shallower water. They stumbled back to relative safety of the bank, both gasping for breath. The horse continued its thrashing, but there was little they could do to release it.

'Thank you,' the squire sputtered, water streaming from his hair and clothes. 'I thought... I thought I was done for.'

'Not today, lad.'

As he helped the boy to his feet, Estienne's gaze drifted back over the dispirited column. How many more would they lose to the treacherous waters before they reached safety? How many had they already lost?

The sound of distant thunder rolled across the flooded plain, and for a moment, Estienne's heart sank. A storm now, on top of everything else? But as he turned his eyes to the sky, he saw no gathering clouds.

The sound only increased, a deep, rhythmic booming that seemed to shake the very earth. Not thunder. Drums.

War drums.

'God help us,' someone shouted further up the column. 'They're coming.'

Cresting over the hill to the east came a flood of horses. Armoured warriors sat atop, helms crowned by turbans, spears flying pennons. A sudden whistle of arrows filled the sky, heralding a deadly rain that splashed down into the muddy floodwaters. Estienne barely had time to shout a warning before the first volley struck, and men cried out in pain and surprise as shafts found their marks with brutal efficiency.

He turned to bellow at the squire to take cover, but the boy merely stared, an arrow shaft protruding from the centre of his chest. Before Estienne could reach for him, the boy fell dead in the muck.

'Shields!' someone bellowed, but the command came all too late.

The Saracen war cries rose like a storm, drowning out the screams of the wounded and dying. Estienne's heart hammered as he saw the massive force descending on them from over the rise, their banners snapping in the hot wind, sunlight glinting off curved blades and shields.

Amalric was already running north, to where the standard of his Order fluttered in the breeze.

'Form up,' Estienne roared as he staggered after his friend. 'Form ranks, damn it.'

But it was a futile command. The crusaders, already disorganised and demoralised by their gruelling retreat, broke at the sight of the oncoming horde. Men scattered like leaves in a gale, some charging forward in a desperate show of defiance, others fleeing into the floodwaters in a vain attempt to escape.

Estienne's instincts took over. He drew his sword as an arrow whizzed past his ear. In the confusion he lost sight of Amalric, as men raced across his path in a panic. Before he could think to join up with his fellow knights, a Saracen warrior charged towards him, scimitar raised high. Estienne met the blow with his own blade, spinning to the side and bringing his sword down in a vicious arc. The Saracen's head flew from his shoulders in a spray of crimson, his body toppling into the muddy water.

No time to think. Another attacker was upon him, and his sword rose and fell once again. A cloven arm, a scream in his face and he was turning to face the next. He felt the sting of a spearhead across his thigh, but the pain was distant, drowned out by the pounding of blood in his ears. Estienne stumbled, desperate to defend himself against the spear wielder, but all was confusion now.

A crusader stumbled past him, an arrow protruding from his eye socket. Estienne reached out instinctively to steady the man, but he was already dead, collapsing into the flood with a splash that was lost amid the din of battle.

Through the press of bodies, Estienne caught sight of a familiar face. Amalric stood atop a small rise, his back to a gnarled tree, fending off three Saracen warriors. Even as Estienne watched, a fourth circled around, raising his blade for a killing blow.

'Amalric!' Estienne's voice was lost in the chaos, but his legs were already moving.

He charged through the melee, heedless of the danger. A warrior loomed before him but Estienne didn't break stride, barrelling into the man like a battering ram. The man went down with a splash and Estienne leapt over him, closing the distance to his friend.

His sword flashed out, catching the creeping Saracen in mid-swing. The man's eyes widened in surprise as Estienne's blade opened his throat. Amalric, sensing the presence at his back, shifted his stance, allowing Estienne to take position beside him.

Three armed men against two. But they were not odds to give Estienne pause.

He snarled as he lunged forward, blade a scythe. It sheared through the arm of one, his curved sword falling to the ground as he staggered back with a high-pitched wail. A thud, and

Amalric had stoved in the helm of a second foe. Estienne managed to lurch back from a jabbing spear, his blade coming up to bat the shaft aside before he rammed his sword into the Saracen's guts.

As the last one fell, Estienne scanned the battlefield. If they did not find their allies and form ranks, they would be done for.

'There,' Amalric shouted, pointing towards a knot of knights near the river's edge, white surcoats bearing the black cross.

Estienne saw him then. Hermann was at the centre of the group, his surcoat stained red with blood. He fought with the strength of a man half his age, his sword rising and falling in a deadly rhythm, bearded face snarling his defiance.

'We have to reach him,' Estienne said. 'Come on.'

Amalric nodded, falling in beside him as they waded back into the fray. The going was treacherous, the uneven ground hidden beneath the floodwaters. More than once, Estienne nearly lost his footing, saved only by Amalric's steadying hand. They were halfway to Hermann's position when Estienne saw it – a patch of relatively dry land to the east, rising like an island amid the chaos. It wasn't much, but it was defensible. A place where they might make a stand.

'Look,' he shouted to Amalric, gesturing towards the higher ground. 'We need to get everyone to that rise. It's our only chance.'

Amalric nodded grimly, and they redoubled their efforts, slogging their way towards Hermann with renewed determination. As they neared the grand master's position, Estienne raised his voice in a battle cry that cut through the din.

'To me, Knights of Saint Mary. To me. Make for the high ground.'

Hermann's head snapped around at the sound of Estienne's voice. Their eyes met across the battlefield and Estienne pointed to the east, and the knot of land above the mire. The grand master barked out orders to his men in the Teuton language, and the remaining knights began to move as one, cutting a path through the Saracen forces towards the patch of dry earth.

Estienne and Amalric fell in with them, following Hermann as they fought their way towards relative safety. The Saracens pressed in on all sides, dogging their every step, and Estienne's sword played a grim dirge as they moved.

Eventually their small band of crusaders clambered onto the patch of land, gasping for breath. Estienne's legs trembled with exhaustion as he helped haul Hermann up the slight incline. Around them, the sounds of battle continued unabated, but for a moment they had found a small respite from the chaos.

'Form a perimeter,' Hermann barked. 'Shields up. We hold this position.'

The Knights of Saint Mary moved with practised efficiency, making a protective ring around their grand master. Estienne cast his gaze out over the battlefield, taking in the grim scene before them.

The crusader army was now scattered and broken. Small groups of men fought desperately against the overwhelming Saracen force, but it was clear that the tide of battle had turned irrevocably against them. The flood waters ran red with blood, countless bodies floating face-down in the muddy torrent.

'We can't stay here long,' Amalric muttered, his eyes darting nervously across the horizon. 'They'll regroup and come for us soon enough.'

Estienne nodded grimly. 'Aye, but where can we go? We're surrounded on all sides.'

'Archers,' someone hissed, before he could think of a plan. 'Horse archers, coming in from the southeast.'

Hermann cursed, raising his arm. 'And mamluks to the north. We'll be boxed in.'

Estienne's gaze fell upon a riderless horse nearby, its former master floating in the mire a few yards away. The animal stood stock-still in the shallow water, eyes rolling in fear but making no move to flee. In that moment, Estienne knew what he had to do.

'I'll draw them off,' he said, gaze fixed on Hermann. 'Make myself a target they can't ignore. While they're focused on me, the rest of you can make a break for it.'

'No,' Amalric snapped. 'There is no way you can—'

'Look around you,' Estienne snapped. 'We're finished if we stay here, and we'll be cut down if we try to run. This is the only way.'

Hermann was silent for a long moment, his weathered face etched with the weight of this decision. Finally, he nodded, a single, sharp movement.

'Very well,' the grand master said, his voice heavy with resignation. 'But I'll not order you to do this, Estienne. It must be your choice.'

'It is, Hochmeister. But I'll need one thing to make this work.' Estienne turned to the standard bearer. 'The standard. I need the Order's standard.'

For a moment, Estienne thought Hermann might refuse. Then, as though seeing the sense in it, he reached for the fluttering banner and handed it to Estienne.

'May God go with you, Estienne Wace,' Hermann said solemnly.

Estienne nodded, then turned and waded towards the waiting horse. The animal shied as he approached, but Estienne spoke softly, reaching out with a steady hand to stroke its quivering flank. After a moment, the horse calmed, allowing him to grab its mane and haul himself onto its back.

A deep breath and he raised the standard, letting the white fabric snap in the hot wind, displaying its stark black cross. Then, with a final glance back at his comrades, he dug his heels into the horse's sides.

'For Saint Mary and Outremer,' he bellowed, spurring the horse forward directly towards the approaching enemy.

The horse surged forward, its hooves churning the muddy water as Estienne urged it on. The standard streamed behind him, a defiant banner that drew every eye on the battlefield. Wind whipped at Estienne's face as he leaned low over the horse's neck, his heart pounding in time with the animal's thundering hooves.

An arrow whistled past his ear. Two more splashed into the waterlogged earth just ahead, sending up sprays of muddy water. Estienne gritted his teeth, fighting the urge to duck or swerve. He had to remain visible, had to draw their attention away from his comrades.

'Come on, you bastards,' he shouted.

His challenge was answered by a chorus of war cries as the horse archers wheeled their mounts, abandoning their advance on the small island where Hermann and the others still stood. Behind them, a contingent of mamluk cavalry broke off from the main force, heavy horses splashing through the flood as they gave chase, the banner too valuable a prize to ignore.

It had worked. The bait was laid, the hounds snapping after it.

Now he just had to hope the hare would outrun them.

48

All he heard was the pounding of hooves and the whistle of arrows. His nameless mount surged beneath him, its flanks speckled with mud, the standard of Saint Mary snapping in the wind behind him, a beacon to draw the fury of his pursuers.

Across the flooded landscape, there was no sign of salvation. The Nile had turned traitor, its waters stretching as far as he could see, every patch of seemingly solid ground a potential mire waiting to swallow horse and rider whole.

Estienne heaved back on the reins, the horse stamping beneath him. Hauling in breath he scanned the terrain, squinting against the hot breeze. There in the distance, a small promontory jutting above the murky expanse. If he could reach it, perhaps he might see a way out of this. A clear path to escape.

He dug his heels into the horse's sides, urging it towards that distant hope. The animal responded with a burst of speed, but his elation was short-lived. A familiar whistle cut through the air, followed by a sickening thud. The horse screamed, its stride faltered, front legs buckling as an arrow shaft quivered in its neck.

He felt himself pitch forward, the muddy ground rushing up to meet him, and he had just enough presence of mind to tuck his shoulder, trying to roll with the impact. The world spun, a dizzying blur of sky and earth, then he hit hard, the breath driven from his lungs in a rush.

For a moment, he lay there, stunned. The standard lay in the mud beside him, its proud white material now stained and torn. With trembling hands, he pushed himself up, seeing his mount laying a few yards away, its legs kicking weakly as it gasped its last. Staggering to his feet, his eyes locked on a thin strip of raised earth – a canal path, barely visible above the floodwaters. It snaked away to the north, a tenuous lifeline in this watery hell.

Looking about he could see he had outrun his pursuers for now. There were no horses charging him from the murk. Perhaps without the horse, without the standard to draw their eye, he could slip away, lose himself in the confusion of the retreat.

Estienne took a stumbling step towards the path, then another. Then he heard it – the sound of hoofbeats and war cries carried on the hot wind.

'Come on, you fool,' he growled to himself. 'Move.'

He broke into a shambling run, canal path seeming impossibly far away, a cruel mirage just out of reach, but still he pressed on. Memories flashed through his mind – fighting for his life on the walls of Damietta, Amalric's laughter around a campfire, the weight of Hermann's hand on his shoulder as he volunteered for this one final task. Had it all been for nothing? Was this to be his inglorious end, cut down in the mud like a dog?

Another arrow whistled past his head, close enough to stir his sweat-matted hair. Estienne stumbled, nearly losing his footing on the treacherous ground, and risked a glance over his shoulder. Saracen riders were closing the distance.

The canal path was so close now, and he could see that a narrow bridge spanned the deep waters. If he could reach it, perhaps he could make a stand, use the bottleneck to even the odds. But with each step, the thunder of hooves grew louder, drowning out the frantic pounding of blood in his ears.

'Just a little further,' he gasped.

Estienne's boots clacked hollowly on the weathered planks of the bridge. The narrow crossing creaked ominously beneath his weight, but he carried on, driven by the wild hope of escape. It wasn't until he reached the midpoint that he saw movement on the far bank. His heart seemed to stutter in his chest as the shapes resolved themselves into mounted warriors, their sabres glinting in the harsh sunlight.

'Shit,' he breathed, the word escaping in a ragged gasp.

He spun around but found only more Saracens closing in behind. The warriors advanced with measured steps, clearly in no rush now that their quarry was cornered. For a moment, Estienne considered leaping into the churning waters below. It would be a desperate gambit, but perhaps preferable to being cut down where he stood. But even as the thought formed, he dismissed it. The current would likely drag him under before he could swim a dozen strokes, and there was no guarantee the Saracens wouldn't simply riddle him with arrows as he floundered. No, if this was to be his end, he would meet it on his feet, with steel in his hand.

Estienne drew his sword with a doom-laden rasp, planting his feet as best he could on the slick planks, and a humourless chuckle escaped his lips.

'Come on then,' he spat, baring his teeth in a feral grin. 'Let's be done with it.'

Just as the nearest Saracen was about to close the distance, a voice rang out, sharp and commanding. The words were in Arabic, incomprehensible, but their effect was immediate, and the warrior froze mid-step, his blade still poised to strike.

Estienne turned to see a figure emerge from the press of bodies on the far side of the bridge. A face that he knew...

Kashta stood like a colossus wrought in flesh and steel. The warrior looked much as he had that day upon the walls of Damietta – armoured in chain and plate, helm rising to a point, sabre huge in his meaty hand. His eyes bored into Estienne's, filled with a mixture of recognition and something harder, colder – the promise of long-awaited vengeance.

For a heartbeat, neither man moved. The distant sounds of battle seemed to fade, and in that moment memories flashed through his mind – Kashta's fury in al-Kamil's tent, their desperate flight across the desert, the Moor's vow to one day claim his revenge.

It seemed that day had come at last.

Kashta barked out a command and the other Saracen warriors fell back, forming a loose circle around the bridge. This was to be a duel then, not a simple execution. The Moor raised his sword in a salute, and Estienne found himself mirroring the gesture. Then, with a cry, Kashta charged.

Estienne barely had time to bring his sword up before Kashta's blade crashed against it. The impact sent him stumbling back, feet slipping on the wet wood as he fought to keep his balance.

Kashta pressed his advantage, raining down blow after punishing blow, his face a mask of focused rage, eyes blazing with madness. Each strike felt like it might shatter Estienne's blade, and it was all he could do to weather the onslaught.

Desperately, he lashed out with a kick, aiming for Kashta's

knee. The bigger man saw it coming, stepping to avoid the blow, but the motion threw him slightly off balance. Estienne seized the opportunity, lunging forward with a thrust that would have skewered a lesser opponent, but Kashta was no ordinary foe.

He twisted at the last moment, Estienne's blade sliding off the armour that encased his body. Before Estienne could recover, Kashta's fist smashed into his jaw, sending him reeling. His foot caught on a loose plank, and for one heart-stopping moment, he thought he would topple over the bridge's edge, but he managed to right himself.

No relenting. Kashta closed the distance once more, and their blades met again and again, the clash of steel echoing. Estienne fought desperately but he could feel himself weakening, and with every swing of his sword he was losing ground. The relentless slog across treacherous terrain, his battle with the Saracens, his desperate flight, were all taking their toll, but Kashta seemed tireless by comparison, his attacks unrelenting.

Estienne was forced back off the bridge, the soft ground giving way beneath his feet. Once more, Kashta's blade whistled past his ear and he stumbled back, losing his footing in the mud. He fell, dropping to one knee, sword raised to catch yet another mighty blow.

It did not come.

Kashta loomed over him, blade poised to strike, chest heaving with exertion. Estienne knelt before him, equally winded, and for what felt like an eternity they stared, captor and captive, victor and vanquished.

Was this some final cruelty, Kashta drawing out this last moment of vengeance? Or was there something else at play, some doubt in Kashta's mind?

The burning hatred in the Moor's eyes seemed to have guttered out, replaced by a mix of emotions Estienne couldn't fully decipher. Was it a grudging respect that flickered between them? A silent acknowledgment of all they had endured together? They had been enemies, then reluctant allies, and now found themselves on opposite sides once more. Yet something lingered...

Kashta barked out an order, his voice hoarse from exertion. Two Saracen warriors stepped forward, roughly hauling Estienne to his feet and prising the sword from his grip. He offered no resistance as they bound his hands and began to lead him away.

As they did, he cast one last glance at Kashta. The Moor stood watching, his expression unreadable. There was no triumph in his bearing, no gloating over his beaten foe. If anything, he looked... tired. As weary of this war and its toll as Estienne felt.

They led him away from the bridge, his steps unsteady on the muddy ground. As he was marched towards the waiting Saracen lines, he could only hope there would be mercy left in the hearts of these men... if he was even worthy of it.

49

The sun hung low as Kashta looked out over the sea of dejected Frankish prisoners on the plain below, once-proud warriors now bent and broken. The piteous stench of defeat hung briefly in the air, to be blown away by the cool evening breeze. This should have been a moment of triumph, the culmination of their struggle against the invaders. Yet as he watched the prisoners shuffling north through the mud, their eyes hollow, Kashta felt only a yawning emptiness.

He and Wasim had dreamed of this moment, of driving the infidels from their lands. But Wasim was gone now, cut down by Frankish steel, and the victory they had yearned for tasted only of bitterness.

His gaze fell upon a young Frank, barely more than a boy, face streaked with dirt. The youth stumbled, falling to his knees in the muck. For a heartbeat, no one moved to help him. Then, with aching slowness, an older knight reached down, hauling the boy to his feet with a gentleness that belied his obvious exhaustion.

These were not the devils they had been warned of, not the

monsters they had been taught to hate and fear. They were men, as fallible as any, following their misguided leaders on a mission of faith and folly.

A group of mamluk warriors passed below, their faces alight with savage joy as they goaded the prisoners with spear butts and snarled words. Kashta's jaw clenched, disgust rising like bile in his throat. This was not the honourable victory he had imagined. This was simply the ugly face of war, stripped of all its gilded lies.

He turned away from the scene, his eyes seeking the distant horizon. Somewhere to the south lay Cairo, the prize that had lured the Franks to their doom. And beyond that, the lands of his ancestors. He had dreamed of returning there one day, of claiming the peaceful life that had been denied him for so long. But as the wind carried the lamentations of the defeated to his ears, Kashta wondered if such dreams were nothing more than a fool's musing. How could there be peace after this? How could any of them find rest with the weight of so much blood and suffering on their souls?

The sound of footsteps drew Kashta from his brooding. He turned to see Hijaz approaching, his old friend's face lined with weariness but his eyes still sharp as ever.

'There you are,' Hijaz said, coming to stand beside on the mount. 'I've been looking for you.'

Kashta grunted in acknowledgment, his gaze drawn back to the sprawl of prisoners below. 'What news?'

'The negotiations are concluded. Al-Kamil has struck a bargain with the Frankish leaders.'

Kashta had expected the sultan to demand nothing less than unconditional surrender. 'What terms?'

'Damietta is to be returned to us,' Hijaz replied, a note of satisfaction in his voice. 'And an eight-year truce has been agreed upon.'

Kashta's brow furrowed. 'Eight years? That seems... generous.'

Hijaz shrugged. 'The sultan believes it will give us time to strengthen our defences, to prepare for the next time the Franks come. And they will come again, make no mistake.'

A heavy silence fell between them, broken only by the distant sounds of the marching below. Kashta's mind whirled with the implications of this agreement. They had achieved their goal – the reclamation of Damietta – but at what cost? The blood of countless warriors, both Saracen and Frank. And for what? A temporary peace, a brief respite before the cycle of violence began anew?

'You don't seem pleased,' Hijaz said.

'Should I be? We've won a great victory, driven the invaders to their knees. And now we treat with them as equals?'

'Politics.' Hijaz spat the word like a curse. 'The sultan sees the bigger picture. This truce buys us time, allows us to consolidate what we have won.'

'And what of justice?' Kashta demanded.

Hijaz's expression softened, a flicker of understanding passing across his weathered features. 'Ah, my friend. Is it justice you seek, or vengeance for all you have lost?'

Kashta turned away, unable to meet that knowing gaze. Among those prisoners, although it seemed they were prisoners no longer, were the men who had ordered the siege on Damietta. A siege that had led to the death of Wasim, and had brought such devastation to their lands. And yet, looking at those men now, Kashta felt only a hollow ache where his rage had once burned so fiercely.

'I don't know any more,' he admitted. 'I thought... I thought this victory would bring some kind of peace. But now...'

Hijaz laid a hand on his shoulder. 'War is never simple, my friend. And peace... peace is often harder.'

Kashta nodded, appreciating the truth of Hijaz's words. His friend offered a nod before making his way back down the hill, taking the long trail back to al-Mansurah. As he stood there, Kashta felt a sudden sense of loss wash over him. Not just for Wasim, or for the countless others who had fallen in this war, but for the man he had once been. The fierce warrior who had believed so fervently in the righteousness of his cause seemed a stranger to him now, a naive fool who had yet to learn the true cost of victory.

Then, amidst the sea of weary, defeated men, a familiar face caught his eye. Kashta recognised the man he had once pursued across the desert, the knight he had faced in desperate combat mere days ago.

Estienne Wace.

The Frank stood tall despite his obvious exhaustion, his bearing still proud even in defeat. His garb was tattered and stained with the grime of battle, his eyes that had once blazed now harboured a quiet resignation, a weariness that spoke of defeat.

As if sensing Kashta's gaze, Estienne's head turned. Their eyes met across the expanse of mud, and for a moment, there was no victory or defeat, no Saracen or Frank. There were only two men who had faced death together, who had seen the best and worst of what humanity could throw at them, and survived to tell of it.

Kashta felt a surge of... something. Not the hatred he had once nursed so covetously, nor the respect that had grudgingly grown during their shared ordeal in the desert. It was a recognition, perhaps, of a kindred spirit. A soul who had been forged in the same fires and emerged changed, if not... broken.

And that, he realised, was why in the end he had spared the man's life.

For his part, Estienne simply nodded, a small, almost imperceptible gesture that nonetheless carried the weight of volumes. Kashta found himself returning the nod, and in that moment, he saw that the revenge he had once sought so fervently held no more meaning. The debt between them, if ever there truly was one, had been paid in full on the field of battle.

As Estienne was swept along with the tide of Franks, disappearing into the crowd, Kashta remained rooted to the spot. The burden of hatred and vengeance that he had carried for so long seemed to have fallen away, left behind in a wordless exchange with a man who should have been his enemy.

The sound of approaching footsteps, and Kashta turned to see a young mamluk warrior regarding him with a mixture of awe and trepidation.

'Forgive me, Kashta ibn Assad,' the young man said, his voice trembling slightly. 'But the sultan has called for you. He wishes to speak with you about your... your reward.'

Kashta nodded his acknowledgement, before the boy began to lead the way. As he followed the young warrior back towards the heart of the camp, he couldn't shake the feeling that he was walking towards something he no longer wanted. It had seemed so simple at the start. That he should fight for his master and accept his reward. Now the simplicity of that had been shattered. The knowledge that there was more to the circle of his life than violence in service to a sultan.

This war might be over, but he sensed that his own journey was far from finished. And for the first time in longer than he could remember, he faced his future not with dread or anger, but with a quiet, determined hope.

50

The gates of Damietta loomed, a sight that should have filled Estienne with elation. Instead, as he shuffled forward alongside the others, he felt only a hollow ache as he saw the once-proud crusader stronghold now seethed with frantic activity, a hive upended and laid bare.

As they passed through the gates, Estienne's gaze swept over the scene before him. The narrow streets that had once rung with the sound of pious prayer now echoed with panicked shouts and the clatter of wagon wheels. All around him, knights and smallfolk alike scurried about in a desperate dance of evacuation, their faces etched with the same weary resignation he felt in his bones. Crates and barrels littered the ground, their contents spilled carelessly in the rush to salvage what could be saved. A woman clutched a bundle of her belongings close to her chest, her eyes wild as she pushed past the line of freed prisoners, heedless of their dejected state.

A group of knights huddled near a crumbling wall, their once-resplendent surcoats now tattered and stained. One of them, an old greybeard with a face like weathered leather, caught Estienne's eye. For a moment, recognition flickered between them – a shared understanding of how far they had fallen. Then the moment passed, and Estienne was swept along with the tide.

As they moved deeper into the city, the signs of hasty evacuation grew more pronounced. Abandoned carts blocked narrow alleys, their contents strewn across the cobblestones. A dog rooted through a pile of discarded food, snarling as they passed. The air grew thick with the cloying scent of rot, a palpable reminder of how quickly their dreams of conquering the Holy Land had turned to shite.

Along the narrow road that stretched to the western dock, Estienne could just make out ships being readied to carry the remnants of their once-mighty host back to the shores they had embarked from. The irony of it all threatened to choke him. They had come to claim this land for Christendom, to plant the cross in Saracen soil. Now, they fled like desperate thieves from a burning building, leaving behind nothing but corpses.

A bitter laugh escaped Estienne's lips, drawing curious glances from those nearby. They had been so certain, so righteous in their cause. And for what? To end up here, defeated and humbled, those grand ambitions reduced to this desperate scramble for escape.

He closed his eyes, letting the sounds of the dying crusade wash over him. Letting the bustle and panic writhe around him like a serpent. All for nothing. God had not been with them, no matter how many times they had told themselves it was true. But no use lamenting. If God had not delivered them the Holy Land, then it was doubtful he would offer any of them salvation now.

Estienne made his way further into the city, to where perhaps he might spot a familiar face. He did not have to walk far when, amid the press of bodies and the stifling heat, he eventually saw someone he recognised.

Savari of Mauléon, the knight who had dismissed him so arrogantly at the outset of their ill-fated campaign, stood alone. Gone was the proud bearing, the smug certainty that had radiated from him. Gone was his sycophantic entourage. The man before Estienne now was a shadow of his former self, his face sallow and drawn, his once-immaculate surcoat stained and torn.

Estienne watched as the man fumbled with the straps of a worn saddlebag, his fingers trembling with fatigue. The knight cursed under his breath and Estienne almost laughed aloud. Almost. Instead, he left Savari to his ignominy, and found himself a quiet corner, away from the press of bodies. Leaning against a sun-baked wall, he closed his eyes, letting the memories wash over him…

Of the countless men who had fallen, bodies left to rot beneath the unforgiving sun. The senseless brutality, the petty cruelties inflicted in the name of a God who seemed increasingly distant and uncaring. What had it all been for? The grand speeches, the lofty ideals, the certainty of divine favour – all of it hollow now, meaningless in the face of their utter defeat.

A memory of Kashta. Their final confrontation on that muddy bridge, the way he had been spared at the end, the moment when vengeance had given way to… mercy? Understanding, perhaps? Or a weariness with the endless cycle of violence that had consumed them both?

Estienne opened his eyes, squinting against the harsh sunlight. The street bustled with activity, moving in a dance of barely contained chaos.

'God's will,' Estienne murmured.

Right on cue, a group of priests hurried past, their robes billowing in the hot breeze. Once, he would have seen them as emissaries of the divine, their every word imbued with holy authority. Now, he saw only men – fallible, uncertain, as lost in this mess as any of them. What did they have to show for all their grand ambitions now? A broken army, a devastated land, and the bitter knowledge that they had been led astray by their own pride and ignorance.

As they disappeared towards the docks, Estienne's gaze was drawn to a small group of Saracen smallfolk gathered near an alleyway. They stood apart from the bustle of the evacuation, their faces displaying a mixture of relief and trepidation as they watched their conquerors prepare to depart. Among them, an old man caught Estienne's eye. His face was weathered by sun and time, his eyes bright with a serenity that seemed at odds with the chaos surrounding them. As Estienne watched, the man knelt, touching his forehead to the ground in simple prayer.

'Fucking heathen.'

A bark of outrage, said with venom, as a burly crusader advanced on the man, face twisted with hate. Estienne moved without thinking, pushing through the crowd to intervene.

'Stop,' he barked, stepping between the cowering man and his would-be tormentor. 'Have we not seen enough bloodshed? Enough cruelty?'

The crusader hesitated, surprised by the interruption. Estienne met his gaze, seeing his anger grapple with confusion.

'There's no glory to be found here, friend,' Estienne said softly. 'Not any more.'

For a moment, he thought the man might persist. Then, slowly, he backed away, melting into the crowd. Estienne turned to the old man, offering a hand to help him up.

'Thank you,' the Saracen said in halting Latin. 'I am sorry you—'

Estienne shook his head. 'No need to say sorry. I am the one who should be sorry.'

Before he was called upon to explain further, Estienne turned and lost himself in the crowd once more. Despite the bustle, a sense of peace began to settle over him. In that small act he had accomplished the truest expression of faith – not conquering lands, holy or otherwise, but one simple act of kindness.

'Wace!'

The call came from down an alley. Craning his neck, Estienne spotted someone he recognised, waving at him from among the crowd. Isaac carried a bundle on his shoulder as he was buffeted by the seething mob.

Estienne struggled closer, until the two were standing side by side amid the tumult. Isaac grinned up at him, a wry smile on his face despite the misery around them.

'It warms me to see you still live, Estienne Wace. But the more times we meet, the more I realise you are a hard man to kill.'

'You're leaving too, old man?'

Isaac nodded. 'I am, my friend. I have a nephew in Venezia. Not my favourite, but he is willing to offer me shelter for a while. Help me get back on my feet.'

'So this is goodbye at last, then.'

Isaac regarded him sidelong. 'It doesn't have to be. You could come with me. I am sure I can find work for a man who knows how to... get things done.'

Estienne thought about the offer for a moment. A new life. A new start, with a friend he could trust. But was becoming strongarm to a merchant what he truly wanted? Was that the purpose he still strived for?

'Good luck, Isaac ben Berachiyah,' he replied. 'Perhaps one day I will come and search you out.'

'In happier times,' Isaac said, eyes filling with tears.

Before they could fall, he grasped his bundle and pushed his way through the crowd toward the docks. Estienne watched him go, glad that Isaac at least was starting anew. That he had a purpose. A road he had chosen for his own.

Then he turned away and continued to wander, as the people around him clamoured to escape.

51

The harbour no longer seethed with life. Now only a few remaining ships bobbed in the choppy waters as the last of the crusaders scurried across gangplanks, arms laden with what meagre possessions they could salvage. The city that had once rung with the sound of triumphant hymns now lay silent and empty. Where banners had fluttered proudly from every tower, only tattered remnants remained, flapping forlornly in the hot breeze.

As the sun dipped lower, casting long shadows across the docks, Estienne felt the weight of indecision settle upon his shoulders. All around him, men rushed to secure passage on the departing ships, desperate to put this cursed land behind them. Yet he remained, unable to take that final step towards... what? Home?

The thought of returning to England felt hollow. He had been cast out from that land, and there was nothing there for him now. The Marshals had turned their backs on him, and he had no other friends. So what now?

'Brooding. Always the brooding with you.'

Estienne could not suppress a grin before he turned to see Amalric. 'Just thinking, my friend.'

'Well think fast. The last boat will be gone before sundown. And I doubt the Saracens will offer you a friendly greeting when they arrive.'

'No, I don't think they will.'

'You know, some of my brothers were certain you had perished, but not me. I knew you would make it. I knew it would take more than an army of Saracens to bring down the Black Lion.'

'I wish I'd shared your confidence, Amalric. For a while I was certain I was done for.'

Amalric offered a sly wink, as though he didn't believe a word of it.

If only he knew.

'So you will come with us?' Amalric said eventually. 'Our boat awaits at the other side of this harbour.'

Estienne turned, unsure of what to say. 'I... I did not presume—'

'What? That you would be offered a place among the Order of Saint Mary? After what you did? Your act of bravery saved us. Drawing the Saracens away offered us the breach we needed to escape. The Order owes you a great debt.'

'I did what needed to be done. Nothing more.'

'Enough of the modesty. Just accept the offer. Come with us, Estienne. You've no home to return to in England, and the grand master would welcome you with open arms.'

Estienne felt a flicker of resistance. 'I'm not sure I belong anywhere any more, my friend. Least of all among warriors of God.'

'Perhaps that's precisely why you should come,' Amalric pressed. 'The Order needs men like you – men who've seen the true face of war, who understand its cost. Yes, we are a military order, but ultimately one that serves God and all those who worship the faith. Our credo is *Helfen*, *Wehren*, *Heilen*. You know what that means.'

Indeed he did. Help, Defend, Heal. Admirable aspirations for any knight.

'I am not prepared to pledge myself to a holy Order. I would not be worthy of—'

'You would not be asked to make vows. You would merely pledge your sword in return for payment. There are many such men who have accepted a similar position.'

'But my faith—'

'Is your concern, my friend. Just come back with us. And who knows, you may feel compelled to defend our lands, keep the peace, uphold the laws. Your sword would be a welcome asset.'

Estienne considered his words, feeling the weight of possibility settle upon him. This war had taught him the folly of following blindly along a righteous path. But despite Amalric's holy orders, he was not asking Estienne to follow. Only to offer his sword in service to a cause. One that might well be justified.

And after all, where else was he to go?

'Very well,' he said at last. 'I'll come. Though I make no promises beyond that.'

Amalric's face lit up. 'That's all I ask, my friend. Come, the ship awaits.'

They made their way across the dock as the sun cast long shadows. A single dromond stood at anchor, deck bustling. On the other side of the gangplank, Estienne saw the grand master waiting to greet them. Hermann's bearded face was lined with care, but his eyes lit up as he saw Estienne approaching.

'Welcome aboard, Wace,' Hermann said. 'I'm glad to see you've chosen to travel with us.'

Estienne nodded, feeling, with every step toward the deck, that this was the right choice.

As the ship cast off, the white sail with its black cross unfurling, he made his way to the rail. The dock of Damietta receded as they made their way north up the Nile. Ahead was a seemingly endless column of other ships leading the way.

Absently, his hand went to the pocket of his shirt. From within it, he fished out the stone he had entirely forgotten was there. A gift from a little girl in the desert. On its surface was the familiar pattern of a blooming flower, and he suddenly realised it was the only thing he had been given of worth in this whole barren country.

Estienne tightened his fist around it and closed his eyes, letting the salt spray kiss his face. Letting the last Egyptian sun warm him one more time before he left it behind, perhaps forever.

When it rose again, with luck, he would be miles away from this ill-starred shore, and on his way to somewhere he might at last belong.

* * *

MORE FROM RICHARD CULLEN

GLOSSARY

Askar – Personal regiment of the Ayyubid rulers.
Cappa – A long-sleeved robe worn by Templars.
Damietta – City in Egypt, part of the Ayyubid Sultanate.
Destrier – A horse specifically bred for war. Also known as a 'charger'.
Dhourra – A type of hard bread made from millet grain.
Dromond – A large medieval ship used commonly throughout the Mediterranean.
Franks – A collective term used by the Saracens for European invaders.
Gambeson – A padded jacket worn as armour. Often combined with mail for added protection.
Hamtar – A type of turban.
Hauberk – A heavy coat of mail, consisting of interlinked metal rings.
Hujra – The barracks for the sultan's personal guard.
Jandariyah – The personal bodyguard of the Ayyubid sultans.
Jund – The military elite of the Ayyubid dynasty.
Mamluks – Slave-soldiers of the ancient Muslim world.

Outremer – Meaning 'overseas', is a term used for the four Crusader States established in the Middle East after the First Crusade (County of Edessa, County of Tripoli, Kingdom of Jerusalem, Principality of Antioch).
Sayf – A straight-edged sword used by the Saracens.
Siyar – The rules of war by which all Muslim warriors must abide.
Surcoat – An outer garment worn over armour, usually marked with insignia to denote allegiance.

ACKNOWLEDGEMENTS

Once again I'd like to thank Caroline Ridding and all the talented folks at Boldwood Books for making this novel happen.

As is usual, a lot of reading happened so I could bring the story of the Fifth Crusade to life, and the following authors should get credit in no particular order: Nicholas Morton, Christopher Tyerman, David Campbell, David Nicolle and Stephen Turnbull.

Finally, thanks again to you, the reader, for following the continuing journey of the Black Lion. Strap in – there's much more to come.

Best,

Richard Cullen

ABOUT THE AUTHOR

Richard Cullen is a writer of historical adventure and epic fantasy. His historical adventure series *Chronicles of the Black Lion* is set in thirteenth-century England.

Sign up to Richard Cullen's mailing list for news, competitions and updates on future books.

Follow Richard on social media here:

x.com/rich4ord
instagram.com/thewordhog

ALSO BY RICHARD CULLEN

The Chronicles of the Black Lion Series

Rebellion

Crusade

The Wolf of Kings Series

Oath Bound

Shield Breaker

Winter Warrior

War of the Archons (as R S Ford)

A Demon in Silver

Hangman's Gate

Spear of Malice

The Age of Uprising (as R S Ford)

Engines of Empire

Engines of Chaos

Engines of War

Boldwood

Boldwood Books is an award-winning fiction publishing company seeking out the best stories from around the world.

Find out more at www.boldwoodbooks.com

Join our reader community for brilliant books, competitions and offers!

Follow us
@BoldwoodBooks
@TheBoldBookClub

Sign up to our weekly deals newsletter

https://bit.ly/BoldwoodBNewsletter

Printed in Great Britain
by Amazon